Redemption
Tattoos and Tears Book 5

By Amiee Louise

I0636932

REDEMPTION

First edition. October 2, 2025.

Copyright © 2025 Amiee Louise.

ISBN: 978-1968759292

Written by Amiee Louise.

"I'd rather burn out, than just fade away."
– The gospel according to Brody Lennon Hart

Prologue

Brody

Redemption

(rɪdempʃən) (ri-demp-shuh-n)

Word forms: plural redemptions

1. variable noun

Redemption is the act of redeeming something or of being redeemed by something.

[formal]

He craved redemption for his sins.

2. An act of redeeming[1] or atoning for a fault or mistake, or the state of being redeemed[2].

3. Deliverance from sin; salvation, atonement for guilt.

Synonyms: paying-off, clearing[3], squaring, honouring.

I'm asked on a near daily basis *'why do you do what you do?'* It's a loaded question but the answer is plain and simple. I'm a fucking rock star, it comes with the territory. The sex, the drugs, the women. The typical, cliché rock n' roll lifestyle. It's every young boy's dream to fulfil their childhood fantasies, all whilst doing what they love best. The music, playing on stage to thousands of people per night. The buzz you feel deep within your soul when the crowd sings back a song that you've written, word perfect. The euphoria, as the screams drive you to sing the lyrics louder and to play that guitar harder than you've ever played before, like your fucking life depends on it. The feeling of blissful rapture when I listen to the sea of people chanting our name, the deep

---

1.   https://www.dictionary.com/browse/redeem

2.   https://www.dictionary.com/browse/redeem

3.   https://www.collinsdictionary.com/dictionary/english/clearing

rumbling roar of '*Vengeance, Vengeance, Vengeance*' echoing in my mind and driving me on, as I lose myself in the music.

When I play guitar, it's just me and my guitar, nothing else exists. Everything is just inconsequential, trivial, fucking white noise. In all my years in the music industry, on the road, touring, meeting, and greeting fans, I never let anything get in the way of that, except maybe my two vices, but these days they stop at ink and class A's (but I was working on the latter)

I was strictly professional, until I met her, Raleigh fucking Storm. She was my next favourite mistake, my saving grace, my fortress of solitude. When she was around, I didn't need the drugs, I didn't need the other women, I didn't need anything, I just needed *her*. The fame meant nothing. When she was around, we were just two fucked-up people falling hopelessly in love.

We weren't without our demons. She was a troubled actress, who had a mighty fall from grace in the glare of the paparazzi's lens. She ended up in rehab because of poor choices and bad life decisions. We both did. In my head, I had some sort of twisted notion that everybody needed saving, when it was really me that needed saving, from myself most of all.

Amongst all of the chaos and carnage, she was the one to save me from the wreckage. She saved me from drowning in a sea of white powder and pills, she made me rise up like a phoenix from the flames. Over the years, I'd seen the most hideous, awful, disgusting things. And yet, even after almost a decade of therapy, I still resorted to my go-to way of coping. I got high, but after I met her, I didn't want to be that person anymore. She made me want to be a better man, a better version of myself, version 2.0. I wanted to overcome my demons and do what normal people do. Go to the pub, go to the gym, and work out excessively, or just fuck her, until I didn't want to get high anymore.

I needed her like I needed oxygen, I loved her like I'd never loved anyone before. This alien feeling, which made my heart soar and my stomach fill with butterflies, it was all consuming, punch-in-the-gut love between two consenting adults. Raleigh Storm had turned me into a sober, monogamous man, who didn't need to shove thousands of pounds worth of cocaine up his hooter, just to feel...something. Being with her made me go from feeling nothing to feeling fucking everything, she made me whole, and that was enough.

Our story from the beginning was messy and unconventional. A rollercoaster I didn't want to get off. She made me fall in love with life again, she was my second chance at righting the wrongs of the past. *She was my fucking redemption.*

1

Brody

Past

The nightmare is back with a vengeance, the same one that has haunted me for fucking years. The boys can't know, no one can, *not this time*. To them, to the fans and to everyone else, I am Brody Hart, from Rancid Vengeance. The flamboyant, outgoing, crazy motherfucker, with the split tongue and the tattooed cock. The guitarist, with the bad boy reputation, who parties all night, the one who works hard, plays harder and fucks like a rock star.

No one needs to see this fucking sweat drenched, snivelling wreck at two o'clock in the morning. They need to see my lively, fun-loving, crazy alter-ego Snake, playing guitar, in my element, bouncing all over the stage. The one who shows the fans a good fucking time, gives them the show they deserve and gives them their money's worth. Not this scared, vulnerable, fucked up, man-child, sitting in the corner of the room, bare chested and clucking for something to take the edge off, to calm my racing thoughts. Something to shake the image of my ten-year-old self, finding my crack whore, junkie mother dead, with a needle hanging from her arm. The acrid smell, the cold, clammy feel of her skin as I touched her.

It feels as if I am that scared ten-year-old boy again, and I do what I always do when this happens. I race to the toilet to empty the contents of my stomach and vomit violently into the toilet bowl. I lean heavily against the wall, pressing my cheek to the cold tiles to cool my damp, heated skin. *Fuck, I need a hit, so bad*. Just a taste of that delicious white powder to obliterate my fucked-up thoughts, to quiet my inner demons and find the true peace I deserve.

The truth is, I was born an addict. *I was fucked from birth*. Everything about me is addicted in some way. My personality, my constant need to get off my face and my extremely unhealthy obsession with self-destruction. I wipe my mouth and splash my face with cold water as I head back into the bedroom. I find myself reaching for my phone and dial the only person who can talk me down from this ledge I seem to find myself on.

"Hello?" he says in his gruff voice that I have become accustomed to over the past fourteen years, and I clear my throat.

"Len? It's me."

I try to disguise the waver in my voice. *I fucking hate it when he worries and knowing I'm the cause, makes me feel even worse.*

"Do you know what fucking time it is, boy?" he growls, his voice laced with sleep. I find myself smiling at Lenny's candour.

"I'm really sorry to call you so late. I'll make it up to you, old man. How about that Jaguar X-Type, I've been promising you?"

He chuckles throatily.

"You know the way to my heart, son. Now, my old man intuition tells me, you didn't fucking call me in the middle of the night just to exchange pleasantries?"

I smile to myself, at his brutally honest words, as I jump off the bed awkwardly.

"I-I had *the* fucking nightmare again, Len. *Bollocks!* I was *fine,* at least the drugs blocked it out, but now - I'm feeling it, to the *nth* fucking degree and I don't like it, not one fucking bit." I say with a tight jaw, and I pound the heel of my hand against my temple.

"I can't deal, Len. I *need* to get high, *fuck me.*" I curse, as I frantically pace the floor, like a caged fucking animal.

"Listen to me, son, you're doing so well. Nance and me are so fucking proud of you. You don't need to shove that shit up your nose anymore, B. You are stronger than this, it's been six months, that's an achievement. Remember all those therapy sessions? All that time spent in rehab, it will be wasted, if you go down that road again. We don't want that for you, you're like a son to us; you gave us purpose after Daryl died. You gave us hope, don't you ever forget that."

I suddenly start to feel bad for calling and unloading on Len when it is coming up to the anniversary of their son Daryl's death.

Daryl Dean Nicholas was Lenny and Nancy's son. He died at the age of twenty of a heroin overdose just like my mum. I was there when he died, I was the one who found him with the needle hanging from his arm. I fell in with the wrong crowd and Daryl was part of that crowd, but he was different from all the others. He just liked to party and to have a good time. We were similar in that respect, which is why we became friends. That is why I ended up crossing paths with Lenny and Nancy. I feel an intense guilt deep in my gut every time he brings up Daryl, I know he doesn't blame me for his death, but I can't help thinking, why him and not me.

"Do you need me to come over, son?" he asks as softly as he can manage with his gravelly voice, from smoking forty fags a day.

"No, course not, don't be silly, Len. I'm all good, honestly. I shouldn't have called, I'm sorry." I say ruefully, hoping to fuck that I sound at least a little convincing.

"*Oi*! Don't you ever fucking apologise for needing to talk to someone, son. It's good that you decided to pick up the phone rather than going to score. That's progress right there and I'm so bloody proud of you for that." There is a hint of gratification in his voice, and I smile at his sentiment.

"Don't you go getting soft on me there, old man!" I tease. I always do this whenever shit starts to get serious, I throw in a joke.

Back in school, I was the class clown, the joker, and the wheeler-dealer, all rolled into one. All to disguise the fact that I was going home to an empty fridge and to find my mum more than likely on the sofa, strung out, with a needle hanging from her arm and one of her many boyfriends zipping up and leaving. I shake that particular unwanted memory away, as Lenny's throaty chuckle fills my ears.

"What have I told you, you cheeky little fucker, less of the old! You're not too old for a clip round the ear, boy!" he chastises, but I know he doesn't mean it. The sound of Lenny's wheezing cough has me feeling more than slightly panicked.

"Fucking hell, Len, you sound like you're hacking up a lung there! You good?"

I try to disguise the alarm in my voice, concerned for the only father figure I have ever known.

"All good, son, don't you worry about me, there's life in the old dog yet!"
I laugh.

"Ah, so you do admit you're old?" I say cheekily.

"*Fuck off!* Go and get some sleep, B. Come by the club tomorrow, we'll have a proper chat then. I've got a thirty-five-year-old single malt that needs drinking. Are you sure you don't need me to come over, son? I can be there in twenty minutes, fifteen if I put my foot down. Just don't tell Nancy! You know how much she worries," he asks again softly, and I smile to myself.

"Yeah, I'm sure, thanks, you get back to Nancy, give her a kiss from me. I think I'll try to get some sleep. I'll catch you tomorrow, Len, bye."

I hang up, grab myself a glass of water and make my way back to bed. I lay there, staring at the ceiling for the longest time, going over and over the past in my head. *What was so wrong with me, that my own mum didn't even care about me?* I torture myself for what seems like hours. But in reality, it is only minutes, and I am resigned to the fact that it is just going to be like any other night, I can't sleep. No matter how hard I try, I can't get my brain to switch off. My mind is like an internet browser with forty-four thousand tabs open...*all at fucking once*. I am lucky if I get two or three hours a night these days.

Before I know what I'm doing, I pick up my phone and dial the one person I've been told time and time again to stay the fuck away from.

"Kev, its Brody." I say rather apprehensively. He is the last person I wanted to call, but I need a fix so fucking badly, my mouth is watering, and I can literally taste it. That chat with Lenny didn't help and my body is craving just *one last* hit.

Kevin Adams is my old drug dealer from Brixton, my old stomping ground. We used to hang out together in the early days, before Rancid Vengeance made it big. He was never really a close friend, simply an acquaintance. He just someone who Daryl and I happened to get high with occasionally. He was someone who could supply us with what we needed for a good time.

"Brody, my man. Long time, no speak." He greets me a little too enthusiastically, and I pause.

Do I really want to go back to my old ways?

"Wondered how long it would be. The word on the street is, you're clean."

I run my hand over my head.

"Yeah, you heard right, it's been a while, but I just need a little something to take the edge off, man."

I try to sound nonchalant, but I'm fucking *desperate*. I need...*crave* oblivion; I need to forget, just for a little while.

"I've been warned specifically not to sell to you; I've been threatened, rather graphically, by your boy Sam if I remember right. Something about cutting off my dick and shoving it down my throat."

Fucking Sam.

"I'd like to keep my tackle intact, thank you very much, so I'm going to have to pass and say no, man. It could damage my business and my reputation, I'm sorry."

I growl. *His fucking reputation? He's a drug dealer for fucks sake!*

"Look, Kev, I'm fucking desperate. No one needs to know. It will be between you and me, I swear. You know I always pay you well, please, I wouldn't ask if I didn't need it, come on." I try my hardest to persuade him. *Fucking junkies will say just about anything to score.* "I was your best customer at one point, I've helped you out more than once, come on, mate, please, you know I wouldn't ask if I didn't need it."

I look up to the ceiling. *Fuck me; I am just about holding it together.*

"Alright, alright, but this stays between us, man. No one can find out about this, not even Sam."

He sounds genuinely terrified, and I roll my eyes.

"You have my word, thanks, man, really appreciate it, usual spot in say..." I pause to look at my smartwatch on my bedside table, "thirty minutes?"

He sniffs.

"Works for me, Hart, usual?"

My whole body is vibrating at the prospect of finally getting a hit, after all this time.

"Make it double my usual, Kev. I'll pay you twice what you'd normally get," I bargain with him, doing my best to sweeten the deal.

"You've got yourself a deal. Thirty minutes and don't be late, Brody."

With those words, he hangs up. I dress quickly and casually in combat trousers, motorcycle boots, a white vest, and a black leather jacket. I grab my motorcycle helmet and leave the house, as quietly as I can manage. *Sam and Peyton don't need to know about this. Just one more hit then I'm back on the wagon.*

I make my way down to the garage and walk casually over to my bike. My electric blue Honda CB1100XX, *my baby*. She is a beast of a bike - a four-cylinder, six speed - and she goes from zero to sixty in ten seconds. I bought her with my first month's wages, when the band made it big. It's not about the extravagance or how fast she goes, it's about the sentiment and sense of achievement I felt when I first bought her. Sam and I have our bikes in common, but unlike Sam, I ride to escape. I ride to feel the road beneath my feet and the freedom that the open road brings. The bike is an extension of my body, the speed and the blur of the horizon whizzing past is fucking exhilarating to me, there is nothing else like it.

I make it to our usual spot in Lewisham in record time; the traffic is practically non-existent at this golden hour. The bell chimes, signalling my entrance to the *Rise and Shine Café*. I have been coming to this café for years, even before we became famous. It is my sanctuary, my place that I go to think and get my head on straight. I have composed some of the bands best and most famous guitar riffs here, so it has a special place in my heart. A picture of Rancid Vengeance, which has all of our autographs on takes pride of place over the counter.

As soon as I step through the door, it feels like...*home.* The smell of home cooking, coffee, the old school décor of worn shabby chic and London themed designs throughout, making me proud to be from the wonderful capital. I order myself a cup of coffee and the girl behind the counter, Emmy smiles brightly at me.

"Brody! It's so good to see you!" she says enthusiastically, and I can't help but return her smile. She really is a sweet kid. Emmy is around five feet eight inches, quite tall for a girl her age, with long blonde hair pulled into a side ponytail. Her eyes are an unusual shade of sea green, which emphasise the smattering of freckles across her nose. Her straight up, straight down, gaunt figure makes her ample breasts look out of place.

"It's good to see you too, kid."

She narrows her eyes at me as I call her kid.

"You know I don't like it when you call me kid, Brody. I was twenty-one last week," she pouts sulkily.

I place my hand on my heart, and she grins shyly. "Happy birthday for last week, babe."

I cock my eyebrow at her, and she sticks her tongue out at me.

"I'm so sorry I missed it; I've been super busy; you know how it is," I say genuinely, and I almost feel guilty that I am here to score drugs. *You are such a prick, Hart.* She pours my coffee and reaches under the counter.

"Here, I saved this for you."

She pushes a large square package, wrapped in tin foil towards me and my heart beat starts to quicken. *Shit, does she know?*

"It's a piece of my birthday cake. I've been waiting for you to come in, and I thought I'd save you a bit. I know how much of a sweet tooth you have!"

She giggles nervously, and I take it as my heartbeat returns to normal. *Of course, she doesn't know, dickhead. Paranoid much?*

"Thank you so much, that's so thoughtful."

I leap up on the counter and kiss her on the cheek, causing her face to flame. I jump down, and she looks away bashfully.

"Birthday kiss, for my best girl."

I wink cheekily and she blushes an adorable shade of pink.

"Thanks for the cake, Ems."

She nods and I go to sit in my usual spot, at the back of the café in the corner. I sit down at the table with a brown and white checked tablecloth with my large cup of coffee. I open the tin foil package to reveal a huge chunk of chocolate cake with a fuck ton of buttercream and icing. *Emmy, you know me well!* I catch her staring at me and mouth the words *'Thank you'* at her.

I am sipping my coffee and munching my chocolate cake with gusto, when I hear the bell chiming, signalling the arrival of another customer. I look up into the cold, vacant, dull, sludgy green eyes of Kev Adams. Emmy observes my exchange with him with cautious eyes. *You're right to be cautious, sweetheart, I wouldn't trust this fucker as far as I could throw him.*

"Can I get another coffee, please, darlin'? Black, no sugar." I ask Emmy to set her at ease, and she nods politely.

"I'll bring it over," she says with a vigilant, wary edge to her voice, and I smile to reassure her.

I gesture for Kev to take a seat opposite me. He pulls the chair out with a noisy scrape, and the sound sets my teeth on edge. He sits down, and it takes him a few seconds of fidgeting to make himself comfortable.

"Brody, it's been a while, man, good to see you."

He reaches across the table and shakes my hand. His palm is clammy, and I instantly feel repulsed, as if I need to wash my hands. *Fucking slimy bastard.*

"You too, Kev."

Emmy, placing Kev's coffee down on the table, interrupts us momentarily.

"Cheers, babe, I'll settle up on the way out."

I wink and she shakes her head, with a small smile.

"I've got this, Brody," she says sweetly and flashes me a cheeky wink as Kev observes our friendly exchange with curious eyes. *Keep your eyes to yourself, fucker.*

"What have I told you, Ems? You're too kind for your own good sometimes."

Girls like Emmy need to be taught that life isn't all unicorns and fucking rainbows. She needs to learn the valuable lesson, that if you give some people an inch, they will take a mile.

I have known Emmy Woods since she was seven years old, she is like the little sister I never had, and I feel oddly protective towards her. A part of me feels responsible for her in some way and she knows I *always* leave her a substantial tip, to make sure she has a couple of extra quid for her, her mum, Mandie, who is the owner of the café and a close friend of mine, and her little brother Malakai, who has autism. She scurries off back to the counter and while her back is turned, Kev reaches across the table, in a swift movement, to give me what I came here to collect. I slide a roll of notes in exchange and tuck it inside the pocket of my leather jacket. I nod curtly, as Kev guzzles down his coffee in one mouthful. He puts the cup back on the table and nods in return.

"Pleasure doing business with you, Brody, as always. You even remembered how I take my coffee after all this time, I'm impressed."

He smiles his rodent-like smile and we both stand up at the same time. We shake hands and he turns to leave. I pick up my coffee, drain the rest of what is in my cup and wrap up the remainder of my cake, storing it in my pocket. I tuck one hundred pounds underneath my cup and make my way back to the counter, with my hands in my pockets.

"Thanks for the coffee and the cake, Ems. I've got to get going, but I'll see you really soon, I promise. If you ever want to go to one of our gigs, let me know, I'll sort you out and put your name on the V.I.P list, call it a late birthday present."

Her face lights up, as I say those words and she kisses me on the cheek excitedly.

"Thank you so much, Brody! I'd love that!"

I beam at her. "You're very welcome, sweetheart."

I wink and turn to leave. The thought dominating my mind, as I make the twenty-minute journey back home is *total fucking oblivion*.

***

I push the bathroom door open and lock it behind me, to make sure I am not disturbed. *That's the last thing I fucking need.* I lift the toilet tank cover and take out a small, black, worn leather toiletry bag that I keep for emergencies. I unzip it; take out an old credit card and a fifty-pound note. *The essentials for a seasoned addict and every rich junkie knows that anything less than a fifty is a waste.* I put the toilet lid down and pull the clear bag with white powder inside from my pocket. I make two neat little lines with the credit card. I hold one nostril closed; my mouth starts to water. I roll up the note, put one end up my nostril and I slide it across the line, snorting until the delicious white powder is up my nose. I immediately repeat with the other line and sniff hard. *Jesus, there is nothing like the feeling of euphoria, as the coke starts to work its way through my system.* The buzz lights me up like a fucking Christmas tree, it makes me feel like I can take on the fucking world. As the numbness begins to set in, I relish the momentary silence. My mind is clear for the first time in months, and I feel so happy, I could fucking burst! I start laughing hysterically to myself, as I make three more neat lines and then three more, quickly hoovering them up my nose with the note. I feel myself floating somewhere between consciousness and unconsciousness, I finally reach the oblivion I so desperately craved.

2

Brody

I remember coming to on the bathroom floor, the memory vivid, sharp, and clear as day. The concerned faces of the people around me, began coming into focus, and the muffled sound of soft female sobs. At that moment, all I could think of was taking another fucking line, then another, and another. I didn't give a shit if I died; I didn't love myself enough to care. No one would miss me; I would become another number, another fucking statistic, another in the long line of dead junkies. Familiar voices registered in my foggy brain, the whispered word *'rehab,'* amongst the idle chit-chat. I vaguely remember muttering something incoherent, as I allowed the darkness to seep into my veins once more.

***

My eyes struggle to process the all too bright room and for a brief, fleeting moment, panic settles in my gut like a lead weight. *Where the fuck am I?*

"Hello? Hello, is there anyone there? What the fuck is going on? Where am I? Hello?"

I notice the quiver in my voice, as I yell, and an ice-cold fear I have never felt before descends through my entire being. My senses are on high alert, as I try desperately to listen out for an indication to where I am. I hear the *'click, click'* of heels across the floor and register a presence. I look up into the concerned chestnut eyes of Jamie-Leigh Chase.

Jamie-Leigh is Jax's mum, she, Sam's mum Lori and Lucas' Aunt Ava, took me under their wings after my mum died. I was a rebellious, scared, lonely ten-year-old, who had lost the only person who ever loved him. I have always had a soft spot for Jamie-Leigh, or Jay as she likes to be called. We have always had a great relationship; she was always my favourite out of the three matriarchs that took care of me. She is the mum I wished I had had growing up. Jay is also a doctor, and she used to work long hours when Jax and his sisters, Shay and Skye, were kids. As her kids have gotten older, she gave up working at the hospital and opened her own state-of-the-art, private healthcare practice called *'Chase Medical.'*

Jay has always had a lot of time for me. She is on the level, and she is the kindest person I know, with zero judgement.

"Hey, you, good to have you back with us."

She smiles softly and genuinely. I suddenly feel like I am that scared, nervous ten-year-old all over again.

"What trouble have you gotten yourself into now, sweetheart?" she asks with a sigh, and I smile mischievously.

"You know me, Jay, can't go anywhere without causing trouble."

I shrug as she moves further into the room and perches herself on the edge of the bed. Her long blonde hair is pulled up into a neat bun on top of her head, which makes her look younger than her fifty-four years.

"Where am I, Jay?"

She leans in to kiss me on the forehead and takes her stethoscope from around her neck.

"I received a call from Mr Richmonde, pretentious twat that he is, asking if he could bring you here, rather than admitting you to hospital. He didn't want the press finding out. Apparently, the bands reputation means more to him, than your health. *Fucking prick,*" she says with more than a hint of bitterness to her voice, and I smile at her tenacity.

"How did I get here? What did I do?"

The underlying fear in my voice is obvious, as she avoids looking me in the eye. "You overdosed and Sam found you unconscious in your bathroom, darlin'."

My eyes widen at her matter-of-fact admission. *Fuck my life.*

"You stopped breathing and Sam administered C.P.R."

I put my head in my hands, humiliated and more than a little ashamed that my best friend found me unconscious, after everything he's been through. *Fucking hell, it just gets worse.*

"Why do you insist on doing this to yourself? Make me understand."

She reaches for my hand and I let her, its times like these I really resent my mum. *She should be here; she should be the one holding my hand.*

"Because it's the only fucking thing that makes me feel, Jay."

A melancholic sadness to my voice and she reaches up to stroke my face softly.

"You're loved, Brody, and you're part of a family, whether you care to admit it or not, Those boys' bloody worship you, my Jackson included."

I shake my head, squeezing the back of my neck. *I wish I could believe her.*

"It's not just about that, not this time."

My voice is barely a whisper as she cocks her perfectly plucked eyebrow and throws me a knowing look.

"You can't bullshit a bullshitter, Brody."

She smirks cheekily, and I laugh. *Typical Jay, this woman knows me so well.*

"There's nothing that gets past you, is there?" I quip sarcastically, and she winks. The distinctive shade of her wide, expressive eyes remind me so much of Jax.

"Call it female intuition, sweetheart." She squeezes my hand. "Let's start with her name then, shall we?"

I shift my gaze, feeling almost embarrassed. *Is it that obvious? Fuck.*

"Only a woman would get you this twisted up, darlin'."

I sigh and my heart slams against my ribcage when I think of *her.*

"You love her, don't you?" Jay says abruptly, and I nod, squeezing my eyes shut briefly, willing myself not to burst into tears like a big fucking girl.

"More than anything and I need her more than my next fix, Jay. The problem is, she doesn't belong to me, she belongs to someone else," I admit with a hint of shame to my voice. She raises her eyebrows and I frown.

"Don't fucking judge me, we didn't plan it, it just kind of...happened." I puff out my cheeks and she sighs.

"Oh, sweetheart, come here." She holds her arms open, and I crawl right into them, desperately craving a hug. She holds me close to her and strokes my head, soothing me. "It's going to be alright, darlin', I promise. You might not think it now, but it will be."

At this moment, I am not sure I believe her.

***

I am not sure how much time passes, but I wake up to hear a commotion outside the slightly open door and I instantly recognise Sam's loud, distinctly angry, gravelly voice.

"WHERE THE FUCK IS HE?" he bellows. Sam is somewhat protective over the people he cares about; some might say a tad overprotective. His temper is almost as famous as his distinctive style and his voice. I've witnessed first-hand the destructive aftermath of his many temper tantrums over the years. They aren't pretty but seem to go hand in hand with his recently diagnosed bipolar disorder, after his most recent episode, which he manages with medication and intense daily exercise.

"HART!" he shouts, shaking off Cole and Jax, as if they were annoying bugs.

He steps menacingly into the room, his nostrils are flaring, his stance loose, as if he's about to strike at any given moment. He has his fists clenched tightly at his sides and his knuckles are white. *Oh fuck, this isn't going to be pleasant.* He moves further into the room and it takes Cole, Lucas and Jax to physically drag him away from me.

"Look, dude, I'm sorry, alright?" I say apologetically, hoping to placate him, and he shakes his head, jabbing his finger angrily in my direction.

"You can shove your fucking sorry up your motherfucking arse! Don't you think we've lost enough fucking people?" He spits angrily as I hang my head in absolute fucking shame. *He's right, we lost nine people that day and I'll remember that clearly for as long as I live.*

"I'll go to rehab, I'll sort myself out this time, I'll get clean, and I'll stay clean, I promise," I whisper sincerely, feeling such shame and regret. *I can't fucking bear the way they're all looking at me.*

"You say that every single time, Brody! It's like an endless cycle, you O.D, you get admitted to hospital, you get your stomach pumped, and you promise you'll get clean. You go to rehab, get clean, come out, go to a few meetings, and repeat the same fucking thing all over again! How many times, man! You're a typical pathetic, weak fucking junkie! I gave you CPR for fucks sake! You've crossed the line this time!" he barks, running his hands frantically through his hair as he anxiously paces the room.

I have the sense to balk at his chastisement. In the background, I hear M.J, speaking in a clipped, business-like tone, as he steps into the room, larger than life. He swipes the screen of his phone, greeting Jay and I, with a curt nod and a cool smile.

"Ah, good to have you back with us, Hart," he says, with a genuine look of empathy on his face, but Jay can't seem to hide her disdain for him.

"The Glades Rehabilitation Centre, in Sandwood Bay on the North Coast of Scotland. They're sending a car for you in an hour. Six months this time, Brody, no arguments. Show us all that you can get clean and stay clean, we all care about you, man."

He places his hand on my arm, in a gesture of reassurance and smiles softly. The tender moment is short-lived, as Jay looks him dead in the eye.

"Bull shit," she spits angrily, jabbing her finger at him. "This is fucking bullshit! What about his rights? He has a right to decide whether or not he goes to rehab!" she raises her voice and Jax puts his arm around her in an appeasing gesture.

"Mum," Jax warns softly, but the look of absolute conviction in her eyes never fails to amaze me.

Jamie Leigh Chase, the mother I always wanted, the mother mine *should* have been, always championing me, always protecting me, always having my back. I gently brush her arm reassuringly.

"Jay, it's ok."

She shakes her head and puts her hand tenderly on top of mine.

"It's not ok, sweetheart. He can't bully you into going to rehab, it's your choice and your choice alone," she argues, and M.J is silently seething at her outburst.

"Honestly, I need to do this, Jay. He's not forcing me, he's just concerned. I need to sort my head out; I need some help to get off the drugs. I can't do it here where there's temptation. I'm just not strong enough to resist. I love you for having my corner, you always have. You're a fucking angel. You're the mum I always wanted, but on this, M.J's right."

I placate softly as I look M.J in the eye. Her gaze softens and she pulls me in for a hug. She squeezes me tightly, and as she pulls away; she kisses me on the forehead with tear-filled eyes. I look from Jay to M.J and take a deep breath, as I realise the weight of the words I'm about to say.

"I'll get clean this time, you have my word, M.J, I swear." I say with absolute fervour in my voice. *I just fucking hope I can stick to my word this time.*

3

Brody

"Would you like to tell the group why you're here and what prompted you to seek therapy, Brody?" The group therapist, with the barely there tits whose name I can't fucking recall, asks. I shrug nonchalantly and roll my eyes. *For fucks sake, here we go again.*

"Hi, my name is Brody Hart and I'm a drug addict." I admit with a bored tone, as the rest of the group applauds, offering silent nods of support. Saying those words out loud and admitting you have a problem, is *'apparently'* the first step to recovery in the twelve step, non-faith-based program. *Not that I haven't heard that a thousand fucking times before.* Personally, I think it's a bunch of bull shit. The sitting in a circle, telling your secrets to strangers, the looks of quiet understanding. All I feel is fucking shame, total and utter shame, at being admitted to this God forsaken hell hole, *again*. I hate admitting that I take drugs purely for the escape it brings, for my demons to finally shut the fuck up and bring with it a quiet calm. For my brain to catch up and give me the peace I so desperately crave.

***

The days go by and seem to all blend into one. *This is a fucking joke, I shouldn't be here, why the fuck should I be punished, for having a good time?* You only live once, right? I head from my room to my daily therapy session, and I lean against the wall outside the door. I notice a young woman, who I don't recognise. *I would have recognised someone as beautiful as her, fuck me, she's a knockout.* I take her in, she's around five feet seven inches tall, lightly tanned, and slender. Her vibrant lilac hair is cut into a short, pixie crop and shaved at the sides in a stylish undercut. She has intricate black and grey tattoos covering both tops of her arms, in half sleeves. Her oblong,

20

black-rimmed glasses, framing her unique, amethyst-coloured eyes. She is wearing a black sleeveless shirt with white stars all over, tied at her midriff, giving me a peak at her flat stomach, denim cut off hot pants, which showcase her tattooed, rockin' legs; I start to imagine them wrapped around my head, as I shamelessly pound her hard. With that thought, my cock jumps in my jeans. *Fuck me, I need to get laid, it's been a while.* The sound of her gnawing on her nails, grates on my every fucking nerve and I hope she doesn't notice my raging hard on.

"Did you enjoy eye fucking me, like some sad, desperate, fucking pervert?" she asks aloofly, and her British accent is tinged with a hint of Australian. I smirk and cock my eyebrow. *I fucking love a challenge.*

"Yeah, I was eye-fucking the shit out of you back then, kitten," I say roughly. *Kitten? Where the fuck did that come from?* I throw her a cheeky wink, as she rolls her eyes, with an amused look on her face. *I am nothing if not honest.*

"I feel thoroughly violated" she says sardonically, and I chuckle softly, as she places her hand on her chest. *A girl with a sense of humour, I fucking love it.*

"So, do I get to know your name, or should I continue to call you kitten?" I say, my voice oozing with charm. *Fuck me, Hart; are you that desperate for a shag?*

"Although, kitten is a cute pet name, I'm far from cute, babe," she says provocatively, as I swipe my tongue across my bottom lip suggestively. She continues to watch me raptly and carefully.

"My mum warned me not to talk to strangers!"

I laugh, and her eyes begin to dance with mischievousness. *Fuck, she is beautiful.* She moves a few inches closer and leans into the door, idly making shapes on the wall with her long slender finger. As soon as her eyes lock with mine, I am a total goner. She is... *fucking captivating.* If she asked me to jump naked off a cliff right now, I would not hesitate. *What the fuck are you thinking, Hart? A girl like her would never go for a fuck up like you.* I clear my throat to quiet the voice in my head and turn on the old Hart charm.

"There's no such thing as a stranger, strangers are just friends you haven't met yet, kitten."

She laughs harmoniously, as I saunter casually in front of her, with one hand tucked into my pocket. The fruity aroma of her perfume invades my nostrils. It takes everything I have not to inhale her distinctly female scent and commit it to memory. I am about to speak again when the sound of my therapists' voice interrupts us. *Talk about bad timing. Fucking cockblock.*

"Brody?"

I briefly close my eyes in frustration, and she chuckles, as she pushes herself off the wall. She ducks underneath my arm.

"Until next time, handsome?" She winks and I nod curtly.

"It's a date," I say softly, and she blows me a kiss, leaving me a desperate mess, panting like a horny teenager, as she turns to walk away. *Un-be-fucking-lievable.*

***

My therapist, Rick eyes me carefully and starts to scribble something down in his notebook. We do this every time we see each other; the silent fucking standoff, to see who backs down first. He inclines his head to the side and clicks his pen in quick succession. I grind my teeth and sink back into my chair. *He knows that sound sets my nerves on edge, fucking prick.*

"So, we've established the fact that you're the sort of person, who doesn't form attachments easily. Yet you seemed quite fond of the young lady out there in the corridor, do you want to elaborate on that, Brody?"

He patronises, in his fucking irritating Mancunian accent, which gets right on my nerves. I have aptly nicknamed him *Rick the Prick*, which suits him perfectly. His smug fucking face, his mid-brown, almost ginger hair, his beady, squinty brown eyes, and his fox-like features.

"Not really," I say with a flat, disinterested timbre to my voice and cross my leg over my knee.

"I understand that you had a tough childhood, and you lost your mum at an incredibly young age, which we've touched upon briefly in our previous sessions. You seem extremely reluctant to talk about it, but do you think your addiction and the fact that you can't seem to form attachments, stems from that?"

What the fuck. He scribbles something down again and I can feel a tic begin in my jaw. *Fucking judgemental twat.*

"You don't know me, how dare you fucking sit there and judge me! You have no idea what I've been through." I raise my voice a few decibels louder than is acceptable, and he quirks his eyebrow as he holds his hands up in defence.

"There's no judgement here, Brody. I'm just trying to find out what makes you...tick if you like? You seem like an intensely guarded person, from what I've observed in previous meetings. You seem somewhat...uncooperative when it comes to sharing your past with me, I'm trying to work out why, that's all."

He states, with a condescending tone to his voice and starts to scribble on his note pad again. The scratch of the pen scrawling across the page, causes me to clench my jaw hard and my leg starts to twitch involuntarily.

Rick's observation starts to imbed its way through my overactive brain. *"You seem like the sort of person who doesn't form attachments easily."*

The truth is, he is only half-right. I never really belonged anywhere, or felt attached to anyone, until I met the boys. We were all so young, with different personalities, but our friendship just seemed to work. I was the joker who craved attention from anyone who would take an interest in me. Sam was the popular one, with the rock star parents and the flash clothes. Lucas was the misfit kid, with the funny accent and Jax was the sweet, brown eyed, blonde haired, boy next door, who everyone liked and seemed to gravitate towards. We were all misfits to an extent, but it all just seemed to fade away when we played music together.

Rick observes me, as if I am some sort of wild animal ready to attack.

"I did what I had to, to fucking survive, I trusted no one, not until I met the boys. To this day, I'm still extremely careful who I trust. You're totally right, I am guarded, because I've *had* to be. Everyone in my life has fucked me over at some point, except the boys. They have always stuck by me, even through the times I didn't fucking deserve it."

It comes out a little more harshly than I intended, but he nods attentively and relaxes back in his chair.

"No matter who I got close to, I was always waiting for the other shoe to drop, ya know?"

I babble, because I am desperately craving a fix, I don't cope well with talking about feelings. *I need something to make this empty fucking feeling inside go away*. I get up from my seat and pace the length of Rick's office. He listens raptly, as I continue, making the odd note in his notebook and I start to loosen up a little. *Maybe he's not so bad after all.*

"Sam's had it easy, he's managed to get by on his looks. Well, that's not strictly true, it's his talent as well. His voice defines our generation, but we're not all that lucky, I've had to get by on my wits, I did what I had to, to survive. I had no one, I had to rely on myself, I had no real family, until I met the boys. It was hard for me to relate when I felt so alone and isolated. I always felt like a bit of an outsider. The boys had a different kind of bond, because Jamie-Leigh was the doctor on call when Sam and Luke were born. She gave birth to Jax a few years after. Sam's parents, Jax's parents and Lucas' Aunt and Uncle all knew each other. They were friends and moved in the same circles. However, soon after Luke was born, he was taken to America and didn't come back to the U.K until he was seven years old. Then there was me, the Artful Dodger of the group, the orphan. I always felt like I was on the outside looking in, but music was always the one thing I clung on to, it's the last true magic in the world."

I don't know why I'm telling him all of this. I fucking detest him; he's patronising and so fucking full of himself. It was a love-hate relationship from day one. I don't talk about my feelings. People can use your words against you, so I just keep it bottled up. It's easier that way, but Rick fucking forces me to talk. The first day I met him, we just sat in silence for a solid hour, him trying to get me to talk, but I was having none of it. After an hour of me avoiding eye contact and constantly looking at the clock, I just walked back to my room and wrote music for the rest of the day. I'd never been that inspired, it was like I was writing down everything I couldn't say out loud.

He nods, for me to continue.

"This one day, it was a few years before my mum died, I'll never forget it. I think I was about eight or nine at the time, I was walking past the school music room and I heard someone playing piano. It sounded amazing, like nothing I'd ever heard before. I moved closer, so I could see who it was and when I looked through the crack in the door, I was surprised to see that it was Sam. I knew he played but didn't realise he was any good, he was singing to himself; he was totally oblivious that I was watching him. To this day, I still remember the song; it was Stevie Wonder *For Once in My Life*."

I smile to myself at the memory and Rick starts furiously scribbling in his notebook.

"I'd never heard him sing or play before, not properly anyway, we were just kids. It was like he was in a world of his own and I craved that so fucking badly. I needed an escape, because I was already starting to rebel, even at that age. I was acting out because my mum didn't give a shit about me. I envied Sam when we were growing up, because he had the perfect life, two loving parents, a stable home life, food on the table, and brothers and sisters, who he adored. But who did I have? *Fucking no one.* A junkie mum who died with a needle in her arm and my dad? I never even knew his fucking name."

I clench my jaw and I can feel myself become more and more agitated with each moment that passes. I am clucking for a fucking fix and it's taking everything I have in me, not to drop the nut on this fucking prick for forcing me to relive this shit.

"So, tell me Brody, why did you turn out like your junkie mother?"

Something in the way he phrases the question, has me stalking across the room, until I am looming over him, with my fists clenched at my sides, trembling with unquestionable fury. He looks up at me and I see a hint of a smirk on his face. *He knows he's getting to me, fucking smug prick. Don't rise to it, Hart.* I unclench my fists and take a deep, calming breath.

"You know what? *Fuck this!* I don't have to sit here and listen to this bull shit!" I roar and storm furiously out of the room, without looking back.

***

I end up outside and in my apparent need to get out my pent-up aggression, I start kicking the living shit out of a tree, that I don't notice that the woman from outside the therapy room. She is witnessing my rather public meltdown. *Fuck.* She clears her throat softly and I look up at her. *Shit the motherfucking bed, she's so beautiful.* Her unusual eyes sparkling in the early spring sunlight, the way the wind tousles her short, lilac hair and the way her legs look like they go on for days, in those tiny, denim, cut-off shorts. *My Daisy fucking Duke.*

"Want to talk about it?" she says, with a hint of sympathy to her voice and I don't know what comes over me, but I stride over to her with purpose. She swallows harshly, and I see the muscles in her neck contract. I remember a conversation I had with Sam once and he told me that's how he knew Peyton was attracted to him. *He's a regular Sigmund fucking Freud.* She is about to speak, and I shake my head.

"No fucking talking," I growl and move forward until we are eye to eye. It is at that moment, I really take her in, she comes up a few inches shorter than me and her figure is to die for. Her lightly sun-kissed skin is flawless and absolute fucking perfection. Her lips are pink, plump, and begging to be kissed. Her breasts are perky and the loose grey top she is wearing, which hangs loosely off her shoulder, makes it blatantly obvious, that she isn't wearing a bra. Her nipples are standing to attention and I have to have my mouth on them. I can't seem to tear my fucking eyes away. *She is the epitome of female fucking perfection.*

"Hello? My eyes are up here just in case you were wondering." she retorts sassily, and I chuckle softly.

"I can see your eyes just fine, babe, and very beautiful eyes they are too...*extremely expressive.*"

My voice low and seductive. She tries desperately to hide her smirk, and she looks so...*innocent.* I cup her face in my hands and I can't stop myself from crushing my lips urgently to hers. She tastes exactly as I imagined her to taste and the feel of her soft lips against mine, coax me to deepen the kiss. The velvet of her tongue teasing and caressing my mouth, greedily begging me for more, causing my heart to stutter in my chest. The unfamiliar feeling has me reluctantly pulling away from her. *Fuck, you're going to wreck her, Hart, walk away.*

"Don't stop, *please.*"

She pants breathlessly and her lips look bruised, as if they have been thoroughly kissed. I war inwardly with myself, as a look of pure vulnerability washes over her features. *Just walk away.*

"My mother warned me about boys like you."

Her tone so soft I barely hear her, and I grin wolfishly at her comment. *You have no fucking idea, sweetheart.*

"If you're looking for a boy, you've come to the wrong place, kitten."

She traps her lip between her teeth and that simple gesture has my cock leaping to attention. *For fucks sake, behave!*

"I'm not good for you, I'm the one your mother should have warned you about," I say, with more than a hint of warning in my voice.

"It's lucky I don't do as I'm told, and I don't listen to warnings. I'd rather make up my own mind."

She smiles a smile so bright; it makes her eyes dance and her whole face lights up. She reminds me of the sunshine, of everything I have ever wanted, a light in my darkness, a diamond in the rough. *Where is all this bullshit coming from? What makes you think that she would want a fuck up like you, Hart?* I swallow harshly to rid myself of that thought.

"Why does it feel like you're trying to force me to walk away? We're obviously here because we've made some bad life choices but that doesn't mean *this* is a bad choice."

Her voice soft, as she gestures between us. "Everything inside me is telling me to walk away, but you've utterly fucking captivated me, and I don't even know your name."

Suddenly feeling unsure of myself and I am never fucking unsure, especially where women are concerned.

"I'm Raleigh."

She pronounces it Ray-Leigh, and she offers me her hand, in a simple gesture. I look down at her outstretched hand, then back up at her. I know as soon as I touch her, I won't be able to walk away. Not even if I wanted to. *Fuck me.*

4

Brody
Present Day

My motto in life has always been, live fast, die young and leave a pretty corpse. I have been out of rehab for three months and it has been the longest three fucking months of my life. Endless nights of restlessness and vivid dreams, endless days filled with exhaustion and fatigue. As I turn to the nameless woman next to me, a soft hand slides across my torso and as I struggle to focus on her, my heart sinks. *Please God no.* I close my eyes, hoping that my eyes are deceiving me, but when I look again, my worst nightmare is confirmed. Lying next to me is Emmy, the sweetest, gentlest, kindest girl I know. *Fuck me; I am going straight to hell.*

I slide out of bed, cursing softly. I desperately try not to wake her, but I can't resist lifting the duvet, to check whether she is naked underneath. *Please tell me we didn't.* I lift it and my suspicions are instantly quelled, as I see she is wearing one of my t-shirts. *Thank fuck.* I let out the breath I didn't know I was holding, and she stirs, as I start to pull on my jeans. She smiles sleepily and snuggles deeper into the pillow.

"Hey you." Her voice is soft and thick with sleep. She rolls over onto her stomach and I rub my head agitatedly. "Where are you going?"

I turn to face her. God, she is...beautiful, in a plain Jane kind of way, but also innocent, she's just a kid. Why the fuck did I have to go there? *What were you thinking, Hart?*

"What's wrong? H-have I done something?" she asks in a small voice and my heart breaks for her. *Why the fuck did I have to pull that shit with her, of all people?* My sweet, innocent Emmy. I drop down on the edge of the bed and she crawls over to me. I turn to her and I feel like the world's biggest prick.

"I need to know I haven't ruined what we have between us, Ems. I couldn't bear losing you, you're like my baby sister."

She smiles tenderly and reaches for my hand. "Of course you haven't ruined things, you donut! You made a drunken pass at me, but I pushed you away. You asked me to come back here with you and I agreed. We ate chicken kebabs in the back of your limo and when we got back here, I put you to bed, and you passed out."

I shake my head. *Fucking classy.*

"*Shit,* Ems, I'm so fucking sorry, you mean more to me than that. I was so drunk, I do stupid shit when I'm drunk, please forgive me," I plead sincerely, as she rests her head on my shoulder.

"There's nothing to be sorry for, chick. It's no big deal honestly, you're funny when you're drunk! Even though you were totally shitfaced, you were still a sweetheart."

She smiles and I wrap my arm around her.

"You're a diamond, Emilia Woods; don't let anyone tell you different. I would never let anyone hurt you, ever. I would lay down my fucking life for you and I don't say that to just anyone." I say, with absolute conviction.

"You're the only pure thing I've got left in my life, Ems. I couldn't bear to think that I'd ruined things between us."

She snuggles closer to me and I squeeze her tighter.

"Of course not, it'll take more than that to get rid of me, Hart!" She punches me playfully on my arm and we stay silent for a few moments.

"*Wow,* I can officially say I slept with Brody Hart!" she squeals and claps enthusiastically and we both laugh.

"Was I good in bed?" I ask teasingly, she pretends to think.

"Hmm, yeah, obviously! You were a total stallion, stamina of an Olympian!" she jokes, and I nod.

"Keep going, my ego needs massaging a little more!" I say wryly and she chuckles softly.

"Let's see, we went at it all night, I could hardly keep up and that thing you do with your piercing..." her eyes roll back in her head.

"*Oh my God,* multiple orgasms all round!"

We both collapse back on the bed, in fits of hysterical laughter and I come to the sudden realisation that I haven't laughed that hard in a long time.

"My one issue, you're not a cuddler, you're more of a hands behind your head, stare at the ceiling, kind of guy."

She says ruefully. Emmy knows me well; she knows every facet of me, just as Sam, Peyton, Lenny, and the boys do. She knows I suffer from chronic insomnia.

I've suffered from insomnia for years and I've repeated the same cycle every night, for the last ten plus years. Most days, I run purely on adrenaline, caffeine, and energy drinks. Other days, I give in to the temptation and do some of the old Columbian marching powder. I can't remember the last time I slept soundly for the whole night. I spend my endless nights reading, experimenting with melodies on my beloved guitar, or just cruising around the city on my bike. But I seem to find my true peace buried in the words of the greats, Koontz, Laymon, Salinger, King, Tolkien and Gemmel. I lose myself in the fictional worlds and the pure escapism it brings to my otherwise chaotic life. Fiction takes me on a journey and the characters allow me to connect with them on a different level, holding me hostage until the final page and final word is read. After music, it's my one true passion and a distraction from mundane reality.

***

In between Emmy leaving and my wayward thoughts, the time seems to pass in a blur.

"Penny for 'em, babe."

Peyton requests and I look up. *She looks stunning; I can see why Sam fell for her so hard and fast.* She drops down next to me, on the edge of the bed.

"How are you, Brody, I mean really, none of your usual bullshit?" she challenges softly, and I laugh at her obstinacy. *I love and hate the way she knows me so well.*

"I'm exhausted, sweets, I might have had six months in rehab, but all I've done is think and I'm tired of fucking thinking," I sigh, as she leans her head on my shoulder and I wrap my arm protectively around her.

"You must have better things to do than listen to me fucking whine."

My lame attempt at a joke, causes her to frown.

"Don't ever say that, I've always got time to listen; I'm here for you, Brody. Always."

I squeeze her and tenderly kiss her forehead.

"In a different life, we would have been good together."

I sigh, half joking, and she rolls her eyes, laughing melodically.

"Is that the life where you swoop in, charm me and it's you I tattoo, instead of Sam? Somehow, I don't think that would have worked out, rock star."

I smile at her term of endearment for me. *She has no idea how important that makes me feel.*

"A man can only hope."

I exhale heavily, and she wraps her arm around me. "Come on, talk to me, Hart," she presses, and I chuckle softly at her tenacity.

"You've got mad fucking deduction skills, sweets," I say wryly, with a cock of my eyebrow and she shrugs.

"It's a gift, what can I say! Now, come on, spill!"

I puff out my cheeks and look up to the ceiling.

"I fucked up, royally. That girl, the one who just left, she's...*so fucking sweet.* She works at the café I've been going to for years. I bumped into her last night, when I was out, and before you ask, we didn't fuck. Apparently, I drunkenly hit on her and she pushed me away, then I bought her back here and I passed out. She's just a kid, why the fuck would I do that to her? What kind of monster does that make me? She doesn't deserve to be treated like that, like she's-*insignificant,* like she's just another hole for me to stick my dick into."

She smirks and crinkles her nose.

"That's a nice image I've got, thanks for that," she says sardonically.

"Sam told me about the married woman you were seeing," she blurts out and at that moment, I could kick Sam in the balls for telling her something so personal.

"Fucking son of a..." I stop myself from continuing and she reaches for my hand, squeezing it in a gesture of reassurance.

"Please, don't be mad at him, Sam's just worried for you because he cares, that's all. I promise you'll never get any judgement from me. We can't help who we fall for. Someone told me once that we all make mistakes, it's how we come back from them that counts."

I roll my eyes. *There she goes with her cliché bullshit, bless her.*

"Should I go downstairs and lie down on the sofa, so I can spill my deepest darkest secrets to you, sweets?" I say drolly, and she chuckles softly.

"My fees are expensive, I'm not sure you could afford me!" she banters back, cocking her perfectly plucked eyebrow, and I laugh.

"I take it back, Sam's fucking welcome to you!" I say cheekily, and she hits me playfully on my arm. I rub my arm and stick my tongue out at her. She giggles and someone clearing their throat interrupts us. I look up to see Sam standing in the doorway, dressed in his running gear, regarding us both intently, as he secures his phone to an arm strap.

"Should I be worried that my wife is in your room, Hart?" I don't miss the possessive tone in his voice, as she rolls her eyes and I chuckle softly.

"I was just showing her my enormous dick; she was so impressed; she's considering asking you for a divorce!" I say with an amused tone to my voice and Sam cocks his eyebrow, as he runs his hand through his hair.

"In your dreams, mate!"

We both laugh.

"Do you fancy coming for a run?"

I nod. *I could do with pounding the pavement to get out some of my pent-up frustration.* "Give me five minutes to get my shit together, man."

He nods curtly.

"Chin up, rock star, don't let the bastards grind you down," she says with a wink and kisses me gently on the forehead, as she leaves with Sam.

I wish it were that fucking easy.

5

Raleigh

I have been out of rehab for over two months now and today my agent, Paul Lyndsey, has set up a meeting with Damien Valentine, for an upcoming film. Damien Valentine is a rival to the likes of Guy Ritchie and Matthew Vaughn and stars from all over the world are queuing up to work with him. As a director, he is easy going, but a hard taskmaster - or so I have heard. I jumped at the chance, when my agent called me and told me Damien was interested in hiring me. I have been preparing, by reading over the script, that Damien had couriered over to me and I loved what I read, so much so that I devoured it in one afternoon sitting. It is sharp, witty, extremely funny, dark in places and beautifully written, with lots of twists and layers to the story.

I'm putting the finishing touches to my make-up and I take a deep breath, suddenly feeling so nervous my stomach is in knots. I apply a final coat of light pink lip-gloss and press my lips together. I am looking good, and I feel fucking good for the first time in a long time. After six solid months in rehab, for my addiction to prescription medication and self-harm, I am back and ready to prove my critics wrong. My short lilac hair is styled sleek and straight, I am wearing a white shirt, with a black vest underneath and black leather shorts, which make my legs look amazing. I finish my outfit, with a pair of cute black and white wedges. I place my thick, black-rimmed glasses on and with one last look in the mirror; I leave my hotel room, hopeful that my career is far from over.

My driver and my bodyguard, Clifford Holt drives the short journey to Damien's office. Cliff has been my driver since I moved to the UK and hit the big-time. I was a young, up, and coming actress, who was making a name for herself, as my first movie was being released. I'd landed a huge role in a UK based soap off the back of it. I was being recognised more and more and it got to a point where I couldn't leave my apartment without the press camped outside. That's when Paul employed Cliff to take care of me and drive me around. Paul knew Cliff from the club circuit years ago, he trusted him implicitly and according to Paul, he was the only man who was up to the job. He's a quiet, stoic man, but he has a heart of gold and would go out of his way to protect me.

As I step onto the curb, I look up and up at the striking office building, in the heart of South Kensington, which houses Damien's independent production company, *Pendulum Productions*. I am in awe, as I enter the stark and bustling lobby. As I move further into the modern reception area, I notice the vibrant red and light grey tones, which gives off a sleek, but professional vibe. I shuffle nervously to the reception desk, to announce my arrival. *Fuck,* I am so out of practice, it has been a while. I clear my throat and paste a smile on my face. *Chin up, tits out, Storm.*

"Hi, I'm Raleigh Storm, I have an appointment with Mr Valentine."

The receptionist regards me with obvious disdain, and I try to school my expression to somewhere in between neutral and indifferent. She taps her acrylic nails on her keyboard and looks up at me.

"Take a seat, Mr Valentine will be down to collect you momentarily, *Miss Storm,*" she says aloofly, and I nod curtly, mentally counting to ten, as I walk over to the plush seating area. I sit down on the large black leather armchair, which seemingly swallows me, as I sit back. I take a few deep breaths and inwardly give myself a pep talk. *Come on, Storm, you can do it. This is the opportunity you have been waiting for.* I breathe in through my nose and out through my mouth, thinking nothing but positive thoughts and willing myself not to let nerves get the better of me. *You got this, girl.*

My thoughts are interrupted by the arrival of a tall, lean man, around six feet one inches tall, with short, dark brown hair, which is shaved close to his head. He has light, ocean blue eyes and he has at least a few weeks' worth of stubble on his chin. He is wearing a pair of dark jeans, which cling to his muscular thighs, a white t-shirt, black military boots and a black suit jacket, with the sleeves rolled up. I notice he has an intricate tribal tattoo, which wraps around his forearm. I struggle to get to my feet, and I can see by the look on his face, that he is desperately trying to hold in a smirk. He offers me his hand and pulls me up until I am upright. I stumble awkwardly into him and looking in his amused blue eyes. I clear my throat, feeling my face burning with embarrassment. *Great first impression, Storm.*

"Raleigh Storm, pleased to meet you, Mr Valentine," I offer him my hand, but his dismisses me with a wave of his hand.

"Please, no formalities here, call me Damien; it's a pleasure to finally meet you. Do you mind if I call you Raleigh?" he asks politely, and I shake my head.

"No, no, of course not," I mutter, and he chuckles softly.

"Try to relax, Raleigh; the press would say my bark is worse than my bite, but you're quite safe...*for now,*" he says, with a charming tone to his voice and I am instantly soothed by his friendly, laid back demeanour.

"If you would like to follow me." He smiles and gestures for me to follow him. I do as he asks, and I trail after him, in an awkward silence, through a maze of corridors, until we get to a set of frosted glass, double doors. The doors have the initials *D.V,* in flowing, script letters etched into the glass. My eyes flick to the sign and he laughs cumbersomely.

"I keep meaning to replace that, it's bloody pretentious isn't it?" he says, with an almost embarrassed edge to his voice and I love how down to earth he seems. He presses his thumb to the device to the right of the door and it clicks open. He steps inside, and I shadow him, taking in my surroundings, as we step through the door. His office is a stark contrast from the rest of the building, it is warm, inviting and feels quite like how someone might have their living room. The slate grey plush velour sofa with a fur rug over the back and a garish, brightly coloured Indian inspired blanket draped over the arm, sits in front of a glass desk, which has a MacBook and a few dog-eared scripts scattered haphazardly across it. The far wall has a large fireplace and mantle, dominating the space, with bookshelves full of books, lining it on either side. On the mantle there are two antique clocks and various photos of Damien with well-known, famous movie stars. A few of which I recognise. There is a television mounted on the wall to the right, which is muted and shows the showbiz news. In front of that shelf is an upright piano and bench in dark walnut. Hanging on the wall above the piano, is a collage of movie posters which Damien has directed. It really is an interesting and inviting space.

"Please, take a seat, would you like something to drink?" he enquires and nodding, I sit down in front of his desk.

"Water would be great, please."

He nods curtly and takes two bottles of water from a fridge underneath his desk. He hands me the bottle, with a warm smile.

"Thank you." I smile and unscrew the lid; I take a long pull from the bottle and it is a welcome feeling on my dry throat.

"Did my staff take care of you, whilst you were waiting?"

He sits down in his large leather chair.

"Yes, thank you," I lie, covering up my deception with a smile. He seems satisfied with my answer, clapping his hands together and kicking up his long legs casually onto his desk.

"Now, to the matter at hand. Did you get a chance to go over the script I had couriered over to you?"

I nod enthusiastically, and I am about to speak, when he abruptly cuts me off.

"I know this is a little unorthodox of me, but I want you to be in my film," he says brusquely, and my eyes widen. I observe that it's more of a statement than a question.

"Don't look so startled, Raleigh," he laughs.

"I'd love it if you would let me tell you a little more about it?"

I nod for him to continue and the smile that washes over his features softens his face, making him look at least ten years younger. He steeples his fingers under his chin, as he begins to speak.

"As you probably gathered, it's about a rock band and it starts off set on a tour bus. It depicts the truer to life, darker, grittier side of fame, kind of a twisted love story, if you will. I want you to play the role of Stevie Lynn, the female guitarist. I have seen you act, and I think you are exactly what I am looking for. You're edgy, different, and exceptional at what you do, it's refreshing. I know most directors audition actresses first, but as you've witnessed this morning, I'm *not* most directors."

I can see why people want to work with Damien. He is a force of nature, he is friendly, driven, but extremely down to earth. I feel instantly comfortable in his presence and I've never had that with a director before. It is a refreshing and welcome change.

"I'd love to be in your film, Damien. I loved what I read, Stevie was feisty, she didn't take any crap from anyone, and she reminded me a lot of myself."

That is before rehab and before Carter, but I don't say those words aloud.

"I learnt a long time ago, that the only thing you believe from the newspapers is the date. Despite what the papers say about you, I think there's a lot more to you, than meets the eye and I'd love to bring that out in you."

He regards me intently and I start to relax a little in my seat.

"Some actors and actresses find me intimidating, but that's only because I want to bring out the best in them. I know you're more than capable of acting the fucking shit out of this role," he says crassly, and I smirk. *I think I am definitely going to love working with this man.*

Our meeting is over quickly, and he promises he will call me as soon as he has details and a contract finalised. I leave the building feeling the most optimistic I have felt in a long time. As I step out onto the kerb, I pull out my phone and dial my best friend Liv. Olivia Rosenberg has been my best friend since we met in theatre school, when I first moved to the U.K. She was my first friend and we have been through everything together. The good times, the bad times and everything in between. Liv is a backing dancer for various artists on the mainstream music scene, has starred in numerous TV commercials and been an extra in a few popular UK based soap operas.

"Hey, what's up, *bitch?*"

Liv greets me, and I laugh to myself. *I love this girl.*

"The sky, bitch! Life is peachy fucking creamy right now and I feel like celebrating. I have news!"

I say excitedly, attracting the attention of a few passers-by.

"Please, tell me you're not pregnant, Rae?"

She asks, and I roll my eyes.

"No, I'm not fucking pregnant, you cheeky bitch!"

She laughs.

"Oh, yeah, I forgot, you'd actually have to get laid to get pregnant! Your vagina hasn't seen any action for a while! I'm surprised it isn't covered in cobwebs!"

I clutch my stomach; I am laughing so hard. I hear a man's voice in the background, and she clears her throat.

"Erm...I'll call you back in ten, Rae! Love ya!"

She says brightly and in a rush.

"Right back 'atcha, Livvy!"

She hangs up and I cross the busy road, with Cliff a few steps behind, following the flow of pedestrians. I go into the small, quaint coffee shop. I order a double shot of espresso and sit by the window, watching the world go by. I'm enjoying the quiet calm and basking in the fact I'm rarely recognised when my phone starts ringing. As I see Damien's name flash up, my stomach somersaults. *He's going to say he's changed his mind, fuck, I feel sick.*

"Hello?" I say apprehensively, taking a sip of my espresso with a trembling hand. *Positive thoughts, Storm.*

"Raleigh, it's Damien, I've set wheels in motion. My legal team are drawing up a contract as we speak, and it should be with your agent by the end of the day. All it needs, is for you, your agent, and a lawyer to go over it. Then I need a signature from you, and we have the green light. From what I've heard you like to research your roles. I have contacts in the music industry; how would you like to go on an upcoming tour with Rancid Vengeance?"

He asks, and my eyes widen. Me, on tour with a bunch of rockers? The very same rocker that I met in rehab. Brody Hart, the charismatic guitarist who sent my hormones into orbit.

"How soon would you want me to go?" I ask apprehensively, biting my lip. He pauses, and I hear the creak of leather, as I picture him leaning back in his chair.

"How does the beginning of next week work for you, for a month? I want a quick turnaround on this film; I want my cast fully assembled and I aim to be shooting within the next eight weeks."

Eight weeks... fuck me. Looks like I'm going on tour with Rancid Vengeance. Who knew?

6

Brody

I finished my run with Sam, and by the time we finish, I'm fucking knackered. My legs are deliciously sore, but my head is finally clear for the first time in months. We are in the car on the way to our record company, for a meeting with our manager, M.J. Michael James Richmonde III, has been our manager for a while now and he has been such a breath of fresh air for us. He is smart and so laid back he could be fucking horizontal. His experience in the industry is second to none. That's one of the reasons why we hired him, he has our best interests at heart, and he gets the direction we want to go in where our music is concerned. He is a welcome addition to the Rancid Vengeance family.

As we all saunter casually into his office, M.J is sitting at his large antique desk, with his cowboy booted feet perched on the edge, looking every bit the rock star manager. He has three buttons on his burgundy paisley shirt undone with his sleeves rolled up, he is wearing dark blue skinny jeans, and he has a grey streak running through his sandy brown, spiky hair. It should look ridiculous on a man his age, but oddly, it suits him.

"Boys!"

He greets us enthusiastically in his familiar soft American drawl that we have become accustomed to. We all mutter our usual greetings to him, and he gestures to the long stylish sofa, in front of the desk.

"Please, sit."

We all sit down, and he pushes a button on the desk phone. "Could we get some refreshments for the boys, please, doll?"

There's a slight pause, as a female voice replies quickly. "Yes, of course, coming up, right away, Mr Richmonde."

A few minutes pass and his assistant, whose name I can never remember, enters the room, with a large carafe of coffee and five cups on a tray. She sets it down on the table and starts pouring it. As she starts pouring, M.J claps his hands animatedly, startling her, and she clumsily spills the coffee on the desk. He rolls his eyes, and we all watch, as Jax gets up from his seat and proceeds to help her clear up her spillage. He gives her a tender look of sympathy, and she mutters her thanks, as she exits the room. M.J leans back in his chair and steeples his hands, as Sam leans forward to grab a cup of coffee.

"Right, so boys, I've got some terrific news! Damien Valentine has been on the phone this morning; he's making a new film. Now! Onto the juicy part!"

He waves his hands in an elaborate, dramatic gesture and I chance a look at Sam who's sitting there brooding, his leg involuntarily twitching. Jax looks like he'd rather be anywhere else but here and Lucas is awkwardly gnawing on his nail, looking bored. I try to hide my smirk, as M.J clears his throat to continue.

"The actress he's cast likes to research her roles extensively before she starts shooting. Which leads me to the next thing, how do you fancy having a guest on the tour bus? Actually, it's guests, plural. Three to be precise."

We all look at each other and Sam, ever the professional, takes charge of the situation. He sets his cup down on the table and straightens, looking M.J dead in the eyes. "Don't you think you should have at least run it by us before you agreed? What sort of guests are we talking about here, M.J?" Sam says, with a hint of prudence to his husky voice. His muscles bulge, as he folds his arms defensively across his chest. M.J leans forward in his chair and rests his elbows casually on the desk. *Where the fuck is he going with this?*

"Raleigh Storm, she's been cast as one of the leads in the film, as a female guitarist in a rock band. Gavin Kincaid, he's been cast as the bands manager and I believe you're familiar with Nick Slade, who has been cast as the band's lead vocalist."

As soon as he says her name, my cock jumps to attention. *Jesus Christ.* I catch the expression on Lucas' face as Nick's name is mentioned and if I'm not mistaken, he squirms in his seat. Crossing one leg over the other, he refuses to meet our gazes. *Hmm, interesting.*

"Damien asked if we minded having a few extra people on the bus, naturally, I said yes, of course, it will be great exposure for Raleigh, Gavin, Nick and for you guys obviously! I thought you wouldn't mind."

He laughs, as we all look cautiously at each other and I swear I hear Sam curse under his breath.

Of all the gin joints, in all the towns, in all the world, she walks into mine. Yes, I am quoting Casablanca. Fuck me.

Raleigh

Some days I love my job, other days I fucking hate it with a passion. Packing for a month on a tour bus, with a bunch of sweaty rockers, is way more difficult than it sounds. *What does a woman like me, pack for a situation like that?* I am standing in my hotel room, surrounded by a mountain of clothes and the room looks like a bomb has gone off. I have just showered, after my workout in the hotel gym and ever since Damien informed me that I was going on tour with Rancid Vengeance, I've been restless and all I have thought about is Brody. How he made me come over and over again, with his expert split tongue, how he tuned my body like an instrument and how I can't orgasm without thinking of him. My thoughts are interrupted, by my phone blasting out *'Zombie by Bad Wolves'*. I smile, as I see Liv's name flash up on the screen.

"Hey girl."

I greet her cheerfully.

"Hey yourself, how's the packing going?"

I sigh, taking in the carnage surrounding me.

"It's not; I'm really not sure about this, Liv, as good an opportunity as working with Damien Valentine is-"

She stops me before I can continue. "No, you're going to stop that, right now, Raleigh Storm. You are going to pack that suitcase; you are going to slap a smile on that beautiful fucking face of yours and you are going to own that tour bus! Amy's fiancé is their bodyguard; the lead singer is Cole's best friend. He came into the studio once, for a photo-shoot, that guy is hot, with a capital H!"

I giggle at her description of Samson Newbolt, lead singer of Rancid Vengeance. *She's right, he is rather delicious.*

"Unfortunately, he's off limits, because he's married now, but the rest of those gorgeous boys, are fair game! Including Mr Guitarist extraordinaire, who you had that juicy encounter with in rehab!"

She laughs, and I find myself laughing right along with my best friend.

"You always know the right words to make me feel better, Livvy."

I flop down on the bed, amongst the pile of clothes. I stare at the ceiling and sigh heavily. "What if he doesn't remember me, Liv? What if I was *that* forgettable? He...he made me feel things, things I haven't felt in...*a long fucking time.*"

I hear her curse softly. "Babe listen to me, if he doesn't remember you, you need to make damn fucking sure he does! What happens on tour, stays on tour, that's the motto isn't it? Why wouldn't he remember you? You rocked his world in rehab, rehab of all fucking places, you filthy slut!"

We both giggle childishly.

"Look, I'm coming over to your hotel; this is your last night before you go on tour, so we're going to make it count. Get your dancing shoes on, because we are going to paint the town all kinds of psychedelic colours! Be ready in an hour, bitch!"

Before I can protest, I hear the click of the phone, as it goes dead. *Looks like we're hitting the town.*

Brody

By the time I was sixteen, I was fluent in the art of seduction and I knew what was required to seduce a woman. I lost my virginity aged fourteen, and I made it my life's mission to know all there was to know about the fairer species. From the moment I realised the difference between men and women, I have been a lover of the female form; so much so, I live by the mantra of the *five F's*: find 'em, feel 'em, finger 'em, fuck 'em and forget 'em. For that reason alone, I don't even have to try, usually a rightly placed word, a wink, or a cheeky smile was all it took to get a willing and able woman beneath me. Women got off on the fact that I'm Snake from Rancid Vengeance and my reputation as a generous lover had gotten around over the years. Yes, I might be a total dick, I might leave her in the morning before she even wakes up, I might not call, or see her again after one night of unbridled passion. But I always made it a night she would never forget and I always made sure she came first. I was an attentive lover, I took my time, getting to know her hot spots and what really turned her on. I'm a master of seduction, a connoisseur of cunnilingus, a guru of sex and fucking God of the g-spot, which was why without fail, they always come back for more. They usually always want more than I can give, which is why I haven't settled down, at least that's the excuse I'm using and I'm sticking to it.

After our meeting with our manager to inform us of our surprise tour guests, we decided to hit a club, for an exceedingly rare boy's night out and blow off some steam. I am spraying some *Dior Sauvage* aftershave, as the door taps.

"Yo."

I call out and the door opens, and Sam stands in the doorway, with a frown on his face, fidgeting with the sleeve of his black blazer. "What the fuck is going on with you, dude, you're not your usual self. You seem-off."

I roll my eyes. Sam folds his muscular arms across his chest and cocks his pierced eyebrow. "Come on, out with it, Hart."

I try to distract myself, by picking up my dirty washing and dumping it haphazardly into the washing basket.

"It's her, isn't it? The married woman that you were seeing, the one who seems to tie you up in knots? She's the reason you're acting like a complete dick."

I'll give the fucker ten out of ten for observation. When I don't meet his eyes, he steps further into the room and closes the door behind him, leaning against it. *He thinks he's being intimidating because of the size of him, but he doesn't intimidate me. Sam Newbolt's secret is that he's a big fucking softie and he always, without fail, cries at Titanic.*

"It's no big deal, Sam, just fucking drop it, yeah?" I snap abruptly, and he just stands there, smirking. *Smug bastard.* "It was nothing," I say nonchalantly.

"Of course it was!" he says with an amused tone to his voice and by the look in his eyes, he's not buying it, and he most definitely isn't going to drop it. I puff out my cheeks, exasperated. *Fucker.*

"Ok, we fucked...*a lot*, end of story, now will you please, just fucking drop it?" I yell impatiently, silently begging him to just shut the fuck up. He drops down onto the edge of my bed. *He's not letting this one go.*

"You're so full of shit, your eyes are turning brown, Hart," he says drily, and I shake my head.

"Since when have you been so interested in my love life, Sam? She tied me up in knots, I fell in love with her, and she chose her husband instead of me, end of! *She's* the fucking reason I went off the rails, is that what you really want to hear?" I raise my voice.

"I begged her to leave him, Sam, I got down on my knees and I *fucking begged* her. I have never begged a woman in my life, ever. She got to me; she got under my skin. *Shit,* it was never meant to be like this, it hurts to see her carrying on, as if nothing happened, ya know. Then she ended it and said she had to focus on her marriage, her career and trying for a baby. She told me we couldn't be together and that's when I lost it. I literally went bat shit. She's part of the reason I ended up in fucking rehab after your wedding, Sam, *she's* the reason I was so messed up."

I start to pace the room, almost frantically and I need a fix so bad, my skin feels like its buzzing. *Fuck, fuck, fuck.*

"I loved her-*Jesus,* I *love* her so fucking much, but it'll never be enough, *I'll* never be enough." I run my hands over my head and Sam looks at me.

"*Shit*, dude, I had no fucking idea, why didn't you talk to me? Why didn't you tell me any of this before?"

I laugh bitterly. "I know you, Sam. I've known you since we were kids, you and the boys would never have let me live it down."

He shakes his head. "That's fucking bullshit, and you know it, Hart," he says matter-of-factly, and I briefly close my eyes.

"Because I was fucking *ashamed!* I was ashamed, alright? I was sleeping with someone else's wife, Sam. She was never mine to begin with, every stolen moment we had together reminded me of that. I had to share her with him, and do you know how that made me feel? I couldn't fucking stand it! I couldn't bear seeing her with him, it fucking hurt!" I raise my voice a few decibels louder and angrily swipe away the tears, that have escaped from me, as I purge everything that happened between Lorna and me.

Lorna Lavelle is the married woman I have been sleeping with for the past four years. She is a West End make-up artist, and we met in the 'House of Burlesque' club, where she used dance part-time. She has skin the colour of café au lait, aquamarine eyes, long red hair, and her legs go on for miles. She is married to Stefan Lavelle, a well-known professional surfer, from Oahu in Hawaii and they have been married for nine years. Even though he beats her, and abuses her physically and mentally, she refuses to leave him.

"Every moment I had with her, was fucking borrowed, I needed her like you need Peyton. She was *it* for me, Sam. I always want what I can't fucking have, it's been that way my whole life. After she said it was over, she just pushed me further away, stopped taking my calls and point blank refused to see me."

The looks in Sam's eyes, says it all and I clear my throat, as I jab my finger in his direction. "Don't you fucking dare feel sorry for me, Sam Newbolt, don't you dare!"

He holds his hands up defensively and I suddenly feel angry at him for forcing me to talk about it. "There's no pity or judgement here, mate, I promise," he says sincerely, and I roll my shoulders, as I check my reflection in the floor-length mirror. *I suppose I'll do.*

"Right, are we going to get fucking shit-faced, or not?" I say a little too brightly and Sam stands up. *I can't talk about this anymore.*

"So, that's it, then? You're just going to fucking carry on, as if nothing's happened?"

I look at him and he glowers at me. *Two can play that game, Newbolt.*

"Yep, that's exactly what I'm going to fucking do."

I grab my leather jacket and don't give him an opportunity to say anything more. *Subject closed – for now at least.*

***

The pulsing beat of Blow by Ed Sheeran, Chris Stapleton and Bruno Mars, blasts through the speakers of *Neon Nights*. The walls are decorated with opulent black, teal and aubergine wall coverings, the main area of the club is open with purple plush sofas all around the edges, and the tables are black granite and chrome. The fully stocked black granite bar takes up the whole back of the venue, as we are escorted into the V.I.P lounge, by our security team and a leggy blonde hostess, who is wearing tiny gold hot pants.

"What can I get you boys to drink?" She purrs, as I rub my hands together and tuck a hundred between her ginormous tits, which are spilling out of her gold bikini top.

"Bottle of your finest Cristal and a large bottle of Jack please, darlin'. Keep 'em coming and put it on our tab."

She nods, fluttering her fake eyelashes at me. *Looks like I'm in there, get in my son!*

"Coming up, hot stuff," she winks and teeters off on her heels, fluffing her hair as she goes. I slap Sam on the back and laugh animatedly, "looks like I've still got it, Sammy!"

Sam rolls his eyes, and we all sit down in a roped off private corner booth.

Nights out seem to be rare these days, and it reminds me how far we have come since the early days. Performing in dive bars, dodging glasses, and stepping over drunks. We are at the height of our careers and so much has happened in the fourteen years since we formed Rancid Vengeance. Sam is settled down, with a wife and two kids, Jax is a dedicated dad to his daughter, Thea and Lucas is just...well, Lucas. I'm stuck in the same rut I have been since we started, battling demons and a fucking drug addiction.

I start to think nothing is ever going to change, when I catch sight of a woman in a striking red dress. As she turns around, I'm stunned into silence, when the realisation hits me, it's Raleigh Storm, the fucking goddess I met in rehab. The one who rocked my world, and I haven't been able to stop thinking about. She is with her friend, the smile on her face is easy, genuine and lights up her whole face. *I can't tear my fucking eyes away from her.* The colour of her dress, as she dances effortlessly and gracefully, across the dance floor. The colour of her lipstick, as she smiles, with that familiar sparkle in her eyes. I am fucking floored by her beauty. She has never looked more beautiful and for the first time ever, as I watch her, I feel weak, vulnerable, and exposed. *A feeling that I have never been overly familiar with.* My thoughts are interrupted by Sam's leg nudging mine.

"Something you need to tell us, mate?" he says, with an amused tone to his voice, as the other boys laugh raucously.

"Nothing at all, dude," I say nonchalantly, with a shrug of my shoulder and a slight shake of my head. I am not ready to share her. *Not yet.* She is too fucking precious for that. I hardly know her, and she is already evoking feelings in me, that are...*alien.* Sure, we know each other intimately. I will never forget the distinct female moans she made, as I licked her to climax over and over again. The way her breathing would increase and the way her body stretched out like a cat, as she reached orgasm. *Fuck, I'm hard just thinking about her.*

"Bullshit," Jax regards me with narrow eyes.

"We've known you for over twenty years, Brody, and you've always been shit at poker. You have so many tells, the way you squeeze the back of your neck, when you're nervous."

I release the back of my neck, and they all laugh rowdily. *Busted.* "See, told you!"

I pout.

"Brody Hart, I do believe you're pouting! He's definitely pouting, guys!" Lucas laughs wildly.

"Fuck you!"

Sam turns to see who has me tied up in knots and cocks his eyebrow. "She's Miss Rehab, isn't she? That's the reason you were so cagey in our meeting earlier. Raleigh Storm, the very same Raleigh, who's coming on tour with us, you filthy fucking animal!"

Jax and Lucas look at each other and then back at me.

"Dude, seriously? You and Raleigh Storm? She's...*fucking stunning*, how did you manage to tap that?" Lucas chuckles at his own joke and I kick him under the table.

"Prick."

Lucas sucks his bottom lip and rubs his leg.

"Asshole," he mutters.

"Why are we always the last ones to find out?" Lucas complains and I roll my eyes.

"Seriously? Don't you motherfuckers have anything better to do, than stick your beaks into my love life? It's really no big deal, we fucked that's all, end of." I try to sound cool and detached, avoiding their scrutinising eyes. Jax snickers and catches Sam's stare. They exchange a silent look, and I look from Sam to Jax.

"What was that fucking look about? I saw that." I narrow my eyes suspiciously, as they both shake their heads in unison.

"Nothing, man." Sam holds his hands up defensively, as he takes a sip of his drink. I am about to stand up when my skin starts to prickle. She is close and as I turn around; I am greeted by those familiar, sparkling amethyst eyes.

Fuck me.

7

Raleigh

As my gaze locks with his, I witness the familiar flash in his eyes, that I saw when we first had sex. Maybe it's the colour of my dress, maybe it's because this is the first time I've seen him since rehab. *Who knows?* I can feel the weight of his sizzling stare, from across the room and boy, is my pussy throbbing to feel him inside me again. *Shit, this man is like a walking aphrodisiac. I feel like a bitch in heat.* My blood is on fire; my pulse is racing and every nerve in my body is tuned to Brody Hart. *Fuck, what is he doing to me?* He's like a force field and I'm a magnet being pulled towards him. I shouldn't feel this way, I shouldn't crave the forbidden fruit, that he so willingly offers. I twirl my ring around my middle finger, and I hear Liv softly chuckle.

"You only do that when you're nervous, or anxious, he's really got to you, hasn't he, babe?" Liv observes and I shake my head to try and dismiss her, but she knows me too well.

"Don't lie to me, Rae, you forget how well I know you. It's ok to want him, there's absolutely nothing wrong with that. You're only human, I must admit, he's smoking hot, it's all about the tattoos."

Liv fans herself with her hand and I swear she fucking swoons. I roll my eyes. *Dramatic as ever, Liv.*

"What?" she feigns innocence, as she sucks her Cosmopolitan through a straw.

"I know I might be engaged, but there's no harm in window shopping. I can look, but not touch, right?" She cocks her perfectly plucked eyebrow. I laugh and take a sip of my rose wine.

"Why don't you go and say hi?" she tries to encourage me.

"Not a chance, he's with his friends, I don't want to intrude," I say in a rush, and she sighs theatrically. "All men aren't Carter Leonard, Rae."

I shudder, as she says the name of my manipulative ex-boyfriend. He's the reason I ended up in rehab. His constant put downs, the sleeping around, the subtle mental abuse that went on for months and the bruises I ended up with after he'd been drinking. I push those thoughts from my mind and focus on the pulsing rhythm of *Bruno Mars 24K Magic*. The beat of the song rolls through me, along with the four tequila shots I just downed to pluck up the courage to go and say hi. *You're pathetic, Storm.* I look at Brody and he is just as stunned to see me as I am to see him. *What are the fucking odds of us bumping into each other?*

"Hey trouble." His voice playful and filled with wicked promise, as I clear my throat, feeling more than a little nervous.

"Hey yourself."

Fuck, he's gorgeous. I have to stop myself from eye-fucking him, his muscles are visible through his leather jacket and white t-shirt combo.

Black tattoos peek out from his leather jacket cuffs, covering the backs of his hands to the knuckles. Both are black and grey, on his left hand is a rose with hints of red and on his right hand is a super realistic eye. He's magnetic and there is an invisible connection between us. An undercurrent of overwhelming desire and need takes over my body. I'm lost and totally fucking blinded by sizzling hot lust. I haven't seen him since rehab and I've craved him every day since I left. He's been my go-to fantasy each time I've been reacquainted with B.O.B.

"What have I told you about eye-fucking me in public, kitten?" he whispers low and suggestively in my ear, the hairs on the back of my neck standing on end, as I feel his warm breath against my skin. He runs his finger down my bare arm, and I have to stop myself from moaning aloud. *This man is seriously bad for my health.*

Liv comes strutting over to us, flicking her blonde hair over her shoulder, interrupting the moment. *Typical Liv, she's a natural flirt.*

"Aren't you going to introduce us, Rae?" she asks with a girlish giggle. *She's definitely had too many cocktails.* For the first time, I notice the rest of Rancid Vengeance, sitting casually in the private booth.

"Sure," I clear my throat, my eyes locking with his and I can't look away. *Fuck me, he's even hotter than the last time I saw him, has he been working out?*

"Liv, this is Brody, Brody, this is my pain in the arse best friend, Liv."

Liv narrows her eyes and pouts childishly, as she offers Brody her hand.

"Nice to meet you, seems we have that in common, darlin'. These are my pain in the arse best mates, Sam, Jack and Luke."

Sam salutes coolly, Jax nods and Lucas sticks his thumb up in greeting. Liv chuckles far too enthusiastically, as she stumbles on her heels into the booth. Sam, Lucas, Brody and Jax all snicker between themselves and I can clearly see the chemistry amongst all four of them.

"Can I get you a drink, kitten?"

I nod and he offers me his arm. I link mine through his and his muscles undulate against mine, as we walk through the throngs of people, in the crowded club. I can feel the warmth of his skin through his jacket, and I am aching to glide my hands all over his ripped, inked body. He half turns towards me and leans in to whisper in my ear, his breath warm against my cheek.

"You as well, huh?" As if he can read my thoughts, he cocks his head towards the door.

"Step outside for some air with me." He makes it clear in his tone of voice that it's more a statement than a question and like a love-struck puppy, I blindly follow him. *What could possibly go wrong?*

Brody

I can feel the heat radiating from her tight little body at my back, as she follows me outside the club. The rush of cold air chills me to the bone; I instinctively take off my leather jacket and wrap it around her shoulders. I'm struck dumb by the smile she gives me in return, as if no other man has ever done that for her before. The sudden change from loud music, to just the sound of our breathing is a welcome change, and I relish in the momentary silence. We both go to speak at the same time and we both laugh.

"Ladies first," I say, with an amused tone to my voice and she nods.

"I was just going to say, it's really good to see you, it's been a while. You're looking...*good*."

I chuckle at her statement, as she licks her lips. "Thanks for the compliment, you look stunning too, as always, but we both know I didn't drag you out here to exchange pleasantries, kitten."

My voice is low and rough. "*Fuck*, I've missed your tight pussy," I blurt out crassly and I can't seem to help it. She brings out a side of me that I don't show easily, and I don't miss the soft moan she lets out as I say those words.

"Admit it; you've thought about nothing else, since we fucked in rehab."

Before I finish my sentence, she's on me. She tackles me and pushes me forcefully against the wall. My back colliding with the cold, hard brick and she practically kiss attacks me, as if she can't get enough. She smashes her lips against mine and slides her hands underneath my t-shirt, running her nails possessively down my abs. She briefly pulls away and the look she gives me is filled with pure carnal lust. Her eyes turn smoky in the dim streetlight.

"Ah fuck, kitten, what are you doing to me?"

She lifts up my t-shirt, claws at my biceps and I growl at the feeling, torturous pleasure mixed with sweet pain.

"I'm taking what's mine, Mr Hart. You have no idea what you've done; you've ruined me for all other men. I can't fucking orgasm without thinking of you and your magnificent cock."

I'm not sure if it's the alcohol talking, but I'm taken aback by her words and fuck, is it turning me on. *At least it's given my fragile ego the boost it needed.*

54

"*Fuck,* I love it when you talk dirty, kitten," I smirk, and she presses her forefinger to my lips.

"Shhh, no more talking. I just want you to fuck me." She crushes her lips to mine and proceeds to undo my belt. *Shit, who is this fucking vixen?* As her fingers wrap around my dick, I am fucking finished. I let out a primal grunt, as she pulls away from our kiss and tugs my lip with her teeth.

"*Shit*, Raleigh."

She sinks down to her knees, unzips me, and wraps her lips around my hardness. I hit my head against the wall, as she starts to build up a rhythm. I try hard not to gag her, as she expertly moves her tongue around my piercing, and I get off on the danger of almost being caught. It's forbidden, a little dangerous, and it's fucking hot as hell. *The press would think their Christmases have all come at once if they caught us right now.*

"*Fuck,* you're going to make me come, so hard."

She sheaths her teeth and picks up her pace. As my breathing quickens, she stops and grins mischievously. *What the actual fucking fuck.*

"I want you to be inside me when you come," she says seductively, as she slides her knickers down her legs and steps out of them, stuffing them in the pocket of my jeans with a cheeky wink.

"Condom," she pants breathlessly.

"Wallet," I manage to grit out, as she reaches into my pocket and takes out my wallet. The hard on I'm sporting, is fucking painful. She pulls it out, carelessly shoves my wallet back into my pocket and impatiently rips the condom wrapper open with her teeth. She envelopes me with the rubber. *Fuck, I hate johnnies.* She jacks me off a few times, climbs me like a tree and wraps her slender legs around me. I position my cock at her entrance and push up inside her. We both shout aloud, as I enter her slick channel, allowing her to adjust to my length and my piercing for a few seconds. *Fuck, I've missed this.*

"*Jesus,* kitten, I forgot how fucking good your cunt feels."

She audibly gasps and throws her head back in ecstasy. *Her pussy is so fucking tight; I think I've found heaven.*

"*Oh, Jesus fucking Christ!*"

Her shout echoes in the quiet alleyway. I spin us around abruptly and slam her against the wall, ramming my cock deep inside her tightness. I quicken my pace, rearing back and thrusting forward, much to her delight. As I push my cock deeper into her, I feel my piercing bump her cervix. I build up a punishing pace, as my cock drives in and out of her slickness, I can feel her pussy undulating around me, and I know she is close. *Fuck, she feels so good.*

"God, Brody, don't fucking stop, don't you fucking dare. It feels too good," she whimpers, as I deliver a punishing thrust.

"I've got you, kitten. Fucking come for me, now!" I encourage, as she leans forward and sinks her teeth into my shoulder. I grunt at the bite of pain, as I feel her orgasm detonate, from deep within her.

"Brody, I'm coming. Oh shit! Fuck! I'm coming!" she pants, as she bites my shoulder harder, and I can't stop myself from exploding inside her with a roar.

"JESUS! FUCK! SHIT! RALEIGH!" I quiver against her, as we both ride out our orgasms. It takes us a few minutes, to catch our breaths, but she unwraps her legs from around my waist and I set her down on her feet. *Wow, just fucking wow.*

***

As I set her down on wobbly legs, she looks so hot and thoroughly fucked.

"You have no idea how long I've waited to do that again, kitten," I say gruffly, as I wrap my leather jacket around her shoulders again. She begins to straighten herself out and finger combs her hair. I smile to myself, and she looks up at me. *Fuck, I need to be inside her again.*

"*Fuck*, you're beautiful when you come, do you know that?" I stroke her face softly and she shivers at my words. As she stands there in front of me, looking a little dishevelled and a whole lot beautiful, my mind starts to race. I know I'm no good for her, I know I shouldn't want her, but I feel like the Joker, and she is my Harley fucking Quinn. What she doesn't realise is, she makes me feel weak, she's breaking down my defences slowly and I am fucking powerless to stop her. She doesn't care that I'm the bad boy and I will ruin her if she gets close enough. I am terrified that if I let her, I will need her the way Sam needs Peyton. *Like I needed Lorna.* But I don't allow myself to think about that. That is exactly why this can't happen again, no matter how much I crave my dick inside her.

She is looking up at me expectantly, she looks so beautiful and almost vulnerable. Her lips are deliciously bruised, and her lilac hair is slightly mussed. If I allowed myself, I could seriously love this woman. *Fuck me, where did that come from?* No, I'm toxic, and I'm no good for her. *You don't deserve someone like her. Fucking walk away, Hart, while you still can.* I clear my throat, as her hand slides over my bicep.

"I'm staying in the Presidential suite, at The Four Seasons Hotel, on Park Lane; we could continue this there, if you want to?"

Fuck. She stands there innocently, twirling her silver ring around her finger, anxiously waiting for me to answer. I try desperately to push those thoughts from my head and just go with it. *Live for the moment, Hart, what's the worst that could happen?*

"How about we go back to my place?" I suggest, and she agrees all too easily for round two. *Shit, why the fuck did I do that?*

***

After calling Trey to come and drive me home. The journey was filled with some seriously X-rated heavy petting. In a blur of hands, lips, and expert tongues, we end up back at my place. We both step out of the car, and I scramble for my keys, in a rush to get inside. As I push the door open, we both go inside in total silence. Before I can get hold of myself, I'm slamming her against the wall and devouring her mouth, as if it's the last thing I'll ever do. I slide the strap of her killer red dress down her shoulder and pepper kisses along her collarbone. She moans softly and reaches down to cup my hardness. I gasp as she unzips my jeans, skating my hand up her dress and feel her warm dampness from our earlier fumble.

"*Fuck,* you're all wet for me, kitten."

She smiles, "Mmm, all for you, baby."

She purrs, she's never called me baby before, but I like it. It makes me feel cherished and important. *Just like when Peyton calls me rock star.* It feels like forever, but she drags me up the stairs, by bunching my t-shirt in her fist, as if she can't wait to get me naked. *I know I can't wait to get her naked, I can't wait to see her tight little body bare again.* She practically drags me down the dimly lit hallway and I pounce on her, taking charge of the situation, as we come to a sudden halt outside my room.

"I can't wait to be inside you again, kitten." My voice thick with need, I manage to shove the door open with my shoulder. She grabs the front of my t-shirt and hauls me inside, kicking the door closed with her heel. As the door slams shut, it's a race who can get naked the fastest. She wins, and she tackles me to the soft, carpeted, floor, not caring if we even make it to the bed. It's in the moment, it's primal, it's frantic and I'm happy to just let her relinquish control and use me the way I've used her.

"Fuck me, Brody," she says fervently.

"I need you to fuck me, *hard,*" she pants and my lips quirk at her demands.

"Demanding aren't we?"

Her lips collide with mine and our tongues entwine. Cupping her pert breast in my hand, I slide my thumb across her already erect nipple. She gasps audibly.

"Touch me, Brody; I need to feel your hands on me, I need to be reminded of what it feels like."

My hands roam all over her body and her skin feels so soft. I commit every inch of her beautiful body to memory, every scar, every mole, every dimple, and imperfection. She writhes as my hands skate over every part of her; I move down her body and settle between her legs. I swipe my split tongue up her wet slit and with that movement, she's lost.

8

Raleigh

From our chance meeting at the club tonight, the night has been full of sexual energy, and I can't seem to get enough of him. I'm naked and ready for him, anticipating his next move. I have never been so turned on in my whole life and I'm needy and desperate to feel him inside me again. Brody moves down and settles himself between my legs. The sight of him causes slick heat to flood my pussy. Brody's split tongue licks a path up my wet centre, and I scream out at the contact. It feels like two tongues, licking me simultaneously, he also has his tongue pierced and the flick of the stud against my sensitive nub, feels amazing.

"You like that, kitten?" His chin is glistening with the evidence of my arousal. I nod, a little too enthusiastically and his deep chuckle resonates in my most sensitive parts.

"Mmm."

As he sucks my swollen nub between his teeth, I'm a total goner and he knows it by the cocky wink he gives me in return. *God, that tongue is magical.* Sometimes, I imagine it uttering the words "*Expecto patronum.*" I push that ridiculous thought aside, as I focus on the absolute pleasure this man lavishes upon me.

"Oh God, don't you dare fucking stop," I pant out, grabbing blindly at his head.

"*Christ,* you have the sweetest tasting pussy," he says gruff with need. "Fuck me, you're dripping wet."

Brody removes his tongue and pushes two calloused fingers deep inside me. I moan aloud and I take my nipples, rolling them between my thumb and forefingers, creating a delicious ache. He builds up a rhythm, his fingers push deeper, and his thumb continues to circle my engorged nub.

"Come all over my fingers, I want you to come hard for me, kitten."

His words are my undoing, and I scream, as his skilful fingers bring me to the most delicious orgasm.

"OH GOD! OH FUCK! YES! YES!" I writhe, and Brody squeezes every ounce of pleasure from me.

"*Jesus Christ*, you're sexy when you come."

Brody's voice is thick with his arousal, as he reaches into his wallet for a condom. He rips the foil packet between his teeth and rolls it down his impressive length. His cock has a piercing, in the end of his bell-shaped head. He also has a tattoo of a snake, wrapped around the length of his eight-inch penis, which I have never noticed before. He winks and I smirk.

"Is that why they call you Snake?" I inquire, referencing his stage name as I look up at him from beneath my lashes.

He nods, almost shyly. He's got absolutely nothing to be shy about; his body is fucking impeccable. His body is all hard, muscular lines, his shoulders are broad, but his hips are narrow and in perfect proportion with the rest of him.

"Like what you see, kitten?"

I nod and bite my lip as I look up at him.

"I need your cock buried inside me, Brody. I want to get lost in you," I say shamelessly, and he roughly enters me with a sharp shove forward.

He fucks me so hard; I feel the slap of his balls with each thrust.

"God, your cunt is so fucking tight, it's like my cock was made for you," he grunts crudely and continues to fuck me hard.

He lifts my leg over his shoulder, and he thrusts so deep I can feel him bump my cervix with each plunge of his hard cock. I throw my head back in ecstasy and moan loudly.

"Oh God! Brody, I need it harder, fuck me hard," I cry desperately, and he increases his deep drives, fucking me like a mad man.

"Do you like it hard?" he grinds out.

"*Oh, Jesus yes!* Yes! I love it hard and rough."

He reaches down and rolls my sensitive nipple between his thumb and forefinger. The combination of pleasure and pain causes me to scream.

"YES! OH GOD YES! THAT FEELS SO GOOD!"

As I cry out, he increases his deep thrusts, fucking me harder each time.

"Let it go, Raleigh, fuck. I can feel you throbbing around my cock, come for me, NOW!" he demands, and my orgasm washes over me, like a tidal wave of pleasure.

I scream out and Brody muffles my cries by putting his hand over my mouth, as he finds his release.

"FUCK!" he growls as his hot seed spurts deep inside me.

As both of our orgasms subside, he pulls out and rolls over onto the floor next to me, pulling me closer to him. He idly traces shapes on my shoulder, and I find myself snuggling deeper into his embrace, resting my head on his chest. I close my eyes briefly, relishing the silence and being in his presence. I start to let myself think of a potential future with him, but I can't allow myself that, at least not so soon. *This man could seriously be bad for my health.*

Brody

For the first time in my life, I'm enjoying post-sex cuddling and shit. Raleigh is snuggled up to me and I feel content just to lie here with her, listening to the sound of her breathing. Words aren't necessary, we're both so wrapped up in each other and right now; there is no place I would rather be. She is stunning and so vulnerable; it hurts to look directly at her. I wish I could frame this moment and keep it with me for all eternity.

As we both lie naked next to each other, I feel her breathing even out and before too long, I notice she has fallen asleep. The longer I lie here, with the warmth of her skin against mine, the more I allow the doubt to creep in. *You don't deserve someone as beautiful and pure as her, you'll taint her with your poison, Hart.* Desperate to quell the demons inside my head, I swing my legs out of bed, pull on some jogging bottoms and head quietly out of the room.

I hate not being able to sleep, no matter how hard I try, I can't get my brain to switch off, and it drives me fucking insane. I feel an overwhelming sense of guilt at leaving Raleigh alone in my bedroom, but I find myself sitting at the mixing desk shirtless, writing lyrics and experimenting with melodies in our soundproof studio. It's the only place in the house I can retreat to and not wake Peyton, Freddie, and Zachary. It's one of the only places I can seem to go to find peace these days, without being drunk or high.

As I pluck the strings of my guitar, I let my mind wander to Lorna. My cock jumps to attention at the thought of her, she was like the forbidden fruit, and I was Adam in the garden of fucking Eden. *I couldn't fucking help myself.* My love for her was like an incurable virus, a soul-sucking, fucking disease that I would never be able to shake off. No matter how hard I tried, she would never love me the way she loved him. *Her fucking scumbag, wife beating, husband.*

I allow myself to think of the day we finally had sex, when we finally succumbed to the burning temptation, we both knew it was wrong, but it felt so fucking right. The way her pussy gripped my cock like a vice, the way her soft mewls sounded in my ear and the way she scraped her blood-red nails down my back to mark me as hers. I could never be hers and she would never be mine. That was the cold, harsh reality of it. Every time we had sex, I sent her back to her husband, full of my semen and as fucking twisted as it sounds, I got off on it. I got off on the fact that I fucking sent her back to him, with a part of me inside her. I knew I should feel disgusted, and I did. It fucking disgusted me that I got some sort of sick satisfaction out of it. But it didn't disguise the fact that, in that instance, I was the *'other'* man.

Every moment stolen, every kiss, every post sex cuddle we shared was never real. It was just an escape from life as we knew it. For her, it was an escape from her mundane, abusive marriage. For me, it was the chance to take a vacation from the shit in my head, escape from my chaotic life as one quarter of the biggest rock band in the world and just lose myself in her.

I know I have no right to be thinking such thoughts, while I have a gorgeous woman lying naked in my bed, but I can't help myself. I start to wonder whether Lorna is the reason I can't allow Raleigh to get close to me, or if it has something to do with my underlying mummy issues. *You know that's the real reason, Hart. Mummy didn't love you enough, you sad, pathetic twat.* I shake those negative thoughts away and try to focus on how Raleigh makes me feel.

She's like the sun and I feel her warmth every time she's near me. I feel like the weight of the world has been lifted off my shoulders and I want to allow myself to bask in that feeling just a little longer. The more time I spend in her company, the more I want her to be more than just a bit of fun. *A man can only hope.*

Raleigh

I wake in unfamiliar surroundings and momentarily feel a crippling sense of anxiety. *I never go home with strangers, ever.* Then it all comes flooding back to me, coming home with Brody, the sex, *Jesus fucking Christ, the sex.* I sit up and I feel a delicious soreness deep inside me, as I move, the memory bringing a wicked smile to my face. I look over at the space next to me, finding it empty and I can't help the disappointment that tears its way through my body. I get up, taking in the environment I find myself in. The room is a combination of grey and mustard yellow tones throughout, with grey and white furniture to match. It is something I didn't expect from Brody, and I find myself pleasantly surprised.

There is a large flat screen TV, mounted on the wall and a set of three photographs on the wall. I recognise a young Brody and the rest of the boys from the band, in the first one. He looks so far from the man I now know, and it makes me smile. The next photograph is of Brody, Sam, Peyton, and a little dark-haired boy. Brody looks ever the cool rock star, wearing sunglasses covering his eyes, ripped jeans, a white shirt open at the collar, revealing his neck and chest tattoos and a black blazer, which looks like it was made for him. The last photograph is of a young dark-haired boy and a beautiful dark-haired woman. I look closer and study the photograph. I identify the boy as Brody, but the woman looks unfamiliar. I start to wonder if the woman in the photograph is his mum and I vow to ask him when I finally find him.

I start to pull on Brody's discarded white t-shirt, go over to the chest of drawers and pull open the top one. I find a pair of black Calvin Klein boxer shorts and pull them on, as I set about looking for him. I pull open the door and I am greeted by a little boy, with jet black hair sticking up in all directions, wearing Batman pyjamas, dragging a toy penguin at his side. He is adorable, as he rubs sleep from his eyes.

"Hello tiger," I smile, and he gives me a toothy grin in return.

"Are you Uncle Bwody's girlfriend?"

I am caught off guard by his question and I feel my face flush with embarrassment.

"Erm...yeah Uncle Brody is my friend," I answer awkwardly, as he takes a moment to take in my answer.

"Will you be my fwend too? This is *Keef*."

He waves his toy penguin in my direction, and I chuckle.

"Well, hello Keith, I'm Raleigh, and what might your name be, buddy?" I ask curiously.

"Fweddie, my mummy and daddy is sleeping, shhh!"

He puts his finger animatedly to his lips and I smile. *This must be Sam and Peyton's eldest son, Freddie.*

"Are you sure you should be out of bed, honey? It's very late."

He shakes his head guiltily and puts his arms out to me, gesturing for me to pick him up. I swing him up into my arms and I feel an overwhelming sense of wanting to take care of him. *I've never been a huge fan of kids, but this kid, he's fucking adorable.*

"Let's go and find your mummy shall we, handsome," I say softly as I pad down the corridor with him in my arms.

"You've got pwetty hair and pwetty drawings like my mummy."

He reaches up to idly play with my hair.

"Why thank you," I beam and continue the walk down the corridor with him in my arms. He yawns dramatically and I chuckle to myself.

"Is someone tired, soldier?"

He nods, as I turn the corner and down the stairs, I find myself heading into the kitchen. I'm greeted by Brody, shirtless in loose fitting, grey jogging bottoms, which hang deliciously from his lean hips. He has a glass of milk on the counter behind him, and he is eating Nutella from the jar with his finger.

"Hey kitten, I'm sorry, did I wake you?" he asks around a mouthful of Nutella. He smiles softly, as he takes in the sight before him. "And you mister, you're supposed to be in bed," he chastises softly as Freddie clutches onto my t-shirt and buries his head into my shoulder.

"Sorry, I found him lurking outside your room, he's adorable."

Brody smirks, as he screws the lid back on the Nutella jar.

"Yes, he is, and he has a habit of wrapping everyone around his little finger! Troublemaker!" He chucks Freddie's chin, and he giggles mischievously. "And don't be sorry, babe, it suits you."

He winks and my stomach unexpectedly flip flops, at the thought of carrying Brody's child. *Where the fuck did that come from, Storm? You barely know him.*

"There you are, mummy's been looking for you, Freddie," a gentle, concerned, female voice says, and we both turn to see Peyton. I set him down and he runs full pelt into Peyton's legs, almost knocking her off her feet. She lifts him up easily and swings him onto her hip.

"What has mummy told you about getting out of bed and wandering off in the night, Freddie Bear?" she says tenderly. His bottom lip quivers and my heart melts.

"It was my fault, I found him outside Brody's room," I offer almost guiltily, as she takes me in.

"It's ok, honey, he's inherited his daddy's charm, unfortunately. Little heartbreaker, he's at that awkward stage."

She rolls her eyes dramatically, as she explains, and she pinches Freddie's nose playfully. Brody looks from me to Peyton, clearing his throat and smiling awkwardly. Peyton cocks her eyebrow curiously and Brody tries desperately to hold back his smirk.

"We're going to head back to bed, sweets."

She nods, with an amused look on her face. He kisses her on the forehead affectionately and kisses Freddie's chubby cheek.

"Night, sweets, night, night, sleep tight, troublemaker."

He salutes, as he leads me back the way I came. He swats my bum, as he walks behind me, and I shriek.

"Ready for round two, kitten?" he says seductively.

"I'm sure I could be persuaded, handsome," I counter.

Who are you trying to fool, Storm? *Round two is inevitable, along with falling for the unreachable rock star.*

9

Brody

I'm no good at early morning pleasantries, especially not before my first cup of steaming black coffee and definitely not before my morning workout. After a full forty minutes of sleep and a night of hot, nasty sex, with the Goddess that is, Raleigh Storm. I wake with a start and reach over to find a cold, empty space in my bed. *Well fuck me running, this is a first, it's usually me who just leaves without saying as much as a thanks for the fuck.* I get out of bed, with a slightly bruised ego. I go about my usual morning routine and try to mentally prepare myself for my therapy session with Rick the Prick. *I could do without this bullshit.*

One of the conditions of my release from rehab is that I still have to see Rick Delaney once a week. After the uneventful and silent journey, I find myself standing outside Rick's London office, in the heart of Greenwich. I'm all sorts of edgy as I make my way into the building, flanked by Trey, one of our many bodyguards, who oddly looks like Jason Momoa.

The receptionist greets me in an overly friendly manner and Rick steps out of his office, leaning casually against the doorframe, as Trey makes himself comfortable in the bright, but clinical reception area.

"Good to see you again, Brody, mate," he says in his familiar, annoying Mancunian accent. *I'm not your mate, dick.*

Nodding curtly, I step into his office with my hands tucked coolly into my pockets. I sit down on the sofa and rub my hands together anxiously. Every time I set foot in this room, I feel twitchy and cluck desperately for a fix. Rick observes me with cautious eyes and picks up his navy leather notebook. After the usual bullshit introductions, he clears his throat and begins to speak.

"So, we've touched upon this in our previous sessions, but I want to discuss it in more depth. Can you describe the dynamic between you and the other guys in the band?" he asks curiously, and I lean back in my seat, steepling my hands in front of my face.

"What do you want to know that we haven't already spoken about? Sam's the most dedicated one, he lives and breathes Rancid Vengeance. To an extent we all do, but Sam's level of dedication is ridiculous. He's the brooding

68

hunk, the reformed bad boy, but he's got something else to live for now, his wife and his boys and I couldn't be prouder of him, to be honest, he's come a long way," I say fondly as Rick scribbles furiously in his notebook.

After a few minutes of solid writing, he sets his pen down and looks up at me.

"Have you ever harboured feelings towards Sam?" he asks warily.

Where the fuck did that come from? Cheeky fucking prick.

"Fuck no! Our relationship is purely platonic, he's like my brother, all of the boys are like my brother's. They're the only family I've ever known. Mine and Sam's friendship, was toxic for years, I was a bad influence, we led each other astray, we weren't good together. He was my wingman, the guy who was always up for a cheeky line or three. After he met Peyton, it was different, *he* was different. I formed a bond with Peyton and that changed our friendship totally."

He picks up his pen and I catch his eye. He thinks better of scribbling in his notebook and puts his pen in the top pocket of his black Lacoste polo shirt.

"What's your relationship like with Peyton?"

I smile thoughtfully when I think of my best friend.

"She's...amazing, she's one of my best friends, she gets me on a level, that no one else seems to. She hated me when we first met and I didn't blame her, I won't lie, I was a complete arsehole back then, but we bonded while we were on tour. We did shots and played a game of truth, we got to know each other, and we've been friends ever since. She's the only woman I've been friends with that I haven't wanted to fuck and it's refreshing, ya know?" I explain as he smiles his Fox-like smile, and I'm instantly transported back to that day on the bus.

Brody

Past

I'm suitably buzzed after those cheeky lines of coke I've just snorted, and I feel like I could take on the fucking world! I'm zipping up my jeans as I come back from the toilet. We're at Neon Nights, unwinding and having a few drinks after yet another epic show. I'm rubbing my forefinger underneath my nose, and I sniff, as someone bumps head on into me. I catch her from falling and as I set her on her feet, I realise it's Peyton. Fucking great. I feel about as thrilled as she does right now, and she looks up at me with big blue eyes, which look startled, like a rabbit caught in headlights.

"Whoa! Where's the fire, sweetheart?"

I grin like a loon. Fucking hell, Hart, you could at least pretend you're not high as shit right now. I clear my throat, and she narrows her eyes on me. Fucking judgemental bitch.

"Jesus Christ, you're high," she says, as if it's a surprise to her.

Fucking hell, are you really that naïve?

"As a kite, babe!" I wink at her and tuck my hand into my pocket. Well, I may as well play up to it, once a junkie, always a junkie. "You didn't answer my question, where's the fire?"

She rolls her eyes, as if my sheer presence is an inconvenience to her. Well, the feelings fucking mutual, sweetheart. I look at her again and notice her nose is bleeding. What the fuck happened to her?

"You're bleeding, babe, come on. Let me take you back to the bus and get you cleaned up."

She swipes her nose with the back of her hand, as I grab her arm and lead her towards the back exit. We step out into the cool night air and Skip drives us back to the o2 arena car park where the bus is parked. I spend the journey silently looking out of the window, uninterested in the woman sitting next to me, who can't get further away from me. She's practically squished against the window. Fuck me, why does she have to be such a bitch. From the corner of my eye, I see her start to shake uncontrollably in the back of the car. Shit that was unexpected.

"Hey, I've got ya, sweets," I say softly and scoot closer to her, pulling her into an awkward side hug.

I have this overwhelming urge to protect her, as I drape my arm around her. She narrows her eyes at me, and I smirk at her reaction. I do have the ability to be a nice guy, on occasion.

"Not that I care, but Sam would kick my arse all over the bus for letting you bleed everywhere," I say indifferently and sniff.

"God, do you have to be such a prick?" she hisses, with an irritated tone to her voice.

"It's all part of my charm, babe."

Skip parks the car and makes his way over to the bus. He checks the bus for unwanted guests, and when he deems it safe, he nods curtly. We step out of the car and onto the tour bus. I lead her to the sofa and sit her gently down.

"I'll be right back; I think Lex has a first-aid kit here somewhere."

I head off down the bus. Fuck me, this night took an unexpected turn. I should be getting shit-faced right now, balls deep in some random groupie. Fuck this, if she's going to insist on ruining my night, I'm at least having a few drinks. I rummage around in the kitchen area; I know I had an emergency bottle of Jack here somewhere. I find it hidden at the back of the cupboard, grab the first aid kit from the drivers cab on the way and go back with two shot glasses. I put the bottle of Jack Daniels on the table and set the first-aid kit down next to it. I sit down casually on the table in front of her and I'm inches away from her. She's fucking gorgeous and definitely Sam's type, but I don't want to fuck her, which is a surprise. Any holes a goal and all that. I flip open the first-aid kit, taking out some antiseptic wipes and some cotton wool. I quirk my eyebrow and look at her regarding me intently.

"Are you not familiar with the concept of personal space?" she says wryly, and I laugh out loud.

She's feisty, I'll give her that. I move closer to her, mostly just to piss her off.

"You really don't like me very much, do you?" I observe casually.

"I didn't say I didn't like you," she states matter-of-factly, and I raise my eyebrows. I don't believe that for one fucking second.

"So, there's hope for me yet?"

I wink cheekily and she rolls her eyes. I choose that moment to swipe the antiseptic wipe under her nose and her eyes start to water instantly.

"Ouch." She winces and I puff out my cheeks. Fuck me, this is going to be a long night.

"Are you always such a baby?" I say wryly, as she hits me on the arm, and I stifle my laughter.

"You could at least be a little gentler," she grumbles and if I'm not mistaken, she pouts.

I hold my hands up in defence.

"OK, I'll be gentle, I promise, scout's honour." I salute as I gently clean the blood from her nose with the antiseptic wipe. "By the looks of it, you had the pleasure of being introduced to the delightful Miss Hudson?"

I laugh. The tenacious Miss Lyla Hudson, Sam's fucking crazy ex-girlfriend. The less said about that psycho bitch, the better.

"Why didn't he tell me about her before? Surely, you were all aware I knew nothing about who she was."

I shrug. Fucking hell, I should be charging by the hour for this shit. Since when have I become Jeremy bastard Kyle?

"Look, babe, I'm not interested in yours and Sam's proclivities, sexual or otherwise. If he wanted you to know, it was down to him to tell you. Personally, I don't give a shit, it's always been bros before hoes, that's just the way it is, darlin'. I know I come across as an arrogant prick, because, well, I guess I just am, but he's turned into a cockless wonder since he met you. We used to have fun before you came along, he was my best mate, we shared women, we took drugs, and every night was a party."

She wanted the truth; I'm giving it to her both fucking barrels. Jesus Christ, I need another few cheeky lines if I'm going to deal with this bullshit, my buzz is starting to wear off. I stand up, throwing the antiseptic wipe in the bin, and go to the sink to wash my hands. I'm a regular Florence fucking Nightingale.

As I go back to the living area, she's pouring us both shots of Jack Daniels, and I push the shot onto her side of the table. We both down them at the same time, and she grimaces.

"I know you think I've taken your best friend away from you, but it doesn't have to be that way. I don't want us to be enemies, Brody. Look, I know what happened to your mum, and I can't even begin to imagine what you went through—"

I stop her by holding my finger up, my eyes widening. What the actual fucking fuck?

"Wait, Sam told you about that?"

She nods, and I pour us both a second shot of Jack, trying to get my head around why Sam would spout my personal business to someone he's just fucking.

"Motherfucker! He had no fucking right; it wasn't his story to tell," I yell.

She reaches for my hand, and I let her. She squeezes it in a gesture of reassurance, and it feels oddly comforting.

"Brody, it's OK to talk, I'm a good listener, and I'm actually kind of starting to like you. You've shown me a different side of you tonight. You didn't have to take care of me, but you did, and I'm grateful for that."

She smiles, and I knock back my drink. Maybe she's not actually that bad, plus I think the alcohol is giving her the courage to open up to me a little more.

"Let's play a game, if you're up for it?" I declare, changing the subject and hoping she doesn't notice.

She knocks back her drink and I find myself smiling at her determination, knowing full well she's enjoying my company as much as I'm enjoying hers.

"OK, I'm up for it."

I take a seat next to her and cross my legs at the ankle, pouring us more shots.

"Let's play a little truth or dare game."

She nods in agreement. This is going to be fun.

"Here are the rules, if you choose truth, you have to take a shot."

I set the rules, and she leans back, taking her heels off. She tucks her legs underneath herself and leans back in her seat, making herself comfortable.

"You start."

"Truth."

I knew she'd choose truth. Pussy. I point to the shot glass, and she takes her shot.

"OK, has Sam fucked you in the arse yet?" I ask and the expression on her face is fucking priceless, as she almost chokes on her drink. "Using the whole 'I want to be the first and last man back here.'"

I put on Sam's deep voice, and I can't help it. She's so easy to wind up. I know I'm being a complete bastard, but I can't seem to help myself, she's such a prissy little Princess. She pauses and honestly, she looks like someone just murdered her puppy. I throw my head back and burst out into hysterical laughter. Sam Newbolt, you dirty fucking dog!

"From the silence, I'm assuming that's a yes. I fucking knew it! That boy has no shame; it's his signature move."

I lean forward, sensing her unease at my line of questioning. She looks like she's going to burst into tears, and I try desperately to stifle my laughter. For fucks sake, does she have to be so fucking sensitive?

"Seriously, don't sweat it, babe. It's not that deep."

She shakes her head, and I almost feel bad for being such a prick. Almost.

"It's fine, really," she says softly, clearing her throat, with a wave of her hand.

"OK, my turn. I take dare."

Let's get this fucking party started!

***

A few hours pass and a whole lot of truth or dares later, we are extremely drunk, after polishing off a whole bottle of Jack Daniels and half a bottle of tequila. Fuck me, I can't see straight, and I'm suitably wasted. I've had a good night getting to know her and maybe she's not that bad after all, I could see us easily becoming the best of friends. I've got to see a different side of her tonight and I feel an overwhelming sense of guilt for being an absolute dickhead towards her since she met Sam. Sam deserves to be happy, and I was a selfish prick for jeopardising it. I've apologised on more than once occasion tonight and I fucking hope she can find it in her heart to forgive me. From those few hours spent in her company tonight, she makes me want to be better, she makes me want to try and she's one of the very few people that makes me feel that way.

"I'm off to bed, babe, I'm fucking fucked!" I slur as I stumble from side to side and we both laugh. "Care to join me?"

I ask cheekily, wiggling my eyebrows. I know I'm pushing my luck, but I can't help myself. The attempt she makes at rolling her eyes, has me belly laughing.

"You wish, rock star!"

Something in the way she says that term of endearment, makes me feel special. I know that sounds lame, but it makes me feel wanted and not even my mum wanted me. No, not going there tonight, I'm in too much of a good fucking mood.

"You don't know what you're missing, sweetness!"

I wink and I manage to stagger back to my bunk on the bus, hopeful that this is the start of a beautiful fucking friendship.

***

Rick's voice snaps me back to the present.

"What about the other boys, describe your relationship with them?"

I lean further back in my seat and make myself comfortable.

"Jax is the baby of the bunch, he's always been the boy next door, and all the women love him. He's a good time guy but we're not as close as we used to be because he saw how I almost destroyed Sam. I'll be eternally sorry for that, I don't think Jax has ever forgiven me for it. His fiancée died in Vegas, after she gave birth to his daughter and he's fiercely protective of her. He's not the same as he was before Ruby, he's so lost and he's a little more broken now, we all are."

I feel all kinds of fucked up, as I think of what happened in the city of Sin. We saw things that no human beings should ever have seen, and we lived through things that no normal people have.

"Lucas, he's...complicated, he's clever, but none of us have ever got close enough, to know the real him. He's guarded, like military grade guarded, he doesn't give anything away and that scares the shit out of me sometimes. Even after over twenty-plus years of friendship, he's still a mystery to me, to all of us. He's closer to Jax now, like me and Sam are, but he's a great listener. He's very observant and extremely intelligent; a definite ladies' man. I think women get off on trying to figure him out, but he doesn't make it easy."

Rick nods and uncrosses his leg.

"Do you want to tell me what happened in Las Vegas?"

I roll my neck and steeple my fingers underneath my chin tautly.

"No, not really," I say flatly and resolutely.

I'd rather stick pins in my fucking eyes.

"It was well documented in the press; it can't have been easy to witness such carnage," he presses.

I take a deep breath to quell the need for a hit and lean forward, resting my elbows on my knees.

"That day will be etched into my consciousness until the day I fucking die. We lost so many people close to us that day, it's still hard to comprehend. I'll never forget the horrific sounds, the sights, it fucking haunts me," I say with a clenched jaw.

The sheer insanity of the whole situation and the events that took place on that fateful day, continue to affect us all, in one way or another.

Rick has stopped scribbling vehemently in his notebook and he's just sitting there listening, in disbelief, as I resume explaining what happened on the tragic day that changed all our lives drastically. Even though I'd rather not talk about it, I know sharing with Rick will put things into perspective and shed new light on an awful fucking event.

"I'll be honest, I haven't been in a good place since it happened. I saw some of the closest people to us butchered in the most horrific ways. The mindless bloodshed and the evil acts of violence. I saw a bullet pierce Ruby's skull; I saw the moment in slow fucking motion. I tried to help her, I tried to reassure her, I was fucking terrified, I was covered in her blood, it all happened so fast, some of it was a complete blur, but I was a total fucking mess. While Jax was unconscious, I lay next to her and held her hand, I stroked her stomach, and I told her everything was going to be fine. I fucking lied to a dying woman!"

I angrily swipe away a tear that has escaped from my eye. I never cry, I've spent so long repressing my feelings and emotions, I've almost forgotten what it feels like to *actually* feel.

"I lied to her, I made promises I couldn't keep, I...tried so fucking hard to help her, but it didn't do any good."

I sob and the look on Rick's face, is one of sympathy, as I'm transported back to that awful fucking day.

Past

Brody

Today is supposed to be Sam and Peyton's wedding, a day of celebration, drunken dancing and me fucking some nameless bridesmaid in the bog. Instead, some unknown fucking lunatic shrouds the room in a constant and relentless stream of bullets. They're ruthless and don't seem to give a shit who they hurt; they're shooting to kill. I'm so fucking terrified, I can barely think, as I lay there under the first pew that I could dive towards. Bullets thunking into the wooden pew and splinters of wood, showering down on me like wooden tears from the crosses on the wall, lamenting the scene of utter fucking chaos. Thunk, thunk, thunk, thunk. I see Alistair's head explode, as he is hit by four bullets, in quick succession. Thick, red, viscous brain and fragments of skull spraying out to decorate the walls and floor, as his body hits the ground with a sound I can barely hear over the cacophonous roar of gunfire and people screaming. There's a Chinese looking kid, can't be more than twenty-five, rooted to the spot in sheer terror. I see countless dark crimson stains start to form and spread out across his pale blue silk shirt, as he looks down with a look of utter confusion. He puts his hand on his chest, looks at his hand and just folds to the floor. Callum runs straight at the maniac with the guns, shouting something incoherent and without hesitation, the guns, which I think are automatic pistols, are turned on him and his head vanishes into brain matter, blood exploding all over the place. It was so sudden that his legs carried on going from the momentum and they kicked up into the air, like Wile E fucking Coyote.

As I listen to the hail of bullets rain down around me, my heart pounding in my chest, my survival instinct kicks in, and I crawl further underneath the pew. I know I'm a fucking coward, but of all the million ways to die, being taken out by a bullet in a chapel in Vegas, of all fucking places, doesn't even register on my list. But as I'm lying on my stomach, stock still, underneath the chapel pew, all that's running through my mind is staying alive. I saw Sam get shot, and it took everything in me to stay hidden, even as I saw his blood seeping from his lifeless body. I hold my breath and remain stock still, as the guns incessant firing made hearing anything else, even rational thought, impossible.

Out of nowhere, I hear a bone chilling scream and what I see is going to haunt me until the day I die. It happens so fast; it almost feels like it's in slow motion. A bullet pierces Ruby's skull, and she's so close to me that I hear a low, guttural moan as she hits the wooden floor, inches away from me. Her scared, glazed hazel eyes lock with mine and I can't stay fucking hidden anymore, I have to help her. I shuffle across the floor on my stomach, I think I saw it in a movie once, I'm a regular John fucking Rambo. I'm at her side in seconds, desperately trying to stay hidden and not attract the attention of the shooter. My heart is pounding and I'm regretting that stack of blueberry pancakes, bacon, and maple syrup I had for breakfast because it's threatening to evacuate all over the floor. I grasp her hand in mine and I'm not sure if she knows I'm here.

"Ruby, it's me, Brody, can you hear me?"

She garbles incoherently and I curse softly to myself, as I start trembling violently. I'm way out of my depth and I have no fucking idea what I'm supposed to do.

"Ruby, listen to me, you're going to be ok, yeah?" I whisper softly, as I stroke her hand.

"You and your baby, you're going to be just fine, I promise."

My voice is shaky and I'm fully aware I'm making promises I can't fucking keep. I shuffle closer to her and place my hand on her large bump.

"You and Jax, you're going to get your happy ever after, the one we talked about once, remember? Fuck! I'm out of my depth here, sweets, help me out."

I swipe a stray tear from my eye, I've never been this scared before, ever. I've seen some awful things and I've done things I'm not proud of, but this utter carnage, is on another fucking level.

I've never considered how I would die, and I've never thought about facing my own mortality. I always thought that I would stare death straight in the eye and shout 'FUCK YOU!' in his face, while giving him the finger. That's more my style. But, as I lie here whispering words of comfort to Ruby, it puts things into perspective for me, that nothing lasts forever, everything, even life is temporary.

I hear more gun shots, and I flinch violently at the sound. I squeeze Ruby's hand, and she doesn't respond.

"Ruby, Ruby, Ruby?" I mutter desperately and shuffle closer to her.

She's still breathing, barely, but I try to awkwardly cradle her lifeless body in my arms and rest my head on her shoulder.

"Ruby, please, please. I need you to wake up! Fuck! Fuck! Darlin', wake up, please!"

At that moment, I'm overwhelmed by the insanity of the whole situation and out of the corner of my eye, I catch sight of a clock hanging on the wall. I'm not sure if it's my mind playing tricks on me, or sheer terror making me delirious, but I convince myself that time has actually stopped.

The firing ceases and the eerie silence makes me let out the breath I didn't know I was holding, and I raise my head to see if I can somehow escape or at least call for help. I see someone charge towards the gunman, I recognise Seb, as I witness him put his hand up under the front of the shooters helmet and wrench so fucking violently sideways, I'm surprised the helmet didn't come off with the head inside. I have never in my life heard such a deafening, sickening snap, as the neck is broken, and the upper vertebrae is severed. Seb launches the lifeless corpse towards the wall, it hits with such force, that I'm sure it must have shattered the spine of that sick motherfucker.

Present

Brody

I'm snapped back to the here and now by Rick's soft voice. A tear rolls down my cheek and I swipe it away angrily, pissed off at him for forcing me to talk about it.

"Ruby's death wasn't your fault, you did all you could, you're a hero, Brody."

Rick tries to gently reassure me, and I shake my head.

"She lived long enough to give birth to her daughter, but I look at that beautiful little girl every fucking day and I see Ruby and that scene playing out repeatedly. It doesn't stop me forgetting that I fucking hid like a pathetic, coward, while my family were lying on some cold chapel floor bleeding out! It's part of the reason why I'm here because I'm not a hero! I'm a coward and I've never admitted it before because I'm ashamed! I'm a selfish, fuck-up, because I can't say no to drugs, because I'm as weak as my fucking junkie mother!"

I spit bitterly and I can't stop the honesty from spilling out.

"I hate myself, Rick. I can't bear to look at myself in the mirror, because every time I look in the mirror, I see her, I see my mum staring back at me."

I get up from my seat, rubbing my hands over my head and start to frantically pace the room. *Fuck me, I'm desperate for a fix.*

"I can't fucking do this. I can't, I just can't."

I repeat, shaking my head and squeezing my eyes shut, trying to quiet the voices in my head. I really don't need this shit right now, I need a hit, just one delicious line. I need to be obliterated to block out these dark thoughts.

"FUCCCCKK!"

I roar, hitting myself in the side of the head, relishing in the sharp pain that barely registers.

"I need to get high, fuck, fuck, fuck!"

Rick observes me carefully and going over the events of Vegas, has me feeling more than a little agitated and a whole lot on edge. I feel the overwhelming urge to get high, I need it so badly; it's making my mouth water, and I can taste it. I start to tremble violently, I feel like I need to throw up, I'm sweating profusely, and my chest feels tight, as my breathing becomes laboured. My last thought as I succumb to the blackness is, *this can't be fucking happening.*

***

I'm not sure how much time passes, but I come around to a concerned Rick, sitting on the floor next to me.

"Brody, you had a panic attack and passed out, mate. Another few minutes and I'd have been forced to ring an ambulance."

He says softly and calmly. I look up at him and the look in his eyes isn't of judgement, it is a look of quiet understanding.

"Are you ok? Can you sit up for me?"

I sit up slowly, and he offers me a cup of water. I take it and sip it with a trembling hand, while trying to avoid eye contact.

"Does that happen often?" he enquires, and I shake my head, with my gaze firmly rooted to the floor.

It hasn't happened in a long fucking time.

"Do you want me to call someone? Sam, Peyton, your sober sponsor, perhaps?" he asks with a furrowed brow, and I shake my head vehemently.

That's the last thing I fucking need. He offers me his hand and helps me to my feet. As I unsteadily get to my feet, I'm hit with this sudden overwhelming urge to run. *I can't fucking be here anymore.* I shake my head.

"I'm...I'm sorry, I can't, I can't fucking be here."

He seems to know what I'm about to do, and he tries to stop me by blindly making a grab for me. I haphazardly shove him out of the way and high tail it out of there, without looking back. *Fuck my life.*

***

I find myself dialling the most unlikely person. I'm not in a good place right now and I need someone to talk to. Someone who was there on that fucking awful day, who knows exactly what I'm going through. The phone rings three times, before it connects.

"Hello?"

I clear my throat.

"Hey Amy, it's Brody."

She pauses.

"What do you want, Brody?" she says with a bored tone, and I laugh at her reaction to my call.

"Look, I know I'm the last person you want to hear from, but I'm fucking struggling here, I'm a fucking mess. I've just come from a therapy session, and I freaked the fuck out. I just need someone who was there at the chapel in Vegas, someone who knows exactly what I'm going through."

I hear her sigh softly.

"I know you don't fucking like me; I'm not under any illusions that we're even friends. I-I just can't go to Sam, the boys, or even Peyton, they're too close. I wouldn't normally ask, but-I'm fucking desperate, Aims."

As I wait for her reply, I hear a loud noise. My hands start to shake, and my heartbeat starts to quicken. *Fuck me.*

"We've had our differences, but I'm glad you reached out. I'll put the kettle on; I'll even stretch to some chocolate biscuits!"

We both chuckle.

"Thanks, Aims, I appreciate it. I'll be there soon. Mines coffee, black, three sugars."

She laughs, "Ok, see you soon."

I hang up, flagging down a cab and climbing in the back, as Trey comes flying out of the building, touching his hand to his ear. I reel off the address on autopilot and my mind is swimming with flashbacks from Vegas, I can't focus on anything, but the sight of Ruby's lifeless body. The sick sound of the hail of bullets, pounds through my brain, as the idle chatter of cab driver barely registers in my jumbled thoughts. I stare absently into space, trying to focus on anything other than the worse time in my life.

"You alright, mate?"

I look up and catch his concerned stare in the interior mirror.

"Yeah, yeah, all good, cheers."

I plaster on a fake smile, as a look of recognition flashes in his eyes.

"Hey, aren't you Snake from Rancid Vengeance?"

I smirk and nod. *Fuck me, here we go.*

"The one and only!" I say cockily, and he smiles a genuine smile.

Why not milk it for all it's worth?

"I'm a huge fan," he says coolly as he clears his throat.

"Thanks, that means a lot."

I smile, but I know it doesn't reach my eyes. He's about to speak again when we arrive at my destination. I give him the fare, and I tip him generously.

"Do you want me to sign something?"

He nods, with an awestruck look on his face. He leans over to root in his glove compartment. He passes me a scrap piece of paper and a pen.

"What's your name, dude?" I ask.

"Darren."

I nod, as I scrawl my autograph on the piece of paper and hand it back to him.

"Here you go."

I wink, as he takes out his phone.

"Do you mind if I get a selfie?"

I shake my head.

"No, course not, man, go for it."

I pose, as he snaps a selfie, and once he's satisfied with the result, he puts his phone on the dashboard.

"Nice to meet you, Darren."

He beams.

"You too, man! See you around!"

I smile as he drives away, and I head down the path with one hand tucked into my pocket. I tap the door softly and Amy answers the door almost instantly. She has short, black hair styled in a neat bob, which has been straightened within an inch of its life. She has flawless, coffee-coloured skin, her eyes wide and almost black in colour. She has a friendly, warm smile, as she greets me.

"Brody," she says softly and invites me inside.

She pulls her cardigan closed and heads into the large open-plan kitchen, with me following behind her. She gestures for me to sit at the breakfast island and places a steaming cup of coffee in front of me. She takes a seat opposite me and takes a tentative sip of her coffee.

"I wanted to apologise for calling you out of the blue, I know we haven't always seen eye to eye, but I was fucking desperate, Aims."

She shakes her head.

"Don't ever be sorry for asking for help, Brody. I don't dislike you; I just think you can be a little reckless, sometimes, but it's not a bad thing. I see a totally different side of you, when you're around Peyton and the boys, you're not the bad boy that everyone else sees."

She pauses to take another sip of her coffee.

"Was I surprised when I saw your name flash up on my phone? Yes, I was, but that was because I didn't expect it, it caught me off guard, that's all. Would I have turned you away? No, I wouldn't, my husband was shot in the hip, I stood by him, even when he tried to push me away, when he called himself a cripple and a failure because he couldn't prevent what happened. I know what it's like because I lived it too. Every day I'm thankful to whoever, for getting us through that dark time."

I look at her and for the first time, I see her, I see the woman behind Cole Benedict. Behind every strong, brave man, is an equally brave, strong, independent woman.

"How do you cope? I mean, every time I close my eyes, I see Ruby and the fucking massacre of that day. I can't hear a loud noise without fearing for my fucking life, I had a panic attack at my therapy session today and I passed out. How fucked up is that? I legged it from his office, because I couldn't cope with him pushing me to talk about it, making me give a blow-by-blow account. I witnessed things that no normal human being should *ever* see. It broke a little piece of me that day, a piece that I'll never get back."

I take a shaky sip of my coffee, and she looks at me with a look of sympathy.

"Don't fucking look at me like that. I can't bear it, I don't want pity, I wake up every morning and I'm thankful that my life was spared, but I go through each day with a crippling sense of guilt that fucking weighs me down."

I take a shaky breath before I continue.

"I held her hand, I whispered words of reassurance, I stroked her stomach, I made promises I couldn't fucking keep. I told a dying, pregnant woman that everything was going to be fine, and I fucking lied! That's what keeps me up at night, that's why I can't hear loud noises, without wanting to hit the deck. I can't go to Sam, the boys, or Peyton, because I'm fucking ashamed, they're too close, they lost so much that day. I can't look Jax in the eye, knowing I held his fiancée, as she was dying in my arms, while he was unconscious. I've carried that guilt around with me for so fucking long."

My voice sounds desperate and unfamiliar to my own ears, as Amy reaches for my hand. "Everything will be ok, maybe you should talk to Jax. Does he know what you did?"

I shake my head.

"You're not to blame, Brody, you tried to help."

I swipe a tear away from my eyes and scrub my hand down my face.

"What if he somehow blames me? He already hates me for leading Sam down that dark path all those years ago. He's stubborn, he holds grudges, and he's headstrong, just like his mum. God, she'd be kicking my arse around this fucking kitchen, right about now, if she heard me talking like this."

I laugh trying to make a joke, but Amy rolls her eyes.

"Don't do that, don't try to make a joke, it's ok to admit you're struggling. I struggle on a nightly basis, when I wake up to hear Cole shouting in his sleep, when I have to console Addison, because she wants to know why her daddy's screaming in his sleep."

It's my turn to reach for her hand and I squeeze it, in a gesture of reassurance.

"It's not been easy for any of us. I see it in the dark circles under Sam's eyes, the faraway look he gets when he thinks no one's watching. I can't imagine what him and Peyton have been through, first J.D, then Savannah, his own fucking sister. We grew up around her, how did we miss that?" I ask rhetorically, shaking my head at the thought of my best friend struggling, just the way I do.

I finish my coffee in one mouthful and place the cup down on the island.

"I toyed with a lot of things, before I decided to dial your number. I was either going to one of three things, score, fuck my ex-girlfriend, or go to Lenny. The latter was a strong possibility; the rest would have landed me straight back in rehab or at least sent me to a meeting. I feel so fucking pathetic. The going gets tough and I end up right back at square one. Two steps forward, three steps fucking back. I don't want to be that person anymore, Aims. I want to face my problems head on; that's the reason I ended up here. I've got no one else I can reach out to, because no one can understand what I'm going through, but you can," I say sincerely, and she smiles warmly.

"I'm just glad I could be of help."

I hear the door slam, and it sounds like a gunshot. I flinch at the sound and Amy regards me with cautious eyes. *Fucking hell, Hart, get a grip of yourself.*

"You here, sugar?"

Cole's baritone voice echoes through the house.

"In here, sweetheart," she calls, as Cole enters the kitchen with his walking cane.

He cocks his eyebrow when he sees me sitting in his house.

"Brody, this is a surprise, mate."

Amy laughs.

"I just popped by to ask Amy for some advice on some girly shit, that's all, no need to get those knickers in a twist, Cole!"

The lie comes easily as I jump down from my seat at the breakfast bar. *He just wouldn't fucking understand the real reason I'm here.*

"I should get going, thanks for the chat, Aims, really appreciate it."

I wink and kiss her on the cheek. I leave feeling lighter and my phone starts ringing. I see Rick's name on my screen. *I could do without his bullshit psychobabble.* I reject his call and head back home with renewed purpose.

10

Raleigh

Monday morning rolls around all too quickly. Today, is the day I join Rancid Vengeance, on the UK leg of their "Symphony of Vengeance" tour. I haven't seen or heard from Brody since that night. We had wild, hot, passionate sex, and I lost count of the number of orgasms he so willingly gave me. I haven't been able to stop thinking about him and find his silence a little unnerving, even though it was me who left before he woke up.

My driver, Cliff arrives a few minutes earlier than scheduled and I mentally go through a checklist. *Hair dryer, check, straighteners, check, contact lenses, check.* I drag my suitcase out of my hotel room, saying a silent prayer to myself *'Please let my new apartment be ready for when I get home'.* As I make my way through the hotel lobby, I spot my agent Paul and he greets me with his usual, warm, beaming smile.

Paul Lyndsey has been my agent for eight years. He's been in the industry for almost thirty and he's at the top of his game. He's such a professional and an absolute wizard at what he does, everything he touches turns to gold, literally. I attended Italia Conti Academy of Acting when I first moved to the U.K, when I was eighteen years old. Over the three years, I got my head down and studied hard, I wanted to be an actress so badly, I lived and breathed it. It was just before I graduated, I'd been attending auditions, and I was tired of the constant knock backs and rejections. Paul taught a workshop as a visiting industry professional, and he was so impressed with me, he asked me to stay after the workshop, and he gave me his card. He invited me to an audition, and he was blown away by my raw and passionate performance as Blanche from *A Streetcar Named Desire.* He signed me straight away and soon after my graduation, I got the job on my first film. That was all thanks to Paul having faith in me, taking me under his wing and guiding me to be the best I could be. He taught me so much in the early days and I'll always have a special place in my heart for him. At sixty years old, he has jet black hair, peppered with grey, he is tall, with olive skin and deep, kind brown eyes. He looks like a distinguished gentleman. He has been married five times and has four kids, two sons and two daughters, and he is currently a mentor on a popular U.K talent show.

"Raleigh, so good to see you, sweetheart, you're looking fabulous as always," he says affectionately, and I smile.

"Hey Paul," I say brightly.

"I've checked you out and Cliff's waiting outside. I've got a great feeling about this. You're going to bloody smash it."

I hope I can live up to his high expectations. Paul escorts me out of the hotel, sliding my Michael Kors sunglasses into place, as I'm met with the blinding flashes of the paparazzi's lens'. I instantly turn on my public persona and give them a shy, reluctant smile. They lap up the attention I focus on them, posing for the camera as they snap away, until they are satisfied with what they have. They allow me to climb into the car and I'm silent on the journey to the tour bus. I'm stuck inside my own head, stewing over what I'm going to say to Brody.

All too soon, we arrive at the tour bus, which is parked around the back of the o2 arena, in preparation for the band's first homecoming gig tonight. Cliff comes around to my side of the car and holds the door open for me. I crawl out of the car, as gracefully as I can muster, and I am impressed with the sight that greets me. A black and silver, sleek, double-deck bus, with heavily tinted windows, and the band's logo down the side. It is exceptionally large and from the look of it, it is armoured. It's eye-catching from the outside and I can't wait to see the inside.

Cliff gets my luggage from the boot of the car and helps the driver load it onto the bus. The driver is around six feet seven inches, average build, with long shoulder length, blonde hair, he has blue, grey eyes, and a beard. He regards me intently and I greet him with a small, shy smile. *I feel like the new girl on her first day at school.*

"You look terrified, love. I promise these guys are pussy cats," he jokes and offers me his large hand.

"I'm George, but these guys call me Gorgeous George, or just Gorgeous, for short!" he says with a strong Bristolian accent, and I shake his hand.

"Hi, I'm Raleigh, nice to meet you, Gorgeous," I greet him.

He instantly makes me feel at ease, as he smiles warmly and nods.

"It's a pleasure, my love, follow me, I'll introduce you."

Paul pulls me in for a hug and kisses me tenderly on the forehead.

"Knock 'em dead, kid. I'll call you in a few days to check in."

I hug him back and follow George onto the bus, wishing I came across a little more confident, than I feel. *This is so unlike me.* I am as amazed by the interior, as I was by the exterior. George leads me into the living area and sitting on the grey corduroy sofa, which spans the whole perimeter of the bus, is Peyton. I know I saw her a few nights ago, but I didn't properly get a chance to take her in. Her photos don't do her justice; she is absolutely stunning, even after having two kids.

Her jaw length, dark brown hair, with electric pink and turquoise flashes, frames her face. Her vivid tattoos stand out on her lightly bronzed skin and the sparkle in her blue eyes makes her look younger than her thirty-one years. She has a little boy perched on her lap and she presses her nose lovingly into his dark hair. I stand there silently observing her for a few seconds, until she realises, she's not alone, and she looks up.

"Peyton, love, this is Raleigh. Raleigh, this is Peyton, she's Sam's wife and one of my best friends," George introduces her proudly, and I nod, trying to manage a more confident smile, but I think I end up looking like I'm in pain. *Great first impression, Storm.*

"Thanks, Gorgeous, we'll chat in a little while, yeah, babe? I've got some wine stashed away somewhere."

He nods. "I was counting it on it, lovely!"

He winks, leaving us to it.

"Hey, come sit, we didn't get properly introduced the other night." She gestures to the seat opposite her and smiles.

"I'm Peyton, but you knew that already! This is Zachary, say hello, sweetheart."

She chuckles, as the little boy in her lap turns to me and I am stunned by how much he looks like Peyton. He has bright blue inquisitive eyes and a dark mop of hair.

"The guys are doing a sound check; they should be back in a little while. I have to say it's going to be nice having another female around. Don't get me wrong, I love all the boys to death, but there's only so much talk of women, shagging, football and Xbox a girl can take!"

She laughs melodically, and I find myself laughing along with her.

"I'm sorry; I'm finding this a little overwhelming, if I'm being honest."

She shakes her head and dismisses me with a nonchalant wave of her hand. "It's fine, honestly, I was the same when I first came on tour, but you get used to it after a while. The boys are pretty easy going once you get to know them."

She leans back in her seat and Zachary snuggles deeper into her. She eyes me curiously and I suddenly feel way out of my depth. She cocks her head to the side and opens her mouth to speak, but she stops herself, which I find odd. I don't say anything, as Zachary idly plays with her hair, twirling it around his chubby fingers. She kisses his knuckles to distract him.

I am about to speak when I hear a commotion towards the front of the bus. Sam strides down the aisle and stops in front of Peyton and his son.

"Angel," he rasps and takes a seat next to her.

He wraps his tattooed, muscular arm around her, and she sinks into him, his sheer size, eclipsing Peyton. *His muscles are fucking huge, surely that can't be normal.* He kisses her on the lips, and the kiss is so passionate and full of love; I almost feel like I'm intruding. He plucks Zachary from Peyton's arms, and he squeals excitedly.

"Hey, buddy, come to daddy."

He turns to me, momentarily registering my presence and nods curtly.

"Raleigh, nice to see you again."

I smile, and he smirks.

"You too, Sam."

A look passes between Peyton and Sam, as Brody and the other boys enter the bus. I remember Jax from the club, his long, honey blonde hair sets off his hazel eyes and he has at least a weeks' worth of stubble on his chin.

"Hi," he says coolly as I look up into the silver eyes of Brody Hart.

He's even hotter than the last time I saw him, which feels like a lifetime ago, when in reality, it was only a few days ago. He's the stereotypical bad boy rocker, he's wearing that leather jacket, a black vest, a black and white skull scarf, dark blue jeans, and black, studded biker boots.

"Kitten," he says with an amused tone to his voice.

The moment my eyes lock with his, I know there's no turning back. *Welcome to the madness of Rancid Vengeance, Storm.*

After an hour speaking to Peyton, I find out that she is thirty-one years old and she's worked for the infamous celebrity tattoo artist, Seb Henry since she was eighteen. I have yet to be tattooed by the legend himself, which is definitely on my bucket list! She met Sam, when she tattooed him at Saint Sinner Ink, and they have two kids, Freddie, and Zachary. Her mum used to be a famous pin-up model in the seventies, and her dad is a renowned and extremely talented, fashion photographer. Her brother, Dexter is a police officer and her sister, Eden owns a beauty salon, just outside Brighton. She doesn't go into detail, but from what I know from the gossip sites, she was kidnapped by the band's former manager, John Dalton and for a year, everyone thought she was dead. As our conversation continues, I find myself feeling strangely comfortable around her, which is extremely rare. I'm never this at ease around someone I hardly know, it's just the way I am, but with her, it's totally different and it's refreshing. She's easy to talk to and I can see us becoming fast friends.

***

We've been on the bus for a couple of hours and the boys have gone into the venue to get ready for their upcoming show, leaving Peyton and me on the bus to bond some more. Zachary, Freddie and Jax's daughter Thea, have gone with the bands' nanny, Marnie, Peyton's brother's new girlfriend, who I've yet to meet. We are getting ready for the show, and we are drinking white wine. As she is applying her make-up in the mirror, she catches my eye.

"One thing you should know about Brody, is that romance isn't in his repertoire, it's not even in his vocabulary. He thinks buying condoms, ribbed for her pleasure is the height of romance!"

We both giggle like a pair of schoolgirls.

"How did you come to know Brody; I mean *really* know him. He won't let me through those impenetrable, steel walls. He keeps them firmly in place," I ask curiously, hoping she will give me some sort of insight into the enigma, that is Brody Hart.

She smiles thoughtfully.

"It wasn't easy, I hated him at first...no, *hate* is a strong word-let's just say I intensely *disliked* him! Him and Sam weren't good for each other; they were a total recipe for disaster when we first met. The first time I came on tour with the boys, on my last night before I was due to go home, I got into a little bit of trouble with one of Sam's exes!"

She pulls a face and we both laugh.

"I punched her in the face and stormed out of a club. I was bleeding quite badly, so Brody took me back to the bus, cleaned me up, and we played a game of truth or dare. We got absolutely fucking wasted. We shared a lot of things that night, and before you ask, nothing like that happened, it was just two people getting to know each other and bonding. I've never told anyone what we talked about that night, not even Sam. It's safe to say, I consider Brody one of my closest friends, he's a tough nut to crack, but the end result is worth it. Once you're in his inner circle, he'll do anything for you. He's godfather to our son Freddie, and they worship each other. He might have his faults, don't we all, but he's such an amazing guy, I'm proud to call him my best friend."

She regards me intently and I'm speechless at her honesty. It is clear the way she speaks about Brody, that I've barely touched the surface at getting to know the real him.

"Just don't give up on him, Raleigh, he's had so much of that in his life already. He doesn't love easily, but he's worth every second and more."

I cock my head to the side and twirl my ring anxiously around my finger.

"How did you become so close?"

She laughs, as she takes a long sip of her wine.

"I think it was because I was the first woman he had actually become friends with, without wanting to fuck me. His words, not mine!"

We both laugh and I take a sip of my wine, enjoying our chat.

"He's so...complicated, I've caught glimpses of who he is around you and the boys today. I can't help thinking, why he isn't like that with me."

She sighs and takes a long gulp of wine before continuing to speak. I have a feeling that it's the wine making her a little loose lipped.

"Between you and me, Brody didn't have the best start in life. It's his story to tell, but the one woman who was supposed to love him and care for him, just abandoned him and left him to care for himself. He has issues with women in general. It's not you, babe, I really wouldn't take it personally."

She smiles warmly and turns around to face me. She is wearing an oversized, off the shoulder customised Rancid Vengeance t-shirt, with spiked studs, safety pins and rips in it, which looks like a dress on her, knee high black Converse and her colourful hair styled into loose tousled waves. She looks amazing.

"How do I look, hon?"

I take her in and whistle.

"You lookin' mighty fine, girl!"

I put on a silly, fake Southern American accent and we both laugh. I feel a lot more relaxed than I did earlier and I don't know if it's the wine or just her company. She's magnetic and so easy to talk to.

"Come on, let's go and see what our boys are made of. You'll love it, I promise."

She links her arm through mine; we head off the bus and into the venue.

***

"London, how the fuck are we all doing tonight?" Sam asks, the crowd lapping up his attention.

The atmosphere is electric, and I can feel their energy surging through the large, sold out venue. We are stood at the side of the stage, with a clear view of all four members of the band, including Brody, who is looking delicious up there, with his guitar casually slung over his broad, tattooed shoulders. He has a black bandana around his head, and his tight black vest hugs his sculpted, well-defined muscles.

"It's so good to be home again, London! You're all looking fucking beautiful out there."

Sam moves to the front of the stage and sits down on the edge, with his long legs, dangling in front of him, with a look of complete awe on his face, as if he can't believe all these people are here to see him and his band.

"Now, tonight for the first time in history of Rancid Vengeance, we're going to change it up a little," Sam says huskily, and the crowd goes crazy.

I look to Peyton questioningly and nudge her with my elbow.

"Do you know what's going on?"

She pinches her two fingers together and makes a zipping motion across her mouth. I narrow my eyes at her and pout. She smiles knowingly, as Sam begins to speak again.

"We're going to perform a brand-new song from our upcoming album called 'I Will Bleed for You', we hope you guys like it."

The crowds' screams seem to get so loud, it's almost deafening, as Sam says those words and the room almost feels like it is vibrating.

He turns to Brody and shuffles nervously forward. Sam hands him the microphone with a wink and an encouraging pat on the back. Sam sprints to the centre of the stage, where a black, baby grand piano, with the Rancid Vengeance logo emblazoned on the lid, emerges from a rising platform. Sam takes a seat behind it and the soft, classical strains of the song begin. Sam plays the piano, his fingers gliding over the keys with effortless grace, as if he were born to do it. The audience, including me, all wait with bated breath, as Jax joins in with the accompanying guitar riff. Brody leans into the microphone, takes a deep steadying breath, softly strums his guitar, and begins to sing. I've never heard him sing before and it's amazing. His voice reminds me of Passenger, but with a tone that is distinctly unique, and it suits him. It's literally the opposite of Sam's voice and it's a welcome contrast.

"I will bleed for you, I will steal the stars from the sky, don't ever ask me why, but I will bleed for you. As the sun burns through the evening shadows, eternal sunlight shines through, I will bleed for you."

I watch him awestruck, his voice is so different from Sam's signature gruff tone and the hairs on the back of my neck stand on end, as his voice echoes through the arena. The crowd are enraptured by him and as the song continues, I see Brody close his eyes and completely lose himself in the lyrics.

"I will bleed for you, I will steal the stars from the sky, don't ever ask me why, but I will bleed for you. The sun is gone, with all that is said and done, I will bleed for you."

Jax moves fluidly across the stage and strums out an impressive guitar solo, as Lucas pounds an energetic drumbeat, and Sam plays a haunting melody on the piano, his fingers flying over the keys with elegance and precision. Brody opens his eyes and catches my gaze, as he looks at me, it feels like he can see into my soul. The smile he gives me is genuine and I find myself returning it. As the closing strains of the song fill the arena, the crowd erupts into a thunderous applause, the euphoria is palpable. Peyton gives me an encouraging side wink, the grin I give her in return is sincere and genuine. She nudges me and cocks her head to the side, as she leans in to whisper in my ear.

"Go get your man!"

She winks and make my way through the crowd, to the side of the stage. Cole nods curtly and lets me pass, as I head backstage to wait for him.

Brody

After the show, I'm fucking buzzed and I feel the adrenaline cursing through my veins. This is better than any chemical fucking high I've ever felt! As I step onto the bus, she's sitting there, looking like a fucking goddess and I can't take my fucking greedy eyes off her. *She's stunning.* I take a seat next to her and she pushes an open bottle of beer towards me.

"Thanks kitten."

I smile, and we sit there drinking in a comfortable silence. A few minutes passes and she turns to me, regarding me intently.

"Who taught you to play guitar?" she asks curiously and her out of the blue question takes me aback.

"My mum," I answer honestly and thoughtfully as I think back to some of the better memories of my mum, Imogen Hart.

"My mum gave birth to me when she was twenty, she was a scared, naïve kid, who was all alone. I never knew my grandparents, according to her, they never approved of her relationship with my dad, so she left home right after she found out she was pregnant with me. She was on the street for a while and that's when she got hooked on the drugs. She was an immature; pregnant junkie, who sold her body for her next fix, and I'll never fucking forgive her for that. I missed out on my childhood because the drugs meant more to her than I did. I was born with neonatal abstinence syndrome, I was born with drugs in my system and experienced painful withdrawal, up until I was three months old.

I never knew my dad, she always said he was going to come back for us one day and we'd live happily ever after. *Turns out she was full of shit.* She died on her thirtieth birthday and the moment I found her, still fucking haunts me.

There were a few rare occasions that she wasn't wasted or high and I looked forward to those moments, so fucking much. I was six or seven, when she started teaching me, she had this old acoustic Fender guitar, it was battered to fuck, but it didn't matter. She taught me how to play, and I took to it straight away. She said I was a natural, I'll never forget the look of pride in her eyes, when I played for the first time. It was only a simple, random little tune, but it was worth it, for her to look at me like that."

I smile softly at Raleigh, as I recall the memory, with such crystal-clear clarity. The way my mum's silver eyes would glisten like diamonds when she was happy. Those moments were so rare when I was growing up, that I sometimes question if they ever really happened at all.

"I was in the school talent show, playing guitar with Sam, Jack and Luke, she promised on my life that she'd be there, but she never showed up."

I sigh at the memory and the look in Raleigh's eyes, breaks my heart. *This is exactly why you shouldn't be anywhere near her, Hart.* I shake that thought away, as I continue.

"I wasn't angry, I was upset and so fucking disappointed. I was seven years old, the first time it happened, and I just remember being so embarrassed. Everyone else's parents were there supporting them, with such pride in their eyes and I step out onto the stage for our performance. I fucking looked for her and my heart broke when I didn't see her. I got home, and she was strung out on the sofa, with a strap attached to her arm and one of her many boyfriends between her legs."

Raleigh gasps as I say those words and I'm transported back to when we were in rehab.

11

Brody

Past

Ever since our first encounter a few short days ago, I haven't been able to get the lilac haired Goddess, who I now know as Raleigh, out of my mind. Fuck me, even her name sounds beautiful. She's been leaving notes under my door and gifts outside; to let me know I'm not far from her thoughts either. She left a book this morning "Women are From Venus & Men are From Mars". A neon pink post-it note stuck to the front of the book which read:

"I'd much prefer Uranus... X"

That put a permanent smile on my face, for the rest of the day. I never really put much thought into trying to meet someone. We were never really in one place long enough, especially when we're on tour. But since Sam met Peyton and Jax met Ruby, it's not really outside the realm of possibility anymore.

When I get to my group therapy session, she's sat down, with those sexy as fuck black-rimmed glasses, which make her look like a naughty secretary. The room is full, and they're all sat in a large circle, the only spare seat is opposite her. I sit down, and I can't seem to take my eyes off her. The therapist, with a voice that would put a glass eye to sleep, starts to speak.

"Welcome back, everyone, who would like to start this week?"

The room falls silent, everyone avoids direct eye contact, as she moves round the circle.

"No-one? Raleigh, how about you?" she suggests, and Raleigh looks up, catching my gaze.

"Yeah, sure, why not?" she mutters quickly as she twirls her ring around her finger.

"Don't be nervous, we're all friends here, there's no judgement. Do you want to start by telling the group why you're here and what prompted you to seek therapy?" the therapist says with all the enthusiasm of a wet lettuce leaf.

Raleigh clears her throat and looks to me for encouragement. I throw her a cheeky wink, and she smiles softly, as she begins to speak.

"I'm Raleigh and I'm an addict. I'm a self-harmer and I'm addicted to prescription drugs."

Everyone in the room, gives her nods of empathy and they all clap softly. She pushes her glasses up the bridge of her nose and clears her throat.

"I started self-harming when I just turned eighteen years old, purely for the release it bought. I started just after my grandma died; she was my biggest supporter. My grandma used most of her life savings to put me through drama school, despite my parents' protests. They've never approved of my career choices, My younger brother, Jagger, he's fifteen and he's the golden boy. He can do no wrong in their eyes, he's the favourite and I'm just a disappointment. I always have been. I left home after my grandma died and I moved to the U.K to go to theatre school. I learned more in that time, than I'd ever learned back in Australia. I continued to self-harm, even then, but I learned to hide it. I always wore long sleeves, even in the summer months. It was my way of escaping reality even if it was just for a little while."

Listening to her describe what she went through makes my heart hurt for her. She's so fragile and vulnerable in this moment, the admiration I feel for her increases with every word she speaks. I can relate to her with having parents who didn't give a fuck about you, who didn't love you enough to let you be you. I look up and her watery gaze catches mine.

"I'm sorry, I can't fucking do this."

My eyes follow her, as she gets up and dashes from the room in floods of tears.

"Right, does someone else want to share?" the therapist asks uninterested, as if Raleigh running from the room didn't happen.

I get up from my seat, scraping the chair noisily across the floor.

"Where are you going, Brody?"

I cock my eyebrow.

"If you hadn't noticed, one of your patients just ran out of the room. I'm going after her, not that I need your fucking permission," I snap with conviction and sprint out of the room with purpose.

I head to her room and tap softly on the door. When she doesn't open it, I try the door handle and walk in.

"Raleigh?"

I'm shocked to my core at what I find. She is perched on the edge of her bed, sobbing uncontrollably, with a razor blade pressed against her wrist, she's about to hurt herself. My heart slams against my rib cage and the overwhelming feeling grips me. Fuck, I can't let her do this. I head warily towards her and sit down next to her, careful not to spook her.

"You don't need to do that, sweetheart," I say softly, gently coaxing the razor blade from her hand.

She lets me and I tilt her chin up to face me. The look in her eyes fucking shreds me. She moves closer to me and before I know what's happening, her lips collide with mine. I tangle my hand in her silky hair, and she kisses me, as if her life depends on it. We devour each other and as the kiss deepens, I feel my erection pressing painfully and uncomfortably against the zipper in my jeans.

"Brody," she moans into my mouth, and I reach out to cup her breast in my hand.

"I can take you to heaven, if that's what you need, kitten," I say with a rough edge to my voice, and her eyes darken with pent-up desire. "I'll take you right to the edge until you can't take anymore, and then I'll fuck you into oblivion. I'll fuck you so hard, you'll beg me to make you come, over and over again."

She lets out a small moan and bites down on her plump bottom lip. She looks so beautiful and natural, her hair slightly mussed, no make-up.

"Tell me to stop or tell me you want me to fuck you, kitten. Your choice."

She grips my t-shirt in her fist.

"Fuck me, Brody. Please, I need you to fuck me."

She pulls off her t-shirt, and she's naked underneath. Her nipples are pebbled into hard, erect buds. I can't take my eyes off her; her tits are perfect. She is fucking perfect.

"Play with your nipples, show me how you like it."

She lies back and does as I ask; she rubs her nipples between her thumb and forefinger. She closes her eyes and the noises coming from her causes my dick to swell in my jeans.

"Mmmm," she moans.

"That's it, baby. You look so fucking hot. Now take off your shorts and play with your pretty pussy for me."

Her slender fingers swipe up and down her wet slit. Her juices dripping, my mouth waters at the sight. Fuck, I'm dying to taste her.

"Show me how you get yourself off." I demand, as I take out my cock and start to slowly stroke myself. "Fuck me, that's hot, I'm so hard," I rasp and her eyes lock with mine.

"I need you to take care of me, Brody. Please, please fuck me," she begs, and before I know it, I'm naked in record time. "I need it hard, please. Fuck me hard, take it away, Brody, please."

I climb on the bed, straddling her and she takes me by surprise by grasping my cock in her hand. I let out a hiss and curse low in my throat.

"Oh fuck."

She jacks me a few times and I slide my hand over hers putting a temporary halt to my pleasure.

"I won't last if you keep doing that, kitten," I placate, and she continues to rub her still erect nipples. "You look so fucking hot."

I start to feel a little weird, that we're about to fuck in rehab of all places, but I'm too far gone to stop it from happening. There's something about her and I'm too weak to say no. I stroke my erect cock, and she bites her lip.

"Just fuck me already," she whines petulantly, and I smirk.

"Someone's impatient." She smiles and if I had a heart, it would be skipping a beat right about now. "Jesus, you're so fuckin' beautiful."

I lean down to suckle her erect nipple in my mouth.

"Brody," she moans inaudibly as I run my finger through her wetness.

I tease her for a few seconds, driving her to the brink of orgasm and I push my long finger in her slick channel, taking her by surprise. She gasps at the feel of my finger moving in and out. I introduce a second finger, rubbing her inner walls with every stroke. Her eyelids flutter closed, and I bite down on her nipple.

"Eyes on me, beautiful."

She opens her eyes, and her eyes lock with mine, as I increase the pace. I take her nipple out of my mouth with a pop, and I twist my fingers inside her, causing her to cry out.

"Oh fuck, Brody, that feels so good."

She strokes my erection, causing me to growl. Fuck, that feels fucking amazing. I pull my fingers free from her pussy, leaving her bereft at the loss of contact.

"Do you have a condom? I don't fuck bareback, kitten," I ask, feeling almost desperate enough to say to hell with it and just fuck her without anything between us.

"Top drawer, oh God," she moans out loud.

I fumble around in the top drawer and manage to find one. I tear the foil packet with my teeth and roll on the condom. I fist my cock for a few seconds, as I find her entrance and I shove forward, impaling her on my waiting firmness. She whimpers softly, as I allow her to adjust to my length and my Prince Albert piercing. I throw my head back, as I cry out with pleasure.

"Oh Jesus, fuck, you feel like heaven."

I pick up the pace, moving in and out of her slick heat. She wraps her arms around my neck. It feels so good, she moans softly in my ear. As my pace quickens, I can feel her orgasm cresting to the surface, her pussy ripples around my cock. She squeezes her inner walls around my cock, and I gasp at the feeling.

"Shit, that felt...FUCK!" I bark as I piston in and out of her, as she explodes around me.

"I'm coming, fuck, Brody, I'm coming," she yells, and I move my hand over her mouth.

My orgasm is right behind hers, as my hot seed spurts inside her, causing a second orgasm to detonate from deep within her. She cries out around my hand and as we come down from our orgasms, the room is silent. The only sound is our breathless, post-orgasmic pants and the thought at the forefront of my mind is, we just fucked in rehab. God damn.

12

Raleigh

The rest of the boys, Peyton, and George crowd back onto the bus. Peyton narrows her eyes and looks from Brody to me.

"Not interrupting anything are we?" she asks, and Brody laughs at her curiosity.

"Na, course not, babe. We were just chatting, unwinding after that fucking epic show!"

The boys rowdily congratulate him, on his first time singing on stage, in front of an audience.

"Beers all round?" Jax asks and everyone all nods in agreement as they pile on the large sectional sofa.

Jax cracks the lids off the beer bottles with his teeth and hands them round.

We have been sitting around the table, shooting the breeze for a few hours and we're all more than a little buzzed. The conversation is flowing easily, and the beer is surging through my veins, making me feel more than a little vocal.

"I've done things I'm not proud of, some I wish I could take back," I say with a melancholic tone to my voice, and everyone regards me with rapt attention.

"We've all done things we're not proud of." Brody breaks the awkward silence, as he takes a long pull from his beer bottle. "Jax ended up fucking a record executive once to secure us a number one! It's those puppy dog eyes; the women can't seem to resist!"

Jax laughs, he stops strumming his guitar; to give Brody the finger and I chuckle at their camaraderie. I notice from my previous interactions with Jax, that his eyes always seem sad, and his smile never quite reaches them. I know from the tabloids and the gossip columns, that his fiancée died, and she managed to live long enough, to give birth to their daughter, Thea. I don't know the full details, I'm too scared to ask.

"What about you, what have you done that you're not proud of, Brody?" I ask, instantly regretting letting my mouth run away with me, as he smiles ruefully.

"Where do I start? I'm not proud of anything I've done in my life, except the band. It's the only thing that's kept me going over the years. That and the drugs, but now, I just have to rely on the music. It's fucking hard, but I can't screw up again. I know without a shadow of a doubt; the boys would give me another chance, but in my mind, I wouldn't deserve it."

Sam squeezes Brody's shoulder and reaches for Peyton's hand.

"Angel," he rasps, and she follows him.

The other boys are not far behind, leaving Brody and me alone.

"Was it something we said?"

Brody chuckles, as I take a sip from my beer and lean back on the sofa.

"Be honest, is our relationship based on just sex?" I ask, fuelled by alcohol and fully aware that I sound like one of those needy girls, who constantly needs to be reassured.

"No, of course not," he says indifferently, idly picking the label from his beer bottle.

"What's it based on then?" I challenge as he quirks his eyebrow.

"Obviously, it's based on my charm, my good looks, sex, your rockin' bod, your impressive rack, sex, my sense of humour, my wit, sex, your smile, your sexy secretary look when you wear those glasses, have I mentioned sex?"

He smirks playfully and I narrow my eyes at his nonchalant answer, but I can't hide my grin, as he tucks my hair behind my ear.

"People put too much stock in relationships, why do we have to define what this is?"

He gestures between us, and I ponder his statement for a few moments, before responding.

"Sam and Peyton, what would you say their relationship is based on, for example?" I push, and he laughs.

"That's easy, their relationship is based on the fact, that they're fucking perfect for each other, almost a little too perfect. They're so in love, it makes me want to vomit, they literally don't argue, and if on the rare occasion they do, the make-up sex, is literally off the chart's explosive. Sam can't function without her, he tried for a whole year, but he doesn't work without her, and she doesn't work without him, they're a match made in heaven, literally."

He sighs and gets this faraway look in his eyes. It's at that moment I wish he'd just fucking open up to me and let me know him the way Peyton and the boys do.

"Theirs is based on two things, love and complete and utter devotion, pure and simple."

As I listen to his explanation, I wonder why he can't put a label on our relationship. *What's so wrong with me, that he can't even admit that there's something deeper between us?* Am I really that hard to love? I sigh audibly, and he folds his arms across his chest, defensively and I swear to God, *he fucking pouts.*

"Stop fishing, it doesn't suit you, why should we define what we are, Raleigh? Why is it so important? We've fucked a couple of times; I'm not proposing marriage. I thought we were on the same page, it's just no-strings fun."

He shrugs nonchalantly, as if his words don't mean a thing. The truth is his words cut deep; just when I thought our relationship was going somewhere. *How fucking dare he?*

"Is that it? Is that all you're going to say on the subject? I thought this was turning into more than just fun?" I spit angrily, and he just stays silent, avoiding looking at me directly.

Fucking prick, I deserve better than this.

"*Jesus!* You're a fucking arsehole!" I curse and he raises his eyebrow.

He leans forward to rest his elbows on his knees, with a cocky look on his face and all I want to do, is punch the ever-loving shit out of him for wounding me so deeply.

"I'm an arsehole? Accurate description, babe. Tell me something I don't know. You sit there, demanding I put a label on our relationship, we met in fucking rehab of all places! I walked in on you trying to open a fucking vein the first time we had sex!"

Low blow, Hart. He's such a dick. I'm so angry with him, before I can get my temper in check, I lash my hand across his cheek, and his head snaps to the side as he laughs bitterly.

"We're both fucking damaged, Raleigh! We're more alike than either of us care to admit. We both turn to self-destruction when things don't go our way, but I'm comfortable enough to admit that are you?" he challenges as his voice gradually becomes a few decibels louder.

He grabs my arm, running his fingers across my healing wounds and I quickly snatch my arm away from him, as if he's burned me.

"You wear your fucking scars like a badge of honour, Raleigh! You're quick enough to call me out on not putting a label on our relationship when you can't even put a label on it yourself! We've both made some shitty decisions, which is why we both ended up in rehab in the first place and I've made peace with that. I know I fucked up, but can you hold your hands up and take responsibility for your actions?"

He sits there, eagerly awaiting my answer, but I'm literally too fucking angry to respond. *Fucking selfish prick.* I take a moment to compose myself, before answering him.

"Do you regret what happened between us? Are you ashamed, is that it? I can't fucking work you out! One minute you're trying to jump my bones, and the next, you're acting like I don't fucking exist! What the hell is wrong with you?" I say with a more than exasperated tone to my voice.

He gets up from his seat and starts to pace the floor. I can see from the look in his eyes that he's desperate to say something, but he seems to be holding back.

"What do you fucking want from me, Brody?" I shriek.

I am not a shrieker. *What the fuck is wrong with you, Storm?* I don't wait for him to reply before I get up and walk away. *Childish much?*

Brody

Once you've seen one hotel room, you've seen them all. For the last fourteen years, I've seen my fair share of them, and this isn't any different. For the first night of our tours, M.J. always books us all hotel rooms, instead of spending the night on the bus. Tonight, we're staying in the Intercontinental Hotel. It boasts four hundred and fifty-three spacious bedrooms and suites in a contemporary design, each with an abundance of natural light from floor-to-ceiling windows, looking out onto the scenic capital.

I've stayed in some of the worst hotel rooms in the early days of Rancid Vengeance, and I've stayed in some of the best the world has to offer. We've spent so long living out of suitcases, I've forgotten what it's like to set down actual roots. I've never had a real blood family; the boys have been all the family that I've needed. We may not be blood related, but that doesn't matter, they have always been by my side, and they have always fought my corner. Despite our differences, I know without a shadow of a doubt that they will always have my back, no matter what. They taught me that you don't have to have the same blood running through your veins to be family. Blood just makes you related, loyalty makes you family, and I considered myself lucky to have them in my life, even if I didn't deserve them sometimes.

In the beginning, I was angry at the world and the hand I'd been dealt, that I couldn't see what I had, and a wise man once told me *'We cannot change the cards we're dealt, just how we play the game'.* I lived by that mantra, so much so I had it tattooed across my back as if to remind myself of that fact on a daily basis.

After my argument with Raleigh, angry at her and myself, I left the bus and went for a drink in the hotel bar. I drank until I was suitably wasted and managed to stagger back to my room, alone. For once, I didn't want company of the female variety, or of any variety, I just craved solitude and to be alone with my thoughts.

As I lie here, start to think of how far I've come since Rancid Vengeance started, and a thought occurs to me. I'd rather just burn out, than fade away. Fading away isn't an option for me. I love being in the spotlight and the attention it brings. I crave it, it gives me a sense of reassurance that someone actually gives a fuck about me, it makes me feel relevant, like I have a purpose.

Four a.m. is a lonely place when you're lying in bed for the eleventh night in a row, staring blankly at the ceiling. My mind is a dangerous place to be. I'd compare it to a warzone. Four a.m. knows all my secrets. It knows what makes me tick, and it knows that dark place in my mind that I go to when I can't sleep. The darkness is my friend, and I embrace it, I wear it like a second skin, I bask in all its glory and in an odd way, it comforts me.

When I think back to the argument I had with Raleigh earlier on. I told her that she wears her scars like a badge of honour. Aren't I the same though? I wear my darkness in the exact same way and instead of pushing it down, both of us in different ways, we accept it, and we encompass it tightly, like a warm hug.

After our argument, she locked herself in the bathroom and I listened to her sob her heart out. I couldn't stand to hear it; I couldn't bear to be the reason for her torment. *I'm such a prick.* It took me back to the times I used to listen to my mum crying after I used to scream at her. I'll never forget the sound of her sobbing after I called her a *'useless, junkie, whore'* and how I wished she were dead.

Past
Brody

We argued the night she died. She missed yet another one of my school talent shows, it was the first time me and the boys performed a song that we had written, and we won. I cried on the way home, and other than that, the car journey with Mr and Mrs Newbolt, Sam and me was silent. I was grateful to Mrs Newbolt for comforting me, as she whispered soft words in my ear and stroked my hair. By the time I got home, my upset had turned to anger. I was so fucking angry, I was trembling, and I stormed into my mum strung out, on the tatty, old, worn sofa in our living room. One of her many boyfriends shirtless and snoring next to her. I laughed bitterly to myself at the sight before me.

"Why am I not fucking surprised?" I muttered to myself.

"Brody, baby," she said in a ridiculous baby voice, which she thought sounded endearing.

It wasn't. It was fucking annoying, and it irritated the shit out of me.

"Don't Brody, baby me, mum. I'm surprised you even remember my god damn name!"

She had the balls to look confused. "What's wrong, baby?"

I rolled my eyes, trying desperately to shove down the mixture of feelings racing through my ten-year-old body. "Do you remember what today was?" I snapped, desperately hoping she would remember.

She gives me a vacant look and, in that moment, my heart broke.

"Today was the fucking annual school talent show! You promised me you'd be there!" I shouted, willing myself not to burst into tears.

I don't cry, only little pussy boys cry. That's what Sam said.

"I'm so sorry, baby. Let me make it up to you, shall we go out for burgers?"

I shook my head.

"Don't you dare! We won, as if you even give a shit! Everyone's parents were there, except for you! Do you realise how that made me feel? Humiliated, worthless. I fucking hate you! You are pathetic, junkie, whore! I wish I were fucking adopted! You don't deserve to be my mum!"

That night, I spewed out every poisonous, hurtful thing, I could think of, and I listened to her gut-wrenching sobs. Every sob pierced my ten-year-old heart, and I went to bed, and I cried myself to sleep.

The next morning, I was ready to apologise for everything I'd said, but I found her dead, and I didn't even get to say sorry. I couldn't take back those awful, hateful words and I've lived with that on my conscience for twenty-plus years. My own mother died thinking her only son hated her.

Present

Brody

I swing my legs out of bed and the memories of that night assault my mind. The image of my mums' lifeless body haunts me to my very core. Instead of pacing, my exhausted body crumples to the floor, as I try desperately to rid myself of the poisonous memory. The craving, that works its way into my cerebral cortex, grips me tight and my chest constricts, as I try anxiously to keep it at bay.

I find myself scrolling through my phone with a trembling hand and dial the person I have always relied on, for fourteen years.

"Len," I say tentatively, swallowing hard a few times to stop my guts from vacating.

"Should I be worried you're calling me this late, son?"

I smile to myself, as I slide open the doors to the hotel balcony. I drop down on the edge of a sun lounger in my Calvin Klein boxer shorts, the cool air a welcome feeling on my clammy skin.

"Nah, I just called to hear your riveting conversation, Len!"

He laughs throatily.

"You good, B?" he asks cautiously, and I sigh.

"Can't sleep... same shit, different day. Just thinking."

I hear a creak of leather and imagine him sitting in his office, with a glass of scotch in front of him.

"Never a good thing, son."

I lean back, feeling guilty for calling.

"Am I interrupting you, Len?"

He coughs.

"Don't be fucking stupid, you could never interrupt me, I've always got time for you. Now stop bloody prancing around and get to the fucking point."

I laugh at his honesty.

"I should be charging you by the fucking hour!" he jokes.

"And here's me thinking you liked me!" I quip, and he chuckles.

112

"Don't go getting all fucking sentimental on me, son."

We are both silent for a few moments.

"My mum died thinking I hated her, Len," I say, breaking the silence.

"Listen to me and you better listen fucking good. Your mum knew you loved her, even though she didn't deserve it. You can't torture yourself with what ifs. You need to let it go and leave the past in the past, where it belongs. Focus on your music and your lady friend, what's-her-name?"

I laugh.

"Her name's Raleigh."

He pauses.

"That's the one, wine and dine her, or whatever you courting kids do these days."

I sit up.

"Courting? Fucking hell, what century are you from?" I say sarcastically, and he laughs gruffly.

"One where I can still give you a clip round your fucking ear! Now call Rachel, or whatever her name is and let this old dog get some beauty sleep!"

I smile to myself at our easy banter and his knack at knowing just the right thing to say.

"Thanks Len."

"Night, son."

I hang up and head back inside, contemplating going to Raleigh's room, but I lay down on my hotel room bed and torture myself on 'what ifs', exactly what Lenny told me not to do.

13

Raleigh
1 week later

Ever since our disagreement last week, I've barely spoken to Brody. If he walks into a room, I walk out. The tension is palpable and I'm starting to feel more than a little awkward. Peyton has been amazing, running lines with me, taking me for coffee and making me feel more at home, we're becoming fast friends. We've been for our daily early morning run and when we both step back onto the bus, out of breath and sweaty, we are greeted by Nicholas Slade and Gavin Kincaid.

Nicholas Slade is a British actor, and he is one of the U.K's *hottest* exports in Hollywood. He started off acting in low budget Brit flicks and moved to the States, where he landed various roles in *Into the Fire, Fix Me,* and *The Photograph*. At almost thirty-eight, he is a huge star, despite his background. He grew up on a council estate in Camberwell and attended an acting school called *'London Academy of Music and Dramatic Arts'* on a scholarship. He earned the scholarship, by taking the lead in various performances in school productions and was spotted by a talent scout. He landed a prestigious role in a play called *'Domino'* at the Old Vic theatre, where he was discovered by Damien Valentine. Nicholas got his big break in British gangster flick, *"Chelsea Smile",* which was a huge success and rocketed his career into oblivion. I've never worked with Nick before, and I've been looking forward to meeting him.

He enters the bus, and it's like all the air has been sucked out. He really is handsome. He is around six-foot-tall, extremely muscular, has lean, narrow hips and his dark brown, almost black eyes remind me of Minstrels. His dark brown hair is elegantly styled into a soft quiff. A tattoo of a set of dice, playing cards, a lucky *'8'* ball and the words *'You make your own luck'*, peeks out of the open neck of his shirt, extending up his throat and neck. He is wearing a pair of loose fitting, baggy, ripped jeans, a black v-neck t-shirt, which stretches across his shoulders and his broad chest, and he wears a pair of black and white checkered Vans. He catches me ogling him and winks. I feel my cheeks burning with embarrassment, as he throws his arms around Peyton and she steps into his embrace.

"Hello love! So good to see you again! Looking foxy as always!"

He laughs infectiously, as Peyton rolls her eyes at his roguish camaraderie.

My embarrassment is soon forgotten, as my face breaks out into a beam, when Gavin catches sight of me. Gavin and I have worked together on a few occasions. He took me under his wing on my first movie 'The Underdog', where I played his daughter. It was a gangster film and my first movie out of theatre school. I was young, nervous, and inexperienced as an actress. Gavin sensed how nervous I was, and he put me totally at ease and it won me my first Bafta nomination. He has become a great friend, confidant, and father figure over the years. I'd just started my relationship with Carter and Gavin saw he wasn't good for me. He was part of the reason I plucked up the courage and found the strength to get away from him, until things took a turn for the worst. In a way, he saved me, and I'll always be grateful to him for that. We've worked together a lot over the years, and we've become firm friends.

On my first morning on the bus, I found out that Nick and Gavin had been cast in 'Rocked' and Nick will be my leading man. Nick has been cast in the role of the band's lead singer, Tripp Squire, and Gavin has been cast as the band's manager, Elias Lincoln. Gavin Kincaid has been in the movie industry for over twenty-five years. He is average height at around five feet nine inches tall; his light brown hair is smattered with grey; he has dark steel-blue eyes and even at forty-six years old, he's still handsome.

"Gavin!" I say excitedly, and Brody's attention is piqued as he looks up from his Xbox battle with Jax.

"Hello sweetheart, you're looking gorgeous as always! It's been a while!"

He sweeps me up into one of his famous bear hugs and it takes everything in me not to burst into tears. *Seeing Gavin after all this time is a little overwhelming.*

"It's been too long! And I told you before, flattery gets you everywhere, Kincaid! How have you been? How's Cleo?"

Cleo is Gavin's daughter, she is seventeen and being an only child, she is spoilt and definitely takes after her mother, Liberty Mitchell-Kincaid. Liberty Mitchell was a household name back in the early nineties. She made her fortune as a glamour model and was always photographed falling drunk outside nightclubs. She played up to the press and was known for her outrageous behaviour. She went on to sit on the panel of a late-night British chat show called '*Girl Talk*' and met Gavin when she interviewed him. The interview went viral because the chemistry was off the charts hot and the attraction was obvious to millions of viewers. They went on to marry and soon after, Liberty became pregnant with Cleo.

After eleven years of marriage and countless newspaper stories of infidelity, Gavin and Liberty divorced. The divorce was high profile, and she took him for a substantial amount of money, declaring him bankrupt a year later. Even though she has been married four times, Liberty seems to be very vocal and bitter about their relationship and is constantly mentioning him on 'Girl Talk.'

Gavin got his second chance, when he was cast in a popular quirky British cop show called *'The Rozzers'* and has worked steadily on TV and movies ever since, clawing his way back to the popularity of his heyday.

"Cleo is demanding as ever, darling, just like her mother!"

I laugh, as Brody joins us, wrapping his arm around my waist and pulling me close to his side. Is this what jealous Brody looks like? *He is definitely staking his claim.*

"Aren't you going to introduce us, *kitten?*" He emphasises my pet name and smiles sweetly.

I clear my throat and nod. *Two can play that game, arsehole.*

"Yeah, sure, Gavin, this is Brody Hart, Brody, this is Gavin."

Gavin smiles and tries to get a read on the situation, looking from Brody to me.

"Brody, pleasure to meet you, mate."

Brody reaches for Gavin's hand and shakes it firmly. *Talk about my dick is bigger than yours, for fucks sake.* I'm getting whiplash from Brody's mood swings. He's spent most of the week avoiding me, and now an old friend comes into the picture, he's acting like some sort of jealous lover. *What the actual fuck?*

***

It's been a couple of hours since Gavin and Nick arrived on the bus and for the first time since I've set foot on this bus, I feel claustrophobic. Everywhere I turn, I can feel his eyes blazing into me, everywhere I go, he's there. It's driving me insane. I'm going over my lines and highlighting parts which stand out for me. It's a process I developed in theatre school and it's my method of learning my lines. *It never fails, even after all these years.*

Every time I look up, I catch him staring at me. I must admit, it's quite a turn-on knowing he's watching me. I find myself playing up to the fact that he's watching. I push my glasses further up my nose and stretch dramatically, giving him a sneak peek at my flat stomach and the tattoo of a song lyric from The Script, which reads *'Every day, every hour, turn the pain into power'* that extends up my ribs. I continue to go through my script, aware that his eyes are rigidly fixed on me. I cross my legs and give him a cheeky flash of my thigh, the other boys totally oblivious to me teasing their guitarist, quite so blatantly and openly. I stand up and make my way confidently to the bathroom, carefully avoiding contact with him. I go to open the door, and he pushes me inside, crowding in behind me, flipping the lock, as he does.

"Are you fucking enjoying teasing me, Raleigh?" he says tightly, and I feign ignorance.

"I have absolutely no idea what you're talking about," I say nonchalantly, and he smiles wickedly.

"We both know where playing games gets you, kitten," he challenges.

"Where might that be?" I say innocently, knowing his answer will be far from innocent.

"Beneath me, kitten. With you screaming my name so loud, even the neighbours will need a fucking cigarette."

Involuntarily, I moan softly at his statement.

"Admit it, admit you want me, Raleigh, tell me," He growls as he pushes me against the sink.

I can't say a word, I'm speechless and so fucking turned on.

"By all means, tease me all you want, it's just going to get you fucked."

I close my eyes briefly and when I open them, his are blazing with pent up lust and frustration.

"I want you, Brody and I'm tired of pretending I don't," I manage to pant out as he lifts me up, causing me to yelp at the action and deposits me on the sink.

He steadies me and pushes my legs apart, settling his body between them. He's so close I can feel his warm breath on my cheek; he smells faintly of beer and of something uniquely Brody. He gently tucks my hair behind my ear and leans in to kiss me deeply. His kiss takes my breath away, his split tongue, duelling with mine, softly licking, and caressing the inside of my mouth. I go lax against him and open my legs wider, giving him the opportunity to get closer. He reaches down and shifts my knickers to the side. It's at that moment I thank my inner vixen that I decided to wear a skirt. His long, callused finger swipes up my aching centre, as he pulls away from our game of tonsil tennis.

"*Fuck,* you're soaked, is that all for me, kitten? Did you enjoy our voyeuristic little game? Did you get off on the fact that might have been caught teasing me?" he says seductively.

"Yes!" I pant. "God yes, it made me wet," I admit, and he smiles like the cat that got the cream.

He rewards me by pushing his finger inside me, building up a steady rhythm until he introduces another finger. I moan softly, aware that someone could possibly hear us.

"*Jesus*, your pussy is gripping my fingers so tight right now," he says softly as his rhythm increases, driving me towards the big O.

"Mmm," I hum softly.

"*Fuck,* you feel so good."

I grip his shoulders to steady myself, as my orgasm rolls through me. He shushes me, as he pulls his cock free of his trousers.

"I'm so fucking hard for you, kitten. You drive me fucking crazy, woman. Do you have any idea how difficult it's been for me to stay away from you?" he admits shamelessly, and I smile.

"So, you've missed me then?" I ask curiously, and he cocks his eyebrow.

"I've missed your wet cunt, kitten," he says crassly, hoping that the disappointment on my face isn't visible to him. "*Fuck*, I need to be inside you," he rasps seductively, and he runs the head of his cock through my slickness.

The feeling of his piercing against my still sensitive clit, makes me want him, even though the rational part of me knows I should walk away. But the rebel in me can't seem to stay away from him. My thoughts are interrupted by Brody teasing my opening with the head of his cock, as he impales me on his impressive, waiting length. I gasp out loud and he puts his index finger to his lips.

"Shhh, you need to be quiet. Or does it turn you on, knowing that everyone on the bus will know what we're up to in here?"

I trap my lip between my teeth, and he chuckles softly.

"Ah, she's thinking about it."

He gradually increases his pace and I'm writhing beneath him, aware that there's hardly any space to move, but I don't care, I'm basking in everything Brody Hart. He rubs his piercing against my inner walls, and I let out a strangled moan.

"Ohhh Jesus!"

The smoky look in his eyes and the ripple of his hard, tattooed muscles is enough to chase my orgasm to the finish line. With a few more expert strokes, it surges through me, like I'd imagine a fire tearing through a bush and in this moment, I've never wanted a man as much as I want Brody Hart... every damaged fucking inch of him.

***

As the weeks go on, I find myself enjoying my time on the tour bus, which are words I never thought I'd be saying. I spend my days running lines with Gavin and Nick and learning what it takes to be a fully-fledged rock star from Sam and the guys, all in the name of art. I spent my nights wrapped up in everything Brody Hart. After our argument, a few weeks ago, Brody apologised, and I willingly forgave him after some explosive make-up sex.

Past

Raleigh

We've been avoiding each other for the past week and the awkward, icy, atmosphere on the bus, you could cut with a knife. I'm running lines with Nick on the bus and Brody is glaring daggers at us. Nick looks up over his script and rolls his eyes. I smirk at his reaction and we both start to recite the script, by heart. It also happens to be a scene in which Nick's character, Tripp and my character, Stevie, declare their love for each other.

"I'm tired of sharing you with the world, Stevie, fuck, I want you for myself. Call me selfish, but I can't stand it. Every man, who watches you out there, doing what you do best, every single one of them, is imagining you naked and in their beds, when the only person that should be in your bed, is me," he recites his lines with genuine passion and conviction, that I almost believe every word he says.

He folds his arms across his broad chest and places his script face down on the table. The next part of the scene involves us kissing and Nick bites his lip to stifle his wicked smirk. I school my expression and get right into character, placing my hand on Nick's face.

"Tripp, I'm done pretending I don't want you, all the women that came before me are insignificant. Shit, you're-everything."

Nick and I move closer to each other, aware that Brody's eyes are trained on us. As Nick's lips touch mine, I kiss him back and impetuously, I feel a firm grip on my wrist.

"That's enough, Raleigh. You've made your fucking point."

His tone is possessive, authoritative, and resolute.

"You and me, we're gonna have words, Slade," Brody snaps menacingly, as he jabs his finger in Nick's general direction.

Nick cocks his eyebrow smugly and gets up from his seat. He flashes a cheeky wink at Brody.

"I expected nothing less, Hart. My work here is done, next time maybe attempt talking to her, instead of childishly pretending she doesn't fucking exist," Nick declares obstinately and leaves us alone.

"Was that really for my fucking benefit?" he spits, and I smile innocently.

"Why on earth would you think that? He is one of Hollywood's most eligible bachelors, I think we would make adorable babies."

I shrug sardonically and Brody growls assertively.

"Don't even fucking joke about that, Raleigh."

I stand up and even though he is a few inches taller than me, I feel small and inferior, as he crashes his lips forcefully to mine. His kiss knocks me breathless, and he tangles his large hand in my hair, pulling my head closer to him. His tongue wrestles with mine and he nips my bottom lip with his teeth, as if he is claiming his territory. He pulls away momentarily and presses his forehead against mine.

"I'm incapable of staying away from you, Rae."

His voice is low and full of want.

"I know I'm no good for you, but there's something about you that makes me want to see where this goes. I'm sorry for acting like a dick, my feelings-overwhelm me sometimes and I don't know how to deal with them. I'm trying so hard, but you make me feel-too fucking much, that's a totally new and different concept for me. Be patient, don't give up on me... on us."

I grasp his t-shirt and for the first time since we met, I see vulnerability in his stormy silver eyes.

"I get it, those feelings are alien to me too, I've spent countless therapy sessions trying to make sense of it, but no matter how hard I try, I can't-I can't stop myself from wanting you."

He squeezes his eyes shut, as if waging an internal war with himself.

"Raleigh," he murmurs roughly, and I see the struggle in his eyes.

"Take me to bed and show me, we can do our talking that way."

I pull away from him and lead him to the back of the bus, by gripping the front of his t-shirt. We pass Nick and I swear I hear him mutter.

"About fuckin' time."

I grin like a loon and as I push the door shut, he's on me. He takes off his t-shirt and the sight that greets me, makes me lick my lips.

"God, you're hot!"

He chuckles softly to himself and winks cheekily.

"Clothes off," he demands gruffly, and I don't need asking twice, as I race to get naked.

We're both naked in record time and eagerly anticipating his body pressed against mine.

"Jesus, you're a sight for sore eyes, Raleigh Storm, how did I get so lucky?"

His voice is soft, almost as if he is saying it to himself. "I need the words, Raleigh. Tell me what you want."

I'm practically panting with raw lust, I'm desperate for this gloriously anguished man and I don't know how to stop myself from falling in love with him.

14

Brody

Today is the last day of the UK leg of our tour. We're playing our final gig at the world famous, iconic Royal Albert Hall, before we embark on our European and U.S leg of the tour. The past few weeks have been a whirlwind and Raleigh, and I have been practically inseparable. During this time, I've got to know what makes her tick and I've come to the realisation, that she isn't the same woman I met in rehab. Yes, she's still fragile, but not fragile like a flower. She's fragile, like a bomb and at any moment she could self-destruct, but I'm determined not to let that happen. I have never met anyone like her before. She's beautiful, smart, funny, and she accepts me for who I am. Despite my flaws, she still wants me. Her soul is equally as damaged as mine, yet we fit together perfectly.

The feelings she evokes in me scare the living shit out of me, but the more I get to know the real Raleigh Storm, the more I find myself becoming attached to her. She spends her days running and perfecting her lines for her upcoming film with Peyton and Nick, and by night, I pleasure her, until the sun comes up. During the weeks that have passed, I've been teaching Raleigh how to play guitar. She wanted to make her film role more authentic, by being able to play for real. She's a natural and tonight she's joining us on stage to play with us. She's dressed in tiny leather hot pants, a white vest - which emphasises her perfect, pert breasts - and knee-high leather boots, with black and silver accessories. She takes a deep breath and looks at me. The look she gives me, practically puts me on my knees, she's so beautiful and she doesn't even realise.

"I'm so fucking nervous!" she laughs uneasily, and I press her against the wall.

"Will this make you less nervous, kitten?" I say gruffly as I crash my lips against hers.

She moans inaudibly and loses herself in our kiss. I briefly pull away.

"Fuck, you're a force of nature, Storm."

I run my fingers through her hair, and she chuckles softly.

"Right back at you, Hart!" I laugh, as I make some last-minute adjustments to my guitar.

"You're gonna smash the shit out of this, kitten, trust me. See you on the other side!"

I wink and steal one last kiss, before we make our way to the side of the stage.

***

We're in the middle of our set, and the crowd is lively tonight. Sam makes his way to the front of the stage, and they go wild. The whole venue seems to vibrate with their enthusiastic energy. It's what I live for, the high is way better than any chemical high I've ever felt.

"How are you doing, London! Wow! So, I don't know if you know, but for the past month, we've had a special guest, on tour with us, the very beautiful, Raleigh Storm."

The crowd screams, as her name is mentioned.

"She's been on the road with us, preparing for her brand-new movie 'Rocked' directed by the legend that it is, Damien Valentine. Whilst she's been on tour with us, our very own Snake, has been teaching her how to play guitar. Our brand-new song 'Rock Me' is also going to be featured on the movie soundtrack and we're going to perform it for the very first time live, for you fucking lucky people tonight!"

Sam sweeps his arm out to the side, and I step forward to introduce her.

"For the first time, please give a warm Vengeance welcome, to the extremely talented and honorary Rancid Vengeance member, Raleigh Storm!"

She steps out onto the stage and the crowd cheer for her. She comes to a stop in front of me and I can see by the look on her face, she is terrified. I sling my guitar over her shoulder and let her adjust it herself. One of our loyal roadies, Donovan runs on stage, with my bass guitar and I fine-tune it quickly, as I lean into whisper.

"Remember what I taught you, kitten. Just relax, you're going to blow them away, I promise. I've got every faith in you, you fuckin' got this!"

I give her a wink of encouragement, and she smiles nervously, as the opening strains of our new song 'Rock Me,' echo through the arena. Jax strums out an impressive opening riff and Raleigh joins in halfway through. She's a total natural, it is as if she was born to play. That kind of talent is so rare. She fingers the fret board effortlessly, as Sam steps up to the microphone stand, gripping it with both hands and begins to sing.

"Faster than a moving train, enraged like a hurricane. She's half woman, half American dream. Mistress of singing, I'm pulling your strings, twisting your dreams, and thrashing your drum. Rock me until the sun comes up. She's blinded by me, and you can't see the strings. Just call my name, 'cause I'll hear you scream. Mistress, Mistress, just call me by my name, 'cause I'll hear you scream. Mistress, Mistress, rock me, until the suns comes up."

The spotlight moves on to her and bathes her in soft light, she looks almost ethereal and otherworldly. She struggled with this particular riff, but I know in my heart, she'll smash the shit out of it. I give her an encouraging nod, to boost her confidence. I mouth '*You can do this*' and she smiles softly. She grasps the opportunity with both hands, and she makes my guitar sing to her. She makes it her slave and for these four minutes and forty-two seconds, she is its master. I watch in awe, as her slender fingers, move lightning fast, up, and down the fret board and I can't quite believe how quickly she's took to playing it. The crowd grows more excited, and the atmosphere is electric. She strums out a solo, as if she were born to do it and the pride in my face must say it all, because she's *actually* performing. She moves to the front of the stage, as the solo ends, Sam growls and begins to sing again.

"A demon nestled somewhere in time. No warnings, no sign. My pretty little judgment day and slowly the villain arrives. Eventually, they all commit their crimes. Just call my name, 'cause I'll hear you scream. Mistress, Mistress, just call me by my name, 'cause I'll hear you scream. Mistress, Mistress, rock me, until the suns comes up. Yeahhh! Rock me, til' the sun comes up."

Jax moves fluidly across the stage to stand back-to-back with Raleigh, as he normally stands with me.

"Let's give 'em a show, sweetheart!" I hear him whisper to her.

"Two-three-four!" he counts her in, and Raleigh didn't just play my electric guitar, she fucking rocked it, and she didn't just rock the guitar; she rocked the whole venue.

As the song draws to a close, the crowd goes wild, cheering, screaming, and stomping their feet. There's no feeling like it, Raleigh jumps up and down and she launches herself at me. I catch her, hyper-aware that this moment will be captured and printed in tomorrow's press. But I don't care, I'm so fucking proud of her.

"Ladies and gentlemen, give it up for Miss Raleigh Storm!" Sam says gruffly, and she beams as she blows the crowd a kiss.

"Thank you! Thank you so much London!"

Donovan runs back onto the stage to swap our guitars, and I sling my guitar over my head.

"London, you're looking so fucking beautiful out there tonight! Now, we're going to take you on a journey back to the very beginning of Rancid Vengeance. Back to when we were four young and fucking stupid teenagers, who had suddenly become famous. It's been a hard thirteen years, but you guys have kept us going, coming out to support us, buying our albums, you all make it all worthwhile and we can't thank you enough."

The crowd begins their familiar chant.

"Vengeance, Vengeance, Vengeance."

Sam laughs.

"Yeahhh! We want everyone in this fucking room to get their phones out. Come on, all of you, get your phones out. We want every single one of you to start recording, live streaming, going live on social media, Facebook, X, Snapchat, Instagram, Tik Tok, because right now, we're going to make a fucking moment!"

The sea of people all do as Sam says, and it never fails to amaze me how he has the audience eating out of the palm of his hand. There is a soft glow of light as the crowd hold up their phones to capture this iconic, defining moment. It is uniquely beautiful. The hairs on the back of my neck are standing on end and I feel goose bumps begin to form on my entire body. There's no feeling like it and every time, feels like the very first time.

"Let me hear Corrupted, Flash."

The opening riff of our first single, which launched our career, fills the room and I feel so fucking high on adrenaline. The crowd go wild and the whole venue seems to vibrate with their enthusiastic energy; this is what I fucking live for.

"Let me see those fucking hands in the air. I need to hear you *scream* for me, London!"

Jax strums out the impressive, complex introduction and I join in. This truly is a defining moment, because it's the moment I conclude, that I'm in love with Raleigh Storm. *Fuck it all to hell.*

15

Raleigh

Everything was going great and today was the final day of touring, with Rancid Vengeance. A part of me didn't want this tour to end, because I had fallen hook, line, and sinker in love with the enigma, that is Brody Lennon Hart. Earlier on this evening, I performed live on stage with the boys, and I understand what Brody meant when he said it's better than any chemical high. I came off stage buzzed and unusually horny. I have some time to kill, before the boys come off stage, so I decide to call Liv to distract myself. I enter the empty dressing room, shut the door behind me and drop down onto the sofa. I pull my phone out of my bag and dial her number; she answers on the third ring.

"Hey Liv!" I greet her enthusiastically.

"Hey, hey Miss Rocker-knickers!"

I laugh at her ridiculousness. *God, I miss her.*

"How's it going, girl?"

I lean back in my seat and sigh heavily, "it's been-eventful to say the least."

She laughs melodically. "Uh-oh, you've fallen in love with him, haven't you?"

I chuckle softly at how well she knows me, and I squeeze my eyes shut briefly, willing the shameless ache that settles in my chest to subside.

"Head over heels and I don't know what to do, he makes it so easy for women to fall at his feet, Liv. He won't let me inside those impenetrable walls, it's impossible. I can't stop fucking thinking about him, he's-everything. *Shit*, I can't stop myself from feeling with him, all those years of therapy and it all gets fucked to hell by a damaged rock star."

She pauses for a second. "*Wow!* His cock must be huge!"

We both burst out into hysterical laughter, her blunt honesty is what I need right now and I'm so grateful she answered my call.

"I'm assuming that's a yes, by your awkward silence?" she asks curiously.

"Hmm, tattooed and pierced too!" I indulge her, and she shrieks.

"O-M-F-G! You lucky bitch! You've hit the jackpot! I've been trying to convince Jens' to get his cock pierced!"

I close my eyes and think of Brody's thick, pierced member. I feel myself getting wet just thinking of him and I bite my lip. *Behave, Storm.*

"Let's just say, it's fucking amazing, Liv! Multiple orgasms all round and I haven't had to fake it once!" I admit brazenly as she laughs dirtily, and I find myself laughing right along with her.

We catch up for a while longer, shooting the breeze and catching up on our eventful and hectic lives.

As I go to speak again, he steps into the room and it's like all the air has vacated. He looks delicious drenched in sweat wearing ripped jeans, which hang low on his lean hips and a tight black vest, which clings to his overwhelmingly, powerful physique. He cocks his eyebrow curiously.

"Liv, I've got to go," I say softly.

"Ah, I see, give him one for me! Love ya! Speak soon!"

I hang up, without saying goodbye and I get to my feet. He moves closer, like a predator trapping its prey. I have nowhere to go, as he backs me against the dressing table. He lifts me effortlessly onto it and he presses his lips to mine. His tongue probing mine, as he deepens the kiss. His lips are unusually soft for a guy, the softness of his lips and his two-day-old stubble is a total contrast, as he pushes himself further into me. His erection digging into my lower abdomen and he is damp with sweat, but he smells of something distinctly Brody Hart. I trace his bottom lip with my tongue, and he buries his hand in my hair, as if he can't get enough of me. The low rumbling sound he makes, lets me know he's more than turned on. I wrap myself around him, telling him wordlessly, that I'm more than ready to rock his world. Brody is broad, muscular and a few inches taller than me, I feel small in comparison. The working out he's been doing in his spare time has really paid off.

"God, you were fucking amazing out there, kitten. I'm so fucking proud of you; I knew you could do it," he grinds out hoarsely and I feel a sense of real achievement at his praise and kind words.

"Is it weird that I'm fucking horny right now?"

I laugh and shake my head, as he thrusts his steel erection into me.

"Not at all, I've thought of nothing else since I stepped off that stage," I confess boldly.

"See, we fit together perfectly." He moves his hand lower and starts rubbing lazy circles over my shorts.

"Oh God, Brody," I moan softly. "Anyone could walk in."

"Fucking let them, I'm pleasuring my girl and I'm not ashamed."

My stomach does a little somersault at hearing him call me his girl.

"Do you want me to take you right here, kitten?"

I bite my lip and nod.

"Does it turn you on that someone might walk in and catch us?" he says seductively as he unzips my shorts and slides his hand inside. He shoves his finger inside my slick channel; I gasp at the intrusion. "God, you're always so wet for me."

I moan softly and as he builds up a rhythm, I'm practically riding his hand.

"We have to be quick; do you think you can come for me? I want you to come hard all over my fingers."

I writhe beneath him, as he continues to finger fuck me shamelessly, on the dressing room table. He introduces a second finger and I'm aware, that someone could walk in at any moment.

"Jesus fucking Christ, you're close, I can feel you rippling against my fingers. That's so hot," he says, as his rhythm increases, driving me towards the finish line.

"Fuck, I'm going to come! Oh God! Brody!"

He expertly twists his fingers inside me, and his thumb finds my sensitive swollen nub.

"Oh fuck! Brody!"

He grins, his silver eyes twinkling with want.

"Come for me, kitten." He increases his pace, and I find myself panting audaciously for him. "I want to watch you come."

His voice is commanding as my orgasm to tears through me like a lightning bolt. He swallows my screams, as he squeezes every ounce of pleasure from my tightly wound body.

"Fucking hell! That was easily the most erotic thing I've seen, watching you come around my fingers like that."

His voice is low and filled with seductive promise.

"Fuck me, Brody."

He shakes his head and tips my chin up to face him.

"Not here, kitten. As much as it turns me on, I don't want other men seeing what's mine."

He says with hard conviction, as he presses his forehead to mine and with those words, I know one million percent, I have fallen hopelessly in love with this beautifully broken rock star.

**

After he made me come perched on the dressing room table, we ended up back at the hotel. He fucked me on and across every surface in the room. There's no doubt in my mind that there's something between us, whether he cares to admit it, or not. We lie there in a post-sex haze, my head resting on his solid pecs and his fingers idly stroking my hair.

"Me and Carter had been together six months when he tried to rape me," I admit and I feel his whole body stiffen and as I say those words, I am instantly transported back to that day.

Past
Raleigh

It was our six-month anniversary, and we had been out for dinner to celebrate. We both left our cars at his place, so we could both have a glass of wine or two and we got a cab to my favourite restaurant, 'The Cave'. I was wearing my favourite backless, cobalt blue, Roberto Cavalli mini-dress and Carter was wearing a dark slate grey three-piece suit. It was just like any other night, we had dinner, chatted easily about our upcoming projects, even had a few laughs, like any normal couple would. But as our night ended, his attitude and whole demeanour totally changed. When he was in this mood, I never knew which Carter I was going to be graced with, the Dr Jekyll part of him, or the Mr Hyde part. On the cab journey back to his penthouse apartment in Mayfair, he was distant, eerily silent, and his mood was intense.

By the time we arrived, I was feeling relatively anxious, as I followed him through the front door. As I shut the door, he hung up his jacket, and I turned towards him, his open palm cracked across my face. It took me by surprise, as I was slammed back against the door. I could hear him yelling, that I was a whore and a worthless slut, for flirting with the waiter during dinner. He continued to shout about how I made him look pathetic. He grabbed me by my hair and dragged me close enough, that I could smell the strong scent of alcohol on his breath and feel his spittle against my lips, as he hissed at me.

"So, you think I'm some sort of fucking pathetic idiot? Do you?"

My mind still reeling from his sudden outburst of anger and violence, I could only manage a pitiful noise that only appeared to enrage him further. He hit me with the back of his hand so hard, that I bounced off the wall next to the door and I crumpled against it. I felt the force of his foot hit my side, a split second before I felt the excruciating pain and I screamed out in agony.

"Please, Carter. I didn't do anything, please, tell me what I've done," I begged pitifully.

"Didn't fucking do anything?" he roared at me.

I felt him grab me by my ankles and drag me across the floor, the carpet burning my back. As I opened my eyes and realised, I was lying on the living room floor. He was on top of me, ripping my dress off my shoulders, and pawing at my tender breasts, the look in his eyes was not like anything I'd seen before. I was terrified, as he moved himself slightly and thrust his hand up between my legs. He yanked my knickers to one side, as I felt him roughly penetrate me with his fingers. I summoned every ounce of strength I had inside of me and screamed in his face for him to stop at the same time as I clenched my fist and smashed it into his face. He looked only slightly shocked for a second, before a sinister grin appeared on his face and it was in that moment, I knew I was in real trouble.

"Is that all you've got, bitch?"

He spat at me, as he grabbed both sides of my head, raised it slightly and smashed it down on the carpeted floor. I could only see colours and strange, psychedelic patterns, as I felt him stand up and rip the rest of my clothes off.

"Why are you doing this, Carter?" I managed to mumble incoherently, and I truly had no idea what I had done wrong.

"You know fucking why, you worthless piece of shit! I saw the way you looked at him! The waiter, you were practically eye-fucking him right in front of me!"

I couldn't comprehend the way he was talking and acting. He bent down to grab me by my hair and dragged me into the kitchen. He jerked me to my feet and slapped me across the face again, throwing me forward, so that I fell to my knees. I heard a bottle clank, as it fell and rolled to a stop against the wall. I heard the clink of his belt and the sound of him unzipping his trousers. He grabbed my legs and dragged me forwards, gripping me by the hips, and I knew what was about to happen. I started to sob and prayed to everything I could think of to make it stop. I was screaming and crying hysterically, he just kept saying it's what I wanted and what I deserved for treating him like an idiot. I heard the bottle clink again, as he attempted to push himself into me, but I didn't allow him to, as I screamed again. I lashed out blindly with my hand and I heard a smashing sound, a second before I realised, I was the one holding that fucking God-sent bottle.

After I knocked him out, I really don't know how I managed to get away from him. Somehow, I'd sliced my arm open. It must have been as I hit him with the bottle, and I was bleeding quite badly. I grabbed a towel from the kitchen and wrapped my arm in it, the blood soaking it almost immediately. I remember every move I made was almost robotic, like I was either on autopilot, or in shock. I haphazardly pulled on my ripped dress, fully aware that he could come around at any moment. I took Carter's suit jacket from the coat rack and pulled it tightly around myself. I was aware that it was Gucci and uber expensive, and his jacket would be totally ruined, but I didn't give a shit. I grabbed my bag with my car keys and left in a hurry without looking back.

Present

Raleigh

Brody takes in a sharp intake of breath. I feel his body trembling against me, with such palpable anger, that I don't doubt his feelings for me for one second.

16

Brody

Listening to her recount the horror she went through with her fucking scum bag ex-boyfriend. How could he treat her like that and still be fucking breathing? *He wouldn't be after I've finished with him.* I knew she broke up with her ex, Carter Leonard from what Cole found out, when I asked him to do a background check on her. *So fucking sue me!* Carter and Raleigh both starred in a popular, well-known UK based, soap opera, called '*The Village.*' They also both starred in a leaked porn movie and there was speculation that it was Carter who leaked it. Raleigh's character was immediately written out, and she was publicly shamed. Carter's management called a press conference, he made an apology to his fans, and his role was immediately reinstated. Not long after, Raleigh was admitted to rehab.

"To this day, I really don't know how I summoned up the strength to get away from him."

I feel a tear drip on my chest, and I realise it came from my eyes. *What is wrong with me? I never fucking cry, at least not in long time.*

"Don't cry for me, Brody. God, I can't bear it, I don't deserve it, I was so fucking weak and pathetic."

I swipe my tears away and tilt her head, so she's facing me.

"Don't you fucking dare do that, Raleigh. How could you think you deserve to be treated that way?"

She shakes her head, almost in disbelief.

"Because he *made* me that way, because I *let him* make me that way, I *allowed* that to happen. We're both damaged, Brody, but whatever anyone says or thinks, we're both survivors."

I clench my jaw, feeling angry on her behalf.

"I really want to hurt him; he needs to fucking pay for what he's done."

She laughs bitterly.

"He's brilliant at manipulating, he's an actor. He's an expert at it, he's good at making people believe what he wants them to believe. He's a liar, but he's great at turning on the charm, when it suits."

I sit up and lean down to face her.

"He doesn't deserve to be fucking breathing for what he did to you, Raleigh. He needs to suffer for laying his hands on you!"

I reach out to stroke her face and she leans into my touch.

"I'm so sorry you had to endure that; I'd never hurt you like that. *Jesus Christ*, the thought turns my fucking stomach," I express incredulously.

She sits up and entwines her fingers with mine, as she continues her story.

"Despite that fact that I'd been drinking, I managed to drive myself home, praying that I wouldn't get pulled over. I went inside, and I tried to fix my arm myself, I tried to bandage it, but there was so much blood. I couldn't stop shaking. I felt woozy, and I was in a lot of pain. By that point I think the adrenaline had started to wear off. I took some pills to dull the pain, and I must have passed out, because the next thing I remember was Paul finding me the next morning. I tearfully spilled out that I had suffered a relapse with the self-harming and was addicted to prescription medication. I admitted myself to rehab, I was so desperate to get away from Carter, I invented a fucking addiction."

A tear rolls down her cheek, and she angrily swipes it away.

"To this day Paul still believes the lie, even though he constantly questions me and tries to pick holes in my story. He's got his suspicions, he's a smart man, but I managed to convince him otherwise and he thinks it was a cry for help. A failed suicide attempt. You're the only person I've ever told but I'm not a drug addict. Yes, I'm a self-harmer, that was never a lie, but I'm not addicted to prescription medication. I'm so sorry I lied."

I am dumbstruck at what I'm hearing. *How the fuck can someone as strong as her, allow herself to be treated that way?* I actually feel physically violent.

"Don't you dare be fucking sorry. You've got nothing to apologise for. He needs to be dealt with, Raleigh. He needs to be stopped, before he does it to some other innocent woman."

She smiles warmly.

"How many other women do you think have tried to go to the press about him, Brody? I've taken out a restraining order against him, so he can't come within one hundred yards of me."

My mouth drops open and I can't believe what I'm hearing. *What the actual fuck?*

"If you think nothing's going to be done about him now that I know, you're very much mistaken, kitten. I will make sure that fucking piece of shit pays for what he did to you and all of those other women. He won't be breathing by the time I'm done; I'll make him beg for his fucking sad, pathetic life, I'll make damn sure of that," I say with absolute conviction to my voice, and I know at that very second, I would do *anything* to protect what's mine.

Raleigh Storm is mine.

***

My mind is still reeling, after Raleigh's earlier revelation and all I can do is just lie there in silence and comfort her. Her head resting on my chest and the warm feeling of her body pressed against me, oddly distracts me from the shit in my head.

"You know whether you choose to believe me is completely your call, but you have the ability to wreck me, Rae. No woman has ever had that power over me before. That makes you the most powerful woman in my life. Fuckin' own it!" I admit shamelessly, and she chuckles softly as I brush my thumb across her full bottom lip.

She closes her eyes, relishing in my touch.

"You sell yourself short, Brody. You're a fucking walking contradiction, you say you don't do romance, but your words and your actions tell me different."

As she says those words, I don't know how to react, because the truth is, I often wondered who the real Brody Lennon Hart was. Who am I, other than Snake, world famous guitarist and one quarter of one of the worlds' biggest British rock bands? Lying here with her, at this moment, I've never been surer of who I am. I'm the man, who's perpetually in love with Raleigh

Storm. This beautiful, annoying as fuck woman, she completes me, she quiets my demons, but she can't ever know. *Fuck my life.*

Raleigh

Our conversation last night, has seemingly bought us closer together and even though I know today is the day I have to say goodbye to Brody, I know in my heart that this won't be the last time we see each other. We're on the tour bus and I'm packing up my stuff, ready to go home. I got a call from Paul this morning, to let me know that my new apartment in Kensington is ready for me to move into. *Thank God!* I have an unusual, but welcome spring in my step today and I'm looking forward to what life has to throw at me. Peyton makes her way towards me with a newspaper under her arm and two Starbucks cups in her hands.

"Hey hon, thought you might need this. Although when you see this, you'll wish I'd bought you something stronger!"

She laughs and hands me the cup, bracing myself for what I'm about to see, as she spreads the newspaper across the table. We both sit down opposite each-other, and the bold headline catches my eye. 'Budding romance for troubled actress and bad boy of rock?' I take a sip of my coffee and read on aloud.

"Veteran rock band Rancid Vengeance made a welcome return to form on stage last night, at the iconic Royal Albert Hall. But the question on everyone's lips was, are bad boy, Brody 'Snake' Hart and troubled actress, Raleigh Storm an item? Brody Hart, 34, is famous for his off-stage antics, his numerous stints in rehab and his links to a string of women. Sources close to the band say, 'They've been getting very close, and they are very much smitten with each other' and 'She may be the one to subdue his wild, rebellious ways.' Raleigh Storm, 29, who has been cast in Damien Valentine's upcoming film 'Rocked', is famous for her previous turbulent relationship, with popular U.K soap hunk, Carter Leonard. The pair are said to have met on the bands' recent tour and judging by the picture, it won't be long before their relationship is official. A spokesperson for both Miss Storm and Rancid Vengeance have declined to comment."

I lean heavily back in my seat and Peyton reaches for my hand, brushing it reassuringly.

"Really, don't let it get to you, honey. When Sam and me first got together, it was hell, they scrutinized every little thing. They dug up random shit from years ago, that wasn't even relevant," she says with an annoyed tone, and I shake my head.

"It's not that, I got used to it when Carter and me first met. It sort of goes with the territory being in the public eye, but I thought we'd have more time to keep us secret, before the media circus got involved, that's all."

She smiles sympathetically.

"I know the feeling, babe."

I am about to speak again when my phone starts ringing. I see Damien's name flash up and I swipe the screen to answer.

"Hi, Damien," I answer brightly as he clears his throat before he speaks.

"Hello Raleigh, how's it going?"

Peyton gets up and leaves, to give me some privacy.

"Yeah, it's going really great, thanks. I've learned so much, it's been such an adventure. I'm looking forward to the start of filming," I say enthusiastically.

"Good, good. So, is there something you need to tell me, Raleigh?"

My heart sinks and my good mood plummets, as the tone of his voice changes. I should have known as soon as I saw his name flash up on my phone that this was the reason for his call.

"I'm not saying this to be a bastard, I'm saying it, because it needs to be said. You need to stay away from Brody Hart. He's self-destructive, selfish and he doesn't care who he hurts. Don't get me wrong, I like him, he's a good guy, but walk away, while you still can. I'm saying this as a friend and an employer, he's bad news for your career, Raleigh. He's a hurricane, a disaster looking for a place to happen. I know you're an adult, but I can see you're fragile, you're vulnerable and he might not mean to, but Brody will take advantage of that. I don't want that to happen, especially not when you're building yourself and your career back up. You're so talented, I'd hate to see that exceptional talent go to waste. He's a genuine guy, but he's impulsive and he's unpredictable. It might seem exhilarating and exciting, but he'll take and take, until there's nothing left. I care about you, Raleigh, as an actress and as a friend. It's good publicity, don't get me wrong, but I want the focus to be on the movie and not some are-they-or-aren't-they romance. I'm not saying you shouldn't date, not at all, I haven't got the right. I'm giving you my professional opinion, some friendly advice if you will. Maybe try and keep it under wraps, at least until the movie's complete."

I am struck dumb at Damien's words, and I can't believe what I'm hearing. *How fucking dare he try and dictate who I can and can't date.*

"Don't let me down, Raleigh," he says abruptly and hangs up without saying goodbye.

He doesn't even give me the opportunity to defend myself. *Prick.* I now understand what Damien said at our initial meeting, his bark is definitely worse than his bite. *For fucks sake.*

17

Brody

I'm about to say goodbye to Raleigh and for the past few hours', she's been oddly quiet. She's never quiet, and it's unnerving me. Her idle chatter grounds me in some way. I don't know how to get through to her. We've just had incredible, mind-blowing sex, and she's lying on my chest idly making shapes with her fingers on my pecs. She's got something on her mind; I can tell by the way she's avoiding eye contact and her overall demeanour.

"Hey, talk to me, kitten," I ask softly, and she shuts down on me.

Fucking women. I lift her gently, get up and I start to get dressed, tugging on my jeans, visibly annoyed. I zip up my zipper and raise my hands in the air.

"What do you want from me, Raleigh? Tell me because I'm fucking confused!" I snap, and she sits up, the sheet pooling at her waist, giving me a full view of her pert breasts. "Put some fucking clothes on, you're distracting me," I say exasperated as I pick up her t-shirt and launch it at her.

She pulls the sheet up to cover herself, deliberately avoiding my stare.

"I don't know what you want me to say, Brody" she says softly as I pull on my t-shirt and zip up my jeans.

"Then don't say anything, just listen to me."

She looks at me and the look in her eyes almost breaks my heart.

"You want to know something, Raleigh? You're so fucking perfect and it scares the shit out of me. How can someone be *that* perfect and still want me? I don't deserve you."

A lone tear slips down her cheek and I wipe it away with the pad of my thumb.

"You're so fucking different from any of the other women I've been with; they're so caught up in the money and the fame, that they don't *see* me, you *see* me, you actually care. You don't just listen to me, you hear me. You're smart, you're brave and *so* fucking beautiful."

I move closer to her and stroke her face.

"Stop, please stop."

She shakes her head, and I start to pace the floor.

"Before you came along, I thought I was beyond saving, Raleigh. You give me hope that I could finally be happy."

She swipes away her tears with the back of her hand.

"You don't need me, Brody, the world doesn't need me," she says with such self-loathing in her voice, and it makes me angry.

How could she think that? I perch myself on the edge of the bed and cup her face in my hands.

"Don't you dare think this world doesn't need you, Raleigh. The world may still see the sun rise and set, but my world would fucking end, if you weren't in it."

My words only cause her to sob harder and that right there, is the reason why I can't admit aloud how I feel about her. *Fuck my life.*

Raleigh

Brody is such a complex, complicated, damaged human being, but he is mine. I belong to him, and he belongs to me, in every way possible. He runs his hands over his head, as if he's waging an internal war with himself. He gets up, putting some distance between us and I sense the moment his mood switches and the shutters come down.

"You know what, actually I take that back. Maybe I am beyond saving, Raleigh. What did you think was going to happen? That you'd show up, and you'd be the girl to tame me? I'm fucking damaged! I've seen things, I've done things, I'm not proud of."

The haunted look in his eyes, all but destroys me and I want to cry for him. I want to cry for the innocent, damaged little boy he was, and I want to cry for the beautifully ruined adult he's become. I reach out to stroke his face and he backs away from my touch, as if it repulses him.

"Don't fucking touch me," he whispers as I try to hide the bitter sting of rejection by tucking my hair behind my ear. "You need to go, as far away as you can get away from me, I'm not a good person, I'm not someone who can give you the happy ever after you fucking deserve. In another life, I could love you, Raleigh. Just not this one, I'm sorry."

I angrily swipe away the stray tears that have escaped and mentally curse myself to hell for giving in to my stupid fucking emotions.

"Don't you get it? I'm damaged too! We're both damaged and yet it doesn't stop me loving you! You fucking selfish prick!" I spit, and he looks taken aback by my statement.

It takes me a few seconds for my brain to catch up with itself and the words that I practically vomited. I just told Brody Hart I'm in love with him. *Fuck it all to hell.*

Brody

Raleigh Storm just told me she loves me. She's in love with me. *Fuck my life.* This isn't happening, this is not fucking happening.

"Say something."

Her voice comes out small and weak. The look in her eyes makes my chest ache, but this categorically can't fucking happen. I thought I could, but I'll destroy her, this beautiful, amazing woman, so full of life. I'll turn her into a shell of herself if she gives me the chance and I can't do it. *I won't let that happen.* I shake my head and steel myself to look her in the eyes, eagerly anticipating my reaction.

"No, no, no! This can't happen, you can't be in love with me, how can you possibly be in love with someone like me? I'm evil, I hurt everyone around me, can't you see that?" I babble.

I can feel myself getting agitated and the craving for a fix is so strong, my hands start to tremble.

"Why are you saying these things, Brody?"

She sobs softly, and I know I'm being a prick, but she *has* to understand.

"Because it's fucking true!" I roar as she sobs harder.

Watching her break down is killing me, but I can't bring myself to hold her like I know I should. *I don't want to give her false hope.*

"I'm not asking for forever, Brody, I'm not asking for a marriage proposal, I just want us, here in the moment, right now. I love you; I love you with every fibre of my fucking being, you make me whole, you complete me."

Hearing her repeat those words, almost shatters my resolve.

"Just go, please, just fucking go, Raleigh. I'm begging you, please, just walk away, for your own sake."

My voice trembles and as I say those words, she lets out a strangled sob.

"Brody, don't do this, please."

She moves closer to me and smashes her lips against mine, taking me by surprise. I know I should be stopping her, but I can't bring myself to do it. She feels too fucking good, and she smells delicious. She smells of Yves Saint Laurent Black Opium and my senses are overwhelmed by the feel of her hands roaming across my biceps and my torso. *Fucking hell.*

"Brody," she says breathlessly as she continues to assault my mouth with hers.

She introduces her tongue and I'm a total fucking goner. I lift her up and she wraps her legs around my waist. My dick is so fucking hard, I could hammer nails with it. I pin her against the wall, holding her up effortlessly, with one arm, as I try desperately to free my cock from the confines of my jeans. I quickly unzip, as she reaches in and grips my dick.

"Oh, fuck," I moan as she starts to jack me off.

It's lucky she's wearing just her underwear after our earlier sex marathon, as I awkwardly shift her thong to the side, giving me full access to her dripping wet slit. As my finger makes contact with her pussy, she pants.

"Jesus, fuck, that feels so good," she whispers as I continue to rub her pussy in slow lazy circles. "Look how good we are together, Brody, can't you feel it?"

As she says those words, I strengthen my resolve and set her down on her feet, putting some distance between us and zip up my jeans. I shake my head, trying to maintain some composure.

"No, Raleigh, we're not good for each other, I'll break you if you let me, and I won't do that to you. You're too pure for that, I'll extinguish that light that burns so bright inside of you, and I can't do that. You mean too fucking much to me, kitten," I calmly try to explain.

She has to understand. She sobs harder as she begins to hit me.

"YOU'RE A SELFISH, FUCKING BASTARD, YOU MADE ME FALL IN LOVE WITH YOU! WHY WOULD YOU DO THAT TO ME?" she screams, punching me harder in the chest. She hits me in the face and my jaw. I just stand there, taking every last beating she reigns upon me. "I HATE YOU! I FUCKING HATE YOU, BRODY HART! I WISH I'D NEVER FUCKING MET YOU!"

I deserve every blow and every hateful word that leaves her pretty mouth.

"What the fuck is going on?"

Sam's low timbre fills my ears, and he looks from me to Raleigh, taking in the situation unfolding in front of him. She stops hitting me and she just breaks down hysterically in a heap at my feet.

"You're breaking my fucking heart," she sobs, and I'm frozen to the spot.

I can't do anything other than just stand there and watch, as if I'm looking from the outside in. Her sobs pierce the hole in my chest and if I had a heart, mine would be breaking right about now too. Sam gets down on his haunches and he places his large, tattooed hand comfortingly on her shoulder.

"Raleigh, sweetheart, let me take you home, yeah?" he rasps softly, and she nods.

He lifts her up and something that feels like jealousy suddenly tears through me. *Fuck, I need to get high that I get so far away from the shit in my head.* It's that thought that makes my brain cooperate with my feet, and I turn around and walk away.

18

Raleigh

After our earlier shouting match when I awkwardly blurted out that I loved him. *Well fucking played, Storm.* I am on the way to my apartment, in Kensington, in the passenger seat of Sam Newbolt's black Ford F-450 Super Duty truck. He sits casually in the driver's seat, wearing a distressed grey Lightning Bolts t-shirt, stretched over his large, muscular body, and black jeans, with a pair of dark mirrored Ray Ban aviators covering his eyes. His raven black hair is styled into his usual messy spikes. He doesn't look at me directly, but I can feel his eyes on me. *Jesus Christ, he's intense and so fucking intimidating.*

"So, are you going to tell me what happened then, sweetheart?" he rasps, breaking the awkward silence between us.

"I told him I loved him, and he went fucking nuclear on me, that's what happened," I say matter-of-factly.

Sam takes off his sunglasses, perching them on top of his head, as we stop at a red light. He looks fleetingly at me, and I can see why women go crazy over him. *Fuck, everything about him screams power and authority.*

"What you should know about Brody, is that he doesn't think he deserves to be happy. He's been punishing himself for years, because of his mum, he's never really gotten over that. He doesn't open up because he doesn't want you to have that in your head. He thinks it's his own problem to shoulder, he doesn't mean to push you away, it is just the way he is. He's complicated, just give him some time to come around, he just needs to adjust, that's all. Don't give up on him, Raleigh, you could be good for each other. I'm telling you this because I like you and he won't," he states pragmatically, leaning my head back on the cars' headrest and sigh audibly.

"I don't know what to do, Sam. The director of my new film called me earlier. He told me in no uncertain terms, that my relationship with Brody would jeopardise my role. He said he's bad news."

Sam nods and cocks his pierced eyebrow.

"Damien Valentine, wow, we've hung out a handful of times and he's directed a couple of our music videos. The guys a legend and he's talented, he's amazing at what he does, don't get me wrong. But Brody's got a thing for married women, he slept with Damien's ex-wife, Kayla, so there's animosity, obviously."

Sam smirks and I can't help but smile too. *Why am I not surprised?* I want to take advantage of Sam's talkative mood and the sadistic part of me is desperate to know how many women there's been before me. But the needy part of me wins out and lays that question to rest for another day.

"That explains the warning then," I muse softly as Sam swiftly changes gear and glances in the interior mirror.

Cursing softly under his breath, he slams his hand angrily on the steering wheel.

"Fucks sake! Think we've got paps following us, sweetheart."

He sighs audibly and pushes a button on his steering wheel.

"Benedict?"

Sam smiles, as the low timbre fills the confined space.

"Cole, it's me, you're on speaker, I'm driving. I've got Raleigh in the car with me, and we've got a slight situation."

Coles deep rumbling laugh comes through the cars sound system.

"Of course you have, you really can't go anywhere without causing trouble, can you, Newbolt?"

Sam laughs, tapping idly on the steering wheel.

"I've said on numerous occasions, I like to keep you on your toes, mate! Look, we've got paps in pursuit, there's two of them."

Sam glances calmly in the interior mirror again.

"I need more than that, Newbolt, give us a clue! And why the fuck didn't you take security with you? That's what I employ them and pay them substantially for," Cole says wryly, and Sam rolls his eyes.

I chuckle softly. "Yeah, yeah, spare me the lecture, man. I've got one on a motorcycle to my right and one directly behind, in a Toyota Prius."

Cole laughs heartily.

"You've got twice the horsepower in your car, I'm sure you could lose a Prius! Just make sure the lady has got her seat belt on."

Sam looks briefly towards me, his emerald, green eyes filled with concern.

"You got your seat belt on, sweetheart?" he rasps.

I make sure it's clipped on and nod.

"Yeah, she's all good, mate. Fuck, please don't tell the wife about this," Sam states nervously and Cole snickers.

"Tell her what? It's all good, man, you don't need to worry, she's gone into work. Seb's been called over to New York... some emergency at his new shop. He's asked Peyton to hold down the fort while he's gone, the boys are with Amy and, she's working from home today. Right, I've tracked your GPS, I've got your location, you need to lead those sons of bitches on a wild goose chase, think you can do that, Sam?"

Sam laughs, his eyes filled with mischief, as he smoothly changes gear and presses his foot harder on the accelerator.

"Of course! This ain't my first rodeo, mate! Although the last time didn't end too well," Sam says with more than a hint of shame to his deep, husky voice.

"The less said about that one, the better," Cole says drily, and I smile warmly at the camaraderie between the two of them.

"*Fuck me*, are they that desperate for a story?" I ask curiously and with more than a little frustration to my voice.

"Unfortunately, they are, they're like a pack of hungry wolves. We'll be front page news tomorrow. I'll have left Peyton, and you'll have broken off your romance with Brody to be with me!"

We both laugh at the ridiculousness of the situation. *Is this really what a relationship with Brody would be like? Wow.*

Brody

I find myself in the last place I expected to be. When I got on my bike, I rode there almost on autopilot. Now, I am standing outside *her* house, in the pouring rain. I tap the door softly and as the light flicks on, I'm met with a feeling of guilt. *What about Raleigh, you prick?* I try desperately to push her to the back of my mind and focus on the only woman who I said 'I love you' to. As I wait for her to open the door, I am instantly transported back to the day I told her I loved her.

Past

Brody

I managed to get away from the boys, it was like a covert military operation, but I managed to check into a hotel, under the name 'Jack Hammer'. Original I know! I haven't seen her for almost seven fucking weeks and I need her like I need my next breath. I'm pacing the hotel floor awaiting her arrival and with each measured pace, I find myself getting more and more antsy. What if she doesn't show up? What if she's realised you're not worth it? What if she's realised she'd much rather have her wife-beating, scum bag husbands cock in her than yours, you sad pathetic fuck. I shake my head, desperate to push those thoughts to the back of my mind. Dude, just chill the fuck out, she'll be here. I try to reassure myself, as I lean down to open the minibar and grab a small bottle of Jack Daniels, unscrew the lid and chug it down neat. The burn as it slides down my throat calms me somewhat. I'm a little calmer as the door taps softly. I take a look at my reflection in the mirror and take a deep breath.

I walk over to the door and the sight that greets me knocks me off balance. Fuck me, she looks even more beautiful than the last time I saw her, if that's even possible. I take in every inch of her and commit it to memory. Her skin looks absolutely flawless and the tender look in her aquamarine eyes, makes my knees weak. Her long red hair is pulled up into a neat bun and her legs go on for miles. She is wearing a knee length black mac belted around her waist and she is wearing sky high, black patent, knee boots.

"Hey gorgeous," she greets me softly in her Northern twang.

"Hey yourself, fuck, you look..."

My words die on my lips, as she backs me into the room, kicking the door shut behind her. She unbelts her mac and underneath she is wearing a black lace bra, black lacy thongs, stockings, and suspenders.

"Am I worth the wait?"

I swallow hard and nod, dumbstruck at how truly stunning she looks. She drops her mac to the floor.

155

"I've thought of nothing else, sweetheart, it's been seven weeks of pure fucking torture," I admit honestly, I reach over and stroke her face. "God, I've missed you, so fucking much."

She shakes her head.

"No talking, tonight is about us, I want to lose myself in you and I want nothing but sheets between us, Brody," she whispers seductively, as she backs me towards the large Queen size bed.

My legs collide with the mattress, and she pushes me down. I'm at her mercy and more than happy to let her take control. My body is on high alert, humming and vibrating for her after seven weeks apart. She cups my erection, which is straining against the zipper of my jeans.

"FUCK!" I grunt.

"Clothes off, I can't wait any longer, I need you inside me, Brody," she pants desperately.

I pull my t-shirt off in one swift movement. She unzips my jeans and slides her hand inside to stroke my already hard cock.

"I've craved your cock for the past seven weeks; I've thought of nothing else. I've fingered myself to orgasm thinking of how you feel inside me."

I groan at her words, she's very vocal about what she wants in the bedroom, I've never met anyone like her. She pulls off my jeans and my boxers impatiently until I'm completely naked. She climbs onto my lap and crashes her lips feverishly to mine. I wrap my one arm around her to steady her, relishing in the feel of her warm skin against mine. I slip my other hand into the cup of her bra, softly stroking her sensitive, erect nipple. She runs her hands over my chest and my shoulders. She moans softly into my mouth, as she shifts her thong to the side to play with her pussy.

"Fuck, that's so hot, I love to watch you play with yourself, beautiful girl."

She throws her head back in ecstasy.

"Oh God, Brody!" she pants out my name.

"Don't come, I want to be inside you when you come, your orgasm is mine tonight," I command as she climbs off my lap, pushes me down on the bed and straddles me.

She takes off her bra and her pert boobs spring free. She moves her thong to the side and impales herself on my already hard cock. It feels so fucking good to *be inside her after all this time. She whimpers softly, allowing her to adjust to my length.*

"Oh Jesus, fuckin' Christ, you feel like heaven."

She picks up her pace riding me, as I move in and out of her slick heat. I move my hand to play with her pussy, as her pace quickens.

"Jesus! Lorna."

She bounces up and down on my cock, I feel the delicious friction of my piercing bumping against her cervix.

"OH FUCK! BRODY! I'm coming, fuck, I'm coming," she screams, and my orgasm is right behind hers as I feel my hot seed spurt inside her slick channel, causing a second orgasm to ignite within her.

As we come down from our orgasms, the hotel room is deathly silent. The only sound is our breathless post coital pants. She climbs off me and comes to lie next to me. I wrap my arm around her, and she snuggles deep into me. I can't hide my feelings for her any longer, all I've thought about over the past seven weeks is her. I've fallen in love with her, even though I promised myself in the beginning that I wouldn't do anything as stupid as fall in love with the woman I'm just fucking. But she made it too easy for me to fall hook, line, and sinker for her.

"What'cha thinking about, babe?" she asks with a soft chuckle.

"I..." I stutter. I've been away from her for seven weeks and I can't even manage to string a fucking sentence together. Get your shit together, Hart. "Fuck, all I've thought about while we've been on tour is you, I've been counting down the hours until I could see you again. I know I promised I wouldn't..."

She shakes her head, as if she knows what I'm about to say. "Brody, don't, don't spoil it by saying things you don't mean."

I lift her up and she sits up, facing me. I cup her face in my hands and press my forehead lovingly to hers.

"I love you, Lorna Lavelle, I love you more than I've ever loved anyone, this goes beyond anything I've ever felt before. You're...fuck...you're everything, I need you more than my next fix, I don't crave the drugs when I'm with you, I just crave you," I admit shamelessly and sincerely.

She squeezes her eyes shut briefly and when she opens them, they're glazed over.

"*This can't happen between us, Brody, I'm with Stefan, I love Stefan. This was only meant to be a bit of no-strings fun. You were never meant to fall in love with me, you deserve someone who isn't afraid to admit they love you back. You deserve someone who's biggest fear is losing you. I know you're not perfect and neither am I, that's why this thing between us has worked for so long. I thought we were on the same page?*"

Hearing her say those words out loud crushes me to my very core. They say love hurts, but I disagree. Rejection hurts like a motherfucker.

"*You don't mean that Lorna, we've been sleeping together for over two fucking years! Tell me you don't feel the same and I'll walk away right now?*"

She opens and closes her mouth as if she's desperate to say something, but she just shakes her head.

"*You love me just as much as I love you, Lorna! You're a coward! JUST FUCKING ADMIT IT! Call me selfish, but I'm done sharing you with that piece of shit husband of yours! Choose me, I'm asking you to choose me!*" I beg.

This is new territory for me, I've never begged a woman in my life.

"*Choose me, Lorna, be mine. I'm begging you, choose me.*"

I'm aware I sound desperate, but she brings out something in me. She makes me want to try; she makes me want more. A tear rolls down her cheek.

"*I'm sorry, Brody, I...I can't, I can't do this, I can't choose you. I'm so sorry.*"

She sobs and I can't look at her, I'll break if I look her in the eye.

"*You're breaking my fucking heart.*"

My voice trembles.

"*I'm laying myself bare for you, I'm putting everything on the line for you, my cards are on the table. I love you, why isn't that enough for you?*" I say through clenched teeth, willing myself not to break down and she swipes away her tears.

"*Because this isn't real, Brody! None of this is real! We both went into this for a bit of fun, to scratch an itch, to distract each other from our shitty lives! If I choose you, then it will be real, you'll get bored! You're a rock star, there's a girl in every city, right? Can you honestly tell me over the past seven weeks there hasn't been anyone else?*"

Truthfully, there hasn't been anyone else because all I've thought about is her. I've had every opportunity to lose myself in a random groupie, but I chose not to because I was saving myself for her. Listening to her excuses is shredding *me and all I want to do is get so high I don't remember how this fucking cruel rejection feels.*

"There's been no one else, all I've thought about is you, whether you choose to believe me is totally up to you, but I can honestly say there's been no one, just you, Lorna, just you. I swear it," I whisper earnestly, as I reach over to stroke her face.

"Don't do this, Brody, please, don't ruin what we've got," she says seductively as she climbs on top of me again, halting our conversation, and I'm too fucking weak to stop her.

Present

Brody

I'm jolted back to the here and now when a shadow appears in the doorway and the door swings open. Every time I see her, she takes my fucking breath away. She is standing there, in a white floral kimono and a long, billowing black skirt, looking so innocent and bohemian. *Fuck me, she is still beautiful.* She seems genuinely surprised to see me, as she folds her arms defensively across her chest.

"What are you doing here, Brody?" Her tone terse, in her soft Northern twang.

"I really don't fucking know why I'm here, Lorna," I admit honestly, and her face softens.

The truth is, after my disagreement with Raleigh, it seemed like a good idea. *We all know where good ideas get you, Hart. Fucked up, in trouble, or back in rehab.*

"Come inside, you're all wet."

I step inside the warmth of her house, and she closes the door. I follow her into the kitchen, and she spins around to face me.

"I didn't believe it when I heard you were out of rehab and clean, you look-good."

She gives me the once over and licks her lips. I smirk.

"Good to know, babe."

She shifts her eyes to the floor and a blush creeps slowly up her neck. I step closer to her and lift her chin up. Her eyes lock with mine and she smashes her lips angrily to mine. Her scent invades my nostrils, as she moans into my mouth and my tongue softly caresses hers. I feel my cock hardening in my pants, and I forgot how... *right* it felt with her. All of a sudden, she realises what's happening and pulls away. She puts some distance between us and scrubs her lips with the back of her hand. She's panting now, and I smile cockily.

"You really shouldn't be here, Brody. I told you before, this can't happen again."

Her voice is weak, and I know she doesn't mean a word she just said.

"I'm trying to play fair, but you're not playing by my rules, sweetheart," I say gruffly and nip her earlobe between my teeth, enveloped in her scent.

Fuck, she smells so good. She gasps audibly and I see her nipples harden through the thin material of her kimono.

"Admit you still want me, L. It will be so much easier for both of us."

Her eyes lock with mine and she doesn't drop her gaze.

"Brody," she says breathlessly, and I chuckle softly at her reaction to me.

I thrust my hips into her, pressing the evidence of my arousal in between her delicious thighs and she moans aloud.

"What do you want? Tell me, beautiful girl, do you want me to relieve you of that ache between your delectable thighs?"

She bites her lip, as if she is having some sort of internal war with herself. I push the shoulder of her kimono aside, to expose her bare skin and kiss along her collarbone. I flick my split tongue up her neck, teasing her with soft licks. She moans softly, and I know she is going to give in. *I'm that fucking confident.*

"Imagine how my tongue would feel on your pussy, how quickly I can bring you to orgasm, how I can give you such intense pleasure, it will make you fucking weep. I'll never forget how you look when you come."

I can feel my control slipping and I don't know how much fucking longer I can hold myself back. *God, I've fucking missed her.*

"Give yourself to me again, Lorna; let yourself feel just an ounce of what we used to feel for each other."

She shakes her head, and I can feel her trembling. I'm not sure if it's because she's scared of her feelings for me, or because she's turned on.

"I can't do this, Brody, not again," she whispers so softly; I barely hear her.

I close my eyes briefly and laugh bitterly.

"Is that all you could come up with, L? Really? You forget I *know* you; I can read you like a fucking book! You know where I've been today? DO YOU?" I bark.

I want her to fucking hurt, the way I'm hurting right now. The way she hurt me all those months ago.

"I was balls deep inside another woman that wasn't you and I ran away like the fucking pathetic coward I am because she told me she loved me! She wants me to commit to her! How fucked up is that!" I confess resentfully.

I know I'm being a complete fucking knob, but I can't help myself. Not when I'm around her, she makes me *fucking irrational*. She makes me say things and do shit that I don't fucking mean. Her eyes flash and her hand lands across my cheek.

"HOW FUCKING DARE YOU! HOW DARE YOU COME HERE AND SAY THAT TO ME!" she screams, her eyes full of fire. *There's my girl.*

"FINALLY! Something you actually fucking mean!"

I raise my hands in exasperation and start to pace the kitchen floor, with the formidable need to get off my face. I come to an abrupt halt in front of her. *Fuck me; she's so beautiful, it's devastating.* She has a figure most women would kill for, curves in all the right places and I could get lost in those aquamarine eyes, which remind me of the clear ocean.

"I'm reckless and irresponsible. Admit it, that's why you were drawn to me in the first place, L. That's why we work, we're the same you and me, because you're reckless and irresponsible too."

She doesn't meet my gaze, and I know it's because she knows I'm right.

"Fuck, say something, please. Let me know I'm not the only one, I stayed away because it's what you wanted but tonight has taught me, I'm incapable of doing that," I say with more than hint of anguish and pure vulnerability in my voice.

As I say those words, her shoulders sag and she finally looks up at me. The sadness and utter devastation in her eyes is visible, and it breaks my fucking heart.

"I'd love nothing more than to be yours, Brody, but I can't. Stefan...he needs me."

My jaw tightens at the mention of her cocksucker of a husband, and I clench my fists at my side until my knuckles turn white.

"I'm nothing without you, Lorna. I can't be with another woman without thinking of you."

She shakes her head. *Why the fuck do I do this to myself?*

"Please, don't make me choose, Brody, I can't. *I fucking won't. Not again,"* she says, with a sharpness to her voice, that I've never heard before.

I move closer to her, and she flinches when I grab the tops of her arms.

"What's he done this time, Lorna?" I ask, with an accusatory edge to my voice and she retreats into herself.

"I-It's nothing," she says quietly, and she hugs herself.

"I'm calling fucking bullshit," I say softly, as I shift her kimono down her other shoulder.

For a minute, I think she's going to stop me, but she doesn't. Beneath the material, is large, angry, purple bruise, in the shape of a set of fingerprints.

"*Motherfucker,*" I curse softly. "Did that fucking *prick* do this?" I hiss furiously, and just by the look on her face, I know the answer.

"Don't fucking call him that! I deserved it, he's ill, Brody. He hasn't been the same since the accident."

Am I hearing right? She's fucking defending him. It was well documented in the press, that Stefan Lavelle had a serious, almost fatal, surfing accident. Where he was wiped out by a fifty-foot wave, in a surfing competition, in Portugal. He broke his neck and severely damaged his spine and shoulder.

"Unbelievable! Why the fuck are you defending him? Don't make excuses for him, L. He laid his fucking hands on you and I'm gonna' fucking kill him, I swear," I say with conviction, and the panic in her eyes sets my nerves on edge.

"You can't, he can't know about us, Brody. He'll kill us both."

She sounds terrified and I shake my head, laughing sullenly.

"Then fucking bring it on, because if he tries, I'll make sure I bury him first, and I will burn every ounce of evidence. That's not a threat, babe, it's a fucking promise," I say, with a chilling edge to my voice.

"Brody," she warns, and my cock jumps to attention at the sound of her voice.

She's like the forbidden fruit. *I can't fucking help myself.*

"What's it going to fucking take for you to realise he's no good for you, Lorna? You deserve so much better than him."

My voice barely a whisper and she hangs her head, avoiding eye contact with me. She busies herself wiping the kitchen counter. *She knows I'm right, she's just too scared to admit it.*

"So, who's this other woman then?" she asks curiously, subtly changing the subject and I perch myself on a stool at her kitchen island, sighing audibly.

So that's the way she's going to play?

"Her names' Raleigh, Raleigh Storm, she's an actress. We've been seeing each other, on and off, we met in rehab," I explain, and she laughs melodically.

"*Wow!* Now there's a story to tell the grandkids!"

I find myself laughing along with her.

"Yeah, I guess it is. She-she's just a distraction," I say flippantly, and she shakes her head, almost regretfully.

"Don't do that, Brody. Don't dismiss it, don't dismiss her, you must feel something for her, or you wouldn't have run away from her, when she said the '*L*' word. You said it to me, what's so different about her?" she says softly, and I hang my head at the memory of when I first told her I loved her.

Not my finest hour, I have to admit.

"She's not you, she doesn't know me the way you know me. *Jesus*, she doesn't get me the way you do," I declare as she steps closer to me, my heart hammering in my chest.

"You need to let her in! How is she supposed to know you if you don't open up to her! Why are you doing this to yourself? You're torturing yourself, over something that's never going to happen, it was great while it lasted, but my life is here, with Stefan."

Listening to those words coming from her mouth. *It fucking stings.*

"Did these past four years mean nothing to you, Lorna? Four years I've watched you choose him instead of me, over and over again! Do you know how that makes me feel? I fell in love with you! How could I not? You made it so easy, you're so fucking beautiful, your crazy compliments my kind of crazy."

I reach out to stroke her face, she leans into my touch, briefly closing her eyes, as my phone starts to ring. I see her name flash up and quickly dismiss her call, as Lorna puts some considerable distance between us, retreating into herself.

"Why are you really here, Brody? Are you asking my permission to move on? Or is it something else?"

I pause for a few moments, to think about her question. Am I asking for her permission, or am I scared of the way I feel for Raleigh? Can I feel the same love for Raleigh, as I felt for Lorna? The love that Sam and Peyton keep speaking about, the butterfly inducing, soul crushing love, that completely takes over your entire being? Suddenly and completely out of nowhere, I seemingly come to my senses. I shouldn't fucking be here, I *can't* fucking be here. I get up from my seat, as if my arse is on fire and pace the kitchen, like a mad man clucking for a fix. I am clucking for a fix, but it's not chemical. *It's her.* I have to go to Raleigh.

"Brody?" she asks softly, and I continue to pace.

"I-I'm sorry, I shouldn't have come here, I should go, I-"

I'm at a loss of how to carry on, so I don't bother with an explanation, I turn and walk away to the sound of her calling my name.

***

After I left Lorna's, I just rode around on my bike for a while, trying to get my head straight, trying to get my feelings and jumbled up thoughts, in some kind of order. I find myself pulling up outside the place I always seem to gravitate towards when I need to put my shit into perspective. I park my bike in my usual spot, and I walk into the Rise and Shine Cafe, the smell reminding me of my home comforts, freshly brewed coffee, and bacon cooking. The bell chiming signals my entrance and I smile at Emmy, who is behind the counter. As usual, she beams at me and rushes towards me and I catch her, throwing her arms and legs around me excitedly.

"Brody!"

I hug her tightly, laughing as she clings to me. "It's good to see you too, Ems."

I laugh at her childlike enthusiasm and set her down on her feet. I look to my left and see that her little brother, Malakai is sitting at the table, with a glass of milk, a plate of Oreos and his colouring book. Malakai is six years old, and he has autism. He hero worships me, and he knows every one of our songs by heart. He is a die-hard Rancid Vengeance fan.

"Hey buddy."

His little face lights up when he looks from his colouring book to me.

"Snake!"

I smile, as he calls me by my stage name.

"Hey Mal, how's it going, my main man?"

He grins, we bump fists, as he pushes his plate of Oreo's towards me, and I sit down opposite him.

"Oreos are my favourite, but I only share them with Snake from Rancid Vengeance," he babbles excitedly.

I pluck one from the plate as Emmy lands a cup of coffee, just the way I like it, on the table in front of me.

"I've missed you, babe. It's been a while."

I dunk my Oreo into my coffee and chew. She smiles shyly, as Malakai continues to colour in his colouring book.

"I know, I've been super busy! I'm going back to college to study Early Years Education and Care."

I take a welcome sip of my coffee and finish my Oreo. "That's fantastic news, I'm so happy for you! It's about time you did something for you!"

She smiles and takes a seat opposite me, regarding me intently. "Thank you, so what's been happening in the World of Brody?"

I laugh, as I take another sip of my coffee. "Same old, same old, Ems. We've just come home from a tour; needed to come and visit my best girl!"

She giggles girlishly, and Malakai looks up from his colouring book.

"Emmy and Snake sitting in a tree!"

He laughs as Emmy blushes an adorable shade of pink.

"Shut up, Mal!"

She pouts, narrowing her eyes on him and he sticks his tongue out at her. I reach across the table for her hand.

"Don't do that, remember, stamina of an Olympian?"

I wink and she laughs at the memory.

"So, why are you really here, Brody?" she asks, and I sigh audibly, leaning back heavily in my chair.

"Woman trouble, Raleigh, the girl I'm seeing. She told me she loved me, and I don't know what to do," I admit, and she nods.

"What's wrong with that? You're easy to love, Brody. Who wouldn't fall in love with you?" she blurts out, and when she realises what she's said, she slaps her hand over her mouth. "Oh my God! Sorry, I-I didn't mean that-well I meant it-shoot, I'm not in love with you!"

I laugh and squeeze her hand. Malakai laughs mischievously.

"Emmy loves Brody!" he says with a slight lisp as she blushes again and I chuckle softly, ruffling Malakai's hair.

"Troublemaker! Don't sweat the small stuff, sweets, life is too short."

I shrug, as she nudges me to continue.

"She told me she loved me, and I bolted like a bat out of hell. Then I found myself at my ex's place, it's all such a mess, Ems."

I put my hand to my head, and she leans back in her seat, studying me carefully.

"It's only a mess if you make it that way, chick," she says cryptically, and I look up at her. She's looking especially pretty today.

Since I started coming here, we have gotten to know each other over the years, and she's become a good friend to me. I've watched her turn from an awkward kid into a beautiful woman.

"How old were you when you first lost your virginity, Brody?" she asks inquisitively and I smirk as I remember the first time I had sex with Hayley Stark, when I was fourteen.

"I was fourteen; it wasn't all hearts and flowers. I was a wham-bam-thank-you-mam, back then! I wasn't the sex God I am now, naturally!" I joke, and she giggles.

I love to make her laugh; something about her tells me she doesn't do it often.

"I want my first time to be special, like it is in the movies. All rose petals, soft music and candlelight."

She rests her head on her hands, and she gets this dreamy, faraway look in her eyes. My eyes widen, as I hear her admit she's a virgin.

"Shit! You're a virgin? Wow! How can someone as stunning as you, still be a virgin?"

She blushes.

"Are you blushing, Ems?" I tease, and she narrows her eyes.

"I just haven't found the right man yet, I haven't had the butterflies fluttering in my belly when I'm around a guy, when I get those, I'll know."

I love how innocently she sees the world. It's rare for someone so young, to have such an old, wise, and sensible head on her shoulders.

"Wise words from someone so young," I say as I take the remaining few sips of my coffee.

This girl makes the best fucking coffee in London. Even better than her mum used to make.

"How come you've never settled down like Sam? He's like mega fit, but you're-you, you're never photographed with the same woman twice, this woman must be special if she told you she loved you," she babbles and gestures animatedly with her hands as I cock my eyebrow, ignoring her previous statement.

"Wow! Does someone have a crush on my best mate? He's pussy whipped, since he got married, his cock is tiny, and he has a lightning bolt tattooed on his arse! My cock on the other hand, has a snake tattooed around it and it's pierced, I'm hardcore! Most women can't handle me, babe!"

I brush off her blatantly trying to figure me out and she must realise, because she pouts.

"Why do you do that? It's like you can't take a compliment," she says perceptively, as she cocks her head to the side, and I shrug.

"I don't take life too seriously; I had a rough upbringing. I did what I had to, just to survive. Sam had it all, his dad was a world-famous rock star, I came from a council estate in Hackney. It didn't get better for me until I met the boys."

I know I'm over-sharing, but like Peyton, she makes me want to be better.

"I didn't have a dad and my mum-well the less said about her, the better. I didn't have a proper positive female influence in my life, not until I met the boys. Lori Newbolt, Jamie-Lee Chase, and Ava Landon took me under their wings, as if I were one of their own. I never knew how to treat women properly until they taught me. I was a tough nut to crack back then. I hated the world, and I was rebellious; I still am to a certain extent. I can't accept it, I'm not sure *how* to love because I feel like I'm not worthy of it. That's why I panicked when Raleigh told me she loved me."

I take a long sip of my coffee, and she reaches across the table for my hand.

"You can't change the past, Brody, but you can't let it shape your future either. You deserve to be happy, look at Sam and Peyton, they seem happy. They're married, and they've got two kids now."

I smile, as I think of my two best friends. *They're so in love, it's fucking sickening.* "They're stupidly happy; they make me want to reach for the sick bucket!"

I roll my eyes animatedly and she smiles, as I look at her. "Talk to Raleigh, tell her how you feel. Pretend she's me, if you like, if it makes it easier."

As I listen to her say those words, I consider that maybe she's right. *Maybe I am worthy, and I do need to tell her how I feel.*

19

Raleigh

After we managed to get away from the pursuing paparazzi, Sam dropped me off at my new apartment in Kensington. We swapped numbers, and he told me to call him if I ever need him. I can see us becoming friends. The keys are waiting at the concierge desk for me with the security guard, who introduces himself as ex-Marine, Aaron Blake. He is over six-feet tall, his broad shoulders and his bulging muscles, make him look terrifying, but his kind blue eyes and dark brown hair, styled into a neat side parting, soften his features.

"Anything you need, ma'am, anytime, day or night, someone will be there to deal with your every need. Someone will be on duty twenty-four, seven and security is of utmost importance."

I nod, and I can't stop the grin that spreads across my face. *I finally have a place I can call home. My* recently renovated, one-bedroom apartment on the lower ground floor is situated in the secluded square of Iverna Court, hidden in an oasis of serenity, with a private, communal garden. Aaron shows me up to my apartment and I'm stunned into silence as I walk through the door. It is modern and decorated in light grey, neutral tones throughout. The large grey corner sofa dominates the space and looks inviting. As I step further into the room, I notice a fifty-inch flat screen TV, on a white lacquer TV stand, in the corner of the room. Aaron stands back, as I take in my surroundings.

"Is everything to your satisfaction, Miss Storm? We furnished it exactly the way Mr Lyndsey requested," he asks, and I turn to him with a beaming grin.

"Yes, everything is fantastic, it's beyond perfect. Thank you so much, Aaron, I really appreciate it."

He smiles and nods curtly. "If there's anything else, the number for the front desk is next to the phone, and my personal number is also on there, should you need my assistance."

I find myself smiling back and nod my understanding. "Thank you."

He nods silently and leaves me to take in my new home. *My fresh start, my new chapter.*

***

I find myself settling in by ordering pizza, a bottle of wine and snuggling on the sofa in my jogging bottoms and comfy top, in front of the TV. I'm watching You on Netflix when I unexpectedly hear a knock on the door. My heartbeat starts to quicken, as no one knows about this place, apart from Sam and my agent, Paul. I get up from the sofa, reluctant to answer the door to my unknown visitor.

"Kitten, it's me, let me in, please, we need to talk," Brody says softly, and I pull the door open.

He is a sight to beholden, he is wearing loose fitting jeans, biker boots, a v-neck, heather grey t-shirt, which showcases his chest tattoos and that leather jacket I love so much. He leans in the doorjamb, which causes his t-shirt to ride up, emphasising the tight, sculpted muscles in his tattooed abdomen.

"Are you going to let me in or are you going to leave me standing here like a dickhead?" he says with an amused tone to his voice.

I step out of the doorway, dumbstruck that he's here, but happy that he is. I let him in and close the door behind him. Instead of looking tall and awkward, he looks at ease, as if it's the most natural thing in the world for him to be here. He tucks his hand casually into his pocket and takes in his surroundings, clearly impressed at what he sees.

"Nice place, babe, Sam told me you'd be here. I promise, I'm not a stalker!"

We both laugh. *He's definitely no Joe Goldberg.*

"Look..."

We both go to speak at the same time, and he chuckles softly. "Ladies first."

I steel myself to say what I need to say to him, but the way he looks at me with those intense eyes of his, almost shatters my resolve. The words almost get stuck in my throat, but they need to be said, they need to be out there in the world, he needs to hear them.

"I'm not looking for an argument, but you need to hear it. You're still so lost in your pain and stuck in the past, that you refuse to let people in. I love you, isn't that enough? I'm still here, I won't give up on you. I'm willing to try for you. I won't leave, I promise. Please, just give us a chance. That's all I'm asking. I didn't want to fall in love with you, but you made it near impossible for me not to. Bit by bit, piece by piece, we're healing the damaged parts of each other, can't you see that?" I explain as he rubs the nape of his neck and squeezes, clearly agitated.

"I didn't come here for a row, Raleigh," he says with an exasperated sigh, and I pause for a few moments, as he starts to speak again.

"You don't get it, do you? I was ten years old when my mum died, I was just a fucking kid! I found her in a pool of her own vomit with a needle in her arm! That image haunts me, that's why I'm a fucking insomniac! Because that image is burned into my fucking retinas and it's the only thing I see when I close my eyes! I don't know how to love because the one person that should have taught me that, abandoned me when I fucking needed her! Everyone leaves eventually, what makes you so different? FUCKING EXPLAIN TO ME, RALEIGH! MAKE ME UNDERSTAND!"

He raises his voice a few decibels louder and I can't stop the tears that fall.

"BECAUSE I'M NOT YOUR MOTHER! I'M FLESH AND BLOOD; I'M LIVING AND FUCKING BREATHING!" I scream, swiping angrily at my tears. "What will it take for you to let me in, Brody?"

I lower my voice to almost a whisper and he shakes his head, causing me to sob harder.

"Don't fucking do that, please, that's not why I came here. I warned you in the beginning not to fall in love with me. Why the fuck didn't you listen?"

He reaches out and wipes my tears away with the pad of his thumb.

"I'm fucking damaged, can't you see that? Inside, I'm still that broken little boy, who found his mum dead. Part of me feels responsible for that, what if I hadn't acted out? What if I'd been the perfect son, the one who did his homework, the one who excelled in all his classes? Do you think it would have turned out differently?"

I know they were rhetorical questions, but he needs answers.

"No, it wouldn't have turned out differently, your mum still would have chosen the drugs over her son. She didn't deserve you. She neglected you. Why can't you see that? I'm trying to stay neutral, but it's fucking difficult for me. My mum hasn't been the best parent over the years, but she at least tried, your mum just gave up! She deserves to rot in the fucking ground for that because you're so much more. You are worthy and you deserve a happy ending. I'm asking you to take that leap with me, the one you mentioned when we first met."

I take his calloused hand in mine and step closer to him. He presses his other palm to the back of my head, guiding me towards him.

"You're my heart, Rae. Don't you get that by now? We've been over this, why should we have to put a label on what we are? I know how I feel about you, that's all that counts. That's all that should count."

Good god, his words shatter my resolve to pieces and makes me practically melt in a pool at his feet.

As his thumb brushes across my full bottom lip, I'm totally lost. The glint in his eyes and the pressure of his hard, muscular body against me, reminds me that I belong to him and he belongs to me. We are two halves of the same coin. Even though, my love for him might not be reciprocated, I have no doubt in my mind, that we are made for each other. *That has to be enough, for now.*

***

The months that followed, I found myself growing more in love with the enigma that was Brody Hart. He was funny, genuine, thoughtful, and even though he would never admit it out loud, he was just as in love with me as I was with him. The more time I spent around him, the harder I was falling for him. He was on a promotional tour with Rancid Vengeance and filming had almost wrapped for 'Rocked.' I was blissfully in love and life was great. The saying is true, that absence makes the heart grow fonder.

Today in between filming, I have my weekly session with my therapist.

"So, what's been happening on Planet Raleigh since our last session?"

She smiles so wide, my jaw aches just watching her. *Fuck me, this woman is always so God damn happy.* She reminds me of one of those children's TV presenters, who is always so full of enthusiasm and energy. I cross my leg over my knee and my leg involuntarily starts to twitch.

"Is there any particular reason my question is making you anxious, Raleigh?" she asks politely, and I ponder her question for a few moments.

"You do realise that the formalities aren't necessary, Mav?."

I smirk and her shoulders visibly relax. She sags back in her chair and rolls her eyes animatedly.

"Thank fuck for that, I was beginning to think you'd been abducted by aliens and replaced with a clone, Rae!"

We both laugh out loud. Maverick Van Straten and I have been friends for many years, her and her parents were our neighbours when I first moved to the UK from Australia to go to theatre school. Liv and me rented this shoe box mid-terrace on the outskirts of Southwark. It was cosy and falling to bits, but it was ours. Maverick is one of my closest friends and like Liv, she keeps me grounded.

Maverick qualified as a counsellor and therapist when she was twenty-three. I've had more therapists than I've had hot dinners over the years, but I never gelled with any of them. I found it hard to open up but when Maverick suggested I see her, I jumped at the chance. It's unconventional and classed as a dual relationship, which is extremely unethical, but it works for both of us. We try to keep both parts of our friendship separate and I feel comfortable telling her my inner most thoughts and feelings. It helps that we're close friends and Maverick gets paid substantially by my parents for the privilege.

"So, are you going to tell me what's going on with you or am I going to have to break out the wine?" she says sardonically, raising her perfectly groomed eyebrows.

I find myself smiling at her bluntness.

"I've met someone."

She squeals and starts clapping excitedly. "Tell me more!" she says spiritedly, and I sigh dramatically.

"I don't know, he's-unpredictable, he's gorgeous, but he's also fragile and he's got baggage. But I can't seem to stay away from him."

Her expression changes and she narrows her eyes at me. "I know that look, Rae, out with it."

I hate that I'm so transparent around the people that know me well.

"He's in a band."

I worry my lip between my teeth and Maverick starts bouncing excitedly in her chair. "Is he famous?"

I drop my gaze and nod, almost shamefully.

"How famous?" She leans forward, practically bouncing up and down on her chair.

"Famous as in, Brody Hart from Rancid Vengeance famous," I say, almost apprehensively and reluctantly as she launches herself out of her seat.

She theatrically starts dancing around me.

"OH MY GOD! OH, MY GOOD FUCKING LORD! RALEIGH STORM!"

She tries to compose herself. "Shut the front door! You're making the beast with two backs with Snake from Rancid Vengeance!"

I roll my eyes at her fervent reaction. *Typical Maverick.*

"What rock have you been hiding under, Mav?"

Her mouth makes a perfect 'O shape, and she makes the sign of the cross, ignoring my question. This woman is married to her job and doesn't keep up with the news. She functions on caffeine, Red Bull and Pro Plus. Sometimes I wonder how she manages it.

"Please, tell me he's good in bed? Ooh, has he got any single mates?" she says in a rush, and I shake my head exasperatedly at her.

"A lady never kisses and tells!" I wink, and she rolls her eyes dramatically.

"Oh, come on, woman! Don't leave a girl hanging! For God's sake!" she shrieks, and I laugh.

"Sam's married, but Lucas and Jax are single."

She fists pumps the air. "Cha-ching! You must introduce us, Rae!" she practically squeaks as my phone buzzes, and she cocks her perfectly plucked eyebrow. "Is that the rock star?" she asks curiously.

"Nosey bitch!" I counter as she pokes her tongue out at me.

"Touché!"

I turn my phone over and as I see Brody's name, my stomach flip flops. *Fuck me, I feel like a teenager again.*

Hey beautiful

I have a surprise for you!

Hope you're not missing me too much!

B xx

My beaming smile must give me away because Maverick chuckles softly to herself.

"Someone's in love."

I idly twirl my ring around my finger and avoid her gaze at all costs.

"Rae, it's ok to admit you've fallen in love. You deserve a man who smears your lipstick not your mascara!"

I chuckle. *Maverick always knows the right thing to say.*

Unexpectedly, my laughter turns to gut-wrenching sobs. Maverick gets up from her seat and envelopes me in her arms. Her familiar scent of Britney Spears Island Fantasy comforts me, as the tears fall.

"Hey, what's bought this on, babe?"

I sob.

"It's all such a fucking disaster, Mav. I outwardly admitted I'd fallen in love with him, and he rejected it like it meant nothing. I've never felt like this before, not even about Carter. He's a huge trigger for me, but I went and fell for him anyway. I tried so hard not to, but it was totally unavoidable. Especially while we were on tour, we were around each other twenty-four seven. He's reckless and he's a pain in the fucking arse, most of the time...but he's my chaos, in a world full of calm. I can't stop myself every time I'm around him. He's so full of charm and charisma."

She rubs her hands up and down my back in a comforting, reassuring gesture.

"He's covered in red flags and he's...so damn complicated, but he made it impossible for me not to fall in love with him. He's so easy to be around and he ties me up in knots. He just gets me, but I'm terrified...*he* fucking terrifies me."

She laughs melodically and sighs dreamily.

"He's...everything." I exhale noisily.

"And does he feel the same?"

As she says those words, I sob harder and shake my head.

"He reckons he's not worthy of being loved, he's more or less admitted he's fucked up, he's had a tough life."

Maverick rolls her eyes. "*Oh please!* Haven't we all? I've seen enough patients over the years that I could write a fucking book, and it would be a best seller! He's so hung up on his past, he can't move on from it, blah, blah, blah! Well, do you know what? *Fuck him and his issues!*"

She makes inverted commas with her fingers and rolls her eyes mockingly.

"He doesn't deserve you, Raleigh Storm! Right, tonight, you, me and Livvy are going out! Strictly no men allowed! You in?"

I swipe the tears away and nod, as I give her a watery smile. *Girlie night out it is!*

20

Brody

It's been over a month since I last saw her, since I last held her in my arms, since I kissed her lips, since I last felt my cock deep inside her. We've both been busy with our respective careers, I've been on a nationwide promotional tour with the band, and she's been filming. Even though we've been in constant contact via text, phone, and FaceTime, it's not enough. It doesn't match up to her unique scent, to her soft skin pressed against mine. We're officially due home tonight after our gig, but she thinks it isn't until tomorrow, so I'm going to surprise her. *Fuck me, since when did I get so sappy and sentimental?*

It's six a.m. in the morning and I'm sitting in the dressing room of a popular U.K morning talk show, *Live @ Breakfast,* waiting for the make-up team to arrive. *Fuck me, I need a bucket of coffee.*

"You look like someone killed your puppy, dude!" Sam laughs, as he sits down in the chair next to me.

"Fucker! You should know after all these years I'm not a morning person," I grumble crankily, taking a welcome sip of my steaming cup of Starbucks coffee.

A triple shot of espresso, I need all the caffeine I can get after a full hour of restless sleep.

"Come on, I'm sensing you're pining for a certain actress by the name of Raleigh Storm?" he says with a wink, and I pause.

"Is it that obvious?" I sigh.

Sam idly plays with his wedding ring, as if he still can't believe he's married.

"You've been distant, and it's not just me who's noticed it. You're working out more, you've lost weight. You're pining, so yeah, of course, it's obvious. We see you every day and I've never seen you like this over a woman, ever."

I exhale noisily and lean back heavily in my chair.

"She's fucking perfect, Sam. It scares the shit out of me; how can someone be *that* perfect and still want me? I don't fucking deserve her. She's so fucking different from any other women I've been with; they're so caught up in the money and the fame, that they don't *see* me. She *sees* me and she actually cares. She listens to me, she's smart, she's brave, and she's so fucking beautiful."

It feels almost cathartic to tell someone how I feel about Raleigh. *It's a fucking pity I can't say all this to her face.*

"*Shit!* I'm falling in love with her, Sam and I don't know what to do about it."

I hear Sam chuckle throatily, as I lean back in my chair and rest my hands on my flat stomach.

"Then fucking tell her! How's she supposed to know if you don't communicate with her? I know it's hard for you, but I can see she's changing you and believe me, that's a good thing. Talk to her, be the man she needs you to be, the man we all know you can be."

I am about to speak, when the door swings open, a tall, curvy woman enters the room. Her auburn hair is tied up in a messy bun on top of her head, secured with a teal bandana. She is wearing a black pencil skirt and a low-cut black polka dot top. I can't help but get distracted by her ginormous boobs practically spilling out of her top. *That is one fucking impressive rack, I wouldn't mind getting my head between those bastards!* She pushes her glasses further up her nose.

"I'm Jen, the agency we use for our make-up is short staffed today, so they've sent us a temp."

Jen says a little too cheerfully and her smile is infectious. *Fuck me, she's way too happy for this hour.* I hear the *'click, click'* of heels across the floor and as I look up, I'm struck dumb at the sight that greets me. *Lorna Lavelle.*

"Morning boys!" she says brightly, but her step falters, as her eyes land on me.

She clears her throat, and I swallow hard, sitting up straighter, trying to appear unaffected but failing miserably. *Fuck me, I can't do this.* I can't pretend everything is normal when I know this woman intimately. She sets her make-up kit down close to me and as she sets it down, I leap up from my seat, as if I've been burned. *Why is she here? Why now?* Just when I was beginning to learn to live without her. *Fucking hell.* I exit the room, but I don't miss the pained look in her beautiful aquamarine eyes. I lean against the wall and look up to the ceiling. *Jesus Christ, I need to get high. Count to ten, Hart, breathe. 1-2-3-4-5-6-7-8-9-*

"*Bollocks!*" I curse under my breath, and I hear a gruff chuckle.

"You good, dude? Was the fuck was that all about?" Sam asks, with concern in his voice.

I shake my head, and I've literally lost the ability to speak. *I can't fucking put into words what I'm feeling right now.*

"Mate, talk to me," he prompts, and I can tell when the penny finally drops. "Is that-is she...?"

He doesn't have to continue as I nod.

"What the fuck is she doing here, Sam?" I manage to string a sentence together, without sounding like a total idiot. "I...I can't fucking do this, I can't. Just when I was beginning to get over her, it shouldn't matter, I'm with Rae now, but she's..."

I stop myself from saying more and start to pace up and down the narrow corridor.

"I literally have no words, mate."

You and me both, dude.

***

After a few words of reassurance from Sam, I finally pluck up the courage to go back into the dressing room to face her. My kryptonite, my drug of choice, Lorna Lavelle. She's touching up Jax's cheeks with some girlie make-up shit when I enter the room.

"You've got really great cheekbones," she says brightly, and Jax chuckles as she sweeps the make-up brush across his cheek.

"Thanks, sweetheart, I'll take that as a compliment."

She chuckles and I noisily close the door. As she looks up, her gaze finds mine. She clears her throat and stands with one hand on her hip.

"Right, who's next?"

Lucas briefly looks up from his photography magazine.

"Go for it, honey," he says nonchalantly, and she gestures to the seat next to her.

I sit down and avert my eyes briefly to the floor. *I can't let her see she's getting to me.*

"Jax, Luke, M.J needs a word." Sam announces as Jax looks from me to Lorna questioningly and I look away guiltily. *Why the fuck should I be feeling guilty? I've done nothing wrong.*

"What about Brody?" Jax asks curiously and looks from me to Sam.

I shift my gaze elsewhere and Sam slowly shakes his head. "He's not needed; it's nothing major."

Sam cocks his pierced eyebrow, and they wordlessly follow him out.

"Was that for my benefit?" she asks softly, and I shrug.

"For your benefit, as in, do they know that we've been shagging for four years? Sam's the only one, so don't worry, I'm still your dirty little fucking secret, L," I spit angrily, and she lets out a sigh.

"It doesn't have to be this way between us, Brody."

I laugh bitterly.

"It can't be any other way because you'll always choose him over me. I thought I was over you, things between Raleigh and me have been really great, after the last time I saw you. I promised myself I'd at least try with her, and I have. I've tried so fucking hard to forget you existed, but here you are, looking gorgeous as ever and now I'm starting to question everything I feel for her again, why are you even here?"

The annoyed tone in my voice is apparent, as she rolls her eyes dramatically.

"Really? You're going to sit there and blame me because you can't fucking move on? I'm here because this is my bloody job! Against my better judgement, I'd already agreed to stand in for Michelle, then they mentioned Rancid Vengeance. I knew I'd made a mistake, but by then, it was too late to back out."

I catch her eye in the mirror and her eyes tell me all I need to know.

"I'll never be over you, Lorna. You're my biggest regret and I'm so fucking sorry I wasn't good enough."

I don't miss the lone tear that runs down her cheek and my heart breaks a little more. I get up from my seat, brushing her hand tenderly, as I turn to leave the room.

21

Brody

We're all sitting on the sofa of popular U.K morning talk show, Live @ Breakfast. Live @ Breakfast is fronted by Shep Goldstein, a tall, lean, middle-aged, outspoken, ex-radio DJ turned chat show host, with sandy brown hair and steel-blue eyes. His partner in crime is Lena Prince, a ruthless, ex-newspaper journalist, she has curves in all the right places, with fiery red hair. She wears purple rimmed glasses, which complement the colour of her eyes. They sit on a long, garish, lime green sofa, smiling almost falsely at the numerous cameras around the studio.

We've been on so many TV interviews over the years, I've lost count and they all blur into one. I hate them with a passion, I hate being told when to smile, what to say and what not to say and how to act. I hate being probed for answers to questions we don't want to fucking answer. I hate the falseness of it all and I can't stand the early mornings. Especially when we've had after show parties the night before and we've been hungover to shit.

We're sitting casually on the sofa, as Shep introduces us with an almost too bright smile.

"Now, these guys have been in the music industry for almost fourteen years and their highly anticipated fifteenth studio album "All Hail Vengeance" is due to be released this coming week. Famous for their guitar-driven, all-out, throw-your-hands-in-the-air, rock anthems, we are incredibly pleased to give a warm welcome back into the studio, Rancid Vengeance."

We all nod our greetings, and I briefly glance at M.J at the side of the studio, as he gives us a thumbs up and a wink of encouragement.

"Welcome, guys, it's so good to have you back in the studio with us at long last!" Shep says over-enthusiastically and Sam nods coolly.

We're always happy to let Sam take the lead in interviews, he's become an expert over the years.

"It's good to be back, Shep, it's been a while. Thank you so much for having us," he rasps and smiles, which brings out his infamous dimples.

Charming fucker.

"It's our pleasure, so, tell us, what have you guys been up to since we last saw you?"

Sam looks briefly to Jax and Jax leans forward confidently.

"Well, we've been on a nationwide, UK tour, we've visited so many places up and down the country. We've had such an insane response from the fans, and it's humbles us each and every time we go out on stage. The amount of fans that turn out for us and the support we receive is absolutely phenomenal," Jax says modestly as he looks back to Sam to continue.

Sam spreads his arms across the back of the sofa and sits up straighter before he answers.

"We love performing, it's what we live for and that's why we do it. We've been doing a lot of promoting; radio interviews, TV and magazine interviews and we've unveiled our brand-new website. Our back catalogue has just been released on all major streaming services for the very first time since we parted ways with Diamond Records and launched our own record label."

Shep and Lena listen intently, as Sam continues.

"We're extremely lucky to have that longevity in the music industry and we owe it to the fans to keep releasing music and to keep touring. We're going on a European tour and then we're touring the U.S and Australia very soon! So, keep your eyes peeled for that!"

Lena pushes her glasses up her nose and she's practically creaming her knickers over Sam. *I literally want to poke my eyes out with fucking forks.* She straightens, before she turns her body towards him, giving him an eyeful of her boobs and asks. Luckily, Sam's professional enough to ignore it and only has eyes for his wife these days. I on the other hand, can't help but get distracted by her perky breasts, which are in full view of my eyeline. *Fucking hell, FOCUS! It's way too early in the morning for this shit!*

"Your career spans almost two decades, that's amazing for a band in your particular genre! I take my hat off to you! So, All Hail Vengeance is your fifteenth studio album. In your long career history, what would you say is your most poignant album you've released so far?" Lena says, and as she says those words, Sam's expression changes.

I can see the mixture of emotions flowing through him. *Fuck my life.* He looks desperately to me for support, and I clear my throat, before answering the question. *Come on, Hart, take one for the fucking team.*

"I think it's different for all of us, all of our albums are poignant in some way or another. They represent different stages of our lives, ya know. But I think we all agree that *'Vengeance Resurrected'* was a significant one, we experimented with a brand-new sound, worked with different producers and it drummed up all kinds of emotions. It signified loss, grief and it dealt with some dark subject matter, because that's where we were in our lives, at the time. I think as a band, as a family, it made us stronger. It connected us with the music. It made it fresh again and I hope it did that for the fans too. Well, it was number one in sixty-five different countries, so I think the fans definitely agreed, Lena!" I joke, and Lena laughs a little over-enthusiastically.

"I agree, it was poignant, and it was such a beautiful album, I have to admit there were some songs on there that made me cry, 'Through the Storm' in particular. What was the inspiration behind that song?"

Sam is literally vibrating with rage next to me and I know I need to take charge of the situation, without coming across as rude.

"It was a mixture of things and events that inspired us, as you all know. It was well-documented that we went through a particularly rough time, but we supported each other through it and what better way to put that across than through music."

I smile almost falsely. I glance over at M.J, who has his head in his hands at the side of the studio.

"Now, you guys are going to be performing a new song from your new album, at the end of the show, which we can't wait for. What can we expect from your new album, boys?" Shep asks a little over zealously.

"It's a typical Rancid Vengeance album, full of play-it-loud, sing your heart out anthems. We've got a few love songs thrown in for good measure and obviously our famous guitar driven rock songs, which the fans all know us for and seem to love! They all keep buying our records, so we must be doing something right! Again, we've worked with some new producers and

Sam's been writing with Jett Powers from Skarlett Ribbon, who have just signed with our label. So, there's a few surprises in there too!"

I tease, with a cheeky wink. *Fuck me, I should do this for a living!*

"That's all we've got time for I'm afraid! We could chat all day! Stay tuned to see Rancid Vengeance perform a song from their brand-new album 'All Hail Vengeance', which is released next week! Thank you so much for coming, boys!" Lena gushes, and we all nod coolly.

"Thanks for having us!" Jax adds, as we wait for our cue to leave and the cameras to stop rolling.

We all simultaneously get up from the sofa, as Sam storms backstage and stops in front of M.J.

"What the fuck was that M.J? Why was she asking those questions? You gave them a list of subjects that were off limits, why would she do that deliberately?" Sam barks, jabbing his finger in M.J's general direction.

I squeeze his shoulder in a gesture of reassurance. He shrugs me off and stalks closer to M.J.

"Sam, look, buddy, you need to calm down," M.J says calmly.

Jesus, this bloke is so chilled he should be horizontal.

"No, I won't fucking calm down, M.J! She fucking humiliated us in front of millions of viewers! What was she playing at! You don't understand what it's like for us to relive that time. I don't expect you to get it because you weren't fucking there! It damaged us, and that damage is irreparable!" Sam roars as M.J tries desperately to placate him.

Trying to placate Sam right now is like trying to tame an angry fucking lion. I don't hear the rest of his tirade, as Lorna approaches me. *Jesus Christ, she looks especially gorgeous today.* She's wearing a long black skirt, a yellow top with a bee on the front, which hangs loosely off her shoulder and finishes off her outfit with white Converse trainers. Her red hair is loose and hanging down her shoulders in loose, curly waves and I can't seem to tear my greedy eyes away from her.

"Brody, can I talk to you for a second?" she asks softly in her familiar Northern brogue and I'm a goner.

I swallow hard and nod in agreement.

"Yeah, sure," I say coolly, feeling anything but cool.

I'm all sorts of nervous and on edge, this is where a nice line of coke would come in handy. I push that thought to the back of my mind and follow her apprehensively down the corridor. She opens a dressing room door, checking if it's empty before beckoning me to come in. I follow her in, and she shuts the door behind us. As the door shuts, she's on me, she pushes me against the door and crashes her lips urgently to mine, frantically clawing and grabbing at my belt.

"I'm done staying away from you, Brody, I can't do it anymore. I want you," she declares breathlessly.

"I've wanted to hear those words for so long, L," I say sincerely.

She manages to unbuckle my belt and unzips my combat trousers, reaching in to grab my erection. I gasp out loud, as her hand makes contact with my cock.

"I want you to fuck me, Brody, like you used to."

The selfish part of me wants to push her away and tell her I'm with Raleigh, but the words get stuck in my throat. I haven't got the strength to stop her, I haven't got the resolve to say no to her, she's my fucking weakness. I reach under her skirt to find she's not wearing any underwear. I skate my hand across her bare pussy, and she moans softly in my ear.

"Oh God, Brody!"

I swipe my finger through her slickness and stroke her engorged nub. I slide my finger inside her with ease and start to finger fuck her.

"God, you're so fucking wet for me, Lorna," I whisper.

She mewls in my ear, while she's stroking my cock. ,"You don't know how long I've waited for you to fuck me again," she admits, almost desperately.

I lean down to pepper her neck with soft, gentle kisses, as I continue to move my finger in and out of her wet heat. I introduce a second finger and push my fingers deeper, my thumb circling her hot button. She pants in my ear, digging her nails into the back of my neck.

"Come all over my fingers, I want you to come hard for me, Lorna."

My words are her undoing, and she screams, as my calloused fingers bring her to the most delicious orgasm.

"Oh God, oh fuck, oh fuck, yes! Yes! Brody! Oh God! Brody!"

She writhes and I squeeze every last ounce of pleasure from her. As I pull my fingers from her, her legs buckle, and she goes lax against me. I lift her up easily, spinning us around so she's pinned to the door. I lift her skirt further up and take my bare cock out of the confines of my boxers. The head of my cock finds her entrance and I shove her up the door, impaling her on my waiting firmness. My cock feels so good inside her. *Fuck me, I've missed this, I've missed her.* She whimpers softly, as I allow her to readjust to my length after all this time. I bite my lip and throw my head back, as I cry out with pleasure.

"*Oh Jesus,* fuck, you feel like heaven. Shit, I've missed you."

I pick up the pace, moving in and out of her slick heat, causing the door to bang with the force of our love making. She wraps her arms around me, and she strokes the nape of my neck. It feels so fucking good, almost too good. She moans in my ear, as my pace quickens, I feel my orgasm cresting to the surface.

"*Shit, FUCK!*" I bark, as I piston in and out of her.

We both explode and find our releases at the same time.

"I'm coming, *fuck*, Brody, I'm coming," she yells, and I move my other hand over her mouth.

I feel my hot seed spurt inside her and she cries out around my hand. As we come down from our synchronised orgasms, the room falls eerily silent. I pull out of her, and we both begin to wordlessly straighten ourselves out. Her hair is wild and mussed, screaming out that she's been freshly fucked. I smirk at the thought, as I gently stroke her face.

"Fuck, you look so beautiful right now," I compliment, and she rewards me with the smile that she knows brings me to my fucking knees.

"God, Brody, that shouldn't have happened, I'm sorry, I really don't know what came over me," she says regretfully, bringing me back to earth with a sharp jolt.

What the actual fuck?

"How can you fucking say that? Didn't you feel what I felt, Lorna? We just fucked bareback! You're the only woman I've ever been bareback with! Surely that must mean something to you. Please tell me it wasn't just me?" I plead, and she shakes her head, determination plastered all over her beautiful fucking face.

"We just needed to fuck each other out of our systems, that's all."

I can't believe the words that are coming out of her mouth. *How could she fucking say that?*

"I could fucking crush you, Lorna. Just like you've just fucking crushed me! I could destroy you, your marriage and your perfect fucking life!"

I am so fucking angry; I just want to hurt her the way she's hurting me right now. I don't want to hurt her in a physical way, I think men who hurt women deliberately are fucking weak pieces of shit. *Men like Stefan fucking Lavelle.*

"You don't mean that. I just want you to be happy with Raleigh, Brody. That's all I've ever wanted for you is for you to be happy with someone that's not me, someone who can love you the way you deserve. I'm sorry, but this is goodbye."

Her voice wavers, kissing me fondly on the cheek and leaving the room before I get to protest.

FUCCCKKK!

Raleigh

After my tearful therapy session with Maverick, Cliff drives me back to the makeshift movie set that has been purpose built, in the centre of Greenwich. I'm now sat in the make-up trailer waiting to be called onto set for the days filming when Nick walks in.

"You're looking particularly hot today, love," he says matter-of-factly, and I smile at his openness.

I'm wearing a pair of tight leather hot pants, a black denim vest, black fishnets, and a pair of black patent Doc Martens. He looks delicious and devilishly sinful today; he's dressed in his costume for our day of filming. He is wearing a pair of tight leather trousers that look like they've been sprayed on, a tight white vest, which shows off his muscles and his tattoos and a pair of leather spiked biker boots.

"You don't look so bad yourself, Slade."

He chuckles softly. "So, how are you and the rock star?"

I blush at his question and lean back in my chair, sighing audibly. "We're...great, thanks."

He rolls his eyes dramatically and I take a welcome sip of my morning coffee. *My elixir for the soul.*

"Are you going to be like Sam and Peyton? Vomit-inducingly in love with constant public displays of affection?"

I almost choke on my coffee and Nick laughs.

"I take that as a yes! Dear God, I don't think I can take anymore!" he groans animatedly.

"I'm fucking sick of being a sad, lonely singleton, love," he admits, leaning heavily back in his make-up chair.

I reach for his hand and squeeze it in a gesture of reassurance. We've become close over the past month, and I hope we can stay friends after filming ends. He sighs and I sense that he wants to say more.

"Something on your mind, babe?" I ask thoughtfully, and he leans his head back, staring at the ceiling.

He keeps a firm grip of my hand.

"I suppose you've seen that ridiculous reality show they've pushed me into. Let's find Nick Slade a wife. I can't think of anything worse to be honest, love." He shakes his head in disbelief.

"I don't want a fucking wife! When are they going to get that into their thick fucking skulls!" he barks sharply, and I flinch.

What the fuck, Storm? You're not that weak willed, downtrodden, punch bag anymore. Get your shit together! I begin to think he doesn't notice until he realises his error.

"I apologise, love, I didn't mean to raise my voice." His voice filled with concern. I shake my head and dismiss him with a wave of my hand, trying to bring a light-hearted tone to the conversation, which has taken a serious turn.

"It's fine, don't apologise, I get you're frustrated. Being in the public eye sucks. Hey Raleigh! Smile! Hey Raleigh, show us your tits! Hey Raleigh, don't date the rock star, it's bad for publicity! I've heard it all, babe, it's fucking tiring!"

I laugh, but he looks as if he's about to burst into tears. "I can't do it anymore, Raleigh, I can't. I can't keep up this ridiculous fucking façade any longer!"

I look puzzled. *What the fuck is he talking about? Has he completely lost his mind?*

"I'm in love with Lucas Landon! I always have been! Always fucking will be! There! I've said it, it's out in the open! Halle-fucking-lujah!"

My eyes widen and he laughs lightly, as if a weight has suddenly been lifted off his shoulders. *Lucas Landon? What the actual fuck?*

"As in, Axeman Lucas Landon? Rancid Vengeance Lucas Landon? Mysterious, shy American boy?" I say almost incredulously, and he smirks.

"Don't look so shocked, love! I've been in love with him for years, it's just taken me until now to admit it to myself. My agent, Chas, bless her heart, she's pushing for this God-awful reality show. Apparently, if the world finds out that I'm a raving homosexual, my career will be over, I'll lose fans, and my brand will be in tatters. That's the only reason she's pushing for it, she's got my best interests at heart, she always has, God love her. I love her to death, but she's becoming quite insistent, I don't know if someone's had a word in her ear, but something doesn't add up. She's never pushed for anything, in all of the years she's been my agent, she's never been this...forceful before."

He explains and I can't believe what I'm hearing. Nick Slade is gay, and he's in love with Lucas Landon from Rancid Vengeance. I want to ask questions, I want to probe him and ask him why, when, what and how, but I hold back. *It's none of your fucking business, you nosey cow and you are not your mother.*

"I can hear the cogs turning, love," he says with amusement to his voice.

"It's just...you and Lucas, I'm stunned! Both of you, don't seem the type!"

He laughs melodically, "I'm very good at what I do. I can convince the world into thinking I'm this charming, English bachelor, when the reality is the complete opposite. I'm not attracted to other men, it's just... *him*, just Lucas, no one else. I'm not gay, I'm not even bisexual, I don't expect anyone to get it, because I don't get it myself half the time, but it's about time I admitted it to myself, I've been hiding it for long enough."

I smile sympathetically and lean back in my chair, desperate to know more.

"How did you meet?" I ask curiously and he smiles softly at the memory.

"I knew Lucas from years ago, way before I knew the rest of the guys. When I was just starting out in the movie business, I'd just been in Chelsea Smile and that was a huge success. It was gaining a reputation as critically acclaimed and off the back of that, I was cast in a film that Lucas' Uncle, Kyle Landon directed. Kyle was the first person in Hollywood that didn't look at me like I was something he'd trodden in. He's an absolute gent, a true saint among men, I've got so much respect for him. This is the guy who hired homeless guys as extras in his films and gave them places to live afterwards. Anyway, I digress. Lucas was in L.A visiting Kyle because he'd got some time in between tours so he came over for a few weeks. It was my first day on set, I was nervous as hell and I'd been throwing up all morning, not because I was ill, just purely through nerves. I really wanted to make a good impression on Kyle, and I just wanted to do a great job on the film, I wanted to build my reputation. At that point, I didn't feel like I'd earned my position. I just happened to be this talented, young actor from England, who had just got lucky."

I listen raptly to his story, fascinated by his vivid recollection.

"I was in the trailer, throwing my guts up, when the door swings open, no knock and there he was, just standing there casually, looking like this fucking statuesque, tanned God. He was wearing a pair of Hawaiian print board shorts and a white vest top, which emphasized his tattoos and his muscles. He was wearing flip flops and a pair of Armani sunglasses perched on top of his head. I think by that point, I was just dry heaving. He's still just standing there, silent. I'm wondering what the fuck he's doing here and why he's just standing there. I finally stop dry heaving, get to my feet, and wash my hands. He catches my stare in the mirror and his eyes are so intense, I clear my throat and ask can I help you; he leans casually back against the wall. By this point I'm wondering if he's mute, or deaf, a bit of a creep, or just plain dumb. I brush my teeth; aware I've got puke breath, and he's still not saying anything. After I'm done brushing my teeth, he just grabs me, pushes me against the wall and kisses me like I've never been kissed before, he's all manly and forceful and I find myself kissing him back, aware that it's all kinds of wrong and anyone could walk in. He knocked the breath right out of me; I'm gripping his biceps and he's just kissing me like his life depends on it. After he finishes kissing me, he finally looks up at me and introduces himself in this soft, cool American accent, which drips sex and mystery. I'm Lucas, Kyle's nephew. Then it's my turn to just stand there with my mouth wide open, staring at him. After that, we'd just meet up when our schedules allowed for sex and to spend time together. We became really close; I'd find myself telling him things I'd never told anyone before. It was refreshing, it was new and the more time we spent together, the harder I was falling for him. He was all I could think about, for months. I told him I was falling for him, and he backed off completely. We still meet up for sex on the odd occasion, but he's distanced himself from me and I can't stand it," he admits, scrubbing his hand down his face and my heart breaks for him.

I can totally identify with the hopeless and utterly devastating feeling of loving someone and that love not being reciprocated. Our moment is interrupted by the door to the make-up trailer swinging open, letting in the cool mid-morning breeze.

"Good morning! How are we today? The agency we normally use for our make-up is short-staffed today, lovelies! So, they've sent us a temp!"

The tall, slender woman explains brightly and animatedly; while scribbling vehemently on the black clipboard she is holding in her hand. Her short black bob perfectly styled, and she is wearing black skinny jeans and a red vest top, teamed with matching red Converse. Nick and me look at each other, shrugging.

"As long as they make us look fabulous there shouldn't be a problem, darlin'."

Nick gives the woman a cheeky wink and I swear she fucking swoons. *Charming bastard.*

The door to the trailer swings open again and a woman enters, she has skin the colour of café au lait, aquamarine eyes and red hair secured on top of her head with a black bandana. She is wearing a long black skirt, a bright canary yellow top with a bee on the front, which hangs off her shoulder and white Converse. Her step seems to falter when her eyes land on me. *Strange.*

"Morning, I'm Lorna," she introduces herself almost shyly in a soft Northern accent, but she can't look me directly in the eye, which I find oddly unnerving.

"Good morning, love! Nick, but I'm fairly sure you know that already, am I right?"

He laughs, offering her his hand, and he kisses the back of it as she nods, fluttering her unusually long eyelashes at him. I roll my eyes at his flamboyant way and chuckle softly.

"I'm going to have to watch you, I think, you charmer!" she jokes.

Oh please! Spare me!

"I was counting on it, sweetheart!" he winks.

"Right, I'll do your make-up first, if that's ok with you?" she directs her question to him, and Nick nods.

"I'm all yours, love."

He holds his hands out to the side, and she sets to work on Nick's make-up. Her and Nick are chattering idly. I pull out my phone and fire off a text to Brody.

Can't wait to see you! Missed you!

R x

Nick groans.

"You've got that love-struck look on your face; I take it that's the rock star?" he asks curiously with a roll of his eyes.

I smirk, quickly stowing my phone away in my bra.

"He's coming home tomorrow; he's been on tour," I explain, as Lorna turns to me.

"I thought I recognised you; you're the woman Brody Hart from Rancid Vengeance has been photographed with?"

I nod and she regards me with piqued interest. "Yeah, Raleigh Storm."

I offer her my hand, and she takes it almost reluctantly.

"Pleased to meet you, I've just done their make-up for a TV interview before I came here, they're a handful those boys!"

She chuckles, almost nervously and I don't know what it is about her, but I find myself inexplicably on edge. Nick keeps shooting me sideward glances, as there is a knock on the door.

"Come innnnn!" Nick says in a singsong voice.

The door opens and Gavin walks in, I have to admit I'm more than a little relieved to see him.

"Hello sweetheart!" he greets me in his familiar tone, and I find myself smiling.

"Hey Gav!"

He kisses me on the cheek and wraps his arms around me from behind.

"Damien sent me here to get my make-up done."

He rolls his eyes, "why does a forty-six-year-old man need his bloody make-up done for?"

I laugh at his reaction and turn my attention back to Lorna.

"So, you know Brody then?" I ask, curiosity getting the better of me.

She continues touching up Nick's make-up with smooth, even strokes.

"We've met a couple of times," she answers vaguely, busying herself with putting the finishing touches to Nick's make-up. "How long have you been together?" she counters, and I can't seem to get a read on her.

"Just over four months, it's been a whirlwind to say the least."

I chuckle softly. *That's a fucking understatement.*

"*Wow!* That's so sweet! I heard you met in rehab?" she enquires, and it's my turn to regard her intently and rather suspiciously.

I wonder if she's been planted here by the tabloids to get a potential story. I push that ridiculous thought to the back of my mind. *Paranoid, much, Storm? Get a fucking grip!*

"Yeah, yeah we did, of all the places we could have met!"

I laugh.

"That's a story to tell the grandkids!"

She giggles and I frown. Those were the exact words Brody used when we left rehab. *Who is this woman? Does she know Brody intimately? Did they used to date?* I find myself too scared to ask.

"Right, that's Nick finished."

Nick looks in the mirror, admiring her handiwork and I have to admit he looks great. She's emphasised his cheekbones and the eyeliner she has used brings out the colour in his eyes.

"Fabulous, love!"

He blows her a kiss and smiling, she turns to me.

"Your turn!" she says a little too enthusiastically.

Nick gets up, kissing me on the cheek.

"See you on set, darling!" he says animatedly, as him and Gavin exit the trailer, leaving me alone with Lorna.

She pulls out an unused make-up brush and sets about starting my make-up. She remains silent for a few minutes, and the atmosphere is palpable and almost uncomfortable. I want to ask her the question that's floating around in my already overactive mind, but I can't seem to pluck up the courage. Every time I try, my tongue feels almost too big for my mouth, and I can't speak, it just comes out like incoherent, garbled gibberish. I bet she thinks I'm a total fucking idiot. I keep catching her gaze in the mirror, but she looks away swiftly, and it comes across as rather guilty.

What the hell is wrong with you, Storm? Where's the feisty, spunky kitten that Brody met in rehab? The ballsy girl who had a smart, quick-witted answer for everything? As I allow my mind to wander, I'm instantly transported back to the time Brody, and I were in rehab.

Past

Raleigh

I slip into the room unnoticed and he's looking delicious holding court with the other patients. He's wearing a pair of black combat shorts, white Vans, and a white vest, which showcases his muscular arms and his vast tattoo collection. He looks particularly relaxed today and the sparkle in his eyes has returned. They're all giggling at his jokes and fawning all over him, hanging on to his every word. His sense of humour and charm is shining so bright, it's...temporarily dazzling. I want to hate him for swanning in with his blatant arrogance and his tattoos, but it seems to go deeper than that. I want to hate him for making me act wild and reckless. I was wild and reckless before rehab; I won't be that girl. The new me is sensible, in bed before midnight (mostly) and doesn't get distracted by boys. EVER. Damn you, Brody Hart. He looks up from animatedly telling his story and his eyes lock on to mine, silencing his giggling fan club as they all turn towards me.

"I'll be back in a sec," he announces to the group of three women, whose names I can't recall.

He brushes the one girl's arm, and her gaze seems to hold his for longer than necessary. I feel a hint of jealousy creep into my consciousness, hands off him, bitch. Whoa! Where did that come from? Focus, Storm! He stands up and approaches me almost cautiously. I try desperately not to blatantly ogle him, as he saunters casually towards me.

"Hey."

I smile warmly, feeling unusually shy around him.

Today is my last day in rehab and as the days have gone on, we've spent time together and gotten to know each other. Even though we've known this day would inevitably come, yet I'm still not prepared for it. I'm not prepared for the goodbye; I'm not prepared to go back to the real world or to my real life. This past six months we've been in our very own bubble and I'm not ready for it to burst. Not yet.

"Hey yourself," I chuckle softly to disguise the waiver in my voice. He avoids meeting my gaze and idly plays with a piece of loose skin on his thumb.

"*Something on your mind, handsome?*" I say sassily.

"*Only you, beautiful,*" he compliments, and I can't help blushing at his sweet words.

I pause, desperately trying to let him know I feel the same.

"*I know we agreed to keep it casual, but I can't stop thinking about you,*" I blurt out, taking him completely by surprise.

But I don't feel panicked, or uneasy about admitting it to him.

"*Ditto, kitten.*"

I swallow hard at his admission, in a desperate bid to keep my emotions in check.

"*I know I'm never going to be the man you deserve but know that I tried for you. Our story was...unconventional, it's one to tell the grandkids years from now! We're not saying goodbye, kitten, just...see you. We're bound to run into each other; we run in the same circles. But I have to say, this is one of the most unforgettable stays in rehab I've ever experienced.*"

He laughs nervously.

"*I've been in and out of rehab for ten fucking years and this is the first time I've met someone I've wanted...more with. I'm not sure how much more I can give you, but maybe we could at least...try? Let me take you out, sometime? I mean...you don't have to,*" he babbles, almost unsure of himself.

"*Like a date?*" I question.

He laughs and nods. "*Exactly like a date, let me show you I can be a gentleman outside of the bedroom.*"

He wiggles his split tongue provocatively and I laugh at his outrageousness. He's so different to men I've been with in the past, I love his carefree attitude, his wicked sense of humour and gentle nature.

"*I don't know how I'm going to go back to my normal life, knowing you're living your life without me in it,*" he admits sincerely, and his honesty makes me want to burst into tears.

My eyes glaze over, and I hang my head, shifting my gaze to the floor. He lifts my chin up to face him, and I can't look him directly in the eyes.

"*Look at me, kitten.*"

His voice a rough command, as I look up to meet his turbulent silver orbs. I catch sight of how handsome he is. Six foot two, lean yet muscular and his dark brown hair cut close to his head, giving me an uninterrupted view of his *devastatingly gorgeous face. High cheekbones, strong jaw, and the sexy scar above his left eyebrow, that's almost invisible unless you're close up. My stomach fills with butterflies and flip flops, as he edges closer. I can feel his warm, minty breath on my cheek. He strokes my face so tenderly and the touch is filled with all the words he can't say out loud. The purple, bruise-like shadows underneath his eyes tell of sleepless nights, all night partying and a lifetime of regrets, broken promises, and never-ending stints in rehab.*

"Our first kiss was life-changing, it was the moment my broken soul found yours. Look for me outside rehab, beautiful. I'll be waiting."

He presses a chaste kiss to my lips, a kiss that's filled with promises of tomorrows, possibly promises he won't be able to keep, but I'm hopeful we will see each other again and with that, he's gone.

Present
Raleigh

I'm jolted back to the present by my phone vibrating in my hand.

Heyyy girl!

Going to have to rain check on tonight's girl's night.

So sorry, something's come up at work!

Looong story!

It's Liv and Jensen's anniversary today, which I completely forgot about!

Another time?

Mav xx

I sigh, as I read Maverick's text message. I hear the door to the trailer open, and Nick enters.

"Bloody hell! Are you not finished yet?" he says dramatically as he catches the look on my face.

He strides over and reaches for my hand.

"Is something wrong, love?"

I look up from my phone, unable to hide my disappointment.

"Me and a couple of girl friends were supposed to be going on a girl's night out tonight, but she's just cancelled. I was really looking forward to it, that's all."

I put my phone on the dressing table and lean back in my chair.

"Well, call me your fairy god father, because your prayers are about to be answered! A bunch of us of going for drinks at a local pub, just down the road after we finish up here, you're more than welcome to join us, love?" Nick says animatedly, and I find myself smiling at his enthusiasm.

"Yeah, yeah, why the fuck not! Let's do it!"

Nick claps.

"Yaaaayy! Now come on, they're waiting for you on set!"

I look up at Lorna regarding me intently.

"All done!" she sings, and I look in the mirror at her handiwork.

She's done an excellent job of making me look halfway decent. I'm so impressed I don't push the issue any further. I've turned into one of those girls who just buries her head in the sand, when in reality I've never been one of those girls. We say our goodbyes and I try to forget all about this mysterious woman who may or may not know Brody Hart intimately.

22

Brody

I don't know how I manage to perform a song on 'Live @ Breakfast'. I managed to smile in the right places and I just about held it together. As soon as the performance was done, I couldn't get out of there quick enough. In a daze, I left the TV studios and I couldn't get Lorna out of my head. *Why the fuck would she willingly have sex with me and then discard me like I meant nothing?* Today was meant to be about me and Raleigh, it was meant to be a bittersweet reunion, after a whole month of being apart, but Lorna Lavelle had to go and shoot it all to fucking hell.

"You alright, mate?"

Sam's low timbre cutting through my wayward thoughts. Jax and Lucas have both gone to the venue for tonights' gig, leaving me and Sam in the car park to follow with two of our security team close by to escort us.

"Yeah, fine, man, yeah, I'm good."

I smile, but he knows me better than that. *Sam's always seen right through my bullshit.* He clears his throat, before he speaks.

"You can't bullshit me, Brody, surely you must know that by now? She's really got to you, hasn't she?" Sam observes, and I can't meet his gaze, knowing that I was willingly unfaithful to Raleigh.

Fuck, I hate myself right now. What the fuck was I thinking? My little head was in control and my big head, he well and truly checked out. He furrows his brow and folds his thick, muscular arms across his broad chest.

"You fucked her didn't you?" he says with a wry smirk, and a sense of utter shame washes over me as I nod regretfully, hanging my head in absolute fucking shame.

I forget how well he knows me sometimes.

"We fucked bareback, then she just left telling me it meant nothing, that *I* meant nothing. Apparently, we needed to fuck each other out of our systems and she expects me to just carry on like nothing happened! How could she do that to me, Sam? After all we've been through!" I say with an incredulous tone to my voice, and he grasps my shoulder in a silent gesture of reassurance.

I briefly squeeze my eyes shut, willing myself not to burst into tears. *She's the only woman I've ever been this fucked up over.* I take a few deep calming breaths and steel myself for his reply.

"I'm sorry, I really don't know what to say, man."

Sam Newbolt lost for words, now that's a fucking first.

I tuck my hands in my pockets and overwhelming, intense urge to get high grips me tight, threatening to choke me where I stand. I stumble to the side and struggle to regain my cool composure. *Shit, that was unexpected.*

"*Whoa!* You good, dude? You don't look so great."

Sam's voice is barely audible, as I feel the colour drain from my cheeks.

"I..." I garble incoherently, blindly grappling for something to steady me.

I feel weak and so fucking out of control. My heart is racing, and the blood is roaring in my ears.

"Brody?"

Slightly dazed, I look up at Sam, as he reaches for me. I frantically and carelessly shove him away. *He can't fucking see me like this.* I shake my head vigourously and desperately claw at my throat. My breath comes in short, sharp, wheezing pants and I can't fucking breathe, as I urgently try to gulp precious air into my lungs. *What the fuck is happening to me?* I stagger in the general direction of the TV studios, my vision suddenly clouding and the floor swaying beneath my feet, as my whole world plunges into darkness.

***

I come around, shaky, disoriented and wondering what the fuck happened. *How did I end up on the floor?*

"He's just come round, I'll call you back, ok, will do, bye."

Sam tucks his phone back in the pocket.

"Brody? Mate, it's Sam. Fuck me, you scared the living shit out of me! What happened? Are you feeling ok?"

Sam's concerned rasp cuts through my foggy brain, as he gets down on his haunches next to me. Unexpectedly, an overwhelming feeling of resentment clouds my entire being and I hate that Sam saw me as that out of control, scared, vulnerable, fucked up man-child I tried so hard to hide from everyone.

"FUCK YOU, SAM!"

I am trembling with inconsolable rage, and I feel myself slowly losing control. Rick told me to count to ten if I ever felt that way, well I say fuck you Rick and your psychobabble bullshit, vodka, a few lines of coke and a bit of pussy is more my style. *Deep breaths, Hart, you don't need that shit anymore.* I get unsteadily to my feet and Sam blocks my path, as I go to walk away.

"Whoa! Fucking stop for a minute, yeah? Are we going to talk about what just happened?" he snaps.

"It was no big deal, just fucking drop it, mate," I say nonchalantly.

He cocks his head and regards me intently. "You just fucking collapsed for no reason! Are you going to tell me what's going on with you?"

I scrub my hands down my face. I really don't need this shit right now; I need something to take the edge off. I need to be obliterated to block out these dark thoughts and the urge to shove Columbia's deficit up my hooter.

"I just want to help, that's all, I'm fucking worried about you."

His voice softens, and I take a calming breath.

"I c...can't talk about it, I..."

I stop myself from continuing, he can't know, he can't find out how much of a fuck up I truly am.

"When was the last time you slept? I mean properly for the whole night?"

I briefly close my eyes, wishing I could confide in my best friend. *You just wouldn't fucking understand.*

"I'm fine, now just drop it, yeah? Now, are we going to fucking rehearse, or not?" I snap impatiently, ignoring his questioning concern.

End of conversation, for now at least.

***

The day goes by in a flash of rehearsals and before I know it, it's time for us to perform a gig in front of a crowd of twenty thousand hardcore screaming fans. It never fails to get my adrenaline pumping and the euphoric feeling never gets old.

"Fourteen years, London! Can you believe that! Wow! We've come a long way since our first album!" Sam says with absolute awe in his voice, as if he still can't believe all these people are here supporting us.

"We've come so far since we released our first album and we performed our first gig in a dodgy back street pub, dodging glasses and stepping over drunks! That has always reminded us to stay grounded and never let the fame go to our heads. As a band, as a family, we'll always be forever fucking grateful to each and every one of you for coming out, spending money on tickets and merch', so we fucking owe you a show, right!" Sam growls into the microphone and the crowd goes wild.

Their cheering is so loud I think they can hear it in the next city over. We all move to the front of the stage and the people in the front row are reaching up, screaming our names.

"Are you having fun London!"

The crowd go crazy, and it vibrates with their energy.

"Tonight, we wanted to come out here and have some fun with our fucking family! Because every single one of you guys are our extended Vengeance family. I know we keep saying it, but we wouldn't be here without you. You've supported us since the beginning and some bands get to where we are and turn into complete fucking pricks, but we are not that band! We'll keep coming out to perform for you, even when we're old and grey! I just wanna' take this opportunity to say thank you for all your support over the past fourteen years! Here's to another fourteen fucking years, London! Give me a riff, Flash!" he growls, turning to Jax, flashing him a wink.

Jax cocks his eyebrow and breaks out into a shit-eating grin. What Jax does with a guitar, is definitely not fucking ordinary, he is a musical genius. Everything vibrates when he turns up his amp and the audience are treated to a rendition of 'Sweet Revenge', a track from our new album.

I follow suit and in a totally different way to Jax, my guitar speaks a musical language to my soul. The strumming sound had a hypnotic, yet soothing quality that I craved, like a non-chemical high. To lose myself to the melody was my idea of a heavenly way to die.

Lucas pounds a complex drumbeat, as I move gracefully across the stage to stand back-to-back with Jax and we give the audience what they came for, a fucking show.

23

Raleigh

After a long, gruelling but productive day of filming, what better way to relax than a few drinks in a nice quaint pub not far from where we have spent our day. I'm looking good, feeling great and for once I'm loving the direction my life is currently taking, I'm finally content. Tonight, I'm opting for a black choker dress, with a rainbow-coloured lion on the front with sky high black ankle boots. My short hair is styled sleek and straight, and my make-up is natural and flawless, making me look fresh faced and glowing.

The pub is called *'The Cutty Sark,'* close to the University of Greenwich and is a quirky hidden gem. It features some of the original brewing tanks from the local Greenwich brewery and has an old, weathered railway sleeper for a bar top. It is old mixed with new and the perfect place to unwind after a long day.

"What you drinking, darlin'?" Gavin asks.

"I'll have a beer, please?"

He winks. "That's my girl!"

Gavin goes to the bar to order our drinks, leaving me and Nick alone. He turns to me.

"So, what did you make of the new make-up girl today?"

I'm about to speak when Gavin puts our drinks down on the table and Nick pulls his phone out.

"Come on, guys, let's do a selfie!"

I roll my eyes. We all move in close and pose, as Nick snaps a picture with his phone. His fingers move lightning fast across the screen of his phone.

"That's one for Instagram!"

He turns his phone to show me, the photo of all of us and the caption:

TheOne&OnlyNickSlade: Ready for our close-up! Drinks after work with @RealRaleighStorm and @GavinJKincaid

I smile at how carefree we all look and take a long welcome sip of my drink. After a while of chatting about our respective day and shooting the breeze, I'm finally feeling relaxed. The door of the pub swings open and as I look up, I see the last person I expected to see. Carter Leonard, my slimy, scum of the earth, grade A, arsehole, ex-boyfriend. My stomach roils at the sight of him, and I can't believe he's here. *What the fuck is he doing here? Is he stalking me?* He spots me almost instantly and smiles his dazzling, boy-next-door smile and I start to question how I fucking fell for his fake, over the top bullshit. *Was I really that weak and desperate?*

He waves and begins to saunter over, don't get me wrong Carter Leonard is a good-looking man, he's six feet tall, he's lean, muscular, with broad shoulders. He has jade green eyes, his sandy blonde hair is styled into a neat quiff, and he has grown a beard since I last saw him. He is wearing blue jeans and a black t-shirt. I start to feel my chest tighten as he approaches us, and I try to hide my obvious fear and disdain for him.

"Raleigh, it's been a while, you're looking gorgeous as always. Rehab really did you the world of good."

He leans down and kisses me on both cheeks, as he does, I momentarily freeze. *What the fuck is he playing at? How can he stand there and pretend like nothing happened?* He forgets how well I know him; there's always a hidden agenda with Carter. He's cold, calculating and so far removed from the persona he portrays to the public. In reality, he's a sociopathic, narcissistic, bully, who gets off on wielding power over weak-willed women. I should know first-hand, as I was one of those weak-willed women.

"How have you been?"

I nod, as I take a sip of my drink and Nick regards the situation unfolding in front of him with rapt interest, but he doesn't say anything. He just silently observes.

"Hmm," I hum, struck dumb at his audacity.

How can he stand there knowing what he did to me and act like nothing happened?

"Honestly, you look absolutely stunning, I hoped we'd bump into each other again at some point."

His tone ostentatious, as Nick looks from me to Carter trying to gauge this awkward scenario.

"Carter, right?"

Nick jumps in and Carter nods, smiling his fake smile, the one he uses when he's in interviews.

"Yeah, Nick Slade? Mate, I'm a huge fan."

They shake hands, my eyes darting around the room looking for Gavin. Gavin is fully aware of my history with Carter and hates him more than I do for the way he treated me and for laying his hands on me. I think he went outside to take a call from his daughter Cleo.

"So, how do you know each other, Rae?" Carter asks with a possessive edge to his voice.

"We've been working together on a film; the set isn't too far from here," Nick explains.

I boldly find myself blurting out, "What fucking business is it of yours, Carter?"

Carter laughs as Nick gets up, leaving us to it.

"You're not a part of my life anymore, so it's none of your business," I snap, and he nods smugly.

"It'll always be my business as long as I'm paying your therapy bills."

My eyes widen. *I thought my parents were paying for my therapy sessions. What the actual fuck?*

"What did you just say?"

My voice full of disbelief, still trying to comprehend the bombshell he's just dropped.

"I thought that might make you sit up and pay attention, it's been me all along. I just want you to get better again, that's all I've ever wanted, precious," he says tenderly, and I'd believe him if I didn't know him so well.

Fucking prick.

"I've always had your best interests at heart, Rae. How could you have ever doubted that?" he says with a sickly-sweet tone to his voice, which makes me want to fucking vomit.

"Why the fuck are you here, Carter? Are you stalking me or something?"

I raise my voice a few decibels louder than necessary and he has the fucking cheek to roll his eyes.

"Oh yeah, equally, I could say you've been stalking me, begging me to take you back, like the pathetic little junkie you are."

I stand up and jab my finger in his general direction spitting mad that he could even say such a thing. *How fucking dare he.* He cocks his eyebrow. *There's the Carter Leonard I know, the cold, calculating prick, who knows how to manipulate people into thinking he's the good guy.* I lean in close to him, lowering my voice so only he can hear me.

"I'm not the pathetic one, Carter, I told my boyfriend Brody what you did to me, every gory, sordid little detail. He thinks you're a weak, pathetic loser for laying your hands on me and trying to take me by force when I quite clearly said no."

Something in Carter's eyes flash and he grinds his teeth, fists clenched tightly at his sides.

"Good to see you, Raleigh."

He nods coolly and saunters off. *What the actual fuck was that?*

I have to call my mum; I have to know if Carter has been paying my therapy bills. If he has, why? I don't get it; I don't understand why he would do that, especially now we're not together anymore.

"Are you ok, love?" Nick asks softly, and I nod.

"Yeah, I'm fine, Nick, honestly, just a bit shaken that's all, we've got history, as you probably already know? I need to call my mum; I won't be long."

He looks at me with wary eyes and I brush his arm in reassurance. *He really is a sweetheart.*

"I'll be fine. I'll be right back, I promise."

He nods in understanding, as I make my way out to the large beer garden at the back of the building. I drop down onto a bench and take my phone out of my bag with shaky hands and go to dial my mums' number, it rings four times before it connects.

"Ah, so the prodigal daughter does have a phone that still works," my mum answers brusquely, without even as much as a hello.

"Hi mum, I'm good thanks for asking. How are you?"

I sigh. My relationship with my mum has always been strained, I've always been a daddy's girl. My mum prefers my younger brother Jagger over me, and she's never hidden the fact. He's a spoiled and entitled fifteen-year-old brat, who can do no wrong in my mum's eyes. I, on the other hand, am the spawn of Satan and do everything in my power to make her look bad. Her actual words she spat at me during a particularly bad argument.

"A phone call once in a while wouldn't go a miss just to let us know you're ok, Raleigh."

I roll my eyes to myself and wish I hadn't bothered calling.

"It's been super busy; you know how it is? I haven't had a second, I'm shooting a new film with Damien Valentine, which you'd know if you'd actually bothered to call and check in with me once in a while," I say snippily, and she pauses briefly before continuing, ignoring my previous statement.

"I see from the newspapers you've got yourself a new boyfriend, don't you think you should have called to tell us instead of us seeing it in the newspapers first? Angela across the street took particular pleasure in informing me first, nosey bitch that she is," she says with disdain to her voice.

My mum, dad and my brother live in Beverly Hills, L.A. My mum, Avril Storm, is an established and highly sought-after District Attorney and my dad Vince Storm, is a former biker turned celebrity chef. He has his own TV show '*Vinnie's Country Kitchen*' and owns his own chain of chic, uber popular hipster restaurants. My mum and dad met when they were teenagers, my mum was the popular cheerleader, Valedictorian, and my dad was the boy from the wrong side of the tracks. They lost touch for a number of years and met again at a close family friend's wedding. They were seeing each other only for a few months when my mum fell pregnant with me. They were married a few months later as my mum didn't want to have a baby out of wedlock. She was all for keeping up appearances and always being bigger and better than her friends, neighbours, and peers. She's the total opposite of me, she's materialistic, obnoxious, and sometimes I wonder if her name is really Karen.

"It's early days. We're just taking it slow and seeing where it goes, no big deal. Look, I actually had a reason for calling. Is it true that Carter's been paying my therapy bills?"

I try to remain calm, but on the inside, I'm dreading the answer. I wait for a few minutes and all I'm met with is silence.

"Mum? Please answer me, has he been paying my therapy bills?" I say through gritted teeth, getting more agitated with every second that passes by.

"He just wants you to get better, Raleigh, we all do! Why can't you see that? He's only got your best interests at heart; I thought it was a sweet gesture. I was hoping you two would get back together eventually and give us those grandchildren you always promised."

I squeeze my eyes shut briefly in frustration. *I can't believe what I'm fucking hearing.* Why would she think those things after everything Carter put me through? The abuse, mental and physical. *Why on earth would she think that's acceptable behaviour?*

"That's never going to happen! He tried to fucking rape me, mum! When are you going to get that through your thick skull? But that's not in question right now, why the fuck would you let him take over paying my therapy bills? Why! Don't you think if I'd known that, I'd have had something to say on the matter? *Jesus Christ!* Don't you see that this is all kinds of fucked up?"

My voice shakes and it's taking everything inside me not to burst into tears. *Deep breaths, Storm, you got this.* I had foolishly told my mum what Carter did to me, in the vain hope she would take my side and be the mother I've always wanted her to be. After I told her, she dismissed me immediately and told me not to over-exaggerate things. My mum has always worshipped Carter from the day she met him, and she thinks the sun shines out of his arse. She always hoped that we'd settle down, get married and have kids one day.

"I've told you before, don't say such absurd things, Raleigh. Carter is a good man, he treated you like a Queen, and this is how you repay him? He was a bit rough with you, he didn't try to rape you, don't be so dramatic."

Is she actually for real?

"Unbelievable! We've been through this before, mum! Was I being dramatic when he held me down and tried to take what he wanted, when all the time I was screaming no? What's it going to take for you to believe me, mum? He's the reason I ended up in fucking rehab after he beat me and forced himself on me! Brody is ten times the man Carter will ever be!"

I raise my voice, but she needs to get it into her thick fucking head.

"Brody's no good for you, he's in a rock band for God's sake! I bet he's got a different woman every night, how can you even contemplate being with someone like that?"

I laugh bitterly, pacing down the alley that runs to the side of the club.

"You don't even know him! And being with someone like what, mum? Like you were with dad? Tell me, mum! Fucking enlighten me!" I scream.

Mine and Brody's relationship isn't that different from my mum and dad's, Brody's the bad boy, just like my dad was, but I'm nothing like my mum. My mum was the prissy Prom Queen and I'm more of the misfit rebel.

Fucking hell, she frustrates the shit out of me sometimes!

"Someone...oh it doesn't matter! You've never listened to me or your father! Not once in twenty-nine years! Why can't you be more like your brother?"

Here we fucking go. I really don't know why I bother sometimes. So, I don't, I just hang up the phone. I put my phone back in my bag and go back inside.

I stay for a few more drinks and I didn't see Carter for the rest of the night, much to my relief. I'm more than a little tipsy as I leave with Nick. Gavin got called to some emergency with his daughter Cleo, which left me with Nick and a few of the backstage crew. As we were getting ready to leave, I called Cliff to come and pick me up. He said he was on his way.

"Are you sure you're gonna' be ok, love? Do you need a lift home?" Nick asks, and I shake my head.

"No, I'm good, thanks for the offer. My drivers coming to pick me up, he shouldn't be too long."

I smile my thanks, as my phone rings. I look at my phone and see Cliff calling.

"Hey Cliff, how far away are you?" I enquire, and he sighs deeply down the phone.

"I'm so sorry, sweetheart, I'm having car trouble, my car won't start so I can't pick you up. I've ordered you an Uber. I relayed the address to the driver, and he's on his way. He was in the area so he shouldn't be too long."

Bless his heart, he's always thinking of me.

"No problem, Cliff. Hope you get your car sorted, thank you so much for looking out for me."

"No bother, sweetheart, take care and call me when you're home. I like to know you're safe when I'm not around."

I smile at his thoughtfulness.

"I will do, thanks again, bye."

I hang up the phone and Nick looks at me.

"Everything ok?"

I nod, as I spot an Uber pulling up across the road from the pub and I kiss Nick goodbye.

"Let me know when you're home safe, sweetheart."

He leaves with a wink, as I stumble into the taxi.

"Iverna Court, Kensington, wasn't it, darlin'?" the Uber driver asks, as I settle back into my seat.

"Yes, please."

The driver catches my drunken gaze in the interior mirror and nods curtly, pulling smoothly away from the kerb.

"You're that actress off that film, that one with Gavin what's-his-name, gruff cockney geezer, he was married to that bird with the big-" he rambles as he makes a gesture with his hands around his chest area.

I giggle to myself and find myself smiling at his enthusiasm. I sink back into my seat and just listen to the taxi driver ramble on at a million miles an hour about famous people he's driven around, as I watch the night slide by in a haze of flickering lights and inky blackness. As the journey continues, I feel my stomach start to roil. *Fuck, I don't feel so good.*

"You alright, love? You're not gonna' throw up, are you?" he asks, and before I know what's happening, I projectile vomit all over seat in front of me.

"Whoa! What the fuck's going on? Did you just throw up in my taxi?"

I wipe my mouth with the back of my hand, the events of the night rushing to the forefront of my mind. Still feeling a bit rattled by my confrontation with Carter, my temper hits boiling point.

"Keep your eyes on the road and don't worry what I'm doing back here, just do your fucking job and take me home!" I yell.

"I don't give two fucks who you are, if you don't clean up the mess you've just made, get the fuck out!"

He isn't going to kick me out of his car, doesn't he know who I am?

"I'm not cleaning up shit! Do your fucking job and drive me home, you prick!" I snap.

Unexpectedly, the car comes to an abrupt halt. "Get the fuck out, NOW!" he roars as I reach for the door handle.

I open my purse, haphazardly throwing a handful of notes at him. "Take that and fuck off! Dickhead!" I stumble unsteadily out of the car and onto the pavement, slamming the door aggressively.

"PRICK!" I shout as he drives off.

I look around, trying desperately to gather my thoughts and get my bearings. Luckily, I'm not too far away from my flat, I can't wait to get home. I need a shower, and I need sleep; it's been a long, eventful day. As I walk along the pavement, I hear the roar of a car engine. I turn slightly, but I'm temporarily dazzled by the glare of the headlights. I shrug nonchalantly and continue walking, I can see my building from where I am like a shining beacon. Unexpectedly and completely out of the nowhere, I'm shoved carelessly into a nearby alleyway. I stumble heavily but I don't fall. I'm shoved again roughly against the wall, and I catch myself, as I turn, I see Carter, seconds before his fist slams into my face. My vision temporarily blurs and my head spins as I fall to the ground. I feel the warm trickle my blood down my face, my heartbeat thundering in my chest and I can feel myself trembling. I am trying desperately to fight back the tears that are threatening to escape and the scream that seems to be trapped in my throat. I hear the distinct sound of a zipper; my thoughts turn to what is actually happening.

"I'd like to see you and your cunt boyfriend laugh at me now! I'm taking back what's mine! I'm the one in fucking control! You hear, whore? ME!"

The hatred in his voice is apparent, as I feel him pull my dress up, slide my knickers to the side and roughly enter me. I have no fight in me, as my body is frozen in place and I pray for this to all be over.

24

Brody

After the gig, I'm high on the feeling and I can't focus on anything else, other than the desperate need to go to Raleigh.

"I need to see Raleigh."

Sam cocks his pierced eyebrow. "Is that such a good idea after what happened earlier, dude?"

I scrub my hand down my face, feeling unexpectedly exhausted. "I don't know, I just know I have to see her, Sam. I need to her to know she's it for me, as fucked up as it sounds, it took me having mindless sex with Lorna for me to realise. There is no one else I'd rather be with."

He nods and smirks wickedly.

"Come on, Romeo, I'll give you a ride."

I'm silent on the journey to Raleigh's place and stuck in my own head. *How could I cheat on her like that, you selfish motherfucker!* She doesn't deserve it, she's a good person, she's my light, she's my fucking salvation, my chance at redemption. She would be crushed if she found out that I'd stuck my dick in another woman. *What the fuck was I even thinking?* Well, I clearly wasn't thinking, I was thinking with my dick as usual. I spend the journey to her apartment stuck inside my own head and by the time Sam stops at the curb, I'm all sorts of edgy and antsy. I fidget awkwardly in my seat and as I unclip my seatbelt, I hear Sam chuckle gruffly.

"You're about as subtle as a sledgehammer, Hart, out with it! I can literally hear the cogs turning, mate, it's fucking painful!"

I lean my head back on the headrest heavily.

"What the fuck was I even thinking, Sam? I can't deny my feelings for Raleigh, but Lorna is my fucking weakness, and she knows it! How could I have been so stupid?" I say, a defeated tone to my voice.

"It is what it is, man, you can't change that it happened but maybe come clean to Raleigh and hope to fuck she forgives you; I don't know what else to say. Grovel as if your life depends on it. I can tell you're genuinely sorry. You don't normally give enough of a shit to care, but I don't doubt your feelings for her. Not for one second."

Sam squeezes my shoulder.

"Look, go in there, tell her everything, beg for her forgiveness and say you want to start over."

I let out a laboured breath, knowing deep down it isn't going to be that easy.

"Thanks, mate, really appreciate you being there for me," I say sincerely, and Sam nods.

"Anytime, man, anytime, call me if you need me, yeah?"

He winks and I get out of the car. I saunter casually into the lobby of her apartment building, and I'm greeted by a man mountain. *Fuck me, I wouldn't want to get on the wrong side of this beast.*

"Evening."

I smirk and he nods curtly. "Good evening, Sir, can I help?" he enquires, and I nod.

"I'm here to see my girlfriend, Raleigh Storm, apartment number 4a?"

He taps on the computer in front of him and shakes his head.

"I haven't been informed that she's expecting company this evening, sir. I'm afraid I can't let you in if I haven't received pre-approval from Ms. Storm."

I roll my eyes. *He sounds like he's practised that, or he's reading off a script. Fuck my life.*

"Look, mate, I've been here before, I wanted to surprise her, we haven't seen each other for a while, I've just come home from a tour, and I just want to see my girl."

I sigh audibly and my shoulders sag, the events of the day catching up with me in a spectacular fashion. The overwhelming urge to fall face first in a mountain of white powder at the forefront of my mind and I can't shake the feeling off. The man mountain regards me with rapt attention and at this point, I'm not above using my status as one quarter of the world's biggest rock band to get past this fucking jobsworth.

"I have to say your face looks familiar, have you been here before?" he asks, and I nod.

"Yes, several times, I'm Brody, Brody Hart."

He taps on his computer, scribbles something on a piece of paper. I don't have the heart to tell him I already have a key, which Raleigh gave me the morning I went on tour.

"I shouldn't do this, I could get fired but just this once, next time you need to ask Ms. Storm to inform me that you're on her pre-approved visitors list."

I nod, relieved that he's finally seen sense.

"Thank you, really appreciate it."

I smile cordially.

"Have a good evening, Mr Hart."

I head up to her apartment using the lift and walk the few yards down the corridor. I take out my key, open the door and I step into her apartment, kicking the door closed with my boot.

"Raleigh? It's me, where are you, kitten?" I call out.

As I step further into the room, I hear running water and soft sobs. I instantly know something isn't right, I empty my pockets and drop the contents in the glass bowl, along with my phone, to the left of the door.

Something feels off and all my senses are on high alert. I walk cautiously through the flat and the sobs get louder with each step I take. Without knocking, I push open the bathroom door and my heart slams against my rib cage. Raleigh sitting on the floor of her walk-in shower, fully clothed and shaking violently. The sight causes a lump to rise in my throat and my protective instincts to kick in. *Fuck*. Without hesitation, I step confidently into the walk-in shower and sit down next to her. The warm water pounding down on both of us and soaking through my clothes, everything else just paling into insignificance.

Up close, I notice purple bruising forming on her arms, a cut above her eye, a lump forming on her forehead, a split lip, her dress is torn, and she has grazed both of her knees.

What the fuck?

I cautiously wrap my arm around her and with the initial first contact, she flinches violently. Her sad, desolate amethyst eyes lock with mine and after a few moments, she starts to relax into my hold. She is trembling, as I hold her tightly and the dam seemingly breaks. She starts to sob hard, soul-destroying sobs. I lean down and place a chaste kiss on her forehead. I taste the saltiness of her tears mixed with the warm water from the shower.

Both of us stay silent for long minutes, as I try to decide how to approach this situation, but something tells me, I won't like the answer. I run my hands gently up and down her back in a soothing motion, as her body moulds against mine. My thick biceps, enveloping her slight, vulnerable frame. I reach up to turn off the shower and she seems bereft at the loss of contact, as I get to my feet. I lean down scooping her up in my arms, grabbing a couple of towels from the heated towel rail. I perch her on the edge of the vanity unit and start to dry her off gently. As I sweep the towel over her legs, she winces.

She's unable to form words, she opens her mouth, as if she is about to speak, then she closes it again. I think she's in shock. *Fuck me, what am I going to do?* I can't leave her like this. *Shit, fuck, bollocks.*

"Raleigh, I need you to talk to me. I need you to tell me what's happened."

I take a deep breath and give her a look of reassurance, willing her to find the words.

The gut-wrenching sob that escapes from her, breaks my fucking heart and I'm somewhere between beating the ever-loving shit out of whoever fucking did this to her and crying right along with her.

"Raleigh? Baby, I can't help if you don't talk to me," I say softly, trying to coax her to start talking, but the vacant look in her eyes is like she's completely checked out.

The thought of someone hurting her makes me feel so...out of fucking control. I can't even contemplate what's going through my mind right now.

"You're scaring the shit out of me, I need you to start talking, or I'm going to lose my fuckin' mind, kitten," I say through gritted teeth, all the while trying to remain calm. "Do you want to tell me what the fuck happened?" I say, as softly as I can muster.

Right now, she's as jumpy as a deer in headlights and I'm trying my hardest not to spook her. She worries her lip between her teeth and the tears starts to slip freely down her cheeks.

"I-It's all my fault," she manages to sob out and the hollow sound of her voice causes my heart to stutter in my chest as I tilt her chin up to face me.

"Look at me, whatever the fuck this is; it's not your fault," I say cautiously, and I'm not prepared for the next words that fall from her lips.

"C-C-Carter r...raped me," she starts to tremble violently and uncontrollably.

The desperate sobs that tear from deep within her, feels like a thousand knives ravaging and tearing at my insides. *Motherfucker. He's had his fucking filthy paws all over my woman. FUCKKKKKKKK!*

"Where does he live? I'm going to fucking kill him; I'm going to tear his fucking throat out. How dare he lay his fucking hands on you!" I roar as she starts to rock back and forth.

I take a step back from her, as a red mist starts to cloud my vision. Rage tears through my body and all I want to do is rip that cock suckers face off, with my bare fucking hands. My broad shoulders heave, with my deep panting breaths, but the sound of her hiccupping sobs, bring me back to the here and now. I move to stand in front of her and wrap my arms around her. She clings and claws at me desperately, as if she can't get close enough. I hold her tight, and she moves to press herself against me, as if she is trying to climb inside me.

"I've got you, babe, you're safe now, I'm here, shhh," I soothe as I start frantically routing through the cabinets.

"Do you have a first aid kit? I need to see to those cuts, they look pretty nasty, I think you might need stitches."

She jumps down from the vanity unit and stumbles into my chest. I catch her by her wrist to stop her from falling and she flinches violently, snatching her hand away from me.

"I'm fine!" she snaps, and I spin her round.

"Look in the fucking mirror, kitten! Look! You are not fucking fine!"

I force her to meet her reflection in the mirror, and she starts to sob again. She collapses, trembling in my arms and all I can do is catch her.

***

After I clean and tend to her wounds, I convince her to come back to my place, and she reluctantly agrees. *She shouldn't be on her own right now.* While she packs an overnight bag, I take my phone from the bowl next to the door, and I dial the number I need. It rings twice, before it connects.

"Son, everything alright?"

Lenny's gruff voice fills my ears, and I pace the flat like a man possessed.

"Len, I need a favour."

He laughs throatily.

"Sounds ominous, son."

I scrub my free hand down my face, and I can't bring myself to say the words aloud. I take a deep breath and squeeze my eyes briefly shut.

"I need someone taken care of, Len. Carter fucking Leonard," I spit out his name as if it's poison.

"That pretty boy off the telly? What's he done?" Len says matter-of-factly, and I laugh bitterly.

"That filthy cocksucker, he...he fucking raped, Raleigh." I swallow hard, desperately trying to keep my boiling temper in check. "He dared to lay his filthy, fucking hands on her, Len. She's an absolute mess and I need him taken care of, like tonight. If I get my hands on him, I'll rip his motherfucking face off on sight, I swear it."

My whole body is vibrating with anger, and I can't focus on anything else other than wanting to be the one to fucking end Carter Leonard.

"Look, Len, can you take care of it?" I say more than a little impatiently, and there is a short pause.

"Yeah, course, son, let me make a few calls and I'll get one of my boys from the club on it. Consider it done. Fucking animal deserves everything he's got coming to him," he says without hesitation.

"Thanks, Len, I appreciate it, and I owe you one. Call me when it's done, bye."

I end the call and tuck my phone back into the pocket of my jeans.

"Brody?" she whispers, and I turn around.

I try to appear unaffected by the cuts and bruises all over her face, as I nod. She's just dressed in a simple white t-shirt with leopard print lips on the front, a pair of loose-fitting jeans and white Converse. I pull my phone out of my pocket, call Trey to come and pick us up. Luckily, he followed Sam and me from the gig and has been waiting outside. I offer her my hand and she takes it, I close the door quietly, as we both leave the flat and make the journey to my house. She is silent and withdrawn on the ninety-minute journey to my place, staring blankly out of the window. I have my arm wrapped around her, trying to provide her some source of comfort, as the landscape zips past. When we arrive at my place, I get out of the car, slam the door behind me and go around to the passenger side to help her out. She lets me and grips my hand tightly. I keep hold of her hand, head up the steps, unlock the door and step inside the house.

"Do you want to use the shower, kitten? I can get you something to eat if you're hungry, I can order in? Or I've got vodka?" I babble.

I haven't got a fucking clue what to do, or how to act around her. She nods in agreement.

"I'd like to use the shower, if that's ok?" she says so softly that I barely hear her. I nod and smile.

"Of course, the bathroom's upstairs, the one in my room is the biggest, you won't be disturbed. Sam and Peyton have gone down to Brighton to stay at her parents' house with the boys until the weekend, so we've got the place to ourselves. There are some fresh towels hanging over the towel heater."

She smiles for the first time since I found her, and I find myself smiling back.

"Thank you," she whispers, and I move closer to her, kissing her gently and cautiously on the lips.

"There's no need to thank me, kitten."

She drops her gaze and scurries off upstairs, leaving me to my thoughts. *What would have happened if I hadn't shown up?* Would she have told anyone, or would she have kept it to herself? *Fuck me, it doesn't bare thinking about.* I find myself trembling, with white hot, molten anger. I decide to go into the gym downstairs and box out some of my frustration. I quickly change into loose grey jogging bottoms and wrap my hands with tape. I set my Spotify on my phone to shuffle and the sound of *Alterbridge Down to My Last,* fills the surround sound speakers. I pull on my boxing gloves and start to punch. *Jab, jab, cross, jab, jab, cross, cross.*

I go on like this for half an hour, until my muscles feel deliciously sore and sweat is dripping from my forehead. I pull off my gloves, throw them down and grab a towel from the hook in the corner of the room. I wipe my face and head back upstairs to the kitchen. I'm pouring two large glasses of vodka, as she walks slowly, gracefully, and apprehensively into my kitchen. She is wearing a Rancid Vengeance t-shirt of mine; it looks so big on her; she could almost pass it off as a dress. It hangs shapelessly off her slim figure, as she moves further into the room. She is barefoot, and her pale lilac hair is damp from the shower. Her face is stripped of makeup, her beauty is marred by the angry cuts and bruises all over her face. Despite the temporary flaws, she looks so innocent, vulnerable, and younger than her twenty-nine years. Her unusual amethyst eyes look almost too big for her face, as she worries her bottom lip between her teeth nervously.

"Did you enjoy your shower, kitten?"

What the fuck, Hart, is that all you've got? She smiles, but it's lifeless and doesn't reach her eyes.

"Thank you, Brody, thank you for being there," she says softly.

I move closer to her and watch her reaction with every step I take. She's wary. She's watching me the way I'm watching her, and I can't take my eyes off her.

"I'm not going to hurt you, kitten. God, I'd never harm a hair on your fucking head, I swear it."

The pain in my voice is evident and I reach out to tuck a strand of her hair behind her ear. She leans into my touch and a tear rolls down her cheek.

"I'm sorry."

She drops her gaze to the floor, and I tilt her chin up.

"Look at me, kitten, you have nothing to be sorry for, I promise you. You're safe, Carter is being taken care of, he won't be bothering you again, by the time I'm finished. If he comes within ten fucking feet of you, I'll know about it and it will be dealt with."

I say, with an edge to my voice. I can't fucking bear the thought of another man's hands on her, I can't stand the thought of another man taking her by force. It makes me feel physically violent. I'm not a fighter, I never have been. I'm not even a lover. I'm a thinker. There's no room for shades of grey, no in between, just black, and white. He took what was mine, he violated her and took what he wanted, without consent. That's not ok, he's going to pay for what he's done and he's going to fucking suffer for it. The thought of someone else's hands on her makes me feel sick, I'd never do anything but worship her, like the Queen I know she is. She deserves the world. *She doesn't deserve you; you're pathetic Hart! You fucking stuck your cock in another woman while she was waiting patiently for you to come back to her, you vile, depraved piece of shit!* I swallow hard to rid myself of that thought, *not now, dickhead.*

She moves further into the kitchen. She perches herself on a bar stool at the kitchen island. I push the glass of vodka towards her, and she picks it up. She knocks it back in one go and pulls a face, as she swallows. She slams the glass down on the counter, I pour her another and she leans forward, lifting the glass with a trembling hand.

"Do you want to talk about what happened?" I ask and she shakes her head defiantly as she knocks back her second glass of vodka.

This time she doesn't grimace when she swallows. She slams the glass down again and looks me dead in the eye.

"Nope, I just want you to fuck me, Brody. I need you to take it away, please."

She pleads with her eyes and I never say no to a beautiful woman. *What the fuck are you doing to me Raleigh Storm?*

Raleigh

I feel a needy ache between my legs, and I need him to take it away. I need him to erase Carter's touch, I need him to replace it with his touch. I need him more than my next breath and by the possessive look in his eyes, he knows it. He doesn't need to say the words out loud.

"Brody," I mewl, and he pulls off his t-shirt.

I never get tired of the sight of him shirtless, he's magnificent. His body is all muscle and hard rippling sinew, his physique has changed dramatically in the past few weeks. He's well-built without being too bulky and heavy set.

"Tell me what you want, Rae, I need you to say the words."

I don't miss the rough commanding tone to his voice.

"I want you, Brody," I pant breathlessly, and he shakes his head with a cocky smirk on his face.

"Ah, ah, not those words, kitten. Tell me what I need to hear."

"I need you to take it away, Brody, please take it away," I plead, almost desperately, as I move towards him.

I push him against the kitchen island and pull off his t-shirt that I am wearing and crush my lips to his in a searing, bruising kiss.

My breasts feel heavy and yearn to have his hands on them. He pulls away briefly, as he leans down and expertly laps my nipple with his talented split tongue. I cry out at the glorious torture and the delicious, sweet ache between my thighs is almost intolerable. My pussy floods, as he continues his assault on my nipples and I feel wanton and shameless, writhing in agony waiting for him to fill me. This virile man, who belongs to me just, as I belong to him, he just can't say it out loud yet. The look in his silver eyes almost pushes me over the edge, as I urge him with my eyes to take me, to fuck me like I need him to. I want him to erase Carter's touch, I want him to take it all away. I try to focus on the searing hot pleasure that's working its way through my body.

"I need you in my bed, Raleigh, I want you to let me worship you."

I nod silently in agreement and let him lead me to his bedroom, both of us gloriously naked. We don't say anything, and as soon as my thighs collide with the bed. It's flesh seeking flesh, lips seeking lips and every one of my senses was on high alert tuned into everything that was Brody Hart. His long, callous fingers squeeze and ravage me like a man possessed. The smoky look in his silver grey eyes reminds me there was a storm brewing, and I was about to get very wet. My heartbeat starts to quicken and I briefly close my eyes, desperately trying to concentrate on the feel of Brody pressing himself against me. *Focus, Storm, it's just Brody.* I open my eyes and look up at him, he gives me an encouraging wink, as he seems to be in tune with my inner turmoil. His erect cock seeks out my pussy and he slips into me with ease. My slick channel welcomes him in, as he shoves forward, his piercing bumping my cervix with each measured plunge of his cock. I try to focus on the intense, mind-blowing pleasure he bestows upon me instead of the rough, violent act that Carter subjected me to.

"Brody," I mewl breathlessly.

"I know, I've got you, kitten. It's just me, I'll take care of you," he placates softly and reassuringly, as if he knows what I need.

He slows his pace and I lift my hips, rising to meet him thrust for thrust and he doesn't take his eyes off me. This isn't just a quick fuck, this is Brody Hart making love. He's so gentle, I could weep. Somewhere in my sex addled haze, I'm vaguely aware he isn't wearing a condom, but I push that thought to the back of my mind and focus on the intense pleasure he is reigning upon me.

"Oh God!" I pant as he continues his slow, sensual pace.

He cups my breast in his hand and gently starts to massage it in lazy circles.

"You feel...fuck...you feel too good, kitten," he grinds out as he increases his momentum with an expert swivel of his lean hips.

"Mmm, fuck, Brody, I'm close. Jesus, I'm so close."

I writhe beneath him and he leans down taking my erect nipple in his mouth. He nips it softly with his teeth causing me to gasp. He releases my nipple with a pop and grabs my hips, slamming me forward onto his rock-hard shaft. His pace increasing with each careful drive. The piercing in the head of his penis rubs my g-spot in the most delicious way.

"Do you like that? Fuck, you feel perfect around my cock, Rae."

He thrusts forward, and that's all it takes to tip us both over the edge. I let out a scream and I explode around his throbbing cock.

"I'm coming, Brody, oh shit! I'm coming!"

My orgasm is intense and feels like a frenzy of simultaneous explosions deep within me.

"FUCCCCKKK! Raleigh!"

Brody growls his release, as he his warm seed coats my womb. He collapses spent on top of me and nuzzles his head into my neck.

"You were the one that stopped my heart from breaking, Raleigh. Just you, I thought I needed other women to fulfil my needs, but in reality, all I needed was you," he whispers almost incoherently, and I'm not sure if he means it, or he's still drunk on the post orgasmic high.

I feel him stiffen, as he pulls out of me and I'm speechless. *Was that Brody Hart admitting he loves me without using the 'L' word I long to hear?* He gets up from the bed and wordlessly goes into the bathroom, shutting the door behind him. I hear the shower turn on and I'm still trying to get my head around his words. *I was the one that stopped his heart from breaking? What the hell does that mean?* He talks in riddles sometimes and I'm so fucking confused.

I'm still trying to process what he said, when he comes out of the bathroom with a towel secured around his waist, beads of water still clinging to his lightly tanned, tattooed skin. I watch him carefully, as he dries himself off. He drops the towel, rubbing his short hair and as he turns around, I'm met with his broad, retreating back. I can't tear my eyes away from the huge black and grey tattoo, which spans his entire back. I can't make it out properly from where I'm lying, I've seen him naked so many times, yet I've never noticed the detail in any of his tattoos.

"Stop looking at my arse, kitten, you'll give me a complex!"

His tone amused and lighthearted. I chuckle softly at his quip and bless him for trying to take my mind off tonights events. I roll over into my stomach, my boobs squished against his cool, rumpled bed sheets.

"Your tattoo is...amazing," I compliment.

He turns to face me, leaning casually naked against the door frame, the light from the bathroom illuminating his perfectly chiselled face.

"Thanks, Peyton did it, it was a work in progress, but it's finished now, do you want to see?"

I nod and he moves closer to me, turning around so I can get a closer look. It is a huge black and grey lion, with four playing cards with the words *"we cannot change the cards we're dealt, just how we play the game"* curved around the left side in bold script lettering. The shading makes the lion look realistic, majestic and fierce. The lines are crisp and clean, some thick, some thin, and I lie there in awe, as I reach out to gently trace the lines. Along the bottom of his back he also has the phrase *"If I walk this world alone, then no one can hurt me"*

"It's beautiful," I say with admiration in my voice, my fingers gliding over the intricate line work. "Why the quote?" I ask curiously.

I feel him stiffen under my touch and his gaze shifts to the floor, folding his muscular arms defensively across his chest.

"I'm destined to walk this world alone, kitten. After all these years, everyone leaves in the end. If I'm alone, then no one can hurt me, the only person that has the power to hurt me, is me."

His voice sounds so full of pain and I hate the self deprecating tone to his voice, it makes my heart hurt. *Why would he think such a thing?*

"Don't try to figure me out. Even the shrinks can't figure me out. I'm a lost cause, kitten."

I feel a lump form in my throat and I'm filled with a plethora of emotions. I can't put into words what I'm feeling listening to him so full of hatred for himself and the world around him. He has to know that it isn't like that anymore, he has to know that he has people that love him and care for him. He moves closer to me and I know he's just trying to distract me with sex again. He takes my chin between his thumb and forefinger, forcing me to look at him.

"Stop, whatever you're thinking, kitten, just fucking stop."

His voice dripping with seductive promise. I'm acutely aware that everytime I'm within touching distance of him, my body is on fire. I almost feel as if I would spontaneously combust if he even brushes past me. Every nerve in my body is tuned into his frequency and there isn't a fucking thing I could do about it.

Everytime he pushes me away, I'm drawn back to him, like a moth to a flame or like a sheep to a fucking fox. I love him with every fibre of my being and I hate him with just as much passion and fire. I hate him for making me want him. I hate him for fucking pushing me away when all I want is to know him like Peyton, Lenny and the boys know him. I hate him for not accepting my declaration of love and most of all I hate him for making me feel as if I'm insignificant, that I don't matter.

My mum always told me never to trust a man who couldn't commit, yet she chose to stay with my dad after every affair, after every broken promise and after every torrent of tears she shed over him. Every time he would come home smelling of perfume that wasn't my mums, every time he apologised with flowers and diamonds. Seeing them almost destroy each other and then put their relationship back together again, piece by piece. As soon as I left home at the age of eighteen, I vowed that my future relationships wouldn't be as fucked up as my mum and dads.

"What's going on in that pretty head of yours, kitten?"

I smile at his tender nickname for me, as he pulls on a clean pair of heather grey boxer shorts with a black waistband. He climbs into bed and pulls me to his side, wrapping his arm around me. I rest my head on his pec and snuggle into him.

"Why did you end up in rehab?" I ask him curiously.

It was a thought that has been bothering me for a while. I always had a sneaky suspicion that he wasn't entirely truthful about the real reason he was in rehab. He idly traces shapes up and down my arm and as I ask him that question, he momentarily stops.

"You already know why I was in rehab," he replies defensively.

"I know, but I always had a feeling that you weren't being entirely truthful about the real reason," I admit candidly. "I know you were a drug addict; you were the stereotypical rocker in rehab. You were literally a fucking walking cliché!" I joke and he chuckles softly.

"That's me, the walking cliché! Yeah, I was a massive drug addict, I couldn't function unless I had some chemical or another running through my veins. I...wasn't in a good place back then, I was a mess. The path I was on I was going to be dead before I hit thirty-five, I didn't want to be that person anymore. The truth is, the drugs were the main reason I was there, but the other reason was a woman, amongst other things," he answers vaguely, with a shrug and I stiffen as he says those words.

A woman? Well, Brody Hart, you continue to surprise me at every turn, I definitely wasn't expecting that.

"Don't be jealous, kitten, it doesn't suit you. You asked me for the truth, and I gave you the truth. I was in rehab because I was fucked up in more ways than one, I was in a dark place. I was battling a drug addiction and the woman I thought I was in love with, rejected me like I meant nothing. I felt like I was that scared, messed up kid, who was rejected by his mother all over again. She made me feel things I've never felt before, but she was never mine to begin with."

His voice is thick with emotion and I've never seen this side of him before. *Maybe this could be a turning point for us?*

"What do you mean, she was never yours to begin with?" I ask, more than a little confused by his statement.

"She was married, babe. I was the other man, and that made me feel so fucking ashamed. I was sleeping with another woman who would ultimately go home and share a bed with someone who wasn't me and that made me feel fucking sick to my stomach."

He unwraps his arm from around me and I feel him distancing himself from me.

"What was her name?"

I ask meekly and don't know why I need to know the answer to that question. He perches himself on the edge of the bed and runs his hand through his short hair.

"It's not important."

He dismisses my question and I feel more than a little disgruntled at his blatant disregard.

"Tonight wasn't about me, are you going to tell me what that cocksucker did to you? He put his hands on something that belongs to me!" he snaps agitatedly.

"Do I though? Do I belong to you, because you sure do a good job of making me think I don't?" I retort bitterly, and he turns to face me.

"Of course you fucking belong to me! How could you even doubt that?" he barks, and I flinch violently.

"Look at yourself, Raleigh. He fucking did that to you! He violated you and took you by force! How can you even just sit there like nothing happened?"

He jabs his finger in my direction and I hide my face away. *I can't bear to see the look in his eyes.*

"Because if I let it affect me then he's fucking won! Don't you see that? Yes I feel like crumbling. I want to hide away and cry my heart out, but that says he's won, and he doesn't get to fucking do that to me, to us!" I yell bitterly, and it takes me a few minutes to compose myself before I can continue.

"Do you want to know the difference between a psychopath and a sociopath? Carter fucking Leonard. What sets Carter apart from being a psychopath was the subtle way he'd manipulate me into believing everything was my fault. I couldn't do anything right, in his eyes I was in the wrong and everything I did, was purely to ruin his reputation and make him look bad. Everything with Carter was about image and keeping up appearances, which is why him and my mum got on like a house on fire. I endured that for months, months of him belittling me, mocking me, making me feel about two feet tall. After our relationship ended, we were forced to continue working together on "The Village." His character Connor Diaz was the soap heart throb and his on off relationship with my character Penny O'Shea was the hot storyline of the moment. Everyone was talking about the 'are they, aren't they', and it was high profile because we were a couple in real life too.

Before the split, we made a sex tape, I'm not proud of that, but he manipulated me into thinking it was purely for our own private pleasure and like an idiot I believed him. After the split Carter, leaked it to the press by making it out like someone had broken into our apartment and violated our privacy. It would ruin our squeaky clean reputation and Carter was forced to make a public apology to the press and to his fans. He admitted we were no longer a couple, and I was painted as the bad person... the fucking Scarlett woman. I was suspended from my role on The Village and later fired for my part in the porn video and I fell epically from grace. It made me sick to the stomach that he could apologise like it was just a slip up and I was sacked. I was so fucking bitter and I wanted him to suffer for it. But being this weak willed woman, he asked me to give us another chance and like a dickhead I went back to him. He took me out to celebrate our anniversary and we all know how that night ended."

My voice shakes and he looks at me with sympathetic eyes, as he settles back down next to me. He pulls me into his side.

"It has been an emotional day. I had my therapy session this morning, and I left there in tears. I went straight from there to the film set to continue filming, I was meant to go out on a girly night with Liv and Maverick, but they cancelled on me last minute. So me, Nick, Gavin and a couple of the crew members from the movie went to a pub near where we were filming. Carter turned up out of the blue, he blurted out that he was the one who'd been paying for my therapy sessions. Why the fuck would he do that, Brody? Why? After everything he put me through?" I ask, not expecting an answer, and Brody kisses my forehead tenderly, stroking my knuckles with his thumb.

"I went to call my mum to ask her if was true but we don't have the best relationship. We're opposites and we have a personality clash. She tries, but it isn't with anyone's best interests at heart, only her own. She admitted it was true and she went on this tirade of how she wished Carter and me would get back together and give her the grandkids she's always wanted. I went nuclear and hung up on her. How could she do that? How could she fucking let him take over paying my therapy bills? It's not as if they can't afford it! *Jesus!* I'd have paid for myself if I'd known! I was so fucking angry! I went back inside and got shitfaced. After I was suitably wasted, I decided I just wanted to go home and have a long soak in the bath and go to sleep. I left the pub, Cliff was meant to pick me up and take me home but he had car trouble. He called an Uber for me and a car pulled up at the curb. We were almost at my place, when I threw up unceremoniously in the back of the taxi, we argued, he kicked me out of his taxi and I ended up having to walk home. I was so drunk."

I'm trembling at thought of what happened next and Brody pulls me closer to him.

"You don't have to continue if you don't want to, kitten."

I shake my head.

"No, it needs to be out there, I saw a car, but the headlights blinded me. I couldn't tell who it was and the next thing I know, I'm being shoved into an alleyway. I banged my head, he punched me, pushed me to the floor and he...he...raped me."

I can't stop the flow of tears that track their way down my cheeks. I sob hard, as he pulls me closer to him and kisses the top of my head.

"Shh, you're safe, kitten, I've got you, he's not going to fucking get away with this, I promise you."

From the pure conviction in his voice, I don't doubt his feelings for me, not for one second.

25

Brody

The contrast of her lilac hair against the crisp white of my pillow, made her look ethereal and almost otherworldly. Even though I was somewhat aware of how fucking creepy it was, I couldn't take my eyes off her. She was beautiful, like an angel sent to redeem every fucking sin I'd ever committed. The way her chest rose and fell as she slept soundly in my bed. I can't resist her, I lean over her and start kissing her at the base of her throat, up the slender hollow of her neck and round to nibble her ear. She squirms, wriggling against me and my boner instantly pops up to say hello.

"Mmmm," she moans as I continue my journey up her neck and across her face. She starts grinding against me and all of a sudden my frisky kitten is awake.

"Hey beautiful," I greet her, slipping my hand inside her camisole, rubbing her nipple between my thumb and forefinger.

She grabs a handful of my hair between her fingers and tugs gently.

"Brody."

I chuckle against her neck.

"I've got you, kitten, I'll take care of you like I always do, I promise. I'm going to make you come over and over again until you beg me to stop."

I settle myself between her legs, alternating teasing her nipple with my teeth and my tongue, as she writhes beneath me.

"Oh God!"

I reach down and I press one finger to her slit and gently rub and tease her wet folds, as I continue to play with her nipples.

"Brody."

The evidence of her excitement was coating my forefinger, as I inserted two fingers easily inside her. Her soft whimpers of encouragement were a clear indication that she was beyond aroused. I continue to finger fuck her;

she's panting and breathless. She grabs her breast in her hand and bites her lip.

"Oh Jesus, I'm close, so fucking close!"

I tease her swollen nub and I can feel her pulsing around my fingers, she's about to orgasm as there's a soft tap on the door. *Are you fucking serious right now?*

"I'm busy!" I shout impatiently as the door taps again but more insistent this time.

For fucks sake. Raleigh moans softly and I leap ungraciously from the bed.

"Sorry, kitten, I'll make it up to you."

I wink, swinging open the door, wiping the remnants of Raleigh's arousal on my boxers. I am greeted by Freddie standing at the door. I thought they were meant to be in Brighton until Sunday evening? He's wearing blue dungarees, a black and white striped t-shirt and black Converse.

"Uncle Bwody, was Auntie Raleigh praying? She was shouting 'Oh Jesus.'"

I try to stifle my laughter.

"Erm...yeah, she was. She goes to church every Sunday."

I bite my lip, desperately trying to quell my laughter. Raleigh snickers and Freddie smiles a toothy smile, looking very proud of himself.

"Where's mummy, mate?" I ask him softly, and he giggles mischievously.

Fucking hell, that giggle melts my heart.

"I thought you, mummy, daddy and Zacky were meant to be at Nana and Grampy's?"

He reaches for me to pick him up and I swing him up in my arms.

"To be continued, kitten? Coffee?"

She nods, burying her head in the pillow and pulling the sheets to cover herself.

"Come on, trouble."

I take Freddie down the hallway and down the stairs into the kitchen. I'm greeted by Peyton, barefoot, in her pyjamas, a black t-shirt with the words *'But first coffee'* and black and white checkered shorts. She's stirring a cup of coffee and she looks up at me as she sees me approach.

"Freddie Bear, there you are!" she coos, and I chuckle, kissing her tenderly on her forehead.

"And a good morning to you, sweets," she laughs, as I set him down on his feet and he takes off at a hundred miles an hour. *Jesus, he's got far too much energy for this early on a Saturday morning.*

"Morning, I'm so sorry, babe, did he disturb you? We were meant to be at my mum and dad's until Sunday, but I got a call from Seb, he's split up with Willow and his mum's been rushed into hospital. I'm covering the shop indefinitely; we drove back last night and into the early hours. I'm fucking knackered and I feel like I've hardly slept. I need to do the shop banking and I've got back-to-back appointments today," she says sounding irritated, which is unusual because she loves her job.

"Is everything ok? You never complain about your job, want to talk about it?"

She sighs and leans heavily on the kitchen island, as I step closer to her.

"I think I'm pregnant, Brody."

My eyes widen and she pauses, putting her hand to her face.

"Holy fucking shit!" I curse excitedly. "Have you pissed on a stick, or whatever girly shit you women do?"

She tries to suppress her smirk at my infamous tactfulness, and she shakes her head. "No, not yet I'm fucking terrified of the result."

She bites her lip, avoiding my gaze.

"Then what the fuck are you waiting for? We need to know whether there's another little Sammy on board. Does he know?"

She shakes her head no again and I move closer to her, wrapping her in my arms. She's showing the same fear that she has in all her pregnancies, she's terrified that Sam's going to run out on her like her scumbag fucking ex did.

"You do know that boy would walk through hell for you and those boys? I get you've been burned in the past, but he's proven to you time and time again that he's committed to you, you're married with two kids for fucks sake!" I try to reassure her, but she bursts into uncontrollable floods of tears.

"Hey! What's with the tears?"

She breaks down right in front of me and it's weird because I have a major issue with crying women, I just can't deal with it. She's the only woman who can cry in front of me and it doesn't set my nerves on edge. I wrap her in my arms and she just clings to me as if her life depends on it.

"Hey, shhh, I've got you, sweets, I've got you."

It takes her a few minutes to compose herself and I squeeze her tighter.

"Do you want to tell me what's going on?" I coax softly, and she's silent for a few minutes, burying her head deeper into my chest.

"Don't hide from me, sweets, you know you can talk to me."

I unwrap her from my hold and tilt her chin up to face me. The look in her eyes breaks my heart, I hate seeing my best friend in obvious pain. She's such a selfless soul, she does everything for everyone else, without a care in the world for herself.

"I'm terrified he's going to have another one of his episodes. He's been doing so well lately I don't want anything to jeopardise that," she admits, almost shamefully and starts to sob softly again.

This time I just wrap her in my arms and allow her to find some sort of comfort there.

Raleigh

He's been gone for an awfully long time, I decide to untangle myself from his bedsheets which still smell deliciously and distinctly of Brody Hart. I inhale them deeply and take in the rich, musky, masculine scent of him, silently grateful he can't see me right now. *Get a grip, Storm.* I pull on a discarded heather grey t-shirt of his and take out a clean pair of boxers of his out of his drawer. I put them on and head out of his room in search of him. I can hear muffled voices and soft female sobs, as I get to the bottom of the stairs. I turn the corner and quietly linger, I spot him with his arms around Peyton. He's talking softly to her and comforting her. I see him tilt her chin up with the tip of his finger and the moment is so intimate and tender I can't help the pang of jealousy that hits me right in the gut. I know deep down I've got nothing to be jealous of, they're just friends, but part of me still can't help thinking why isn't he like that with me? I round the corner and make my presence known. He doesn't jump back from her, he kisses the end of her nose.

"Come and find me in a little while, babe? We'll talk more?"

He winks and spins around to face me.

"Morning, kitten," he purrs, and I chuckle softly.

"Good morning to you, handsome."

Peyton rolls her eyes, scrubbing the wetness away from her red, puffy eyes.

"Get a fucking room!" she quips, and he kisses me chastely on the lips.

"I'm going for my morning workout, fancy joining me?"

I decline and as he heads down to the basement, I'm left in the kitchen with Peyton. She swipes her eyes again and sniffs, as she turns to me, regardingly me intently.

"What's on your mind, girl? You look like you need a chat?" she enquires softly, and I sigh, perching myself on the tall lacquered stool at the kitchen island. I'm silently grateful that she doesn't mention anything about the cuts and bruises on my face.

"He never gives away anything of himself. He's locked up tight, trying to get anything out of him is like pulling teeth, it's fucking painful."

Peyton chuckles softly.

"Oh, he gives himself away alright, that's why he's shit at poker, the guys love to play with Brody because it's an easy win! He's got so many tells it's ridiculous! He might think he's being subtle about it, but trust me he isn't! Not at all!"

We both laugh.

"He's not hard to figure out, he's a simple creature, all men are. I'll let you into a little secret, you just have to work out what makes them tick!"

She winks and I find myself smiling right along with her. She turns to the kitchen island and ties her hair into a loose ponytail with a hair tie she pulls from her wrist and she turns around to reveal a *'Mrs Newbolt'* tattoo in flowing script lettering on the back of her neck.

"Mrs Newbolt?"

I've never seen it before and I wonder curiously, as she giggles girlishly.

"Ah, you spotted that, huh?"

I smirk.

"Sure did! Come on, spill it, I'm sensing there's a story?"

We both laugh.

"I lost a bet! Do you know the story? Sam earned his stage name *'Bolt'* because he has a tattoo of a lightning bolt on his arse! And I'm sure you're familiar with the story of why they call Brody *'Snake'*?"

I lick my lips at the thought of the snake tattoo wrapped around Brody's cock.

"Down girl! Well, Sam and Brody are the most competitive members of Rancid Vengeance and I wanted in, obviously!" she explains on a dramatic eye roll.

"We all piled in to Saint Sinner one night. The bet was for one of us to be blindfolded and a person chosen at random was to tattoo the person who was blindfolded. Brody tattooed me and I guessed wrong. He tattooed a smiley face and a love heart behind my ear."

She turns her head to reveal a perfectly lined smiley face and a red love heart.

"I guessed it was Sam who tattooed me, the loser had to get a tattoo from the person who they guessed it was, so Sam tattooed Mrs Newbolt on the back of my neck!"

We both giggle at the ridiculousness of it and she places a cup underneath the coffee machine. There's a momentary silence while the machine whizzes and whirrs as the cup fills. I'm desperate to know what she talked to Brody about, and I turn to her thoughtfully, opening and closing my mouth to speak but nothing comes out. She chuckles softly as she pushes the now full steaming cup of coffee towards me.

"You can ask me, you know?" she declares, and I shift my gaze elsewhere, suddenly feeling guilty for my nosiness.

"Ask you what?"

I feign ignorance and she throws her head back on a laugh.

"What Brody and me were talking about, that's what you wanted to ask, right? It's ok, I don't mind."

I shake my head. "I'm not one of those needy girls, it's not that I don't trust him, I do, with my life, I just wish he'd talk to me the way he talks to you."

She moves towards me and I shift my eyes up to look at her.

"Gives him time, you're still getting to know each other, don't push him, just...let it be!" she sings and we both laugh.

The laughter is short lived, as her next words shock me to the core.

"I think I'm pregnant again."

I instantly feel bad for forcing her to admit something which was quite clearly personal. *Well played, Storm, well fucking played.*

I'm about to ask her about it when we're interrupted by Freddie's excited squeals.

"Mummy! Mummy!"

I laugh, as he bounds into Peyton's legs. She swings him up into her arms and she covers his face in kisses. I watch with rapt attention at their interaction and a thought crosses my mind.

"When did you realise you were in love with Sam?"

I ask and a dreamy look crosses her face.

"I knew the minute he set foot into Saint Sinner that I was going to marry him. I knew I loved him the moment he took my breath away and kissed me for the first time."

She sighs.

"When did you know you were in love with Brody?"

Her question catches me off guard and I stutter my answer.

"I...I don't, I'm not in love with him."

She chuckles softly.

"Bullshit."

Freddie plays with her hair and idly twirls it in his fingers.

"Mummy bullshit!"

Peyton goes an adorable shade of pink.

"Now you know you don't say bad words, Freddie. That's very naughty, don't say it again, please, or mummy will be very cross."

She says sternly and his lip quivers.

"Sorry mummy."

Her faces softens, as Sam walks in wearing a loose pair of jogging bottoms, which hang low on his hips. His hair is perfectly mussed, and he chucks Freddie's chin.

"Hey, what's up little guy?"

Freddie looks at Sam.

"Mummy said a bad word."

Peyton's eyes narrow and Sam cocks his pierced eyebrow.

"Did she now? I think mummy needs a good spanking don't you, buddy?"

Sam rasps and Peyton blushes furiously. I find myself smiling at their dynamic and hope that someday Brody and me could have the perfect relationship. Just like Sam and Peyton.

26

Raleigh

When you've hit rock bottom and survived, there are very few things in life that can scare you. Sometimes, you have to get knocked down lower than you have ever been, to stand back up taller than you ever were. For the past few weeks, this is the first thought that enters my head when I wake up in the morning, it's the first step to positive thinking. My sessions with Maverick have been long, emotional, and often, paired with yoga and the gym, I'm feeling good for the first time in a long time.

I stretch out like a cat in Brody's queen size bed and turn over to find an empty space where Brody should be. I've stayed over at his place since the night Carter raped me and I'll be forever grateful to him for being there for me that night. He was my saviour; my guardian angel and I don't think I could love him more. Brody is an insomniac, and it's exceedingly rare that I wake up next to him in the mornings. He usually goes for a morning run, then comes back, showers, I do my morning yoga and he cooks me breakfast. That's been our routine for the past two weeks and I couldn't be happier.

I swing my legs out of bed and head downstairs to the open plan living room, which opens out into a large, modern spacious kitchen, its slate grey floor, cold against my feet. The kitchen is immaculate and neat with everything in its place. The dark grey marble worktop and cool light grey tones to contrast, with appliances to match the theme. It looks suitably stylish and matches the cool, neutral interior of the rest of the house.

I'm wearing Brody's Motorhead t-shirt from last night. The material is soft against my naked body and it looks like a dress on me, but it smells of him. The sight I am greeted with stops me dead in my tracks, Brody stark bollock naked, cooking in his kitchen. His physique never ceases to amaze me, his narrow hips, his muscular thighs, and his broad, tattooed shoulders. His hair is growing out and is styled into a short, messy, faux hawk and he has a weeks' worth of stubble on his face, he looks rugged and delicious. He turns on the coffee machine and carries on with what he's doing, while softly humming to the music that is playing in the background, I recognise the song as Hinder What Ya Gonna Do and I take a moment to study him. Brody is extremely muscular and a few inches taller than me, I actually fell small in comparison. The working out he's been doing in his spare time has really paid off, he is all muscle and sinew. I'm admiring the view when I hear him chuckle softly to himself.

"Enjoying the view, kitten?"

He spins around, my eyes locking with his.

"Mmm," I manage as he stalks towards me gloriously naked.

When he reaches me, he pulls me close to him. I let him take charge and I don't stop him. He presses his lips to mine, his tongue generously probing mine, deepening the kiss with every stroke of his tongue. His lips are unusually soft for a guy and the softness of his lips and his week-old stubble is a total contrast, as he presses himself further into me. His erection digging into my lower abdomen, I trace his bottom lip with my tongue, and he buries his hand in my sleep mussed hair, as if he can't get enough of me. The low rumbling sound he makes, lets me know he's more than turned on. I wrap myself around him, telling him wordlessly that I'm more than ready to rock his world.

"Someone's woken up with the horn!" he grins.

He lifts me effortlessly off my feet and I wrap my legs around his waist. His lips don't leave mine, as he strides with purpose back up the stairs to his bedroom and deposits me as if I weigh nothing in the middle of the bed. His muscles undulate with his precise, animal-like movements, as he crawls up the bed, settling himself between my thighs. He presses a kiss to my inner thigh and my skin breaks out in goose bumps at his feather light touch.

"You like that, huh?"

His voice low and rough.

"Yesss," I hiss as he lifts his t-shirt to find I'm not wearing any underwear.

"Fucking tease!" he whispers, swiping his split tongue up my soaking wet slit.

"Oh God!" I mewl, desperate for him to take care of the luscious throbbing between my thighs.

"*Fuck*, you're beautiful, you know that?"

I smile shyly and he reaches up to grip the back of my head.

"Do you know what you do to me, kitten? You drive me fucking insane, every time you're near me, I want to bury my cock so deep into you, that we both never forget what it feels like. I want to smear your lipstick and I want the neighbours to know who you fucking belong to."

His words are my undoing, as I crash my lips urgently to his and I squeeze the back of his neck almost territorially. I can't get enough of this man, he's so beautifully damaged and so perfectly imperfect, that I couldn't let him go if my life depended on it.

Brody

The day goes by in a blur of slow, lazy weekend sex and just enjoying being in our own little bubble together. She's been asleep for a while and I find myself envying the fact she gets a full night of uninterrupted sleep. The nightmare which has haunted me for years, is back with a vengeance, for the fourteenth night in a row. There isn't a night that goes by that I don't wake up thick with perspiration and my nightmare clinging to me like a cloak of absolute despair. *Fuck me.* As I lie in my queen size bed, staring up at the ceiling, the silence fucking taunts me.

Ever since the incident with Carter, she's stayed over at my place. Life couldn't be more perfect, I had a beautiful woman lying in my bed. Naked may I add, yet instead of lying next to her sleeping form content to just lie next to her, I'm pacing the bathroom floor, the nightmare still fresh and clear in my brain. I sit down on the closed toilet lid and drop my head into my hands. *When will this shit stop fucking haunting me?* I get the familiar roil in my stomach and I leap ungracefully into action. I just about manage to lift the toilet seat up, as I projectile vomit into the toilet bowl, catching sight of my reflection in the mirror. *Fuck me, I look like shit.*

I hear a soft tap on the door. *Shit, shit, shit, I didn't want to wake her.*

"Babe, is everything ok in there?" she asks softly with concern in her sleep addled voice.

I tear off three sheets of toilet paper and wipe my mouth, flushing the toilet before I answer.

"Everything's fine, kitten, I'm sorry I woke you. Go back to bed, yeah? I'll be out in a sec," I reassure her.

She rattles the door handle.

"Why's the door locked? I heard you throwing up, are you sure you're ok?"

She persists. *Fuck my life.*

"I had a nightmare that's all, I didn't want to wake you, I'm fine," I admit, aware I sound anything but convincing.

"You can talk to me, you know? I'm a good listener," she asks apprehensively, and I smile to myself at her thoughtfulness.

If only she knew, I can't allow her to know the poisonous things that roam free in my mind. She rattles the door handle again.

"Open the door, Brody."

I lean my damp forehead against the cool tiles next to the door and briefly close my eyes. I need to get away from here, I can't do this with her now. I'm exhausted and I need some perspective. I swing the door open and her concerned gaze locks with mine. She reaches out to stroke my face, a frown settling on her beautiful face.

"*Jesus*, you look awful, are you sure you're ok?"

I place my hand on top of hers and nod, absentmindedly smiling to try and pacify her.

"I'm fine, look, I just need some air," I say brusquely as I start to dress.

I pull on some loose grey jogging bottoms, a black t-shirt and trainers. I run my hand through my hair and back away from her. I can't have her anywhere near me right now, I'm too tightly wound. I shake my head, grabbing my keys and my phone.

"Brody, just fucking talk to me! I thought we were finally getting somewhere?" she snaps, and I let out a laboured breath, feeling my chest tighten.

"I can't do this, I just can't, not now. I need some air, I'm sorry," I say wearily as I turn around and leave, slamming the door behind me to the sound of her softly cursing.

I run down the stairs and out of the front door. I gently jog towards the gate and signal Jace in the control room to let me out. The gates start to swing open, and I salute my thanks, as I begin my nightly stroll. I have no particular destination in mind, as I continue my brisk walk, I just know I have to get as far away from her as I can get. I don't want to infect her with the vile thoughts that invade my mind. I just can't do that to her, not after everything she's been through, she's too precious for that. She's damaged as it is, she doesn't need me making it worse for her. She's healing and taking it one day at a time and I'm so fucking proud of her for that. She's battling on, despite the shit life's thrown at her, we're the same, we're survivors. She's a warrior and I've got so much fucking respect for her for just battling through. She's so much stronger than she gives herself credit for.

As I walk, the light rain, becomes heavier and the usual need to get high, causes my veins to buzz and my body to physically ache with need. The craving to just forget is at the forefront of my mind and it's all I can fucking think about. I begin to walk faster, and my walk turns to a full-on jog. I jog with renewed purpose until I get that delicious soreness in my calf muscles and my mind becomes clearer. I'm aware of the ridiculously late hour and I feel awful for turning up here unannounced, but it's the place I seem to gravitate towards when I'm feeling particularly out of control.

I sniff and knock on the door tentatively, almost instantly regretting it. I'm considering turning around and walking away, as I see a shadow in the frosted glass door. The door swings open and I'm greeted by Lenny's looming figure in a burgundy dressing gown, black silk pyjama bottoms and his salt and pepper hair dishevelled. *He reminds me of Hugh Hefner.*

"Fuck me, son."

Lenny's gruff voice, thick with sleep oddly comforts me.

"Len, who's that, love? Do they not know what time it is?"

I hear Nancy call out and I find myself smiling.

"It's just Brody, sweetheart, go back to bed," he placates her, and he beckons me inside, closing the door behind me.

I step inside, the heat and cosiness of the house, feels like home. *This is what my home should have been like when I was a kid.*

"I'm sorry," I say quietly as a wave of guilt washes over me for just showing up without calling ahead.

A look of concern mars Lenny's features.

"Don't be silly, I know there's a good reason for you to turn up here so late, out with it."

I hang my head, following him into the kitchen.

"I had the nightmare again, Len, when will it just fucking stop? It's exhausting, *I'm* exhausted."

The kitchen is blue and white, the appliances match the style of the kitchen, including a blue kettle, a blue microwave, navy, and chrome built-in cooker, a blue Smeg fridge with various magnets of past holidays him and Nancy have been on, a few Polaroid pictures, including one of Lenny, Nancy, and Daryl, bringing back once happy memories of my friend. Blue tea, coffee, and sugar canisters neatly lined up on the blue marble worktop. Over the cooker are blue and white splash back tiles, and the floor consists of blue linoleum. Tucked away in the corner of the kitchen, is a round white table with four blue chairs around it.

I stand awkwardly off to the side, suddenly feeling like I shouldn't be here. Lenny breaks me from my dark reverie by throwing a towel in my direction. I catch it easily and begin to dry myself off from the downpour.

"You want the truth, boy? It will eventually get easier, but it won't stop. Not until you make peace with it, I know you feel responsible for it in some way. Surely you've got to know by now, you were just a kid, your mum made a choice, in my opinion, the wrong fucking one, but that's probably just my fathering instinct kicking in. For all Daryl's faults, he was our son, but he was responsible for his own destiny that night and there's no one else to blame but himself. Just like you weren't to blame for Imogen's death."

He pours us both large glasses of Haig Club whiskey and gestures to the table. We both pull out chairs and sit down. I lean my head on my hand, suddenly feeling exhausted, both mentally and physically.

"I'm so fucking tired of it all, Len," I sigh as he takes a long slug of his whiskey.

"Did I ever tell you about my time as a copper?"

My eyes widen at his admission. *What the fuck?* After over fourteen years of knowing Lenny Nicholas, I thought I knew everything about him. He laughs throatily, taking another sip of his drink.

"Don't look so shocked, son. I know what you're thinking, how could a corrupt, dodgy, old fucker like me, have ever been a man of the law?"

I smirk. *It's like he read my mind!*

"Amongst other things, Len! How come you never told me any of this before?" I ask, curiosity getting the better of me as I take a sip of my whiskey and place the glass on the table.

"Because I was a copper long before all the corruption. I was a copper when there was integrity in the job, when bringing people to justice meant something. I gave up that game a long fucking time ago."

He looks into the distance thoughtfully and I cock my eyebrow.

"I'm sensing there's more to it than just that. Don't hold out on me, old man!"

I try to make a joke of it, but he doesn't smile.

"I watched my partner get murdered, stabbed to death. The bloke who did it, he got away with it, insufficient evidence, total fucking bullshit, but I couldn't prove a fucking thing. Trevor Queen was the best man I knew, and we'd had each other's back since the first day of training at Hendon. But do you know the worse part about it? I couldn't fucking save him, that's what sent me into my downward spiral. I couldn't sleep at night; I'd wake up in a cold sweat. All I'd hear was Trev screaming, don't let me die, Len. I'll never forget that, for as long as I live." He runs his hand through his salt and pepper hair and his gravelly voice trembles. "Fucking hell, it's been years since I talked about this. You're killing me, son."

He flashes me a watery smile and I tap his arm.

"You've been there for me for over ten years, Len. It works both ways, you've listened to me whine so many times... *Fuck me*, what I'm trying to say is, I'm here for you. You're like a father to me, you're the best man I know. You're there when no one else is. Besides the boys, you're the only constant in my life."

He places his hand on mine.

"Don't go getting all sentimental on me, boy," he says wryly, and I smile softly.

"It's ok to talk about it, I spent years bottling up my feelings and look where that fucking got me, a drug addiction and ten fucking years in and out of rehab. I'm every shrinks wet fucking dream, action packed with issues. But all those years, I wouldn't trade them for anything, Len. It bought me closer to you."

He leans over and pulls me in for a hug.

"Come here, you soppy fucker!" Lenny laughs gruffly.

"You good though, B? You're more than welcome to stay here, the spare beds always made up."

I smile at his thoughtfulness and shake my head.

"I'm good, Len and thanks for the offer, but Raleigh's staying over at my place."

He cocks his eyebrow.

"It must be serious with this one, son. That's what, two weeks she's been at your place?" he asks curiously, and I smirk.

"Stop fucking fishing! We're just taking it slow, one day at a time and all that," I say nonchalantly, and he nods.

Lenny has an uncanny knack of seeing through my bullshit, which is both a good thing and a bad thing all at the same time.

"Course, son, course!"

He laughs gruffly and squeezes my shoulder. I look at the time on the clock above the fridge, two fifteen. *Fuck, I didn't realise it was that late.*

"Now, are you going to fuck off and leave this old dog to get his beauty sleep?" he jokes, and I laugh.

"Yeah, I'm sorry for turning up so late," I say apologetically, and he pulls me in for a hug.

"Never apologise for needing an ear to bend, son."

I cling to him for dear life, I'd be lost without this man. He's put me back together, and he's been there when it's felt like no one else has been. I owe him my life. I'll be forever grateful to have him.

"Tell Nance' I'm sorry for turning up so late and give her a kiss from me."

Lenny nods and looks at me with concerned eyes.

"Are you sure you don't need the spare bed, B?"

I know Lenny's silently asking me if I'm going to score and I smile softly at his quiet concern.

"I'm sure, I'm going home to my girl."

Lenny nods curtly, as we walk to the front door.

"Call me if you need anything at all. It doesn't matter what time it is; I'll be there."

I slap his shoulder.

"Thanks Len, I'll call you, I promise. Night."

I walk back down the street and the darkness spurs me on to pull my phone out of my pocket. I dial the number I seemingly need right now, and it rings five times before it connects. I'm well aware I'm taking a risk calling her at this late hour, but I have to see her. I need to see her, I'm incapable of staying away from her, even after our last encounter.

"I know I have no right to ask you, but please, L, I need to see you."

I'm hyper aware of the desperation in my voice, but she's my weakness. She makes me feel weak. I've had time to think, and I couldn't let it go, not after what happened a few weeks ago. The overwhelming silence on the other end of the phone, convinces me that she's hung up on me.

"Lorna, are you there?"

I hear a soft sniffle.

"Yeah, I'm here," she says quietly.

She's fucking crying because of you, you fucking absolute arsehole.

"Please don't cry, look, I need to see you. I can't stop thinking about what happened between us, we need to talk."

She clears her throat.

"What about Raleigh, I thought it was serious with you two?"

I smile to myself. "Is that jealousy I hear, Lavelle?"

She chuckles softly, "me, jealous? Course not!"

I laugh.

"No, course not, because that would mean admitting you care about me."

I know I sound bitter, but I don't mean to.

"Brody, don't, we've been over this."

The tone of her voice tired and defeated.

"Look, I need to see you, are you alone?"

She sighs audibly.

"Stefan's away at a conference in Munich."

As she says those words, I feel more than a little optimistic.

"Can I come over? We need to talk about what happened between us the last time we saw each other."

There's a slight pause and I think she's hung up until I hear the words I was praying would leave her lips. "Yes, you can come over, we've got unfinished business."

I find myself smiling like a loon. "Ok, I'll be there soon."

I hang up with hope of a reunion between me and Lorna.

***

I make my way over to Lorna's in record time and I feel wide awake all of a sudden. I walk up the path and I tap softly on the door. I see the light flick on and her shadow appears in the doorway. She opens the door tentatively and my heart slams against my ribcage as I catch sight of her. Her hair is piled up on top of her head in a loose bun and her black silk dressing gown is pulled tightly around her. She doesn't say anything, she just steps away from the door to allow me inside. She closes the door behind me and the silence that I'm met with is discernable.

"Are you not going to say anything?"

I break the silence which has become uncomfortable.

"What else is there to say that hasn't already been said, Brody? I think I made myself clear the last time I saw you."

She exhales quietly and I hear the bitter tone of her voice. It cuts me deeper than I care to admit, so I remain quiet and contemplative for a few moments before I continue.

"I've got plenty to say, Lorna and you're going to fucking listen to me," I say with a dark edge to my voice.

"Do you remember the night we met?" I ask, curious to know.

She nods slowly, as if she's remembering every spoken word, every touch, every kiss.

"I remember everything about that first night, L. I remember how you came apart beneath me, I remember what you were wearing. I remember every little fucking detail!"

I feel my heart pounding in my chest. I can feel myself getting more and more agitated because she's refusing to look at me. Her pained gaze is firmly fixed to the floor.

"I remember how you panted as I licked you to orgasm. I remember every kiss, every touch, every fucking word we exchanged! But what I don't understand is why you think it's ok to play fucking games with me! Tell me why! Or so help me God!"

My voice is a few decibels louder and I'm aware I'm scaring her, because she's retreated into herself. She's hugging herself and she's sobbing softly. She's never reacted like this before and I step closer to her. As I approach, she flinches violently and with every step forward I take, she takes a step back until her back collides with the wall.

"What's he done this time?" I ask on a soft rasp, and she shakes her head.

"It's n...nothing," she replies meekly, and I tip her chin up to face me.

"Look me in the eye and fucking tell me it's nothing," I counter as a tear slides down her cheek. I catch it with my thumb and rest my forehead against hers. "I'll ask again, what the fuck has he done to you this time?"

She squeezes her eyes shut, refusing to look at me.

"He's ill, he's not been himself," she says defensively, and I laugh bitterly.

"Ill? He's a fucking wife beating psychopath! He laid his hands on you, Lorna, when are you going to realise that's not okay? He should be worshipping you every single night, not beating the shit out of you! How can you stand there and defend him? I want to be the one to worship you, I want it to be my name you scream! I want you for the rest of my life, Lorna! But you'll always choose him and I'm tired, I can't fucking do this anymore. I'm exhausted. Loving you is exhausting and I'm done. I'm so done."

I swallow, desperate to maintain some sort of composure. I can't let her see that she's broken my heart. I take a few steps back, putting some distance between us.

"I wish I could go back in time so I'd met you first," she confesses.

"I wished it was you I'd walked down the aisle with, I wished it was you who I fall asleep next to each night and woke up next to you each morning, I have so many regrets, but you're not one of them."

She sobs softly and hearing her admit those words out loud is sobering. But I strengthen my resolve and shake my head.

"That doesn't change anything, I'm sorry, this has to be goodbye."

I turn to leave and she grabs my arm, pulling me back to her.

"Why did you come here, Brody?"

I briefly squeeze my eyes shut, before I answer her.

"You know he's going to be the one to end your life, don't you? Please don't let him snuff out that light in you, Lorna, please, promise me?"

She sobs and moves closer to me, pressing her forehead to mine, cupping my face in both of her hands.

"Brody, don't," she whispers.

"Promise me?" I plead. "Promise me you won't let him hold that power over you? Promise me that one day you find that fucking strength that I know you've got inside of you and leave him. You leave him and you don't look back, do you hear me?" It's taking everything I have inside of me not to burst into tears, but I know deep down this is the right thing to do. I have to let go and I have to say goodbye. "Promise me, L," I whisper, barely audible.

She sobs uncontrollably, until she manages to nod. My shoulders sag and I press my lips to hers one last time, as I turn and walk away.

Goodbye Lorna Lavelle, it's been an adventure.

27

Raleigh

As I study myself long and hard in the mirror, I notice my eyes have their familiar sparkle back, my shoulders are relaxed and my posture straight. I'm standing tall and proud for the first time in forever, despite a trying few months, I'm the happiest I've been in a long time and I'm in love with Brody Hart. I smile at my reflection, my smile is genuine and for the first time, it reaches my eyes. I apply some bright pink lip gloss and press my lips together.

"Are you ready, babe?" Liv asks with a hint of concern to her voice.

I nod and take a deep breath, as I straighten and smooth out my white Stella McCartney dress, with a bold turquoise leopard print neckline. The dress' plunging neckline makes my boobs look amazing and emphasises my killer figure. I feel confident and ready to face the critics. After a whole day of preparing and pampering, the moment I step onto the red carpet is edging ever closer.

"Ready as I'll ever be, Livvy!" I say enthusiastically, and she claps excitedly.

Tonight, is the premiere of Rocked. After almost three months of gruelling filming and endless hours of reshoots, my first film working with Damien Valentine was complete. Tonight, we were going to be celebrating the release and I couldn't wait to share our hard work with the world.

"Are you sure you're ok, Rae?"

I nod, suddenly feeling sick. I take a deep breath, pressing my hand to my abdomen and I can't stop my stomach from roiling. I rush to the bathroom and drop to my knees, emptying the contents of my stomach into the toilet bowl. Liv gets down on her haunches next to me and rubs my back.

"Fucking hell, what bought that on?" she asks softly as I put my hand to my mouth and shake my head.

"I'm just nervous that's all, babe. Really fucking nervous. It's been a while and I'm a little out of practice."

Concern mars her face, as I manage to smile. I take a few sheets of toilet roll and wipe my mouth. I get to my feet, wash my hands, and check my reflection in the mirror once again. Liv straightens my dress and tucks my hair behind my ears. I smile, as I reapply my lip gloss.

"Will I do?"

I give her a twirl and Liv grins.

"I'd do you!"

We both laugh like a pair of naughty schoolgirls. *I'm ready as I'll ever be, you can do this, Storm.*

***

Nick is my date for the premiere tonight to take away the spotlight from mine and Brody's romance. Tonight, we are arriving separately to throw the press off the scent of our blossoming romance and for the main focus to be on the movie. I step out of the limo to blinding camera flashes. No matter how many times I do this, it always overwhelms me, I can't help it. It sets my nerves on edge and makes me feel anxious. Nick moves closer, placing his hand at the small of my back, it instantly grounds me and calms me. My breathing returns to normal and we pose easily for the eager paparazzi.

"We're going to be front page news tomorrow, Mr Slade," I manage to whisper so only he can hear.

"I'd be disappointed if we weren't, love."

I hear the amusement in his voice, as he turns to me and winks. *Fucking charming bastard.* We make our way along the red carpet. Cliff is a safe distance away, wearing his perfectly tailored Men in Black suit, complete with matching sunglasses. We pose for pictures along the way, stopping to answer the reporters' questions.

"Hi! Juliet Thomson from TMZ. Tonight, I'm joined on the red carpet by the stunning Raleigh Storm and Nick Slade for the premiere of the eagerly awaited release of 'Rocked'. It's been described as Damien Valentine's love letter to rock music; do you think that's accurate?"

I smile, as she thrusts the microphone in front of me.

"It's definitely an accurate narrative. Damien's an amazing director and I've wanted to work with him for so long. It's important when you're acting in a movie that you trust the direction it goes in, ya know? Damien's so lovely, he made us all feel at ease. I loved the script when I first read it. It was witty, sharp, and dark in places, but we had so much fun filming and preparing for it! I think it's definitely one of my favourite films I've worked on in my career so far!"

She laughs in an over-the-top fashion and I'm inwardly rolling my eyes.

"Wow! We can't wait to see the movie! How did you prepare for the movie? Rumour has it you went on tour with Rancid Vengeance, how was that?"

Nick subtly brushes my arm, taking the lead in answering the question.

"It was great! I've known those rascals for quite a number of years! I consider them close friends! It's always an adventure and a total experience that's for sure! They're so professional, they love what they do, and it was fun going along for the ride! They taught us a lot and we can't praise them enough!"

Nick answers enthusiastically and I'm grateful for his intervention. Juliet nods and seems happy with our answers.

"Thank you so much! I've been joined by Raleigh Storm and Nick Slade here at the premiere of Rocked!"

We both nod curtly, and I let out the breath I didn't realise I was holding.

"Breathe, love. Fuck me, I need a drink!"

We both laugh, as the cameras continue to flash wildly. We make our way, inside the Odeon Theatre, in the heart of London's Leicester Square. Nick and I are posing for more pictures, that's when I spot him, Brody Hart.

He is wearing a classic black and white pinstripe suit, with a white vest underneath. He teams it with a wide rimmed black fedora and mirrored aviator sunglasses. I'm quickly learning that his unique style is just another part of him I'm discovering. He poses for the paparazzi, as if it's second nature to him. He's chewing gum and casually standing with one hand tucked in his pocket. He's playing up to the cameras, engaging with the fans and acting the cool, playful, and rebellious rock star, that the press describes him as. It's moments like these I treasure. He takes off his sunglasses and finds my eyes across the crowds of people, occasionally giving me a subtle wink, or a casual smirk. This is the Brody I have fallen hopelessly in love with.

I make my way towards him, and looks me up and down, checking me out.

"Wow! Fuck me, you look knockout, kitten," he compliments, both of us aware that the spotlight is on us.

The press and paparazzi watching and scrutinising our every move.

"Let's give them a picture!"

He smirks, playfully pulling me to him. I turn side on into him, deliberately pressing my breasts to him and I swear I hear him growl. I chuckle softly, as he wraps his arm around me, the flashes firing continuously, causing my head to throb. He buries his head in my neck.

"Fuck, you smell good, I've missed you so much," he breathes.

"You literally saw me this morning!"

We both laugh easily, acutely aware of the attention we're attracting.

"You do realise the press are eating your PDA up with a fucking spoon?" I whisper wryly, as he presses a kiss to my cheek.

"Fuck 'em!" he says cheekily as he bows elaborately in front of me and whisks me off into the large auditorium.

He is magnetic and every morning waking up next to him, I find myself falling more in love with him. With every day that passes, he's showing me more and more facets of himself and I'm enjoying every single moment.

***

After the preview screening of 'Rocked', we head to the after-show party at Neon Nights. It's a who's who of the celebrity world with music, TV, and film stars alike in attendance, it's quite the gathering. I'm sipping my glass of champagne, my stomach still roiling from earlier. Liv and Jensen come over to where I am standing.

"Oh my God, Rae! That was amazing! I'm well jel' of you getting to work with Nick Slade! Hottie alert!"

Jensen rolls his eyes at her theatrics and I laugh. He leans in to kiss me on the cheek.

"Hey Rae! Kudos on the film, it was really great!" he says in his deep Texan timbre.

Jensen Starr is my best friends fiancé, and he's a genuine guy. Jensen is a billionaire world class, F1 racing driver. He drives for Starr Inc. which he owns and he's one of the hottest and most talented drivers hailing from Austin, Texas. At thirty-four years old, he's one of the best drivers of our time, rivalling Michael Schumacher, Max Verstappen and Lando Norris, with a string of pole positions and world lap records under his belt.

He is over six feet tall, he has green eyes, light brown hair styled into messy spikes and only he can rock a burgundy suit, with a white shirt, black braces, and a matching burgundy dickie bow. He and Liv complement each other and together they make a stunning couple.

"Sooo! I want all the gossip on you and the rock star!" Jensen laughs low and hoarsely.

"There's nothing much to tell!" I say coyly, and he nods.

"Right, of course there isn't!"

He says wryly in his rich All-American accent, I shift my gaze to the floor and Liv brushes my arm reassuringly.

"Don't listen to him, babe, Jensen stop winding her up!"

She chastises him and he rewards her with a teasing pinch of her arse. I giggle at their familiar camaraderie and at that moment, we are joined by Brody. He casually slings his arm around me, and I melt into his side.

"Ah, the best friend?" Brody says with a smirk, and Liv cocks her perfectly plucked eyebrow.

"Ah, the boyfriend?" she laughs wryly.

"Nice to see you again, this is my fiancé Jensen."

Brody nods and reaches out to shake his hand. Jensen takes it politely and I can see in their eyes that they are silently sizing each other up.

"Pleased to meet you, mate," Brody says with that cheeky smile I have become accustomed to.

"Likewise," Jensen says coolly, and I see Liv stiffen as her eyes wander to the other side of the room.

I turn around to see what's caught her attention and my eyes land on Carter. *Oh fuck, fuck, fuck, please God, not here, not now.* Brody turns to see what has me spooked and I feel every part of his body tense. He clenches his fists at his sides, and I grip his bicep in warning.

"Take me home, Brody," I blurt out, but he laughs bitterly.

"Fuck that, kitten, this is your night and I for one am not going to let that piece of shit ruin it for you, I'll escort him out myself if I have to, but he's coming nowhere fucking near you, not on my fucking watch," he grits out, and I can feel the tension in his entire body.

A visceral fear descends through my body and I'm frozen to the spot. I can't speak, visions of that night flashing before my eyes, reminding me of how weak I was for not fighting him off, that somehow it was all my fault.

"Breathe, kitten."

He leans in close, whispering in my ear. He's so close I feel his breath on my cheek and out of the corner of my eye I see Liv regarding the situation unfolding in front of her with careful, narrow eyes.

"Rae?"

I barely hear her over the whooshing in my ears, Brody's soft, calming words and the comforting feel of him stroking my hand.

"Do you want to tell me what's going on?" Liv asks impatiently, and Brody flashes her a warning look.

With everything going on, this past few weeks, me and Liv haven't had a chance to catch up. She doesn't yet know the full extent of my ordeal with Carter. I flinch violently as I hear the sound of Carter laughing loudly and obnoxiously, obviously trying to get a rise out of Brody. I grip his thick bicep harder, digging my nails into his flesh. I'm desperate for him to not cause a scene and draw attention to us, especially with the press so heavily present. Brody steps away from me for a second and I feel bereft at the loss of contact.

"I'll be back in a minute, kitten, I need to speak to Sam."

He kisses me on the forehead, and I see him head straight for Sam. I observe their brief exchange and Liv spins around.

"You and me, we're gonna' talk, Missy."

She taps her heel on the floor and Jensen laughs throatily.

"Good luck with that one, Rae."

As he turns and leaves me to handle the wrath of Olivia Rosenberg. *This isn't going to be pretty. Fuck.*

Brody

Watching him stand there without a care in the world is making my fucking blood boil. Knowing he forced himself on my girl makes me feel positively murderous. It's taking all the strength I have not to pound his fucking smug face into the ground until he stops moving. Sam follows my death glare and puts his hand on my shoulder.

"It's not worth it, man. But I get it. If that was my Peyton, then I'd rip his motherfucking throat out and hand it to him as he takes his last breath."

He says those words with utter conviction, and I don't doubt for a second that he would. He knows how unpredictable and how erratic I can be sometimes. My thought process can be irrational due to lack of sleep and the fact that my mind is constantly running at a million miles an hour. Sam of all people should understand that. We're the same, which is why we were so bad for each other back in the early days.

"I can't imagine what she went through, the thought of someone laying their hands on my girl like that, it doesn't fucking bear thinking about."

He clenches his teeth, as if to rid himself of such an awful thought and twirls his wedding ring idly around his finger. He half turns to see where Peyton is, and Nick Slade has his arm slung casually around her. They're laughing wildly, as he makes animated gestures with his other hand. Even though, they're married now I still see that hint of jealousy in his eyes, as he continues to watch.

"Have a fucking day off, man, she's wearing your ring, and it's you that's going to be sleeping next to her. Anyway, I think you're barking up the wrong tree, he'd be more interested in you than her."

I laugh and Sam cocks his pierced eyebrow, as I see Carter out of the corner of my eye leaving the main vestibule of the club. My eyes follow him, and I turn to leave as Sam grabs my arm.

"Don't do anything fucking stupid, man."

Sam's husky voice has more than a hint of warning in it and I shake my head, coolly brushing him off.

"I won't. I just want a little chat, man to man, that's all."

Sam nods curtly and I stride with purpose after him. I catch up to him, as he exits the men's toilets.

"I wondered how long it would be until we bumped into each other," he says with a hint of malice to his voice.

"Did this have something to do with you?"

He points at the fading black eye on his face, and I smirk.

"Well, you did lay your hands on something that was mine, so turnabouts fair play. You're lucky I didn't fucking kill you, you piece of shit!" I say through clenched teeth, and he cocks his eyebrow.

"Are you threatening me, Hart?"

The cocky look in his eyes and his stance, makes me think that this isn't going to be pretty.

"Oh no, it's not a fucking threat, Leonard. It's a fucking cast iron promise. You dared to lay your hands on someone that no longer belongs to you. Did you think, even for a fucking second, I'd let you just walk away from that? Without consequences?"

Carter cocks his head to the side and stands a little taller.

"I have no idea what you're talking about."

He schools his expression. Raleigh said he was a good actor; I didn't realise he was *that* good.

"You know full fucking well what I'm talking about, but if that's the way you want to play, then its game on."

As I say those words, I hear a distinct female clearing her throat. I half-turn to see Raleigh observing our confrontation. *Shit.*

Raleigh

I quietly observe their heated exchange for a few minutes, before alerting them both of my presence. *Holy fucking hotness.* Listening to him defend me so willingly and so passionately is a huge turn on for me.

"Until next time, Hart," Carter spits out, regarding me with disdain.

I try hard not to react as he casually saunters away without a care in the world. Brody is standing in front of me in a few short strides, I swallow hard and clear my throat before I speak.

"Is it wrong that I want you to fuck me right now?" I say.

My voice is dripping with allure, and he smirks cockily.

"Is it me asserting my masculinity, kitten? Is it making you wet for me?"

His voice low and seductive.

"Hmm."

I bite my lip provocatively.

"*Fuck*, you're beautiful, you know that?"

I smile shyly and he backs me against the wall, gripping the back of my head.

"Do you know what you do to me, kitten? You drive me fucking insane, every time you're near me, I want to bury my cock so deep into you that never forget what it feels like. I want to smear your lipstick and I want the neighbours to know who you fucking belong to."

I crash my lips urgently to his and I squeeze the back of his neck. I can't get enough of this man.

"Meet me in the corridor in a five minutes?"

He makes it clear that it's not a question and more a demand. I nod in agreement, as I walk back into the main vestibule of the club.

"Having fun, love?" Nick asks as he approaches me, kissing me affectionately on the cheek.

"You and Hart, it's fucking sickening! You're definitely going to be front page news tomorrow! Congrats, I'm happy for you both, he's a wild one, but I'm sure you can tame him, just like Peyton tamed Sam."

Nick cocks his head to the side, gesturing towards Sam and Peyton. Sam is dressed in black skinny jeans, black Doc Marten boots, a David Bowie t-shirt and a black blazer with the sleeves rolled up to reveal his thick, corded tattooed arms. His hair is styled into his signature spikes. He has his arm wrapped protectively around her shoulder. She is wearing a black floor length floaty gown, with gold skulls all over. She is wearing black Doc Marten boots with gold, glitter stars all over and matching gold accessories. Her dark hair with electric blue and turquoise flashes is perfectly tousled on one side and shaved on the other side. She looks every bit the rock stars wife.

I observe them and the chemistry between them is obvious. The way he looks at her as if she's the only woman he's laid eyes on. *It's the way Brody looks at me, yet he still won't admit he loves me back.*

"Sam Newbolt! Stop!"

He laughs heartily and I find myself smiling too.

"Stop trying to dazzle me, you handsome bastard!"

He cocks his pierced eyebrow, and she blushes an adorable shade of pink.

"Do I dazzle you, angel? Even after all this time?" he rasps, and I can't help feeling more than a little jealous of their perfect relationship. It seems so easy and carefree.

"I need some air," I say softly, and Nick cocks his eyebrow.

"I know what kind of air you need, you filthy bitch!"

Nick laughs dirtily and I roll my eyes at his flamboyant personality. I head out into the dimly lit corridor and find Brody waiting. I observe him for a moment, taking every inch of him in and committing him to memory. He's leaning against the wall with his hand tucked casually in his pocket, looking every inch the bad boy rocker. He looks delicious and I lick my lips at the sight of him. I walk further towards him, clearing my throat, letting him know I'm near and he cocks his eyebrow.

"*Fuck,* you're a sight to behold, Storm."

He offers me his hand and I accept it willingly. He leads me down the corridor and unlocks a door with a key. I look at him curiously and he winks.

"Perks of knowing the owner! He said we could use his office."

I nod and follow him inside, as he locks the door behind him.

"We won't be disturbed, kitten," he says seductively, stalking towards me until the backs of my legs collide with desk.

He tips my chin up to face him, pressing his lips to mine. The kiss becoming more desperate, as if he is starved for me. He lifts me up easily, perching me on the edge of desk, before briefly pulling our mouths apart.

"Do you want me?" he rasps low in his throat and runs his hand up my leg, his lips never leaving mine.

"*Fuck,* I want you."

I throw my head back, as he edges closer to my pussy. He slides my knickers to the side, swiping his long, calloused finger through my wetness.

"Jesus, you're fucking soaked, I knew you were wet for me, kitten. I've had a hard on all night, I need to be inside you," he whispers.

My body instantly responding to his touch. He rubs my pussy in deliberate circles, and I writhe with pleasure, trapping my lip between my teeth.

"*Fuck!*" I gasp.

"Do you like that?"

I nod wordlessly and he unzips his trousers, releasing his already solid cock. His cock never fails to amaze me, the vibrant, colourful snake wrapped around the length and the piercing through the bell-shaped head. My nipples are still swollen nubs of aching desire, my pussy is oozing moisture. I want him to fuck me hard. His eyes turn smoky with pure lust as he starts to stroke himself. Seconds later, I feel him pressing against me, the tip of his hard cock nudging my wet opening and vaguely aware he's not wearing a condom, not for the first time, but I'm too caught up in the moment to care. All I want is Brody Lennon Hart, I want all of him, any which way I could get him.

He rams his way into my tight channel and begins shamelessly pumping into me.

"Tell me you're mine, kitten," he demands roughly.

"I'm yours, Brody, all yours, only yours," I moan blissfully as he thrusts harder, his breath coming in harsh rasps.

"Ah, fuck, kitten, you're gonna' make me come so hard," he pants as I feel the heat gathering inside me, bunching up and then unravelling until I feel like I'm going to explode.

Hot rivers of pleasure flow through my veins, like molten lava and I moan incoherently.

"OH GOD!"

I can feel the hot bloom of pleasure expanding within me, swelling, igniting until it flows along my nerves and through my entire body. It was like I was having an out-of-body experience. It flows through my arms and legs, to the tips of my fingers and toes.

"OH FUCK, BRODY!" I moan, arching my back as I come hard, spread over the desk, and shuddering with pleasure. Wave after wave of my orgasm crest through every inch of my body. His release isn't far behind mine.

"OH, JESUS FUCKING CHRIST! FUCCKKK!" he roars as I feel his hot seed coating my insides.

Our bodies tremble with tiny aftershocks of our lovemaking and I'm lying across the desk spent and satiated. He pulls me upright, nudging my legs open, he presses his forehead to mine and cups my face in his hands.

"Fuck, you know you slay me, kitten, every time I'm near you, fuck...I..."

My stomach fills with butterflies and flip flops at his sweet words, as he edges closer, squeezing his eyes shut briefly. I wordlessly will him to continue, is this the moment where Brody Hart finally admits his feelings for me? *A girl can only hope.*

28

Brody

She wordlessly wills me to continue, but I can't. My words get trapped in my throat and I'm fully aware I probably look like a gormless fucking guppy fish my mouth opening and closing. *Why can't you just admit you love her, you absolute tosser?*

"Why can't you just say you love me the way I love you? Why is it so fucking difficult?" she retorts. "I can't do this anymore, Brody, I can't."

Tears start to fall freely down her cheeks, and I have no fucking idea how to deal with crying women. I just about cope when Peyton cries, but this, this is completely new, unknown fucking territory. It scares the living shit out of me and sets my nerves on edge all at the same time.

It reminds me of my mum and how she used to use tears to manipulate me into doing whatever she asked. I squeeze my eyes shut to quell the memories that threaten my cool, calm composure and she jabs her finger in my direction.

"You're so...detached, so emotionless, heartless. It's like you don't feel anything at all..."

It feels like more of an accusation than a statement and I drop my head into my hands. *If only she fucking knew.*

"I feel everything to the nth degree, I feel too fucking much! Don't you get it? My feelings overwhelm me until I feel like I might collapse beneath them. If I close myself off, it might stop me from drowning," I admit shamefully and honestly.

Her watery gaze locks onto mine and I reach out to stroke her face tenderly. She leans into my touch and her amethyst eyes utterly captivate me and I can't look away. Demanding my attention, she presses herself closer to me and cups my face in both of her hands.

"Whether you choose to believe it, or not, you're the worst and best part of me, Raleigh. You're...everything, you're the reason I'm still walking this earth, you need to know that. You need to believe that."

I don't know how else I can tell her how I feel without actually saying the dreaded L word out loud. I walk around the desk and drop down onto the large leather office chair and sink back into it, I sigh audibly.

"I wish I'd met you before..."

I stop myself from continuing, aware of how pathetic I sound. *Get a fucking grip, Hart. Pull your big boy pants up and stop being a pussy.*

"Met me before what, babe?" she probes, and I find myself taking a deep breath before I answer.

Just tell her how you feel. Follow Ricks advice for once in your sorry fucking life.

"Before I was broken, before my light went out," I admit as she reaches for my hand. I've never been more fucking sincere in my entire life. "I want to give you the best part of me, you fucking deserve the best of me, Rae. You deserve to be treated like the fucking Queen that you are," I murmur as she moves lithely around the desk, climbs onto my lap, and straddles me, cupping my face in her hands.

"I love every single part of you, even the broken parts, Brody, because together we're whole. For years, I kept making bad decisions, kept choosing the wrong men, using my problems as a justification for my behaviour. Then I met you, you taught me that I am not my mistakes. You taught me that, I'm the woman I am now because of you."

Her eyes glisten with tears and as she says those words, I come to the sudden realisation, that she's not the same woman I met in rehab. She's strong, she's brave, and she's the woman I love and adore with every fibre of my being. I just wish I wasn't so scared to say the words out loud. What's the worst that could happen? *She could reject you, she could realise that you're not worth shit and walk away like you mean nothing. Like Lorna did.* My heart slams against my ribcage, as I desperately try to push that thought away. She presses her soft lips to mine and we momentarily lose ourselves in each other.

I have never met anyone like her before. She is beautiful, smart, funny, and she accepts me wholeheartedly for who I am on the inside and on the outside. Despite my flaws, she still loves me. Her soul is just as damaged as mine, yet we fit together perfectly. Despite her body being flecked with scars, it is a puzzle of near misses, mistakes and important life lessons, some that she would never make again. Her scars are a road map of a journey she doesn't care to repeat and as long as we're together, we won't repeat the mistakes of old. We'll make our own mistakes and we'll learn from them, we'll create our own brand of normal, together.

***

I look down at my smart watch and kiss the end of her nose.

"Look, I should go, Luke and Jack should be here by now. But I'll catch up with you in a little while and we can go back to my place and you can let me worship you a little more."

The smile she gives me in return almost puts me on my arse.

"I'll look forward to it, handsome."

In that moment, I know wholeheartedly that I'm in love with this beautiful, brave woman. I get up from the chair and wrap her in my arms. I kiss her as if it's the last kiss we will ever share and I allow myself to get caught up in the moment, as her warmth is pressed up against me.

"You might want to leave it a few minutes before you leave."

I reluctantly pull away from her, leaving her with a wink. I open the door, striding down the corridor and down the stairs with the biggest grin on my face. As I turn the corner, near the back entrance of Neon Nights, I'm stopped in my tracks by Carter fucking Leonard. *Jesus Christ, I can't get away from this prick.*

"You just can't stay away can you, Hart. People will talk!" he mocks in a blatantly attempt to goad me.

I stalk towards him and I can't seem to restrain myself.

"If you lay your filthy fucking hands on her again, I swear to God I will rip your mother fucking throat out, Leonard, and that's a promise."

He smirks cockily and I slam him against the wall, feeling every ounce of control slowly draining from my pores.

"Do you think this is funny?" I say low and menacingly, loosening my grip on him. "That jealous streak will be the death of you, Hart; I just hope she's fucking worth it."

I feel every ounce of resolve slowly slipping away from me, but I desperately try and cling to it like a life raft, a safety net.

"Give me one good fucking reason why I shouldn't just bury you right now," I say through gritted teeth.

"Because deep down you know she's full of shit, she was gagging for it, practically offering her snatch to me on a silver fucking platter, just like old times," he says smugly, and I move closer to him.

"Don't fucking test me, Carter, I've got friends in high and low places. One word from me and I can make your life very fucking miserable."

He folds his arms and lifts his chin defiantly.

"Then I'll tell the press about your little indiscretion with Lorna Lavelle."

My blood turns to ice. *How the fuck did he know?* He chuckles.

"Walls have ears, Hart."

My eyes widen. *This is bad, very fucking bad. If Raleigh found out about me and Lorna, it would destroy her.*

"Here's how it's going to go, Hart, you're going to finish things with Raleigh, break up with her. Make it convincing, break her heart and in exchange, you buy my silence. I won't breathe a word of what I know to anyone, not the press, no one."

He makes a zipping motion across his mouth with his fingers and all I want to is tear him, limb from limb. I won't allow him to blackmail me, I won't let him have the upper hand. No one ever gets the upper hand on me, ever.

"And what, you expect me to go along with you fucking blackmailing me? You expect me to forget you raped my girl? You're fucking twisted, Leonard, you're sick in the head!" I roar, and he continues to stand in front of me smirking like the cat that got the cream. I clench my fists at my sides until my knuckles turn white and I'm trembling with burning rage. "I won't give her up, not for you, not for anyone. If you want to air my dirty laundry in public, go right ahead, just don't fucking test me, because you will lose," I annunciate the last three words.

He folds his arms across his chest and nods.

"If that's the way you want to play. I admire your bravery, or stupidity, whichever way you decide to look at it."

He grins cockily and all I want to do it smash his fucking face in until he's choking on his own teeth. He steps closer to me and even though he's tall, he's no match for my stature. He looks up at me and I cock my eyebrow.

"Tell me, exactly why is it that you continue to protect her, to defend her?" he asks with a wave of his hand.

I move forward, causing him to back up with each step I take.

"Because I love her, I love her with everything I am! I would fucking die for her; I would take a thousand bullets for her; I would sacrifice myself just to protect her. There's nothing I wouldn't do for her. She's everything to me and I won't let you take her away from me, EVER!" I admit.

He smiles and shakes his head.

"Brody, Brody, Brody, oh dear, oh dear," he says smugly.

It's taking everything I have not to rip his fucking head off his shoulders.

"Although, she was begging me to fuck her. She was gagging for my big juicy cock! She was desperate for it, telling me you didn't satisfy her the way I did! So I just had to satiate her primal needs."

As he says those words, I grit my teeth and the red mist fucking descends. With his words ringing in my ears, I smash my head into his nose as hard as I can. I only wish I could do it a billion times harder. I hear his nose crunch as my forehead makes contact, he shrieks in pain like the pathetic fucking cretin that he is, and I grab him around his throat. With a surge of adrenaline flowing through every inch of my being, I launch him towards the glowing, green sign of the fire exit.

Raleigh

My heart is hammering in my chest as I lean my head against the cool wood of the office door, which is ajar. My hand is hovering over the door knob and I know I shouldn't have, but as I was about to leave, I heard raised voices. I stood there for a few moments listening to Brody arguing with Carter and I wanted desperately to make my presence known, especially as I heard him declare his love for me.

"Because I love her, I love her with everything I am! I would fucking die for her; I would take a thousand bullets for her; I would sacrifice myself to protect her. There's nothing I wouldn't do for her. She's everything to me and I won't let you take her away from me, EVER!"

I slap my hand over my mouth to quell the sob I can feel caught in my throat and I try desperately to compose myself. *He just admitted he loves me, out loud! He might not have said it to my face, but he still said it, it's out there in the world now.* I turn, catching my reflection in the mirror above the desk we just had sex on. I look like a hot mess; I definitely look like I've just been thoroughly fucked. *Shit.* I take a few steps closer to the mirror and start to finger comb my hair. *I need to go to the ladies to freshen up.* My hair looks considerably neater than before. *It'll do.* As I make my way back towards the door, I hear Carter's words.

"Although, she was begging me to fuck her. She was gagging for my big juicy cock! She was desperate for it, telling me you didn't satisfy her the way I did! So I just had to satiate her primal needs."

As I hear him utter those disgusting words, I feel bile rise up in my throat threatening to vacate my guts all over the floor. How can he stand there and say those awful things to my boyfriend? How fucking dare he! I snatch the door open with my hand and I don't know if it's the three glasses of champagne I had before I came in here giving me the confidence to stand up to him, but I'm ready to give him a piece of my mind. I step out of the office and I see Brody's head connect with his nose, spraying blood everywhere. My stomach somersaults seeing my past and present colliding in a spectacular fashion. I stand there frozen to the spot, like a spectator looking from the outside in. As I witness Brody launch Carter out of the fire exit, I know I have to do something to stop him. *No, no, no! I can't let him do this, I just can't.* My feet kick into action and I have to find Sam, he's the only one who can stop him, he's the only one big enough to stop him. I'm practically jogging with purpose down the corridor, my feet throbbing and protesting in my heels, as I make my way back into the crowded main vestibule of the club. The music pumping and *The Weeknd's Blinding Lights* blasting through the speakers. I'm barely aware of my surroundings, but I manage to spot Sam amongst the sea of people; he's head and shoulders above the crowd and I march towards him like a woman on a mission. He's leaning casually with his back against a mirrored pillar, holding a glass of amber liquid in his hand. He smiles lazily as I approach and when he spots the look of anguish on my face, his brows knit together, and he frowns.

"Sweetheart? Is everything ok?" he rasps, sounding like he's swallowed a bag of nails.

"I..."

I can't find the words and I feel the tears threaten to spill down my cheeks. I can't let Brody get hurt because of me. Sam places his glass on a nearby table and he places both of his hands on my arms. I flinch violently as his hands connect with my arms, his eyebrows raise, and he drops his hands like I've just burnt him.

"I need you to talk to me, sweetheart, I can't help if you don't talk to me."

I take a deep breath, willing myself to find the words to explain accurately what the fuck is going on.

"Brody...he...he's...Carter...you have to stop him."

I swallow in a rush, unable to coherently string a sentence together.

"Please, Sam, you have to stop him, I'm scared he's going to get hurt," I plead, and Sam curses low in his throat.

He races out of there with renewed purpose and I'm unsure of whether to follow him, terrified of what I might witness. My feet are rooted to the spot and I can't seem to make my legs co-operate all of a sudden. *Come on Storm, pull yourself together you silly bitch.* I mentally chastise myself and I take a few calming breaths, preparing for what I could potentially witness, as I turn on my heel and head toward the exit.

Brody

"Whose laughing now you twisted cunt?" I say through gritted teeth as I punch him full in the face and watch him crumple to the floor.

He's babbling something that I don't give enough of a fuck to listen to, and I bend to pick him up, spotting a shiny red BMW i8 directly opposite us. I slam him face first into the door, then pull him back to do it again. All the while I am as silent as a ghost and I feel so fucking angry that I don't know if I'll ever be able to stop. Red hot molten rage flows through my veins and I can't focus on anything else other than the cold hard fact that I want this twat to suffer for what he's done to my girl. He has to know there are consequences to his fucking actions and even though he's got away with violating women in the past, I won't let him get away with it this time. It's time Carter Leonard paid for his filthy deeds. As I let him fall crying pathetically to the floor. He just sits there slumped against the car, blood dripping from his face. This utterly fucking vicious feeling spurs me on, I feel like I could drink lava and shit fire. I slam my foot into his crotch, and he screams in agony as I feel something give against my foot, I smile at his agony and bend a little to his level.

"You ever fucking lay your hands on her again, I will make you pay, you evil bastard," I say as I grab him by his hair and yank him to his feet.

I punch him in the gut and as he doubles over, my knee smashes into his face. *I'm enjoying this way too much.* This absolute piece of shit deserves so much more than this minor beating, I think as I pound my fists into his stupid, smug fucking face. Every modicum of self-control and every measure of anger I feel, comes spilling out like the poison inside me. All I want to do is smash the living shit out of this fucking cockroach. I can't seem to stop myself, I feel so out of control, as the shutters come down. The nauseating sounds of every blow and the spray of blood seems to encourage me to carry on. As I haul him upright, I look him square in the eye and I smash his head through the passenger window, causing the alarm to sound and glass to spray everywhere. I hear a noise behind me, I spin around with fists flying and the time that ticks by is a total blur, as I register it's Sam who's lifted me like I weigh nothing. I'm struggling against him, as he restrains me, but his death grip doesn't relent. *The man is a fucking machine.*

"BRODY! It's fucking done! Just walk away!" he roars as I sag in his hold, suddenly exhausted.

"You good?" Sam's voice softens and I nod.

He sets me down on unsteady feet and I stagger against the BMW i8 that I launched Carter into. I straighten myself out and my shoulders slump in defeat, as I push the heels of my hands into my eyes. I stand there for a few precious moments, trying to maintain a degree of calm, as I look up and register my surroundings, the pained violet eyes of Raleigh greet me. *Fuck.*

29

Brody

"Raleigh," I mutter quietly, taking in the enormity of the situation that has just unfolded.

She stares right through me, as Sam looks from her to me and back again. He tucks his hand into his pocket and hangs his head awkwardly. My problem has always been do now and face the consequences later. I have no doubt in my mind that Carter deserved every single punch I threw at him, I couldn't help myself. I won't apologise for my actions because I know deep down I was justified, but the look on her face pierces me to my very core and I'm the one who put that look in her eyes. *Fuck my life.*

"I'm sorry you had to witness that, babe," I say finally to break the eerie silence that hangs between us.

She launches herself at me, clinging to me as if her life depends on it. She buries her face into my neck.

"Thank you," she breathes, and I squeeze her a little tighter than necessary, letting her know that I feel it too.

Sam clears his throat and turns to face me.

"I've got a pretty good idea, but are you going to tell me what the fuck that was all about?" he blurts out matter-of-factly.

I puff out my cheeks exasperated, as Raleigh lets go of me and I wrap my arm around her. Unexpectedly, I feel an overwhelming emotion wash over my entire body. I swallow hard and take a few deep calming breaths to quell the onslaught of emotions that are threatening to drown me.

"I had every fucking reason to beat the shit out of him, Sam."

I raise my voice a few decibels louder than necessary.

I don't doubt for a second that Sam would have reacted the exact same way, because he's a lover not a fighter, but when it comes to Peyton and his boys, he's a warrior who would fight to the death.

"I've never felt that out of control before, it's an alien feeling to me. He dared to lay his fucking hands on someone that belongs to me! He had it coming!" I bark, jabbing my thumbs into my chest aggressively.

Raleigh flinches at my harsh tone and I pull her closer to me, planting a chaste kiss on her forehead.

"Go back inside, kitten, I'll be back in in a while I just need to talk to Sam about something?" I ask softly, and she nods, kissing me tenderly on the lips as she turns and heads back in the direction of the club.

I squeeze my eyes shut briefly and scrub my hands down my face, unable to hold back any longer.

"Do you know what it's like to walk in on someone you care deeply about trembling and sobbing in the shower covered in blood because he ex-boyfriend raped her? It destroyed me!"

Sam doesn't say anything. He has an uncanny knack of knowing the right words to say in certain situations, or when to shut up and not say anything at all.

"I can't fucking pretend anymore that I'm ok with some piece of shit shoving his cock in her by force! I can't stand it, it's all I can do to keep it from consuming me. Consuming us, I see how it affects her, she has nightmares, I see that terrified look in her eyes every time we have sex, it kills me that bit more every time, Sam and I can't, I just can't. I beat him tonight because I couldn't stand to watch him act like he did nothing, like he's the innocent party in all this because he's guilty of so many fucking things. He stood there and goaded me into it, he deserved every punch and so much more. I wanted him to suffer the way he makes her suffer on a daily basis. I would have killed him if it weren't for you, I have no doubt in my mind. I couldn't stop, I wanted to beat him until he stopped moving, I wanted to wrap my hands around his throat, while I watched the light fade from his eyes. I wanted to rid the world of another sick fucking predator who preys on women. I'd already accepted that I was going to prison for a long time, but it would have been worth it to have my girl feel safe again."

I swallow, feeling more than a little out of control. I take a deep breath and shake my head, as if to rid myself of my previous thought.

"I love her, Sam, so fucking much. Seeing her tonight, seeing the way she froze as soon as she saw him. Seeing that terrified look in her eyes broke something in me." I shudder at the devastating thought. "I don't ever want to see that look in her eyes ever again, it tore me apart."

Sam places his hand reassuringly on my arm.

"It makes me feel sick, but she can't know. She can't ever know I feel that way because it would destroy her. It would destroy us. I'm trying to be supportive; I'm trying so fucking hard. In all of the online posts and forums, none of them tell you how the partners supposed to feel, and I know it's selfish and I know I shouldn't feel this way, but it's killin' me, Sam."

That's when it hits me full force in the gut and that's when that damn fucking fortress I've spent weeks building around my heart splinters and shatters like delicate glass. I let out a strangled sob, which turns into heart rendering, gut wrenching sobs of despair and it feels good to finally let it out.

***

After my heart to heart with Sam, I spend my sleepless night going over in minute detail the events of the evening, wrapped up in my girl. We didn't have sex, both of us just content with lying silently in each other's arms. The next morning, I wake with a start to an empty bed and fifteen missed calls and five voicemails. *What the fuck.* There's a note on the bedside table and I reach over, brushing over her careful, elegant handwriting.

I've been summoned to a meeting with Damien.
Wish me luck in the lion's den!
Call you when I'm done
R x

I smile at her words, as I set about my morning routine of workout, shower, and breakfast. After I'm done, I'm standing in the kitchen bare chested, in loose grey jogging bottoms and making coffee, while I listen to the voicemails.

"Brody, it's Tate, call me when you get this, thanks, bye."

I roll my eyes at our P.R manager's message as I skip to the next.

"Brody, it's Tate, again, call me back," he snaps.

I swipe the screen to listen to the next.

"Brody, it's Tate, answer your fucking phone!"

I delete that one and skitter my phone across the marble worktop, hearing a deep throaty chuckle from the other side of the kitchen.

"You should call him back; he's doing his nut!" Sam says with an amused tone to his voice.

"He'll give himself a heart attack if he carries on like that, no wonder he's starting to go grey!"

We both laugh, as Sam's face grows serious.

"Mate, you need to call him."

I cock my eyebrow, as I look questioningly at Sam. I pick my phone up and dial Tate.

***

I've been hauled in to the office for an emergency meeting with Tate, our head of public relations. I'm sat in front of him feeling like a naughty school boy being hauled into the Headmaster's office. I'm in a daze wondering how I went from my mundane, normal morning routine to this in such a short space of time.

"I don't know if I can keep this out of the press, Brody. They're about to run the story, I tried to call in a favour, but you're clearly seen in the CCTV footage, what the fuck were you thinking! This has happened way too often! I can't keep calling in favours to defend you anymore. My reputation is on the line and it's starting to become questionable."

The defeated sound of Tate's voice fills my foggy, fucked up brain, as I try to process his words. My fight with Carter was caught on CCTV? I should have fucking known; how could I have been so stupid? *Shit, I screwed up again. He's right, what the fuck was I thinking?*

"Are you even listening to me, fuck nuts! No, of course you're fucking not! This needs to stop, when are those boys going to stop cleaning up your mess, Brody? They don't deserve you bringing them down, do you even care that you're damaging their reputations, as well as your own?"

I puff out my cheeks and let out a laboured breath, as I try to process the extent of my epic fuck up. Brawling in full view of closed-circuit TV cameras, I was naïve to even think I could have got away with this Scott free. I have to admit it wasn't my finest hour, but I have to live with the potential fallout. *Fuck.*

"When are you going to learn, that there are fucking consequences to your actions?!"

I remain silent, because I can't think of anything to say, no witty one liner, no joke, not even a quip. *Nothing.*

"Say something then, this is the perfect opportunity for you, to at least defend yourself, use the 'I was drunk, I was high' excuse, as per usual, but you and I both know you've been clean for almost six months! So, I'm out of options on that one! Bloody hell, what the fuck were you even thinking?"

Tate raises his voice a few decibels and I sigh audibly. *Quite clearly, I wasn't fucking thinking.*

"The fucking bottom line is, I don't know if I can keep this out of the press, Brody! I'm trying my hardest to stall them; but they're starting to ask more questions and they've drawn their own conclusions on this one. We need to put something in place...call it damage control. We need to issue a statement, call a press conference, anything to stop this fucking shit show!" Tate says matter-of-factly and drops his head in his hands.

"I know I fucked up again, and I'm sorry," I say genuinely.

"So, he does speak! The press don't care about sorry, they just want their fucking pound of flesh and that pound of flesh, unfortunately is yours. I don't know if I'm able spin this at this point, as much as I want to. I get that it's your reputation, but I told you, my reputation is on the line too," he repeats his earlier words, but by this point, I've had enough of him fucking talking at me.

"You're so fucking bothered about your reputation! It's not just about that anymore! How many more times can I say, I'm sorry? How many more times can I say, I fucked up? Walk a mile in my shoes, Tate, spend a day in my fucked-up head. I'm not wired like the other boys, I'm damaged! I've spent my whole life in Sam's shadow, I know I'm not perfect, but cut me some fucking slack! I had a damn good reason to beat the shit out of that fucking prick! He had it coming after what he's done!" I say with fire in my voice.

"*For fucks sake!* Spare me the pity party for one, Brody! Number one, it doesn't suit you and number two, *cut you some slack?* I've spent years cutting you some slack! How many more times are people going to cover for you?

How many more times are they going to wipe your bloody arse for you? They've hidden the fact that you were a fucking junkie for years! I know I'm supposed to be subjective, but I've sat back and watched them lie for you. *Jesus,* I've been part of that lie! Those boys are like family to me, you included, I've seen you shipped off to rehab so many times, but you've crossed the fucking line this time, Brody. Whether you had good reason or not, it was caught on CCTV, you can clearly see it's you from a mile off, you'd have to be blind not too, the guy you battered, he's blurry and you can't tell who it was, but you could be up on an assault charge if this gets out! Even I can't make that go away!" he says with venom in his usually calm voice, and I hang my head in absolute fucking shame.

What the fuck have I done?

Our discussion is interrupted by M.J entering the office. He is wearing ripped jeans, a black shirt open at the collar with the sleeves rolled up and matching black cowboy boots.

"Not interrupting anything, am I boys?" he says a little too calmly and enthusiastically. "Can I get you some coffee, tea, something stronger?" he asks as I look from M.J to Tate and we both shake our heads.

"No, thank you," I decline politely as he pushes a button on his desk phone.

"Can I get some coffee, please, precious? Yeah, milk, three sugars...thanks honey!" he says a little over zealously, which sets my nerves on edge. Tate unfolds his arms, glances briefly to the floor, and looks down at his smart watch. "I've got another meeting in twenty minutes; I should get going."

He nods curtly at M.J and looks at me.

"This isn't over, not by a long shot, Brody. I'll FaceTime you later and we can continue our... discussion, explore our options," he says abruptly and leaves the room.

M.J sits down at his desk and the creak of leather makes me turn to face him.

"Something you want to tell me, Hart?" M.J says coolly as he puts his cowboy booted feet up on his desk, resting his hands on his stomach.

"Look M.J, I know what you're going to say, and I don't know how many times I can say sorry..."

He puts his finger up to stop me.

"See, this is where we have a problem, Brody, you need to start talkin' so I can understand this fuck up a little better and none of your usual bull shit, *capiche*'?"

His Brooklyn accent becoming more prominent. I hang my head in shame and puff out my cheeks exasperated. *Fuck me, I wish I'd had the sense to stay in bed.*

***

After I received not one, but two epic dressing downs from our management team, I think to myself I must be a gluten for punishment, as I'm sitting opposite Rick. He regards me intently, his pen hovering over the page in his notebook. He crosses his leg over his knee and clicks his pen in quick succession. It no longer annoys me the way it used to, and I feel more relaxed than I've ever felt in his sessions. He looks like he's troubled and struggling to find the words. Rick never struggles with words if anything it's me that struggles with words. *Fuck me, this must be bad.*

"Look, I'm going to level with you, Brody. The last few sessions, I feel like we've been making progress, in a good way."

I nod and lean back in my chair. He's right, we have. It hasn't been a chore to attend my appointments. I no longer dread our sessions, which is a huge step forward for me. He smiles his fox-like smile, but this time, it just makes him look like he needs a shit.

"Where are you going with this, Rick?" I say defensively.

"From our previous sessions and the subjects, we've touched upon, I think you're suffering from Post-Traumatic Stress Disorder."

What the actual fuck? P.T.S.D? What the fucking fuck is he going on about?

I get up from my seat and start to pace.

"Do you want to talk about how you feel about this?" he asks, and I laugh bitterly.

"Do I want to talk about you thinking I'm some sort of shell-shocked motherfucker? The answer to that would be a resounding no! I'm not...I..."

I stop myself from continuing, because for the first time in all my thirty-four years, I'm fucking speechless. I've got not witty retort, no sarcastic comment, nothing.

As I start to process his words, I try to piece together how he came up with this conclusion. Post-Traumatic Stress Disorder is something I've read about in books and seen in films. It's not something I've ever come across in a social situation before and that's the fucking scary part. Yes I have an aversion to loud noises, I have insomnia, but I've suffered with it for years. I just put that down to the nightmares and now he's telling me I have P.T.S.D? I'm struggling to process, and it takes my messed-up brain a few moments to catch up.

"H-how did you come to that conclusion? Out of curiosity." I say quickly, terrified to hear his answer.

"You mentioned you suffer from insomnia, the nightmares, you also mentioned your recent aversion to loud noises. It's been going through my mind for a few days now since our previous session. I'm genuinely concerned for you, Brody. You've come so far, and you've managed to stay clean for six months, that's such an achievement. I'm proud of you and you should be proud of yourself. I'd hate for you to go backwards; recovery is all about moving forward. From what I've observed of you in our sessions, is you seem to avoid certain conversations and situations, which is also a contributing factor. Now, I'm no expert and I'm not qualified in P.T.S.D counselling, so I want to refer you to a colleague of mine, Allegra Gutiérrez, who specialises in patients diagnosed with P.T.S.D. She'll give you a proper diagnosis, talk about possible medication and she'll potentially take over our sessions."

What the fuck? I start to pace again and run a trembling hand through my short hair. My heart starts to race, my chest begins to tighten, and my breaths come in short, sharp, laboured pants. I stumble into Rick's desk and my whole world becomes dark. *Fuck me, not again.*

***

"Brody? Brody, my name's Megan, can you hear me?" the female paramedic says softly as she shakes me gently.

I struggle to focus on my surroundings and I groggily turn my head to see Lenny having a hushed conversation with Rick in the corner of the room. *What the fuck?* I start to tremble and my vision blurs, as I try to sit up, but the paramedic tries to encourage me to stay still.

"Hey! Hey! Brody, it's going to be ok, I need you to stay calm for me, can you do that? You passed out, your counsellor said it was because you were discussing a particular emotional trauma? Your anxiety could possibly be the trigger, Mr Delaney said it's not the first time this has happened?"

My tongue feels almost too big for my mouth and I can't speak. I'm struck dumb at the sudden turn of events and I feel myself start to become damp with sweat.

"*Jesus,* you look like death, what trouble have you got yourself in this time, boy?"

Lenny's gruff voice cuts through my hazy thoughts and my head is spinning. I'm so disconnected from my mind and my body.

"Len?"

I'm fully aware my voice sounds thick with unshed tears and I feel like I'm losing control.

"Give us a minute, love?" Len asks the paramedic with a wink and she nods curtly, leaving us to it. He sits down on the floor next to me.

"It's alright, son, everything's going to be just fine," he says softly, and I shake my head.

"I can't do this anymore, Len, I can't."

He reaches for my hand and I let him, his touch somehow grounding me.

"Rick filled me in on what happened before you passed out, it's nothing to be ashamed of, son. You're stronger than that, you've been clean for six months, that's a huge achievement in itself and I'm so damn proud of you. You've got yourself a lovely girl, you get to perform to thousands of fans every night, you're living the dream," he tries to reassure, me and I shake my head again.

"It's not enough, it will never be enough. You don't understand! I'll never be enough!" I yell as I jab my forefingers carelessly into my temples, relishing in the sharp pain that follows.

I allow the torrent of tears to flow free and I sob harder than I've ever sobbed before, the events of the past few months bombarding my mind and bulldozing every corner of my brain. I feel my breathing start to quicken and the familiar tightening in my chest. The paramedic rushes to my side and I'm shaking uncontrollably.

"I can't-I-I can't fucking...breathe."

I wheeze, clawing at my throat, trying desperately to force precious air into my lungs.

"Brody, I need you to breathe for me."

I can't focus on anything else but the events of last night, Raleigh, Carter and the whole sorry mess that I created with Lorna. The weight feels like it's bearing down and it will crush me where I sit if I let it. My head spins, as I succumb to the blackness once more.

30

Raleigh

The thought that is floating around my brain as I'm standing outside Damien Valentine's office, more terrified than I've ever been, is how the fuck did this happen? I'm all sorts of edgy, biting my nails, twirling my ring around my finger and I feel so out of control, it's not even funny. I'm so far out of my comfort zone, that I'm considering just turning back around the way I came and just going to get totally wasted.

I'd rather be anywhere else than here at this moment in time, I'm exhausted. I spent the night in Brody's arms, more content than I'd ever been and this morning I got a call from Paul summoning me to a meeting with Damien. I'm about to receive a dressing down from the director of my new movie. *Happy Friday to me!* He warned me when we first met that his bark was worse than his bite and I still don't think I'm fully prepared for it. I was full of confidence when I received a standing ovation at last nights' premiere, and I was optimistic that my career was no longer in the gutter. *From the gutter to the stars, that's how the saying goes isn't it?*

My thoughts are interrupted by Damien's assistant's nasally, shrill voice.

"Miss Storm, Mr Valentine is ready for you now."

She smiles and even though I've met her a handful of times, she still can't hide her disdain for me. I stand up as Damien approaches, he's dressed casually today in a pair of black jogging bottoms, a white v-neck t-shirt, and a pair of black and blue Skechers. His short hair is shaved closed to his head and a five o'clock shadow graces his chin. He has a large cup of Starbucks finest in his hand. *Fuck me, I'd give anything for one of those right now.*

"Raleigh," he greets me with a curt nod of his head.

Fuck this is going to be worse than I thought. I smile vaguely, desperately trying not to burst into tears. *You can do this, Storm.* He cocks his head, gesturing for me to step into his office. I take a deep breath and follow him in, closing the door with a loud click behind me. I notice the initials *D.V,* in flowing, script letters etched into the glass has been replaced with a plain frosted glass door. He smiles.

"It was time for a change, and it was pretentious as fuck!" he remarks drolly.

"Please, take a seat, Raleigh, I haven't dragged you here for a lecture, don't look so worried."

He looks amused and I let out the breath I didn't realise I was holding. I put my hand to my chest, and that's when it happens. I burst into uncontrollable floods of tears. *Fucking great.*

Damien takes a tissue from the box on his desk and passes it to me. I take it, sniffing rather ungracefully and unladylike.

"Thank you, I'm sorry," I sob as Damien waves his hand.

"You blatantly ignored everything I told you about Brody Hart, I warned you, but you chose to disregard that warning. Now, I'm not going to make a big deal out of it, that's not my style, but hey, sales of the movie are up by sixty-two percent, publicity is key in this business, sweetheart. It's mutually beneficial, for both of us. We've got some press conferences and interviews lined up; I'll forward the details to Paul. If you could just do one thing for me, dodge the questions about the rock star for now, I'll let our publicist handle that. Make the focus purely on the movie."

I nod shamefully, as my stomach roils. I swallow hard and vomit all over the floor of Damien's office. *Fuck my life.*

***

After my meeting with Damien, Cliff drove me home. I spent the whole journey in complete silence and stuck inside my own head. I couldn't focus on anything else but the sickening sounds of Brody's fists connecting with Carter's body. The loud pounding of flesh striking flesh, the spray of crimson as it flew from Carter's mouth as if in slow motion. I felt like I was watching a scene from a movie and even though I knew I should look away; I couldn't help but keep my eyes fixed on the scene playing out in front of me. At that moment, I had no doubt in my mind that Brody loved me just as much as I loved him. He just couldn't say it out loud and in that window of time, I made peace with it and I accepted it. My thoughts are interrupted by Cliff's concerned timbre.

"We're here, love, are you sure you're ok? You haven't said a word since I picked you up?"

I paint on a smile and look up, catching his gaze in the interior mirror.

"I'm good thanks, Cliff, it's just been an eventful morning, that's all. I'm fine honestly."

He cocks his eyebrow as if he calls bullshit on everything I've just said. He pulls to a stop at the curb, steps out of the car, comes around to my side to help me out, as a photographer leaps out of nowhere, flashing his camera in my face. Cliff nudges him forcefully out of the way with a growl and I smile my thanks, as he sees me inside the building.

"Call me if you need me, sweetheart, I'm never far away."

He leaves with a wink as I head up to my apartment, nodding my polite greeting to Aaron on the way through the foyer. I kick my shoes off, shut the door with a click behind me and my exhausted body crumples to the floor. I struggle to process the events leading up to today and I can't comprehend the enormity of it all.

With every emotion barrelling through my exhausted body, I manage to get to my feet, and head into the bathroom. Closing the door with a click behind me and flipping the lock, I hit the play button with the remote control and the distinct sound of Johnny Cash, singing about how he can make me hurt, fills my ears. I open the bathroom cabinet and reach inside the small make-up bag I keep hidden at the back. I take my place on the floor, leaning up against the side of the bath and take out a razor blade. My hand shakes, as the blade makes its first slice into my skin. A feeling of silent relief washes over me and the euphoria of the bite of pain that follows, allows the endorphins to spread through my entire body, making me feel high. Like a drug, the effect soon wears off, and the need to mark my skin again overwhelms me and takes over my very being. The second slash, I go deeper until the crimson of my own blood, surges like a stream down my arm. I moan aloud, as the feeling rushes through me like nothing I've ever felt before. I'm hooked, I never want to stop feeling this fucking high, this relief, is like no chemical high I've ever felt, it's euphoric, it's...addictive.

As I make the next careless cut, I all of a sudden feel nothing. Gone, is the feeling of euphoria, gone is the relief. With the fourth and fifth slice, comes the shame, the bitter sting of tears, the tennis ball size lump that forms in my throat, threatening my composure. The sixth and seventh slice, the feeling of dread settles itself firmly in my gut and my stomach roils. I squeeze my eyes shut and I feel like I'm going to either throw up or pass out. The contrast of the dark red of my blood on my pale skin, doesn't stir anything inside of me. *I'm numb to it all.*

I lean my head back against the wall and a tear slips down my cheek. The dam keeping my tears at bay, seemingly snaps and the sound that escapes from me, sounds like a mortally wounded animal. I continue to audaciously hack at my skin, and the blood drips to form a pool on the floor at my side. I am startled by the sound of Brody shaking the door handle.

"Raleigh, open the door."

I recklessly make another haphazard slash; and I let out a scream, as the pain becomes almost too much for my body to bare. He rattles the door handle again.

"Raleigh!"

I sob hard, as my vision blurs and the endless flow of blood down my arm causes my head to spin.

"Get away from the door, Raleigh, I'm gonna break it down if you don't open it, so help me fucking God!" he bellows impatiently and a few short seconds later, Brody's foot connects with the door, splintering the wood and sending the door hurtling against the wall with a thud.

The look in his eyes breaks my fucking heart as he gets down on his knees next to me, causing me to sob harder.

"Fuck, Raleigh," he whispers softly, the pain in his voice evident.

"I'm sorry, I'm sorry, I'm so sorry," I chant softly as my vision becomes fuzzy, and my world is plunged into darkness.

Brody

Of all the situations I've found myself in over the years, this has to be the most difficult and definitely the most fucked up. As I hold the woman I have fallen hopelessly in love with, in my arms, I try desperately to stop the bleeding, by putting pressure on her forearm. I don't care that I'm covered in her blood, I just want her to be ok. *Please let her be ok.*

"What the fuck have you done, kitten?" I ask to an empty room.

I get that her ex dared to lay his fucking hands on her, and I get more than most, but why she would resort back to old habits when the going gets tough. Why couldn't she have just talked to me, instead of marring her beautiful body?

"Raleigh, it's me. Come on, baby, talk to me," I say softly while stroking her face tenderly.

I pull my phone out of my pocket; I need to call an ambulance. She's losing consciousness due to blood loss, and by the look of the cuts on her arm, she needs stitches. I run my finger across the jagged cuts and my heart slams against my ribcage. *Fuck, that's new, I've never felt that before.*

"Brody," she whispers and as she looks up at me, her eyes so sad and desolate. She destroys my fucking soul.

"It's going to be alright, kitten, I promise."

I try to smile, as a gesture of reassurance, but she starts to sob softly.

"Brody, it hurts."

I stroke her cheek and take her hand in mine.

"I know, I know it does, it's gonna' be ok. Shhh, I've got you, everything's gonna' be just fine."

As I'm saying the words, I'm not even sure I believe them.

***

The beauty of having a doctor in the family helps immensely when found in situations like this one. As soon as I dialled Jay's number and she answered after less than three rings, her voice instantly comforted me, and I knew everything was going to be ok.

"Hello, my darlin', to what do I owe this pleasure?"

I chuckle softly at her greeting.

"You know me too well, Jay."

She laughs melodically. "That I do, darlin', now come on, out with it, what trouble have you got yourself into this time?"

I pause for a few seconds, as I think how to explain this fucked up chain of events.

"There's this girl I'm dating and..."

She stops me mid-sentence.

"This is a new one, a girl you're dating? Why am I always the last to know?"

It's my turn to laugh.

"Believe me, no one is more shocked than me, Jay, it just kind of...happened."

She listens raptly.

"We met in rehab, she's a recovering self-harmer, her ex...he-raped her and she's injured herself," I say in a rush, and she gasps.

"I hope that motherfucker has been dealt with, darlin'. If not, I'll cut his fucking balls off myself, with that rusty scalpel I've been holding onto."

I laugh at her obstinacy. She never fails to make me chuckle with her Mama Bear mentality.

"Of course, do not doubt that he's been dealt with. Lenny took care of it. Look, Jay..."

Before I can finish my sentence, she jumps in.

"Bring her to me, I'll patch her up, how bad is it?"

I look at her lying on the bathroom floor, with her head in my lap. "Pretty bad, Jay, she's lost a lot of blood and I think she needs stitches."

Jay clears her throat, as I stroke Raleigh's hair away from her face.

"Ok, bring her to me, I'll fix her up, darlin'."

I breathe a sigh of relief. "Thank you so much."

"You ain't got to thank me. I'd do anything for you boys, you're family," she says sincerely, and I don't doubt that for one second.

"Bring your girl to me, Jude will meet you at the front door and I'll take care of the rest. Drive safe and I'll see you soon."

She hangs up before I get the chance to say goodbye. I pocket my phone and scoop Raleigh up in my arms. I catch sight of myself in the mirror, I'm covered in her blood and my face is still pale from my earlier episode.

I can't help but let my mind wander, as I head down the fire escape with her in my arms, desperate not to be seen by the paparazzi. I start to think that addiction is a powerful thing. Once it gets a hold of you, it refuses to let go. I once asked Rick if two people with addiction could hold down a healthy relationship and he told me in no uncertain terms that yes they could, as long as long as they trusted each other and were one hundred percent open and honest about their feelings. As I look down at Raleigh with blood trickling down her arm, I'm not sure I believe him, not one fucking bit.

31

Brody

I make the fifteen minute journey to Jay's medical practice, in Beckenham, with one hand on the wheel of my burnt orange Lamborgini Urus and one hand stroking Raleigh's hair, comforting her and letting her know I was there for her. As I pull up at the curb, I am greeted by Jax's dad, Jude. He reminds me of an older version of his son, with shoulder-length blonde hair and crinkles in the corner of his eyes. *He looks like he should be in an eighties hair band.*

"Brody."

He nods and I open the passenger door, carefully scooping Raleigh up into my arms. She lost consciousness from blood loss on the journey here. My nerves are on edge, as I stride up to the door with purpose and head inside. Jay greets me, wearing purple scrubs and her hair piled up on top of her head.

"Fuckin' hell, darlin'," she says softly as she leads me down a short corridor and into a small side room.

Inside there is a hospital bed and beside it is a metal table. I put Raleigh down on the bed and I sink down to the floor, crumbling under the pressure of finding my girlfriend carelessly hacking at her wrists and covered in blood. *So much fucking blood it brings back unwanted memories of that day, but I can't allow myself to dwell on that right now.* Jay sets to work on her and I cover my face with both of my hands, allowing the true extent of the day to sink in.

***

I'm sitting on the floor in the corridor with my head leaning against the wall when I hear the familiar 'click, click' of heels across the floor.

"She's gonna' be just fine, sweetheart, I've managed to stop the bleeding and I've stitched her up. Her arm is a fucking mess. I've sedated her and given her something for the pain, she'll be sore for a few days, but she'll be ok," Jay says matter-of-factly, and I puff out my cheeks as she sits down the floor next to me.

She links her arm through mine and leans her head on my shoulder.

"Wanna' talk about it? You look like death by the way!"

I chuckle softly at her brutal honesty. "Love you too, Jay!"

She laughs.

"The whole thing is just a fucking mess," I admit. "I-I passed out at my therapy session this morning. I got taken to the hospital."

Jay unlinks her arm from mine and looks me in the eye.

"You're exhausted, it was only a matter of time before your body told you enough is enough."

I smirk.

"Is that your subtle way of saying I told you so?"

She cocks her perfectly plucked eyebrow. "You need to start looking after yourself properly, Brody Lennon Hart."

I know I'm in trouble when she uses my full name. I squeeze my eyes shut briefly and she reaches for my hand.

"Why are you not resting?"

I roll my eyes.

"Do not roll your fucking eyes at me! You might not be my son biologically, but I love you, you can't keep doing this to yourself, please tell me you didn't discharge yourself?" she asks, and it sounds more like an accusation than a question.

"I needed to see my girl." I shrug nonchalantly. "It's lucky I did, I can't think about what would have happened if I was ten minutes later. It doesn't bear thinking about."

A chill works its way down my spine at the thought, as she moves closer to me and wraps her arm around me.

"You've fallen in love with her, haven't you?"

I nod and lean my head down on her shoulder, the day suddenly catching up with me. *Fuck me, I'm exhausted.*

"I love her so fucking much, Jay, I can't imagine my life without her in it. Neither of us are perfect, far from it, but we just fit. She's everything and I don't fucking deserve her. I've ruined everything, I battered the shit out of her ex at the premiere of her movie last night and I've created a nightmare for our P.R guy. He gave me a dressing down this morning, so I'm kind of avoiding him right now."

She laughs.

"Keeping them on their toes, eh? Fuck 'em!"

I smile. "I'm terrified I'll need her the way Sam needs Peyton, I've never needed anyone, Jay, ever! This is fucking alien to me and I don't know how to deal with it. I don't do romance, I don't do exclusivity, I don't do the girlfriend thing! It's been so long I've forgotten what it's like to be with someone for more than one night. I'm scared shitless that she's going to realise what a fuck up I am and she's going to run screaming in the other direction," I babble shamefully.

"Now you listen to me, and you better listen good! You deserve to be happy, sweetheart, more than anything. You learn from your mistakes and so fucking what if you're terrified, that's what love does! It's supposed to scare you! It wouldn't be real if it didn't. And that girl in there, something tells me that she feels the same too."

I squeeze my eyes shut briefly.

"Then why can't I admit that I love her too, out loud? Everytime I feel like I want to say it, the words get caught in my throat and I just shut down! We've had so many arguments and disagreements about it. She just desperately wants to hear it, but I can't say it! It's not that I don't feel it because I do! So fucking much, it causes my chest to ache, I feel too much when I'm with her and I've never felt like this about anyone. My mum told me once that I'd never fall in love because I was too much like her, a free spirit."

Jay scoffs and I cock my eyebrow at her, trying to hide my smirk. Jay has an extremely strong opinion when it comes to my mum.

"Free spirit isn't a phrase I'd use to describe your mum, darlin'," she says drolly as I pull her closer to me.

I let her comfort me, the way my mum should have.

Raleigh

My eyes flutter open and I find myself in an unfamiliar environment. A feeling of dread settles itself in my gut like a lead weight and I feel like I need to throw up. I swallow it down and take a few deep breaths, in and out, until the feeling dissipates. The door is ajar and bright fluorescent light from outside illuminates the room. I hear voices from outside, a male voice which I instantly recognise as Brody. I'd recognise his voice anywhere. I don't recognise the soft female voice, it seems unfamiliar to me. *Where am I?* My heartbeat starts to quicken and as I go to move, my arm throbs. *Fuck, that hurts.* Then the vivid memory of today's events flood my foggy brain. *The razor blade, the pain, the blood, so much blood.*

"*Tell her how you feel, darlin', you might surprise yourself how easy it comes out.*"

I hear the female say. *What's she talking about? Who is this woman? Is she yet another person who knows Brody better than I do?* My attention focuses on their conversation and I'm aware that I'm eavesdropping, but I can't help listening to what comes next.

"*I need to admit it to myself first and I need to accept it. She told me she loved me and I freaked the fuck out like a total idiot! I've been in love before and she rejected me like I meant nothing! I tried to kill the part of myself that still wanted to save our relationship, even after she walked away while I was drowning in a sea of white powder and addiction. I won't allow that to happen again, the only other woman I've ever loved, I ended up in fucking rehab because I couldn't handle the way she rejected me so cruelly. I felt like I was that scared ten-year-old boy again, I felt so alone and so fucking angry! I can't put myself through that again. I won't. I won't survive it next time.*"

Hearing the obvious pain in his voice causes my heart to slam against my ribcage. *Who is he talking about? Is he talking about the married woman he was seeing?*

"That girl was a fucking fool, sweetheart."

I listen to their idle chatter for a few minutes longer, as I take in my surroundings. It's quite modern and spacious for a hospital room. There's a large navy suede chair in the corner, an array of abstract artwork adorns

299

the walls, it reminds me of a plush hotel room. On the wall is a plasma TV screen, and the décor is all pale pastels with clean lines, which are elegant and calming all at the same time. The large square window has an open light grey blind on it and the floor matches the colour of the blind.

"I was numb to it all when I was using, but since I've been clean and sober, I feel everything, and I can't deal with it. My feelings overwhelm me. I've spent so long going over and over it with my therapist and I still can't wrap my head around it. I'm fucking exhausted, Jay. I mean really exhausted, I'm lucky if I get an hour a night these days, I think today was my body telling me enough is enough."

He actually sounds exhausted and I'm curious about what he means. *Has something happened? Why didn't he tell me? Because you were too busy opening a vein and bleeding half to death, that's why, you selfish bitch.*

"I can prescribe you some sleeping pills, a low dose to start if that's what you want, sweetheart, just say the word."

I'm not sure who this woman is, but from what I've heard of their conversation they're close and she seems kind. She cares about him and I feel a sudden pang of jealousy.

"I don't want to rely on sleeping pills and I don't need any more addictions in my life, Jay. I'm a recovering drug addict, for fucks sake, I'd just be replacing one with another."

There's a pause and I see a shadow in the doorway, that's when I catch sight of him. He looks pale and dishevelled, but still distinctly handsome. His jeans are ripped, and he's wearing a distressed grey Linkin Park t-shirt, which showcases his tattooed muscles and he's wearing those sexy as hell biker boots that I love so much. He's a sight to beholden.

"Kitten."

My stomach flip flops at the way he says my pet name and goosebumps erupt on my arms.

"Thank fuck you're ok, you scared the absolute shit out of me."

His voice sounds depleted and so full of emotion, as he steps into the room almost cautiously, followed by the woman he was talking to. She's beautiful, she is a few inches shorter than Brody, with her blonde hair is piled up haphazardly on top of her head. She is wearing purple scrubs and white

trainers, she has deep hazel eyes and the wrinkles around her eyes tell me that she laughs a lot.

"Hello, sweetheart, I'm Jamie-Leigh Chase, I'm Jackson's mum," she introduces herself brightly, and I find myself smiling right along with her.

"I'm Raleigh," I say, barely audible, as she busies herself checking my vitals, humming softly at intervals.

"How are you feeling, darlin'?" she asks with a genuine smile, and I find myself nodding and smiling right along with her.

She's infectious and as I observe her a little more, I start to piece together their relationship. She must be one of the mother figures he talked about in our previous conversations.

"Ok, I think, just a bit sore."

She smiles sympathetically, stroking my hand gently and I let her, feeling oddly comforted by it.

"It will be a bit sore for a few weeks, I stitched you up as best as I could and the scarring will be minimal if you take good care of it."

I smile in return, not knowing what to say, so I don't say anything at all, as Brody starts to pace the floor impatiently. He does that when he's feeling particularly anxious, along with the squeezing of the back of his neck, which he does at frequent intervals.

"Don't ever fucking do that to me again!" he bites out sharply, and I flinch at his harsh tone.

Jamie-Leigh continues to busy herself checking me over, ignoring his outburst, as he stops pacing. He stands in the middle of the room and stares up at the ceiling.

"I can't fucking do this! I just can't! I'm sorry."

He practically runs out of the room without another word, before I get the chance to protest and that's when the tears come. Jamie stays quiet for a few minutes and I take a few deep, calming breaths to try to compose myself.

"I'm sorry," I say quietly, and I wonder if she heard me.

As I look up from beneath my lashes, she shakes her head.

"Don't be sorry, sweetheart, I've seen worse, I've seen all those boys grow up and I've got daughters, it comes with the territory."

She chuckles softly and I start to wonder what role she plays within the Rancid Vengeance family. She wraps a blood pressure cuff around the top of my arm and hums softly, as she pumps the rubber device in her hand. The cuff tightening uncomfortably on my arm.

"Don't break his heart, darlin', he's had his fair share of that in his life already. He might not admit it out loud yet, but he loves you, give him time. He just needs to admit it to himself first," she says softly, and I regard her intently.

"I can't help asking myself, am I really that unloveable that he can't admit the way he feels? And I can't help feeling I'll never truly know him as well as you, Lenny and the boys know him. He's a puzzle I'm desperately trying to figure out," I finally confess, comfortable enough in Jay's presence to voice my feelings.

Even though I met her minutes ago, I feel oddly as ease in her company. Her soft, mild manner coaxes me to admit everything I've been struggling to say out loud for the longest time.

"Trust me, I've seen girls come and go over the years. Sometimes I considered installing a revolving door!"

She laughs wryly and that pang of jealousy hits me without warning.

"I know you probably don't want to hear that, but that was before. I've never seen him like this over a woman and I can see he cares deeply about you. His childhood traumas haunt him far more than he lets on, you just need to ride out the storms and that sunshine he's been hiding, will shine so bright it will blind you. He's a good man, he's not had an easy life but I think you could be the girl that changes that."

She cocks her head to the side and regards me with careful eyes.

"I love him, more than I ever thought possible. He made it so easy for me to fall, he's...fucking hell I can't believe I'm telling you this, but as soon as we met I knew, I knew he could be bad for my health and he could ruin me with his infectious charm, but I couldn't help it. From the very beginning I found myself falling deeper, and with my track record, I wanted to be cautious but he made it fucking impossible."

I lean back heavily on the pillows and my eyes fill with tears.

"Sweetheart, I knew from the moment he met you you were special, something different. The women who have been in his life, none of them have ever lasted for longer than a few nights, with one exception, but that's not my story to tell. He's never introduced me to one of his girlfriends before, actually come to think of it, I don't think he's ever had a girlfriend before, so consider yourself lucky. I pride myself on being an extremely good judge of character, and you my darling, are going to be the girl who finally tames Brody Hart."

As I continue to listen, there's weight behind her words and I don't doubt them, not for one second.

32

Brody

After Vegas, Sam and Peyton moved into a purpose built, three storey, eleven-bedroom property in Chislehurst, Kent. It also boasts twelve acres of land, which we all contributed to building three luxury ten-bedroom mansions in our very own gated community, aptly named '*Vengeance Estates.*' Today is the day I flee the sanctuary of Sam and Peyton's house and move into my very own house, somewhere to call home, to finally call my own. Our houses are built in a spacious semi-circle and we all live near each other. It's unconventional, but we're all happy to live in relative peace and calm away from the glare of the paparazzi's lens.

From the outside, my house looks like a large, rustic, grey brick farmhouse, with large sash windows and a large round gravel driveway with a large fountain in the centre, the houses built around the circumference. Inside, it is quite the opposite, it's light, airy, and open. The large living space has light grey walls with azure blue accents. A large navy U-shaped sofa dominates the space, as does a large TV mounted on the wall. The artwork is minimal, and the walls are decorated in photos of me, the boys, our album covers and our platinum discs.

For the longest time, music has been my life. I live and breathe it, it's the only thing that's kept me going over the years. It's the one constant in my life and I'll always be grateful to whoever, for gracing me with the talent to do what I love and be afforded the lavish, rock n' roll lifestyle that I have become accustomed to.

Fourteen years and I still never get bored of performing to thousands of adoring, die-hard fans. I'll never get tired of the elation and the pure rush I feel, every time I go out on stage with my guitar in my hand. The familiar chant "Vengeance, Vengeance, Vengeance!" never gets old. It makes all of the shit we've been through as a band, individually and as a family, all worthwhile. That's why I'm so fucking proud to finally lay down solid roots

304

and call this place my home. I moved around a lot as a kid, never settling down, never staying in one place long enough to belong anywhere. The only place I felt like I belonged was with the boys, wherever they were, they were my home. But as I lay back on my sofa, the more I think about Raleigh and how she's become my home.

In the weeks that followed her relapse we spent time rekindling our relationship and getting to know each other again. She helped me move in and settle into my new place and I've never been happier. She's getting stronger by the day and if anything, the relapse made me realise my true feelings for her, even though I still couldn't find the courage to say it out loud. After a whole day of lazy, unhurried love making, we are lying in my king size bed, the sheets draped over our bodies haphazardly. I'm idly tracing shapes with my fingers across her collarbone, her head resting on my chest. Our breathing perfectly in sync, the silence comfortable. She sighs audibly and I smile to myself, brushing her hair away from her face.

"Something on your mind, beautiful?" I ask hoarsely, and she shifts in my hold.

"How did you meet Lenny?"

I stiffen, unprepared for her line of questioning. I reach up to squeeze the back of my neck, as I remember the day I met Lenny Nicholas.

Brody
Past

The bitter taste in the back of my throat, the numb tingly feeling in my face, the unlimited amount of energy, the rush of absolute pure pleasure, my head shattering in white explosions and the feeling that I could take on the fucking world. Ten minutes later I want another hit and another. But the crash was always the worst, suddenly the feelings of euphoria and energy were replaced with extreme angst and exhaustion that all I wanted to do was close myself off from the world and hide away. It had gotten to a point where I started to need that fix every night to reverse the agonising comedown that seemed to become all too frequent. I'd been a cocaine user for a few years now and it was a habit I dabbled in a little too often. It was readily available in the circles I moved in and it was always on hand to help me unwind after a blow job and a show.

A few nights ago, I found one of my close friends dead, exactly the way I found my mum. With a dirty fucking needle hanging out of his arm, foam coming from his mouth and piss staining his jeans. Daryl Dean Nicholas was one of my best friends, he was someone outside of the band and the time we spent together, I relished it. It was an opportunity for me to forget who I was, I forgot our growing popularity and I forgot all the things that came with being famous. It was just two guys shooting the shit and getting high. I'm so fucking buzzed off my pickle right now, I feel numb. The image of Daryl convulsing, the light fading from his eyes playing on a loop in my mind. I shook him, desperately trying to revive him, but he was too far gone, it was too late. I rang an ambulance and got the fuck out of there, with our growing popularity, it wouldn't be wise for a rock star to be caught high as a kite, with a dead junkie. My career would be over before it had even begun. Seeing someone I had grown close to over the years die in front of me should have put me off the drugs for life, but all it did was spur me on to get so high I couldn't feel the crippling devastation of seeing yet another person's light extinguished because of the drugs. It bought all of the demons that have followed me and haunted me since I was ten years old to the front and centre of my brain. I couldn't seem to comprehend all of the feelings that lay dormant in my head, those feelings overwhelmed me and all I wanted to do was forget. I can't focus, I can't fucking see straight, a mix of vodka and cocaine flowing through my veins, creating a floating feeling.

My phone buzzing interrupts my thoughts, and I don't recognise the number. I cautiously connect the call.

"Hello?" I answer apprehensively.

"Hello, is this Brody?"

I pause for a few seconds, trying desperately to place the voice on the end of the phone, but failing miserably.

"Who wants to know?" I reply, aware that my manners are nowhere to be found.

"You don't know me, but I'm Lenny, my son was Daryl Nicholas."

As he says those words, it feels like a lead weight has settled at the base of my stomach and I feel like I'm going to throw up. How the fuck did he get my number? I swallow hard to rid myself of the feeling.

"Look, I'm not pointing any fingers, but were you with my son when he died? I just need to piece together what happened, for closure... I don't know."

His voice so full of grief, it causes my heart to slam against my rib cage, followed by a feeling of pure dread and I contemplate just hanging up. But he doesn't deserve that, not after his son had died. I was the last one to see him, he deserves the truth.

"Yeah, yeah, I was with him," I admit reluctantly, clearing my throat and wondering how tonight took such a turn.

"Could we meet? I'd like to know what happened, and your name appeared quite frequently in his phone. I'm assuming you were close?"

I pause, surprised at his request. I scrabble feebly for an excuse, my drug addled mind coming up with nothing and I'm aware I've been silent for far too long.

"Hello? Are you still there?" he asks, suddenly unsure of himself.

"Erm...yeah...yeah, we were good friends. Yeah, sure we can meet up. Where and when?"

He coughs and then clears his throat.

"There's a little café, The Rise and Shine Café? You know it?"

I smile to myself, as I think fondly of Mandie and her daughter Emmy.

"Yeah, I know it."

There is a pregnant pause.

"Are you free tomorrow at all?" he asks expectantly.

"Sure," I agree tersely and monosyllabic.

"Tomorrow at ten thirty a.m.? Does that work for you?"

I can feel the crash creeping slowly through my body and I'm exhausted, even my bones feel weak.

"Yeah, that works for me. See you tomorrow."

I hang up the phone, wondering what the fuck I've agreed to.

***

I spent the rest of the night mentally trying to talk myself out of meeting with Daryl's dad. Why does he want to meet me? Is it a trap? Am I going to get arrested? Does he blame me for his son's death? Does he wish it me and not Daryl? All of these thoughts barrelled through my coke addled brain, as I fell into a fitful night's sleep.

I wake with a start and throw myself into a warm shower, feeling almost human again. J.D drops me off at the café and I make my way inside. The bell signals my arrival, and the homely café is busy this morning, it's full of builders in hi viz vests and teenagers in tracksuits, noses buried in their phones. Despite being rushed off her feet, Mandie rushes up to me and throws her arms around me, kissing me on the cheek. I find myself smiling widely.

"Hey gorgeous!" I greet her.

I think she's got a thing for me. She's very attractive and given half the chance, I would smash her back doors in. I rid myself of that thought, as she flicks her long blonde hair over her shoulder.

"Usual, handsome?" she asks, and I nod.

She knows me well since I've been coming here since I was fifteen years old.

"You got it, beautiful!" I say with a wink, and she giggles girlishly as she makes her way back around the counter.

I make my way to a free table at the back in the corner. I sit down, a feeling of unease settling deep in my gut and I find myself relieved that I skipped breakfast. My cup of coffee lands on the table in front of me and I look up to meet Mandie's eyes. I'm sure she's undone a few more buttons on her fitted denim shirt and I can't seem to stop my eyes from wandering.

"There you go, handsome."

She brushes my hand with a wink.

"Cheers, darlin'."

She nods with a beaming smile and walks away, leaving me to my coffee. A few moments pass and as I look up, I'm faced with a set of desolate and devastated pale blue eyes, rimmed red. He looks a little dishevelled, his dark grey three-piece suit crumpled. I take him in. He is average height with slicked back salt and pepper hair. He regards me with wary, careful eyes and I shift my gaze back to the floor.

"Brody?" he asks gruffly, and I nod. "Lenny," he introduces himself, and I shake his outstretched hand, gesturing to the seat opposite. He sits down, looking oddly overdressed and out of place.

"To be honest, I didn't think you were going to show up," he admits honestly.

"I almost didn't," I answer flatly, suddenly feeling way out of my depth.

Why is he really here? He's about to speak again, when Mandie places a cup in front of him.

"Is everything ok, Brody?"

I look up at her and smile.

"Yeah, everything's fine, sweetheart."

I don't elaborate and she seems satisfied with my answer, as she turns on her heel, leaving us to it.

"So, you were with Daryl when he...when he..." he struggles to get the words out.

"Yes, I was."

I don't finish his sentence; I just give him the answer and he nods his gratitude.

"I just want a clearer picture, that's all, son. I know what he was, I'm under no illusion. My son was a raving, fucking junkie. Me and my Nancy tried so hard to help him, but you just can't help someone who doesn't want to be helped."

I take a sip of my coffee, just for something to do because I don't know what to say. I'm literally lost for words.

"Look, son, I'm not a cop. I'm just a father who's lost his son."

His gruff voice trembles and I instinctively reach across the table for his hand, as a tear rolls down his cheek. I know we don't know each other, but I can tell he's a good man. He deserves to know what happened.

"*Daryl and me, we'd been friends for three or four years, we met through a mutual friend. We weren't close, it was the sort of friendship that if we needed company or someone to get high with. I know you probably don't want to hear that, but you wanted to know what happened. I'm no better than him, I'm an addict too. You see, I've just signed a record deal with a huge label. I'm in a rock band, it's been pretty full on lately and I just wanted some sense of normality... I don't know.*"

I take a long sip of my coffee, suddenly desperate for something to take the edge off. It's barely even lunchtime and I'm craving oblivion. Fucking hell.

"*We met up, we did a few lines of coke, then he said he'd managed to get hold of something else. Said his dealer gave him a freebie for a favour he'd done for him. He didn't go into detail, but he pulled out a foil wrapper. I'd seen it before, my mum was a heroin addict, so I don't touch it. He offered it to me, and we argued... I kept telling him no. I tried to convince him not to, I tried! I found my mum with a needle hanging out of her arm when I was ten years old, and I didn't ever want to fucking see someone I cared about go out like that. I tried to grab it off him, pleaded with him not to, he used his belt to find a vein. I kept trying to stop him, but he injected it and he kept saying he was fine. Part of me thought he was doing it to prove a point, but we were similar in that respect. We've both got addictive personalities so he was just doing it because he could, because he was chasing the high. He was like a kid, screaming and whooping, saying how he felt like he could take on the world. I don't know how much time passed, but he started convulsing, foaming at the mouth, his eyes were rolling back in his head...*"

I'm the one crying now and I can't help the flood of emotion that surges through me. I press the heels of my hands into my eyes and a deep breath, before I continue, but Lenny holds his finger up.

"*Stop, just stop, I've heard enough.*"

His voice so full of anguish and pain.

"*I'm sorry, I'm so fucking sorry,*" *I sob, and Lenny reaches across the table for my hand.*

"*It wasn't your fault, son, thank you for telling me that. I know it must have been hard for you, losing your mum at such a young age and seeing a friend go the same way. Look, I know we've just met, but I couldn't help my own son, maybe I can help you? You seem like a good kid who's lost his way, that's all. Daryl was a lost cause, he was beyond help, but you're not, I can see that in you."*

Maybe I'm not beyond saving, maybe I can give this man a second chance. With that thought at the forefront of my mind, I find myself nodding and agreeing all too easily with this gentle man who's just lost his son.

Brody

Present

I'm snapped back to the present by Raleigh shifting in my arms and she sighs contentedly.

"Thank you," she says softly.

"What for, kitten?"

She squeezes me tighter.

"For telling me that and for letting me know you a little more."

I press a tender kiss to her forehead and bit by bit, day by day, I'm letting my defences down. I'm lowering those walls I've built so high around myself and it doesn't feel so bad anymore. She's right, we are healing each other. Maybe she's the cure I've waited all my life for. *I can only hope.*

Raleigh

After our early morning love making session and our little chat about Lenny, I feel like I was getting ever closer to knowing the real Brody Hart. I had just finished a successful and productive Zoom meeting with Damien, and I feel more optimistic for the future. I change into my work out clothes, a pair of tiny black lycra shorts, a black and purple crop top and black and purple Skechers. I head down to the basement where Brody's state-of-the-art home gym is located. As I get to the bottom of the staircase, I spot him in all of his tattooed glory, he's shirtless as he launches a pair of boxing gloves at me.

"Put these on, kitten."

I catch them awkwardly and pull them on, letting him help me fasten the Velcro around my wrist. He leads me over to a long, oblong leather bag hanging from the hook in the ceiling with a wink and positions me in front of it.

"Right, first lesson, let your fist be an extension of your arm. Show me what you've got," he instructs, the sexual tension in the room is thick and almost suffocating.

"Jab, jab, cross, jab, jab, cross, cross, jab. Come on, faster."

The authority in his voice is a turn on for me and it hits all my hot buttons. I do as he says, and he smiles at my progress. He is seemingly unaware that I want him to throw me against the wall and fuck me like I need to be fucked.

"Good, you know if you want to learn self-defence, you should probably talk to Peyton. She took lessons when she lived in Santa Monica," he says.

Before I know what I'm saying, curiosity gets the better of me and I blurt out, "What happened to her?"

He shakes his head and smirks.

"It's not my story to tell, babe. She doesn't like to talk about it, but let's just say, she did what she had to, to keep Freddie safe," he explains cryptically, and I want to press him for more information, but I don't.

"She protected that boy with her life, I've got so much respect for her for that. It was a time we'd all rather forget, but it bought her back to us. It gave us hope that happy ever after isn't so out of reach after all," he says ruefully, and I find myself smiling at his words.

"Who knew Brody Hart was a hopeless romantic!"

He rolls his eyes and laughs. "I've got no idea what you're talking about, Storm."

He cocks his eyebrow and I start to bend down provocatively, giving him a full view of my breasts. I pretend to stretch, and he chuckles throatily.

"Do you need something taken care of, kitten?" he asks gruffly, and I reach down to touch my toes.

I purposely brush his growing erection with my bum and lightning fast, he grabs me around the waist.

"Now play fair, kitten. It's not nice to tease."

He pins me to the wall, pulls off both of the boxing gloves, discarding them to the floor. He holds both of my hands prisoner in one of his above my head. I can feel his warm breath gust out against my face, as I take in his features: the angular slope of his nose, his sharp cheekbones, the dimple in his chin, the defined set of his biceps and the curve of his delicious arse. *Fuck, he's gorgeous, but he doesn't seem to know it.* His stormy silver eyes are hooded and blazing with white hot lust, as he cups my tender breast in his other hand. He ghosts his finger across my nipple, and I bite my lip, softly mewling. I can't describe the feelings he evokes in me, as he presses his solid erection into my pelvis.

"You make me so hard, every time I'm near you, kitten, my cock betrays me."

He chuckles softly as I writhe in his grip.

"Ah, ah, not yet I want to pleasure you until you can't take it anymore, I want to take you right to the edge, until you're begging for your orgasm," he rasps seductively and roughly tears my lycra shorts from my body, the noise echoing throughout the room.

He cocks his eyebrow as he realises I'm not wearing any underwear beneath my shorts. I wink cheekily at him and he shoves two fingers inside my brazenly drenched pussy. I cry out in pure unadulterated desire, as he expertly and thoroughly finger fucks me.

"BRODY!"

He curls his rough, calloused fingers deep within my searingly hot channel. I am squirming, my legs about to give under the intense pleasure he is reigning upon me.

"I've got you, kitten, I've got you."

He introduces another finger and rubs my aching clit in deliberate, slow circles.

"OH FUCK!"

I'm so close I can feel my orgasm rising to the surface.

"BRODY! DON'T STOP! PLEASE! FUCK! DON'T STOP!"

I'm aware that my voice sounds breathy and desperate, but I'm too far gone to care. Suddenly he pulls his fingers free, leaving me needy, wanting, and fraught. He frees my hands and I try to catch my breath. I watch him carefully, the corner of his lips quirking upwards. I'm a quivering mess of pent-up frustration.

"What the fuck was that?" I pant, struggling to maintain my cool composure, and he winks.

"That was just a taste, kitten. Do you want more?"

I bite my lip at his suggestive question and nod. His body is damp with sweat and his dark brown hair is longer than it's ever been, it's deliciously mussed and I'm itching to run my fingers through it. His long basketball shorts hang low on his hips, revealing the deep set 'V', which leads down to his tattooed and pierced, eight-inch member.

"Your pleasure belongs to me, Raleigh, I know what gets you off, I know what turns you on, I've memorised every inch of your body, every imperfection, every scar, every dimple, every little detail."

He leans down to kiss a burning trail from my neck and across my collar bone, I shiver at feather light touch. I briefly close my eyes and whisper.

"Oh God, I love you."

He's silent, as his lips continue their journey down to the swell of my breast. I lose myself in him and I let him take control, pushing down the disappointment of him not being able to admit his declaration of love out loud, even though his actions tell me a different story.

"I want you naked, kitten," he demands, and I pull off my crop top in one lithe move.

I'm stood naked before him, as he drops his basketball shorts to the floor, allowing his steel erection to spring free. I lick my lips at the sight of him.

"See something you like?"

I nod, teasing my nipples between my thumb and forefinger.

"Hmm," I hum as he reaches over and traces my arm with a feather-light touch.

Heat blossoms through me, and his name leaves my lips on a ragged pant. The throbbing between my thighs is almost unbearable, as I feel the broad head of his cock probing my entrance. The look in his eyes full of the words he can't say out loud, as he pushes into me on a strangled bark. I cry out with each measured drive of his length, waves of warmth spread through me, as his piercing rubs my inner walls deliciously, creating a friction. I move my hips upwards, encouraging him to go faster.

"Tell me what you want, kitten."

His hands roam all over my body and I lift my hips again, moving with urgency.

"I want you to fuck me, Brody!"

I gasp, my world spinning on its axis, as he flips me onto my back, withdrawing and plunging deep inside my slick channel and I can't help screaming out.

"OH BRODY! YOU FEEL TOO FUCKING GOOD!"

He pounds into me with the fury that he's been holding back, as he grips my hips from behind. Each thrust brings with it new waves of pure unadulterated bliss, each stroke more intense than the last.

"Do you want me?" he asks with desperation etched in his voice.

"God, yes, I want you! So fucking bad," I breathe, and he seems satisfied with my answer as he expertly swivels his hips, causing those familiar flutters deep within me.

"I've got you, kitten, come with me."

With those words, the rapturous ball of heated pleasure at my core, explodes and I swear I see stars. I cry out, throwing my head back and my pussy contracting around his cock, milking every last drop with strong, fluttering pulses.

"OH FUCK! FUCK! FUCK BRODY! I'M COMING!"

He grunts, pumping harder, as he tenses, finding his release. His breathing hitches as he comes long and hard, cursing low in his throat. My body trembles and twitches with post-orgasmic aftershocks, as he pulls out of me. This man makes me crazy with desire and I don't think I could want him more than in this moment. We lie there satiated and spent on the padded floor of his gym, our breathing in sync and returning to normal after our love making session. As he wraps me in his arms, I begin to torture myself with plans of forever.

A girl can only dream.

33

Raleigh

I've been feeling off for the past couple of weeks, but I just put it down to stress. I've just got back from an audition, as Liv sits down next to me, holding my hand and narrowing her eyes on me.

"When was your last period, babe?" she asks curiously, eagerly anticipating my answer.

"What?"

I consider her question for a few moments and try desperately to recall the last time I had my period. My periods have always been irregular, but for the past few years they've evened out and they're usually regular, give or take a few days. *Fuck, I can't be pregnant can I?* Brody and I have always used protection, except for those few occasions when we both got caught in the moment and fucked bare. *Shit.* I bite my lip, as I come to the sudden realisation that I could well be pregnant with Brody Hart's baby. I get up from my seat and start to anxiously pace the floor.

"Talk to me, Rae."

I am rendered speechless by the revelation and I can't speak. I end up just standing in front of the mirror, opening, and closing my mouth looking like a demented fucking goldfish.

"I take it by the silence you've missed a period?"

I nod, full of shame. *What the fuck was I thinking?*

"*Fuck,* Rae. You need to take a test; you need to be sure."

I nod. *How am I going to look him in the eye knowing I could potentially be carrying his kid? This can't be fucking happening.*

"This can't happen, Liv, it can't! Our relationship is fucking fragile as it is, what am I gonna' do!"

I start to panic. My breathing becomes erratic and my chest tightens. *Fuck, fuck, fuck!*

"Breathe, Rae, breathe, it's going to be alright."

She cups my face in her hands, as my breathing starts to even out and I shake my head.

"What if I am and he freaks out? I can't raise a baby on my own, Liv!"

I panic and she rolls her eyes.

"If you are, he's just going to have to fucking suck it up! It takes two to make a baby, it's equally on him as it is on you," she says diplomatically.

"Do you want me to go and get you a test? You have to know, Rae, the sooner you know, the sooner you can start making plans, this is a big deal," she says softly, reaching for my hand.

"I can't do this, Livvy, I can't."

A tear slips down my cheek and I can't hold it in any longer, I start to sob hard. Liv cups my face in both of her hands again, her scent enveloping me and looks me in the eye.

"Look at me, Raleigh, you need to be rational about this, yeah?"

I nod, trying desperately to calm myself down.

"Just how late are you?"

My mind spins trying frantically remember just when my last period was. The truth is, I don't fucking know. I can't remember, which causes me to sob harder and uncontrollably. This can't be happening, what the fuck was I thinking?

"Shh, shh, listen to me, I'm going to nip out to get you a test, I'll be quick and I'll come straight back. Everything is going to be fine, you need to sit tight for me, yeah?"

She placates and kisses me on my forehead, leaving me alone with my thoughts. *Not fucking smart.*

***

I stand in front of the full-length mirror in my bedroom and turn to the side. *Do I look pregnant?* I run my hands across my stomach, don't be fucking stupid. You wouldn't be showing that quick you silly cow. *Relax, Liv's right, everything is going to be fine.* I try to busy myself running through another new script I was sent this morning, not really taking in the words, as my eyes skim across the pages.

I'm not sure how much time passes, but I am startled by the slamming of the door.

"Only me!" she sings.

I get up from the sofa and she empties the contents of a white plastic bag on the marble worktop.

"I got a few, just in case!"

She winks and I find myself laughing right along with her at her ridiculous wild ways. There must be about thirty pregnancy tests currently scattered across my kitchen worktop right now. She gives me a handful of tests and shoos me away.

"Now go and shake your lettuce, babe, I'll wait out here. As much as I love you and even though I've seen your cooch a thousand times, I don't need to see that shit!"

I laugh at her attempt to see the funny side of this absurd situation I find myself in. I go into the bathroom, shutting the door behind me with a click and sit down on the toilet. I take the test out of the box with trembling hands, briefly read the instructions and I pee on the stick, as I wait for the results develop. There is a light tap, tap on the door.

"You ok in there, Rae?" she enquires softly, and I clear my throat, trying to sound confident.

You're fooling no one, Storm.

"Yeah, fine, babe."

A few minutes pass, and I steel myself to look at the result. The test reads *'pregnant +3 weeks.'* I slap my hand to my mouth and stifle a sob. *Fuck it all to hell!*

"Rae, Rae, is everything ok in there? Open the door," she says with a panicked edge to her voice.

I'm just sitting on the toilet seat in pure fucking shock. *I'm pregnant with Brody's baby. This can't be happening, what the fuck was I thinking?* I can hear my mum's shrill voice in my head.

"You silly, silly, little girl."

I'm startled from my meltdown by the door swinging open and Liv walking in. The click, click of her heels as she walks across the floor and gets down on her haunches in front of me.

"Rae? Talk to me."

I open and close my mouth and thrust the test at her.

"I-I-I'm pregnant, Liv."

Her eyes widen, as we both utter the words *"Oh fuck!"* at the same time.

34

Brody

As I lie awake, next to the woman I love, I start to think, that I've never really given much thought to how I would die. From an early age, I always had this feeling I would die young. Kurt Cobain, Amy Winehouse, Jimmy '*The Rev*' Sullivan, James Dean, Heath Ledger, all dead before they were even thirty. Don't get me wrong, I'm not thinking of offing myself or anything, I could never be that weak. I just often find myself thinking, what if my life had taken a different path? I'm grateful for the hand that life has dealt me - mostly. I have an amazing life, a jaw-droppingly, stunning woman, a roof over my head and I'm lucky to be surrounded by people, who love me. I can't help but think of the life I had before. The life I had before I became a world-famous guitarist, the life where I lived hand to mouth, where I had to beg, borrow, and steal, just so I could eat, so I could fucking *survive*.

"What's wrong, baby? Can't sleep?"

Raleigh's sleep induced voice fills my ears, interrupting my dark thoughts, and I'm instantly calmed. I turn to face her, as I catch just how devastatingly beautiful she is. Five feet seven inches tall, slender, her short, lilac hair, cut into an adorable, pixie crop, tattoos covering both tops of her arms, in half sleeves. As my silver eyes find her unique amethyst-coloured ones, my stomach fills with the familiar butterflies, as she edges closer to me.

"Something on your mind, handsome?" she asks curiously as I turn on my side to face her.

You have no fucking idea, babe.

"Nothing you need to worry about, kitten."

I tap my finger to the end of her nose, and she smiles, temporarily knocking the breath from my lungs.

"You know you can tell me anything, don't you?" she says innocently, and I know she's just trying to help, to get me to open up.

But the truth is, she can't help. She can't chase away the demons in my dreams, I wish it were that easy. The things I've done, the things I've seen, I can't subject her to that, *I just can't*. I turn onto my back and place my hands behind my head.

"For fucks sake, Brody! Let me in! Talk to me!" she persists, but she'll never know what it's like to be inside my head.

The darkness that contaminates my brain on a near nightly basis, is toxic, there's barely room in my head for it. I can't infect her with it, she's too pure, and she's too...fucking *good,* for the bad things, that I've suffered through over the years.

"When are you going to trust me enough, to tell me what goes on in that fucked up head of yours, Brody? I thought we were finally getting somewhere."

She sighs and I turn to face her. As I move closer to her, I can smell her arousal. My lips collide with hers and I relish the feel of her velvet tongue, sensually dancing with mine. I thrust my hips into her, pressing the evidence of my arousal, in between her delicious thighs and she moans aloud.

"Brody," she pants breathlessly as her hands start to wander over my bare chest.

I crave her, like that first hit of cocaine. Her taste, her touch, her scent; everything about her fucking overwhelms me. *I don't deserve to be this happy*. I try desperately to push those wayward thoughts aside and just feel my girl. She softly caresses my face and she shift back from me, as if she has just come to her senses. She puts her arm over her eyes, shielding herself from me.

"Don't do that, Brody. Don't fucking distract me with sex."

I chuckle wickedly, and she moves her arm away from her face, the look in her eyes conflicted.

"I never mentioned sex, babe, but I'm sure I can be persuaded."

I wiggle my tongue suggestively and she shifts further away from me.

"Do you have to make a joke out of everything? Why can't you be serious, just for once in your fucking life!" she snaps, and I shrug nonchalantly.

"Life's too short, what can I say?"

She raises her arms in frustration and yells almost incoherently.

"You're fucking impossible!"

I throw my head back and laugh. She shakes her head, exasperated.

"We've been together almost eight months, Brody! I just want to know you!" she all but screams at me.

Fucking women.

"You do know me, why can't you see that? How could you doubt the way I feel about you?" I roar at her as she rakes her hands through her already sleep mussed hair. "You're my heart, Rae, you complete me. You're the reason I'm still fucking *breathing*," I say softly and sincerely, but she cuts me off abruptly.

"I don't doubt that for a second, but I just want to know you the way Sam, Peyton, Lenny, Jay and the boys know you! Why can't you see that?" she protests.

I really can't be fucking arsed with this shit.

"It's different with them, they're all I've ever known. They might not be blood, but they're my *family*!" I counter with more than a hint of frustration to my voice.

Women are so fucking infuriating.

"But don't you want kids, a family of your own?" she whispers melancholically.

As she says those words, I get up and perch myself on the edge of the bed, suddenly feeling exhausted.

"No, I don't want kids, no, never. I made that decision a long fucking time ago. Why do you think I've never been in a long-term relationship? I hurt everyone around me, can't you see that? For years, I influenced Sam, I set him on a path that wasn't good. I almost destroyed his relationship with Peyton before it had even begun!" I babble.

I can feel myself getting agitated and the craving for a fix is so strong, my hands start to tremble.

"But why, Brody? Make me understand! You deserve to be happy!" she begins to sob softly, and I know I'm being a prick, but she *has* to understand.

"I've spent over a decade in and out of rehab and I've seen enough shrinks to know that I'm not good father material. My mum didn't want me, and my dad was gone before the fucking sperm got to the egg! I could never do that. I could never infect a child with my poison. I don't want my child to go through the same thing I did... the poverty, the hunger, the loneliness. I might be a lot of things, but I'm definitely not fucking stupid. Yeah, I've got mummy issues and I've got abandonment issues, is that what you want to hear? Because that's the fucking bottom line, Raleigh!"

She swipes a tear from her eye, and I find myself totally fucking unprepared for the next words that come out of her mouth.

"Brody, I'm pregnant."

35

Brody

How the fuck did this happen? Obviously, I know how but I always make sure my little gentleman is wearing a suit, the only woman I've ever been bareback with was Lorna. Raleigh sits up and waits patiently and expectantly for me to say something.

"S...say something for fucks sake," she stutters, but I'm at a loss.

"H...how?"

Those are all the words I can manage. *Fucking hell, Hart, get it together.* She chuckles sardonically.

"I'm fairly sure you know how, Brody, your penis entered my vagina..."

I stop her from continuing by holding my finger up.

"I'm not a fucking idiot, Raleigh. We've *never* gone bareback, *Jesus Fucking Christ!"*

I run my fingers through my hair, get up from the bed and start to pace. When suddenly the reality of her revelation hits me like a ten-tonne truck. *She's pregnant with my baby. I'm going to be a father.* Fucking hell, this can't happen. She seems to sense my inner conflict, and she jabs me sharply in the chest.

"*Oh fuck no!* You don't get to do that, Brody Hart, there's no way I'm getting rid of this baby. I've made my choice, I'm...*we're* doing this, with or without you."

Her voice trembles on those last few words and my heart breaks, but I know categorically that I can't allow this to happen. I can't infect a baby with my poison as well as Raleigh. *What if I can't be a good father? What if I can't be what he or she needs?*

"I'm already in love with a child I haven't met yet, Brody. I'll admit as soon as I saw the word pregnant, I was fucking terrified. But I knew once I'd had time to think about it and process, I was all in, no half measures. I want to right the wrongs my parents did to me, I'll never do that to our child, *never.*"

She moves closer to me and places my hand gently on her flat stomach.

"We deserve this, Brody, don't you want to give this baby what your mum didn't give you?"

As soon as she says those words, I rip my hand away from her and she visibly flinches.

"Don't you fucking dare, Raleigh. Don't *ever* try and lay that shit on me! My mum was a selfish fucking cunt, who didn't give two shits about me! I'd never ever do that to my child! I'm not going to get the opportunity, because I don't want anything to do with that...*thing* inside of you!" I yell angrily as she breaks down at my feet and starts to sob uncontrollably.

She cradles her stomach, and her sobs pierce my soul.

"Please, don't do this, please, we need you! *I* fucking need you, Brody! I can't do this on my own!"

I shake my head.

"After everything I just said, you lay that on me! No, no, I can't, I can't do this. I fucking *won't* do this."

I swallow the lump that has lodged itself in my throat and walk out of the door to the sound of her gut-wrenching sobs.

It breaks my fucking heart, but I know deep down it's the right thing to do. I'm breaking my own heart in order to protect her from me and the poison that runs through my veins. *Fuck, I'm going to be a dad.* I swipe away a stray tear from my eye and head down to the garage, taking my phone out of my pocket. I dial the first number I think of, feeling more out of control than I have in months.

"Kev, it's Brody," I say, trying to sound more confident than I feel.

"Brody, my main man, how's tricks? You looking to score?"

I pause, looking down at my smart watch, one eleven a.m.

"Yeah, mate, the usual, plus a bit extra, I'll meet you in the normal place in twenty minutes."

My heart is pounding as I wait for his answer.

"Prices have gone up, inflations a bitch. It's double what you usually pay."

I don't argue. I haven't got it in me to argue right now, I just need to forget, I need oblivion.

"You got it. Twenty minutes and don't be late."

I hang up abruptly without saying goodbye and swing my leg over my precious bike. I start her up and feel the vibration beneath me. I push the button to open the garage door and I speed off into the night.

***

I make it to *Rise and Shine Café*, the bell chiming as I push my way through the door. I'm suddenly hit with heat, a stark contrast from the chill of the night air outside. I'm not greeted by Emmy, but her mum Mandie. It's been years since I saw her, she's still as beautiful as I remember her, if a little older.

"Brody!" she greets me, beaming her familiar grin. She steps out from behind the counter, taking me in. "Looking as handsome as ever, darlin'!" she compliments, and I smile as I hear someone clearing their throat.

I turn to see Kev sitting towards the back of the café.

"Friend of yours?" Mandie enquires quietly, and I nod as I head towards Kev's table.

"Usual?" she calls.

"Please, sweetheart."

I take a seat opposite him.

"Brody, good to see you, mate, as always."

He reaches across the table and shakes my hand with a smile. *Jesus, this guy has given me the fucking creeps for years.*

"You too, Kev."

Mandie places Kev's coffee down on the table, and she busies herself wiping the neighbouring table. Her arse mere inches from me and Kev winks.

"Think you're in there, mate!"

I swallow hard, trying to divert my gaze elsewhere as she straightens and heads back behind the counter. As soon as her back is turned Kev reaches across the table in a lightning quick move to give me what I came here to collect. I pass him a roll of notes in exchange and tuck it inside the pocket of my leather jacket, satisfied that the deal is done. I take a long gulp of my coffee, the hot black liquid burning my throat as I swallow. I shift my chair back, nodding curtly to Kev. I slap a handful of notes onto the counter and leave without saying goodbye to make the journey home. All I'm focused on is getting so high I reach that rapturous void I have been craving for so long.

I make it back home in record time and as I lean against the wall in the garage, I rub the delicious cocaine around my gums, I feel the euphoric high enter my system almost instantly. I laugh hysterically at the ridiculousness of it all, my shitty fucking life, the fame, and the fact that I'm going to be someone's fucking dad! I'm high because when I'm high, I can't feel anything and right now, I don't want to feel anything. I don't want to think about becoming a dad, I don't want to think about the look in Raleigh's eyes, as I fucking left her sobbing.

I need to get my head on straight and the only way I can do that, is to go for a ride, I know I have to be as far away from her as I can get, I need to ride. I straddle my bike, pull on my helmet and push a button on the handlebar to open the garage door. I kick the kickstand, twist the throttle, and rev the engine. I signal for Jace to open the gates and manage to salute my thanks, and I pull out onto the open roads of Chislehurst with a roar. Even at this hour it is busy and there's nothing like the rush of adrenaline, as I zoom down the street. The blur of the quaint village zipping past, as I manoeuvre my bike down the narrow roads. I feel free, like nothing else exists. Like the conversation I had with Raleigh before I left the house didn't happen. It's just me, the open road, and the invigorating, heady feeling, as the rumble of the engine grows louder. My mind grows clearer, with each mile that I travel, riding is the ultimate escape for me, and has been ever since I passed my test when I turned seventeen.

Suddenly, as I head from Orchard Road onto Sundridge Avenue, I take the corner a little too fast and a car travelling in the opposite direction hurtles towards me. I hit the brakes and both of them lock up. Time immediately slows down and all but stops. It proceeds to provide me with a frame-by-frame record of me facing my own mortality. In a last attempt to prevent the inevitable accident, I grab a fist full of brake, pump down hard with my foot, and hold on for dear fucking life. The car doesn't quite stop in time, and I crash head on into the car. I'm flung forwards into the air, I hit the asphalt with a bone-crunching thud and my whole world becomes dark.

The End

Stay tuned for the epic conclusion in Absolution!

Page

www.ingramcontent.com/pod-product-compliance
Lightning Source LLC
Chambersburg PA
CBHW060421030726
47495CB00003B/679